LOVES OF LAKESIDE ROMANCES
THE COLLECTION - BOOKS 1-3

Lakeside Love

LOVES OF LAKESIDE ROMANCES
THE COLLECTION - BOOKS 1-3

Lakeside Love

MIMI FRANCIS

4 Horsemen
Publications, Inc.

Published By: 4 Horsemen Publications, Inc.

4 Horsemen Publications, Inc.
PO Box 417
Sylva, NC 28779
4horsemenpublications.com
info@4horsemenpublications.com

Cover and Typeset by Valerie Willis
Editor JM Paquette

Library of Congress Control Number: 2024948636

Paperback ISBN-13: 979-8-8232-0676-1
Hardcover ISBN-13: 979-8-8232-0677-8
Audiobook ISBN-13: 979-8-8232-0679-2
Ebook ISBN-13: 979-8-8232-0678-5

Table of Contents

OUR TWO-WEEK, ONE-NIGHT STAND 165

ABOUT THE AUTHOR 283

BOOK CLUB QUESTIONS..285

Run Away Home

Chapter One

Serena

$\mathcal{J}$orce of habit made her check her surroundings before she shoved open the car door. No one was around, not in this neighborhood on a late September evening. Deserted condos lined the lake this time of year. Most of these were summer homes, occupied only during the warm Montana summers.

Serena pushed the car door closed, put her arms over her head and stretched, working out the kinks in her back from the eighteen-hour drive. The scent of fresh rain washed over her. She took a deep breath; after years of living in smog-riddled Los Angeles and its kissing cousin, Phoenix, she'd forgotten how wonderful the air in Montana smelled. It dredged up memories of barbecues, swimming in the lake, boat rides to the islands dotting Flathead, and antiquing with her parents.

Happier times, better times. She closed her eyes, a smile dancing across her lips, and breathed it in. It was good to be home.

Serena turned in a circle, re-familiarizing herself with the area. She froze when her eyes met those of a tall, muscular, brown-haired stranger leaning on the balcony railing of the condo across the way, a mug in his hand, steam rising from it. A scowl marred his handsome features as he took her in, then he pivoted and went inside.

"What the hell?" she muttered under her breath. She didn't recognize him; not that she would since it had been years since she'd been here. Her father might know who he was. She'd have to ask him when they talked.

She unloaded the car and dragged her meager belongings inside, pushing the stranger and his angry scowl out of her head. She'd had enough of men and their disdain for women. She tossed everything in the bedroom and peeled off her clothes. Before she did anything else, she needed to wash the last two days from her skin, along with Arizona and Trace.

Serena found a bar of soap and some hotel shampoo and conditioner in one of the bathroom drawers while she waited for the water to warm up. She stood under the shower head, shivering as the lukewarm water washed over her. She'd grown accustomed to the Arizona heat. It was going to take some time to get used to the cold.

She held the tears at bay until she cleaned herself up, then she sank to the bottom of the bathtub as sobs wracked her body, bending her in half, tearing out of her like she was expelling a demon.

A demon named Trace.

She stayed on the bottom of the tub until the water ran cold and the shivers tore through her, then she shut off the shower and stepped onto the tile floor. The towels were under the sink, beneath the room-length mirror.

The bruises stood out in stark contrast to her pale skin, the harsh fluorescent lights of the bathroom making the purple, blue, and yellow marks look worse than she'd thought—one in the shape of a handprint on her upper arm, another on her wrist, several on her thighs, and the worst of them, a huge blood red oval shaped bruise on her side where she'd run into the door.

Serena turned her back on the mirror, snatched a towel off the top of the pile, and wrapped it around herself, then she threw open the bathroom door and stumbled across the hall to the bedroom. She yanked some clothes out of her bag, pulled them on, and dropped to the end of the bed, her head in her hands.

Droplets of water hit the floor between her legs and her wet hair clung to the back of her neck. She shuddered, her entire body succumbing to the emotions racing through her. Every muscle in her body ached, her eyes burned, and her throat felt like she'd swallowed grains of sand. Exhaustion held her hostage, weighing her down.

She towel-dried her hair, used her fingers to comb it, and pushed it out of her face, then she stretched out on the queen-sized bed, pulled the handmade quilt folded at the end over herself, and stared out the window at Flathead Lake, the stars sparkling on the water like diamonds. She'd forgotten how beautiful it was. It had been years since she'd been up here—not since she was a freshman in college. Life got in the way, kept her away. But the last fight with Trace sent her racing across the country to the one place that had always been her home.

She hoped it would be the one place Trace wouldn't find her.

Trace's temper hadn't been an issue when they started dating. Six months into their relationship, he'd begged her to move in with him, and that was when she noticed the change. He was quick to anger, often over the silliest things—losing a life on a video game resulted in the destruction of a game console, something not working the way he expected caused a blow-up of epic proportions, irritation over a missed phone call or an unanswered text caused an over-the-top argument. When she came home later than expected from a night out with the girls, Trace had punched a hole in a wall.

The first time he hit her, it had shocked the shit out of her. Her parents, in particular her father, were tranquil, quiet people. In her twenty-five years on the earth, she had never seen her father lose his temper, not once. Violence and anger were not a part of her life.

It happened less than two months after they moved in together. She'd worked late and failed to call Trace to tell him she was running behind. She stepped in the front door of their shared apartment and called his name, an apology on her lips. She found him leaning against the kitchen counter, his arms crossed, a cold, dead look in his eyes. Serena stopped in front of him and before she could open her mouth to explain, his hand connected with her cheek, whipping her head to the side and making her eyes water.

"That's for being late," he growled. He grabbed her arm, twisted it behind her back, and yanked her close. Serena bit her lip to hold back a cry as her shoulder wrenched and throbbed. Trace grabbed her hair with his other hand, wrapped it around his fingers, and pulled. "Don't do it again. Use your fucking phone." He released her, pushing her away from him.

Serena stumbled over her own feet and fell, her jaw rattling as her teeth clamped down on her tongue. Trace stepped over her and walked away, the bedroom door slamming closed behind him. She burst into tears, shame and guilt overwhelming her.

After a few minutes, she pushed herself to her feet and splashed some cold water on her hot cheeks. She contemplated gathering her things and leaving, but she didn't know where to go. Her parents didn't like Trace; both had told her on separate occasions they had a bad feeling about him. She'd been adamant they were wrong. How was she supposed to go to her parents and tell them he'd hit her? Her sister was at school in Alabama; she couldn't stay with her. She didn't have any close friends; after she and Trace started dating, she'd lost touch with most of them. She had nowhere to go.

Her cheek throbbed, so she grabbed a bag of frozen peas from the freezer and wrapped it in a kitchen towel. She gingerly held it to her cheek and sat on the couch.

Half an hour later, Trace emerged from the bedroom. He pressed a kiss to the top of her head, poured her a glass of her favorite wine, and turned on one of her favorite movies. He sat beside her and wrapped an arm around her waist, his nose brushing against her neck.

"I'm sorry, baby," he murmured. "I was just so worried, and I got all worked up. I lost my temper. It won't happen again—I promise."

Except, it did happen again. And again. And again. Repeatedly over the next eighteen months.

Serena left after Trace nearly killed her. They'd argued over something stupid, and in his anger, he'd shoved her, knocking her into a wall before punching her repeatedly in the kidneys. She'd curled into the fetal position, her arms wrapped around her head, begging him to stop as he pummeled her. The only reason he'd stopped short of beating her to death was because his phone rang, drawing him out of whatever weird, crazy trance he'd fallen into. He'd stopped, spun around, and walked away, leaving her a bleeding, bruised mess on the floor. He disappeared into the bedroom, typical behavior after he abused her. She knew she didn't have a lot of time before he returned.

It occurred to her if she didn't leave Trace, he might kill her. It was sheer luck he hadn't yet. If she didn't leave, she might not live to do it at all. She crawled across the floor, snagged her purse off the table, and texted her father two words.

Daddy, help.

It had taken all her strength to get off the floor and out the front door. She'd dragged herself down the street to the corner store and hid inside to wait for her father, keeping in constant contact with him by text message.

That had been the start of a year of running. Trace did everything in his power to get her back, but she held strong with her parents' help. She moved out of her and Trace's house and out of the city. She got a new job, bought a new car, moved into a new apartment, and tried to start over.

But Trace kept finding her. It didn't matter where she went or what she did, he would show up within weeks of her moving or starting a new job. When her sister, fresh out of college, took a job in Arizona, Serena moved there, too. Another fresh start. After three months, she thought maybe things were getting better. She hadn't heard from Trace or seen him since she'd left California; she believed it was over, for good this time.

She got too comfortable, too complacent.

He'd been waiting for her when she got home from work, sitting in her living room, drunk off his ass. He tackled her as soon as she walked through the door, his hand over her mouth. She bit him and kicked him, somehow by the grace of God connecting with his balls. He released her, allowing her to get away. She locked herself in the bedroom and called 911. The police showed up and arrested Trace, but she knew how it worked; he wouldn't be in jail long. With her sister's help, she'd loaded up her car and left, driving to Flagstaff before calling her father and asking him what she should do. They'd decided Montana was the only place she could go.

———

Serena awoke with a jerk, tumbling from the bed to the floor, a muffled scream clawing its way out of her throat, vestiges of the dream still eating at her psyche.

She pushed herself to her hands and knees as angry, frightened tears fell on the dusty wood floor. She reminded herself nothing could harm her; Trace was not sleeping in the bed beside her, Trace wasn't hiding down the hall or behind the door. She was far away from him. He wouldn't find her. Not here. She took a deep breath, swiped a hand over her damp cheeks, and stood up. She needed coffee.

"Shit," she muttered under her breath as she stared into a bare kitchen cupboard. She opened several others, finding them empty as well. No food in the house. Her parents stocked the house with linens, kept the electricity and the water on, but there was no reason to keep food in a house no one lived in.

The lake house, a condo, was in Lakeside, Montana on Flathead Lake, the largest freshwater lake west of the Mississippi. When she was a kid, her parents bought the condo—an investment according to her father—and every summer growing up, they packed their daughters into the car for the long drive across the country from California to Montana to spend anywhere from two weeks to two months soaking up nature—if nature included a pool, a marina, and an eighteen-hole golf course within walking distance. After Serena and her sister moved out and started their lives, her parents tried to keep up the tradition of visiting every summer, but it had gotten more difficult with every year that passed. It had been ten years since she had been there and at least two since her parents had visited. She hadn't realized they still owned it until her father offered it in a last-ditch effort to keep her safe. Serena agreed, and he'd called ahead to have Clint, the year-round maintenance guy, get the place ready. Apparently, that hadn't included stocking the place with food.

Serena grabbed her phone to search for the nearest grocery store, but before she could, her father's picture popped up on the screen. She forgot she'd promised to call him upon her arrival. He was probably worried sick.

"Hi, Daddy," she answered.

"Goddammit, Serena," Mel Chasey grumbled. "What did I tell you?"

"I know. I'm sorry. I fell asleep after I unloaded the car, and I just woke up. In fact, I was about to look for the nearest grocery store. I need food."

Her father mumbled something under his breath, and she could picture his face—resigned and irritated. "Alright, you're forgiven. How was the drive?"

"Long," she replied. "Exhausting. I'm glad to be here though. Thank you for this. I appreciate it so much."

"I would do anything for you, sweetheart," he murmured. "Anything. All that matters is you're safe."

Fresh tears sprang to her eyes. Serena sometimes forgot how much of a burden the last two years had been on her parents. Swallowing around the lump in her throat, she pushed away the fear threatening to overcome her.

Her father cleared his throat. "You got the credit card I gave you?"

"Yes." It was in her wallet and her only source of income.

"I'm working with the lawyer to get everything moved into new accounts, undetected," he continued. "We'll figure it out. I promise."

"I know you will. Hey, I'm gonna go. I'm starving. I need to get some food. And coffee."

Mel chuckled, then he gave her directions to the nearest grocery store, less than two minutes away. Serena thanked him for the millionth time, said her goodbyes, and grabbed her keys and purse.

A chill shot through her as she stepped outside. Late September in Montana differed from late September in Arizona. It was still in the nineties there, while here, the expected high was in the mid-fifties, and right now it was slightly above forty degrees. The shorts she wore weren't warm enough, but she was desperate for something that wasn't gas station food, so changing clothes would have to wait.

She locked the door behind herself and made her way to the car. As she backed out, she noticed the guy from the condo across the drive walking a beautiful mahogany and black dog in a service vest. She'd never seen a dog quite like him, similar to a German Shepherd, though she didn't think it was. The man was tall, long legged with broad shoulders and thick muscles. He had long chocolate brown hair pulled back in a ponytail, and he'd pushed the sleeves of his sweatshirt up, revealing an intricate tattoo on his left arm. Sunglasses covered his eyes. She waved as she passed him; he ignored her. As she waited for the electric security gate to open, she texted her father.

[Serena: Who's the guy in the condo across from ours? #3, I think?]

She dropped the phone in the cup holder while she drove. It vibrated with an incoming message as she pulled into the grocery store parking lot. She parked and opened the text.

[Dad: His last name is Brooks if I remember correctly. I only talked to him a couple of times. Seemed nice. I believe he's a widow. Moved from NY after his wife's death.]

A widower. And a grouchy one at that. The last thing she needed was another short-tempered jerk in her life. She'd have to do her best to avoid him. She thanked her father for his response, climbed out of the car, and shoved the phone in her back pocket. First thing on her list: coffee. She'd worry about avoiding her new neighbor later.

Chapter Two
Van

Van heard the gate rise before he saw the car. Cars didn't come into the gated community this late, not this time of year. He took his cup of coffee and stepped out on the patio, Soldier at his feet, and leaned on the railing. A woman climbed from the white crossover, the lone streetlight illuminating her. She stretched her arms over her head, her shirt pulling up to reveal her stomach. She turned his direction.

She was tall and curvy, her long caramel-colored hair pulled up in a messy ponytail on the top of her head. A worn pair of shorts and a long-sleeved t-shirt covered her. She was stunning.

He took a step back, startled at the thought bouncing around his head. It had been more than three years since he had found anyone attractive or even looked at another woman with any interest. He'd been too busy hiding from everyone and everything, too busy letting his grief consume him to notice anyone else existed.

He scowled, irritated his thoughts had wandered that direction. He spun on his heel and went back inside.

His phone vibrated from the end table. He snatched it up and hit the button.

"You are the only person who calls me this late," Van growled. "You know that, right?"

"It's because I'm the only person who knows you don't sleep," Lincoln, his best friend, chuckled. "You have a cup of coffee in your hand right now, don't you?"

Van grunted and rolled his eyes. Sometimes, he hated how well Lincoln knew him. He dumped his coffee in the sink and rinsed out the cup. If it wasn't in his hand, he didn't have to lie to Lincoln about it.

"How are you, Van?"

"I'm fine," he grumbled.

"You're a terrible liar." Lincoln sighed. "Seriously, how are you? Are you getting any sleep?"

"A little." Van shrugged, even though Lincoln couldn't see him. "A couple of hours a night, I guess. Better than nothing, right?"

"I guess." Lincoln paused, waiting for his friend to talk. Van kept quiet. "Anything new happening?" he pressed.

"Some woman is at the condo across the drive," he blurted, his mouth getting ahead of his brain. Why the hell had he said that?

"Oh. Um, okay." Lincoln cleared his throat. "You say hi or anything? I mean, you two have to be the only people up there right now."

"Sam and his wife were here last weekend," he muttered.

"Evan." Lincoln rarely used his full name. It meant Van had irritated him.

"No, I haven't talked to her," Van said. "She *literally* pulled in ten minutes ago." Through the windows along the front of the condo, he could see the woman outside pulling a duffel bag and a suitcase from the car. She looked over her shoulder every few seconds, taking in her surroundings. His curiosity piqued, he watched her as she hurried to take her things inside, her eyes darting around as if she was looking for danger. He saw the nervous, frightened look on her face.

"Nobody's stayed over there in forever," he continued, turning away from the window after the woman armed the car's alarm and went inside. "The owners live in California and haven't come up in a couple of years. I met them once or twice. It looks like she might stay for a while, though."

"Huh," Lincoln mumbled. "You should definitely say hi."

"Maybe. Look, I gotta go. Soldier's sitting by the door staring at me. I gotta take him for a walk before we go to bed."

"Sure. Hey, I thought I'd come up next week. Stay for a few days. I need a break, and I've got a few business things we should discuss."

Van knew what his best friend was doing and why. Every fiber of his being screamed at him to tell Lincoln to stay home, but he could use the company. He *needed* the company. Especially with the three-year anniversary coming up.

"Yeah, I'd like that." He pictured the smile lighting up Lincoln's face. He didn't want to listen to him gloat. "Gotta go." He disconnected the call before his friend said anything else.

He hated to admit it, but he missed Lincoln. They grew up together, joined the Army together, and served in Afghanistan together. They had seen things no man should see and come home still friends. Even though he missed his childhood friend, he couldn't bring himself to move back to New York. Not now, maybe not ever. Too many painful memories. And even though it meant he had to run their security business alone, Lincoln didn't complain or push Van to come home. He did nothing but support him. Van didn't deserve a friend like Lincoln Dunn.

He snatched the leash off the counter and kneeled next to his Belgian Malinois, Soldier. He rubbed the dog's flank, attached the leash to his collar, and pressed a kiss to the top of the dog's head before rising to his feet.

"Let's go, boy," he sighed, opening the door.

———

She kissed him on the corner, damn the paparazzi, before she laughed and skipped up the street, smiling back at him and waving over her shoulder. Her contagious enthusiasm made him smile. He shouted after her to wait, but she ducked into the coffee shop, her laughter floating back to him, sweet and vibrant over the sound of the busy New York streets.

Van sighed. What was the point of a bodyguard if she wouldn't let him protect her?

The first scream he heard wasn't hers, but it had him shoving the street vendor who'd stopped him out of the way and darting through the crowd, knocking aside the shocked bystanders. He reached her just as Stockwood dropped the match, the gas igniting with a giant whoosh that knocked the air out of him and sent him stumbling backward. He threw himself at her, the fingers of his left hand twisting in her blouse, the flames dancing up his arm—

Van shot out of bed, clutching his left arm, phantom pains burning into the muscle and bone. Startled, Soldier barked, his loud yip stinging Van's ears. He fell to the floor, shoved himself to his feet, hit the wall, and fumbled for the light switch, the breath tearing in and out of his throat, head pounding, eyes burning with unshed tears. He got the light on before he slid to the floor, still clutching his arm.

Soldier jumped off the bed and sat beside him, whining.

"I'm okay, boy," he mumbled. He lifted his arm, allowing Soldier to slip under it and curl up beside him, his head on Van's lap, staring at his master. Hot tears slid down his cheeks and a sob clung to the back of his throat. He gasped for air, his fingers twisting in Soldier's fur. He dropped his head, burying his face against the dog's flank, the sobs breaking free.

Once he could breathe again, he stood up, pulled on some jeans and a Henley from the closet, and grabbed the bottle of scotch from the floor beside the bed. He pushed open the sliding glass door, stepped onto the small balcony, dropped into the lone chaise lounge chair with a heavy sigh, and set the bottle on the floor. He checked his watch, the illuminated dial informing him it was just after three a.m. Two hours of sleep.

He looked out at the lake, the full moon sparkling like a gem on the water. Soldier slipped past the curtain covering the door and walked to Van's side. He absentmindedly patted the dog's head, his thoughts consumed with images from the past. The dog climbed onto the lounge chair and settled himself between Van's legs, his head on his master's stomach.

"Oof." Van grunted as the seventy-plus pound dog climbed on him. "You're not a lapdog, dude."

Soldier gave him a look, and Van swore if dogs could scoff, he would have. Instead, he closed his eyes and fell asleep.

Van relaxed into the chair and scratched between the dog's ears, staring at the surrounding night, sipping from the liquor bottle on the floor. He loved the lake this time of year; it was quiet, and the summer guests had gone home. He was the only year-round resident in the condos, though that hadn't been the plan when he and Adelaide purchased it six years ago. Now and then, some of the other summer residents—those who lived in Missoula or northern Idaho— would come around for a weekend, but no one else was there year-round.

Summers stressed him out. The sleepy town overflowed with vacationers and tourists, strangers mixed in with the familiar faces of the town's residents. He always felt a sense of relief once Labor Day passed, knowing the tourists would leave. The college students were hard to deal with, but he'd gotten good at avoiding them over the years, staying close to home and out of the popular hangouts. It still wasn't as crazy as living in New York.

A light came on in the condo across the way, reminding him of the unexpected visitor. He saw her moving behind the closed blinds, then a few minutes later, the kitchen light came on. The woman who appeared out of nowhere was a curiosity. She seemed skittish and nervous; he was always hypervigilant about those things, noticing the little things others didn't.

His breath caught in his throat, an unwanted memory forcing itself to the surface. He scrubbed a hand over his face. He didn't always notice everything; the one time he should have, the one time it had mattered more than anything, he had failed miserably. A shiver raced through his body, and tears filled his eyes again. He swiped at them, furious with himself. It had been months since he'd had a breakdown, months since he'd let the memories of that day consume him. The approaching anniversary weighed heavily on him.

Van grabbed the bottle and downed the rest of the alcohol inside. God, he'd give anything for a good night's sleep. Surviving on three or four hours—or less—a night for the last three years was slowly destroying him. Two days ago, he'd noticed gray hairs in his beard and several strands in his hair. Wrinkles had appeared on his forehead and at the corners of his eyes. He felt out of sorts, unable to function as he once had, doubting every choice, every decision. He didn't trust himself anymore. Not like he had before Adelaide—

"Nope. Not going there," he grunted, lifting Soldier off his legs and throwing the blanket to the side. He slipped on his shoes, then he whistled for the dog. "Come on, boy. Let's go for a walk."

Chapter Three

Serena

The trip to the grocery store exhausted her. Constantly looking over her shoulder, worrying Trace would appear out of nowhere, messed with her psyche. By the time she filled the cart with all the groceries she thought she might need, a thin layer of clammy sweat covered her, her hands shook, and her heart pounded so hard it hurt. Checking out seemed to take an eternity, the man behind the register chatting about every item she purchased. She nodded politely and smiled, though she was sure it didn't reach her eyes. Once her things were bagged, she mumbled her thanks and rushed out the door.

Back at the condo, Serena backed the car right up to the side door and hurried to unload. After everything was inside, she slammed the door, threw the deadbolt, and slid to the floor, her head in her hands, her breath tearing in and out of her throat. It took a few minutes to get herself under control before she could put everything away.

She'd hoped she could get to the retailer at the edge of town to buy some warm clothes, but after the grocery store, she wasn't sure she could deal with another trip away from the condo. Not right away. Instead, she hauled blankets out of the second bedroom and pulled a few of her favorite movies from the drawer under the television. She made a pot of coffee and a bagel, then she settled in for the day, content to stay inside, hiding away from the world.

Halfway through the second movie she wasn't watching—it was background noise while she drifted in and out of consciousness—she glimpsed the guy from the condo across the way and his dog heading toward the marina. She sat up and watched as they walked down the pier and climbed aboard a beautiful gray speedboat. Within minutes, he was in open waters, headed who knew where, the dog perched on the stern, his mahogany and black fur ruffled by the wind.

Serena sank back into the cushions and closed her eyes. Her curiosity about her neighbor surprised her; after everything she'd been through, men should have been off her list. All men, even handsome, mysterious widowers who lived across the street.

———

Serena pulled the blanket tighter around herself, shivering as the cool air hit her bare feet. After going to bed at 8 p.m., she woke up around 3:30, forcing herself out of a nightmare, the same one she'd had for months, dreams of Trace chasing her. She stumbled around in the dark and tried to find the light, smashing her toe into the corner of the wall, bringing tears to her eyes.

After injuring her foot, there was no sense going back to sleep. Not that she would anyway, not when she couldn't shake off the vestiges of the past or the recurring nightmare.

She should be grateful she had slept at all. Prior to coming to Montana, she'd been lucky to get an hour or two a night. She felt better since her arrival, more at home than she'd been in the last year and a half. Her house in California was the stuff of nightmares and horror movies, more frightening than comforting. The half a dozen apartments she'd lived in after she left California were nothing more than stopping points on the road to freedom, a freedom she could never quite grasp. Arizona had felt like home until Trace had ripped it away from her, forcing her to run. Again.

Here in Lakeside, Serena felt normal. Free. She'd always loved the small college town. It was beautiful, pure, a wonderful place to live. Every summer, she begged her parents to move from their home in California to Lakeside. Over time, she'd forgotten how much she loved the Montana town. It had taken less than forty-eight hours for her to fall in love with Lakeside all over again.

No one from her old life—the one she'd shared with Trace—knew about this place: only her family. They would never tell. Her family craved her freedom almost as much as she did. She prayed this time it worked. She could make a home here, settle down, start over. Maybe she'd go back to school; her degree in marketing wouldn't do her much good here, but maybe she could find a new passion. A fresh start.

Serena pinched the bridge of her nose and sighed, sinking deeper into the couch, deeper into the blankets. She was wide awake, her eyes burning. She wanted to sleep for a week, maybe two. The muscles in the back of her neck and in her shoulder twinged, drawing a weary groan from her. She pushed herself to her feet; she needed to move, to shake off the stiffness the lack of movement caused.

If she were going to live here, she needed to make it her own. Get rid of the old stuff belonging to her parents, bring in some things that belonged to her. She'd start by cleaning, which was cathartic for her. She spent the next couple of hours dusting, wiping down walls, vacuuming, cleaning the bathrooms, and rearranging things, boxing up some old, outdated knick-knacks and even moving the furniture. As she cleared away several years of dust and rearranged things, she realized she was still missing a lot of supplies, along with warm clothes, socks, boots, and a coat.

She was at the store as soon as the sun came up, her cart loaded with long-sleeved t-shirts, sweaters, jeans, socks, a few sweatshirts, a heavy jacket, gloves, and a hat. She picked up a new comforter for the bed and some new sheets, a few candles, some cleaning supplies, and a couple of books she'd been meaning to read. The credit card took a hit, but she knew her father would understand.

By nine, she was back at the condo. She made coffee and breakfast while she watched the news, and the new comforter tumbled around the washing machine. After she put it in the dryer and started the sheets, she grabbed a book and sat on the chair in front of the immense picture window overlooking the lake. Instead of reading, Serena stared at the water lapping gently against the shore.

She tossed the book on the table, tugged on one of her new sweatshirts, and stepped outside. It was a cool cloudless morning, leading her to wonder if it might warm up in the next few hours. She considered going for a walk, but the thought had her gasping for air and gripping the porch rail so tight her knuckles ached. Doing something so normal scared her. Nothing about her life had been normal for years. *Could I go back to the way things were so easily?* It seemed impossible and frightening.

"Fuck it," Serena muttered to herself. "I can do this." She sucked in several deep breaths and stepped off the porch.

She strode across the small lawn and up the road. There was a small bench in the park on the other side of the marina; if she could make it there, she'd be okay. She could do it. Her fear was unnecessary; Trace was over a thousand miles away on the other side of the country. He couldn't hurt her. Once she started down the road by the golf course, she could see the bench. She focused on it and the calm, blue water on the other side of it, repeating to herself she could do it.

When she lowered herself to the bench, a smile playing at the corners of her mouth, it was as if someone had lifted a weight from her shoulders. It had been almost freeing, the walk to the park. For the first time in what felt like forever, she could breathe. She leaned back and closed her eyes, soaking up the morning sun.

Something cold nudged her hand, startling her, and she squeaked in surprise. She opened her eyes to see the gorgeous mahogany dog sitting by her feet, a beat-up tennis ball in his mouth, his tongue somehow hanging out the other side.

"Well, hi there." Serena laughed.

The dog dropped the ball in her lap, tipped his head to one side, and waited expectantly, tail wagging. She picked up the soggy ball and tossed it ten feet away, near the edge of the water. The dog took off like a shot, snatched up the ball on the go, whipped around, and brought it back to her. He dropped it in her lap, then he turned, waiting for her to throw it again. Before she could pick it up, a loud voice boomed behind her.

"Soldier! *Komen*!"

The dog's ears perked up, and his tail wagged faster. He grabbed the ball off Serena's lap and took off at a dead run. She twisted around in time to see him drop the ball at the feet of the guy from the condo across the street. Like the previous day, his hair was in a ponytail, pulled away from his face, and the sleeves of his long-sleeved Henley pushed up, allowing her a brief glimpse of the tattoo on his arm. He crouched in front of the dog and murmured something to him. The dog dropped his head and rested it on the man's knee, his big, brown eyes staring up at him. He ruffled the dog's fur, kissed the top of his head, picked up the ball, and threw it, much harder than Serena had. It soared through the air so fast it whistled.

"Sorry if he was bothering you," he called. "He's overly friendly."

"It's okay," she replied, rising to her feet. "He wasn't bothering me. He's sweet. What kind of dog is he?"

The man smiled and chuckled under his breath, his gray eyes flashing. "Don't tell him he's sweet. He'll get a big head." He cleared his throat and took a step closer. "He's a Belgian Malinois. His name is Soldier. And I'm Van."

"You live across the street." Serena mentally smacked herself; he knew where he lived.

"I do." Van smiled. "And you are?"

"I'm Serena Chasey." She didn't move closer, but neither did Van. They stood a few feet apart, eyes locked, the only sounds the water slapping the shore and Soldier's panting. After about thirty seconds, he cleared his throat again and shifted from foot to foot.

"Are you here long?" he asked.

"I don't know." She shrugged. She honestly *didn't* know. "It's...it's kind of up in the air right now."

Van nodded and crouched beside Soldier, who was staring up at him, the ball in his mouth. He attached the leash in his hand to the dog's collar and rose to his feet. "Well, it was nice to meet you, Serena. I'm sure I'll see you around. After all, I do live across the street."

Serena caught his wink as he spun around and walked away. "Bye," she mumbled, raising her hand in a half-hearted wave.

Heat flooded her cheeks as she stared at Van's retreating form. *When did small talk become so difficult?* She'd be lucky if Van ever gave her the time of day after her abysmal conversation skills. It had been so long since she'd had so much as a casual chat with anyone, male or female, she had forgotten how to act. She pushed a hand through her hair and for the millionth time, cursed Trace's existence. She returned to her seat on the edge of the bench and stared out over the water, wondering when—or if—she would feel normal again.

Chapter Four

Van

By the time Van got back to his condo, he was shaking and sweating. He ran up the stairs, Soldier on his heels, and shoved open the door, slamming it closed behind him and stumbling to the kitchen. He splashed some cold water on his face, but it did nothing to make him feel better, so he grabbed the bottle of Xanax sitting beside the sink, spun off the lid, dumped out two pills, and swallowed them. Not even bothering with a glass, he sucked the water straight from the faucet, then he dragged himself to the couch and sat down, his head in his shaking hands.

Soldier whined, creeping closer, his leash dragging behind him. He rested his paw on Van's leg and whined again.

"I'm okay, boy," he mumbled, resting his hand on the dog's head. "Come here." He patted the sofa beside him.

Soldier didn't hesitate, jumping up on the couch and curling up beside his human. Van slipped off his leash and tossed it on the side table. He rested his head on the back of the couch and closed his eyes, desperately trying to shake the fear clutching his heart.

What was I thinking, talking to that woman? If his damn dog hadn't been the friendliest creature on the planet, he might have gotten out of the park without having to talk to his new neighbor. He wasn't good with people; shit, he wasn't good *for* people. Everyone he got close to got hurt. Keeping to himself was for the best.

As if to prove him wrong, his phone rang, Lincoln's name popping up on the screen. He contemplated not answering it, but if he didn't, Linc would keep calling.

"Yeah?"

"Is that how you greet your best friend?" Lincoln chuckled.

Van grunted something incoherent as he scrubbed a hand over his face.

"What's wrong?" Lincoln asked.

It shouldn't surprise him Lincoln knew something was wrong; he always did. It's what happened when you'd been best friends with someone your entire life; they knew you inside and out.

"I talked to the girl who's staying across the street," he muttered.

"That's a good thing," Lincoln said. "Right?"

"It was until I freaked out," Van grumbled. "The second I walked away from her, I came unglued. Shaking, sweating, trouble breathing. I'm not even sure how I made it back to the house. I popped two Xanax, and now I'm sitting here cursing myself out and hating myself, so guilty I think I might puke."

"Van—"

"Don't say it, Lincoln. Don't tell me Adelaide would want me to be happy. Don't tell me she'd want me to move on. I can't, not after..." He blew out a shaky breath. "I love her. I'll always love her—"

"You don't have to stop loving her, Evan," Lincoln interrupted. "Nobody is asking you to stop loving her. It's been three years, and it's time for you to live again. Maybe getting to know your new neighbor could be a start?"

Van's mouth snapped shut. He scrubbed a hand over his face and through his hair, pushing it out of his eyes. Lincoln was right.

"I'm gonna be there Friday," Lincoln said after several seconds of silence.

"You don't have to come."

"Already bought my plane ticket, dude. I'll rent a car in Missoula and drive up. Go buy some steaks and take the cover off the grill you bought. I expect dinner when I get there."

"Yes, sir." Van sighed. "I'll see you on Friday."

He disconnected the call and tossed his phone on the table. He toed off his boots and kicked his feet up, stretching out on the couch. Soldier huffed, got to his feet, rearranged himself between his master's legs, rested his head on Van's knee, and fell back to sleep.

He closed his eyes and breathed deeply, concentrating on relaxing, like all those therapy sessions taught him. Not that he'd cared or even tried, but now and then the things he learned came in handy. He focused on the sounds coming through the open door and windows—the waves lapping against the shore and the birds in the trees. He ignored the sound of his neighbor's door slamming closed, refusing to let himself be curious about her.

Van dozed off, the image of Serena smiling and petting Soldier behind his closed eyes.

———

The steaks, a couple huge potatoes, and a bunch of asparagus sat on the counter while the beer chilled in the cooler on the patio. Lincoln had called after his plane landed, and he'd gotten his rental car. Van expected him in an hour if the weather held.

He finished making up the extra bedroom and straightened up the bathroom, then he went downstairs to start dinner. He enjoyed being busy; it kept him from thinking too much about Adelaide. He'd already ignored calls from his sister, Rebecca, and Lincoln's mom; he knew they meant well, and they wanted to check on him, but he couldn't talk about it. It had been three years since he'd talked about it; nothing had changed.

Once he had the steaks marinating and the potatoes ready to go in the oven, he grabbed a beer and Soldier's leash. He was out the door and halfway down the stairs when a large white SUV rounded the corner. It parked in his driveway and his best friend stepped out.

Soldier took off like a shot, yanking his leash free of Van's hand to dart down the stairs and into Linc's arms. Lincoln stumbled back into the SUV, laughing at the dog's antics. He set him down, the dog's leash wrapped around one hand, his other hand raised in greeting.

"Loser!" Van yelled, trying and failing to keep the smile off his face. It was good to see Lincoln, especially today. His friend had a way of keeping him centered, keeping him sane. Whether he wanted to admit it or not, he was glad Lincoln was there.

He met Lincoln at the base of the driveway and let his friend pull him into a one-armed hug.

"It's good to see you." Lincoln grinned.

"As much as I hate to admit it, I'm glad to see you, too." Van laughed. "Thanks for flying across the country to hang out with me."

"How are you?" Lincoln asked.

"Really, Linc?" Van sighed.

His friend shrugged. "You knew I was gonna ask. Might as well get it out of the way."

"Same. I hate this day." Van scrubbed a hand over his face. "I don't want to talk about it." He cleared his throat. "Let me take Soldier for a walk, and then I'll start dinner."

"I'll tell you what," Linc said. "I'll take Soldier for a walk and *you* start dinner. I'm stiff after flying across the country and driving for the last two hours."

"It's because you're getting old," Van joked. "All right. You take my dog for a walk, and I'll get dinner ready. Give me your keys."

Lincoln tossed him the keys, clicking his tongue twice to urge Soldier to follow him as he took off down the road toward the lake. Van watched them go. After Linc rounded the corner, Van grabbed his duffel bag from the SUV, locked it up, and went inside. He fired up the grill and cut up the asparagus while he waited for the grill to heat.

He'd just put the steaks on and the asparagus in the steamer when the door opened, and Lincoln called his name. Van stepped back inside, only to come face to face with his new neighbor.

Van froze, his mouth dropping open. He glanced at Lincoln, who gave him a sheepish grin as he crouched down to take off Soldier's leash.

"Uh... hi, Van..." Serena mumbled. "I... I hope this is okay."

Lincoln bounded to his feet. "I ran into Serena outside, and we got to talking. She's all alone over there, so I invited her for dinner."

Van raised an eyebrow and grunted. He swallowed and nodded. "Sure. It's... it's great. We've got more than enough food." He spun on his heel and hurried out the back door. He grabbed the tongs and flipped the steaks, muttering under his breath.

"Van?"

He forced a smile on his face before turning around.

Serena stood in the doorway, smiling shyly. "Are you sure you're okay with me staying for dinner? I know you weren't expecting me." She pushed a hand through her hair and shrugged. "I understand if you want me to go."

God, I'm a jerk. She was the only other person in the neighborhood aside from Clint, and he was being an asshole. It wouldn't hurt to let her stay for dinner. Besides, it might keep Lincoln from talking about Adelaide.

"I'm sorry," he murmured. "I'm being an ass. I don't want you to go. I was surprised. You're more than welcome to stay. Would you like a beer?"

"I'd love one." She nodded.

Van grabbed a beer from the cooler and handed it to Serena. "Sorry, I was kind of a jerk. I wasn't expecting company."

"Don't let him fool you." Linc chuckled from behind them. "He's a jerk."

Van shook his head and glared at his friend over Serena's shoulder. Lincoln shrugged and disappeared back inside.

"How do you like your steak?" Van asked.

"Medium rare. If you don't mind?"

"Woman after my own heart." He smiled. "A steak and beer kind of girl."

Serena laughed, raised her beer above her head, and nodded. God, she was beautiful, especially when she smiled. It lit up her entire face and made her eyes sparkle.

He took a drink of his beer. "What brings you to Montana in the off-season?"

A shadow crossed Serena's face, and she swallowed, her throat clicking. She shifted from foot to foot and stared at something over his shoulder.

"A fresh start, I guess. My parents own the condo. When I needed a place to go, they offered it to me. We used to come up here during the summer, but it's been years since I was here. Funny, this place always felt like home, even though I was only here a few weeks a year."

Van nodded. "I get it. There's something soothing about this place. Aside from how gorgeous it is, it just feels right. My wife and I fell in love with it when we visited, and when we found this place, she was ecstatic. She'd never been happier." A lump rose in his throat and his eyes burned. He hadn't meant to bring up Adelaide, especially not today, but talking to Serena was easy. He wanted to talk to her; he wanted to tell her about himself. He took a drink of his beer, wiped his mouth with the back of his hand, and cleared his throat. "I should check the potatoes."

Serena put her hand on his arm. "I'll do it. I might even set the table." She winked at him and squeezed his arm. "Lincoln knows where things are?"

"He does." He pointed in the kitchen's direction. "Don't let him get out of helping you. He's a lazy bastard."

"I heard that," Lincoln yelled from inside.

"I wasn't trying to be quiet!" Van yelled back.

Serena's laughter followed her inside and made Van smile. He could get used to hearing it.

By the time he finished with the steaks, the potatoes and asparagus were done, and the table set. Lincoln had even started a fire, warming the chilly room. Van shucked his sweatshirt, and Serena took off her heavy sweater.

Dinner was a tremendous success. The food was perfect, and the beers were ice cold. To his surprise, Van didn't think about Adelaide once throughout the entire meal. After they cleared the table and put the dishes in the dishwasher, Serena ordered Van to make coffee before she darted out the door, yelling over her shoulder she'd be right back. Ten minutes later, she was back with a plate covered by a towel.

"Dessert." She whipped off the towel to reveal an enormous stack of home-made chocolate chip and sugar cookies.

"You might be the best neighbor ever." Van chuckled.

Serena blushed and scrubbed a hand through her hair, laughing nervously. Lincoln swooped in, assuaging the awkwardness by playing server and taking everyone's coffee order. They got comfortable in the living room, chatting while they sipped coffee and ate cookies.

Lincoln told Serena about his and Van's security business in New York, going into detail about some of their more colorful employees and a few of their eccentric clients. Van sat back and let him talk. It had always been Linc's strongpoint: small talk, engaging conversations, getting people to open up to him. He was good at it.

Van had no idea how long they sat in front of the fire talking; time seemed suspended, frozen. He couldn't take his eyes off Serena; she enthralled him, watching her, listening to her. There was something under the surface, something hurting her, bothering her. He could sense it, feel it. That was *his* strongpoint, understanding people on an emotional level. It was why he and Linc made such superb partners; Lincoln got them talking and Van got to the heart of the matter. He'd missed it.

"I gotta get some sleep," Lincoln said, rising to his feet, drawing Van from his musings. "My time zones are all out of whack. Serena, it was lovely to meet you. Don't be a stranger. Van could use another friend beside me."

Van scowled. Nothing like telling Serena he only had one friend.

Serena smiled at Lincoln and nodded. "Thanks for inviting me, Linc. This was... it was nice. I've had a great time." She stood up, too. "I guess I should head home, too."

"I'll walk you." Van shot to his feet before Lincoln could volunteer.

"You don't have to. It's across the street..."

"It's dark, though. I don't want you to walk alone." He grabbed his sweatshirt and held Serena's sweater out to her. "It's not a bother. I promise."

Lincoln stopped halfway up the stairs and ducked his head to look at them. "There's no sense in arguing with him. He's chivalrous to a fault. Let him walk you home."

Serena grinned. "I won't argue." She took the sweater from Van, waved goodbye to Lincoln, and let Van lead her out the door.

Van may have been chivalrous, but walking Serena to her condo was a little foolish. It was across the street, and it took them less than two minutes to get down the stairs and across the road to her door. The light on the porch wasn't on, so the only illumination came from the streetlight on the corner. It cast a dim glow over her front door. They stood in the pale-yellow light, staring at each other like they had the first time they met.

She tucked a strand of hair behind her ear and cleared her throat. "Thanks again for letting me stay for dinner. I'm sorry if Lincoln overstepped his bounds by inviting me."

"Linc frequently oversteps his bounds." Van chuckled. "Especially when it comes to my life."

Serena shook her head and grabbed the doorknob. "He worries about you. At least, that's what he told me."

"He does." He smiled. "I love him for it."

"He's a good friend."

"He is. A better friend than anyone can understand."

Silence fell over them again. Serena scraped her shoe in the dirt next to the doorstep while Van desperately tried to think of something to say. Serena beat him to it.

She pushed open the front door. "Thank you for walking me home."

"You really should lock your door," Van scolded. "Crazy things happen, even in a small town like this."

A funny look crossed Serena's face and her eyes darted around. "I... I didn't think about it. You're right of course." She pivoted to look behind her, her elbow bumping his arm when she turned, her foot coming down on his, causing her to stumble into him. Van grabbed her elbow and the doorjamb to keep them both upright, pulling her against his chest at the same time. The top of her head hit his chin, knocking his head back. He grunted as pain shot through his jaw.

Serena's hands landed on his chest. "Oh God! Van, I'm so sorry."

"It's okay," he muttered, rubbing his chin. "Trust me: I've had worse." He squeezed her arm. "Are you okay? I didn't mean to scare you."

"I'm fine." She smiled, though it didn't reach her eyes. "Being in a new place makes me nervous, I guess." She moved backward, pulling herself free of his grip as she stepped through the door. "I'll talk to you later." The door closed in his face.

Van exhaled and pushed a hand through his hair. He must have said something to upset her. He didn't know what or how, but he'd done something; otherwise, she wouldn't have reacted that way. A hard knot sat deep in the pit of his stomach. Things had been going so well; he'd had fun for the first time in forever, and he hadn't thought about Adelaide or the fact it was the anniversary of her death even once. *How do I always fuck things up?*

He stared at the closed door, wishing he could think of something to say or do to fix whatever he'd broken. For the first time in three years, he felt alive, like he could breathe. A slamming door had knocked that right out of him. He spun around and stalked back across the street. He didn't know why he'd even tried. He wasn't good for anybody; the world would be better off if he kept to himself.

Chapter Five

Serena

She shut the door in Van's face and sank to the floor, her back against the door, her knees pulled up to her chest. She wanted to stay outside and talk to Van, maybe invite him in for a few minutes, but sudden fear gripped her heart. She needed to get inside where it was safe, away from the oppressing darkness of the night and the possibility of Trace appearing.

Serena wrapped her arms around her head and prayed, prayed for respite from Trace's insane hold over her. She'd hoped the opposite side of the country would be far enough away from the asshole to end it forever.

She pushed herself to her feet and peered out the window, watching Van cross the street, his shoulders stiff. She should open the door and call after him, but the fear wouldn't let her go. Instead, she threw the lock and wandered deeper into the house.

She'd had a good time, a great time. Lincoln was funny and easygoing, while Van was more intense and serious. She could see how they made excellent business partners; they offset each other well. She was insanely curious why Van was in Montana and Lincoln was in New York when they had a business to run. It had to be because of Van's wife. Her father said he was a widower and the things Lincoln told her confirmed it. But what happened?

The more important question was why she was so interested. It wasn't like she was looking for a new man. She didn't want or need a man in her life, not after the way the last one treated her. She should swear off men forever.

So, why can't I stop thinking about my neighbor?

Her interview for the receptionist position was at eleven in the president's office. She'd once been a marketing executive at a high-end advertising firm in Beverly Hills, but she wouldn't find a job like that in Lakeside. She'd applied for several positions at Lakeside University, including the receptionist to the university president. She hadn't expected to interview for it, not when she had zero experience, so getting the opportunity was a blessing. There wasn't a lot to choose from in a town this small—it was the college or nothing, especially during the tourist off-season.

Every time she thought about the upcoming job interview, her stomach churned, and her hands shook. No matter how many times she interviewed for a job, it rattled her. She tossed and turned for hours, drifting in and out of sleep until she finally gave up and got out of bed well before the sun. Wrapped in a heavy sweater, she sat on the patio with her coffee, watching the sun sparkle on the lake as it rose behind her. A breeze came in off the water, making her shiver.

Voices rose in the air behind her; two men laughing and the playful yipping of a dog. Van and Lincoln. They walked past her condo, headed down the road toward the marina. She considered calling after them, but she bit her tongue and watched them walk by.

Two gorgeous men: one broken and the other longing to help him heal. When she'd run into Lincoln on Friday, and he'd invited her to dinner, he had warned her Van might not love the idea of her being there, even explained why. She'd tried to beg off, but he was insistent, persuasive, reminding her she should get to know her neighbor. He'd promised to be a buffer, but it hadn't been necessary. Van had been wonderful.

They got on the same boat she'd seen Van get on last week. A few minutes later, they headed for the middle of the lake, Soldier sitting on the stern, an adorable doggie grin on his face. Serena wished she were with them, though she didn't want to insert herself in their friendship. She was a neighbor who barely knew either of them.

It wasn't like she had time for fun anyway. The job interview was less than two hours away. Getting a job was at the top of her to-do list. She couldn't keep relying on her father for money; it didn't feel right.

She needed more coffee. Lack of sleep made caffeine a priority. She stood up and watched Van's boat speeding across the water for a few minutes before she went inside. Nervous energy kept her moving; she straightened up the living room, washed the few dishes in the sink and put them away, then she made another cup of coffee.

Despite her exhaustion, she felt energized and ready to conquer the day, if not the world. A shower helped wake her up, and the familiar routine of getting ready calmed her nerves. She went easy on the makeup—she didn't have much anyway—then she dried her hair until it cascaded over her shoulders and framed her face. She pulled on a pair of dark gray cords and a blue sweater, shoved her feet into her favorite boots, and switched the few paltry items in her backpack to her purse. A last glance in the mirror on her way out gave her a boost in confidence. For once, she didn't look or feel like she was on death row.

Maybe things were going to take a turn in a good direction.

———

Charles Ross shook his head and chuckled. "You're seriously over-qualified, Ms. Chasey. You have a bachelor's degree in marketing, and you're applying for a position as an administrative assistant. I feel guilty even *suggesting* you take the job."

"Are you offering it to me?" Serena smiled.

"Yes," Charles replied. "But are you sure this is what you want? There must be something better out there for you. Maybe in Missoula?"

"I live here in Lakeside, Mr. Ross. I want to work here."

"Then the job is yours," Charles said. He rose to his feet and held his hand out. "Can you start next week?"

"I could start tomorrow." She laughed, shaking the university president's offered hand.

"Well, I think my current assistant might take offense to getting kicked out a week early." He grinned. "I look forward to seeing you next week, though. Stop and see Marcie on your way out. She'll give you your paperwork and tell you where to return it."

"Thank you so much, Mr. Ross," Serena gushed. "I can't tell you how much I appreciate this." She prayed he didn't notice the tears gathered at the corner of her eyes. She would cry once she was in her car.

"Call me Charlie." He shook her hand. "I'll see you soon."

Serena floated out the door, her feet inches off the ground. Marcie was extremely helpful, even putting her cell phone number at the top of the employee handbook so Serena could contact her with questions. Marcie invited her to come in on Friday for a few hours so she could acclimate herself with the office and ask questions. Serena readily agreed.

On her way home, she decided she should celebrate. She stopped at the store and grabbed a couple bottles of wine and a sour cream cake with a brown sugar glaze. She also picked up a rotisserie chicken, a salad, and some vegetables. It was too much food for one person, but at least she'd have leftovers for a few days.

Back at the condo, she noticed Lincoln's rental wasn't in the driveway anymore. Maybe he and Van had gone out for burgers at the country club or something. If she remembered correctly, they had exceptional burgers.

Serena parked next to her condo and stepped out of the car. Van came around the corner, Soldier walking beside him, off his leash. As soon as the dog saw Serena, he darted up the road and slid to a stop in front of her. He bumped his head against her leg, pushing her against her car.

"Hey there, buddy," she murmured, crouching beside him.

"Wow, he is really taken with you." Van laughed. "I'm sorry he keeps bugging you."

"He's no bother at all." Serena scratched Soldier behind the ears, earning herself a sloppy kiss on her cheek. "He's sweet." She bounded to her feet. "I thought maybe you and Lincoln went to grab a burger or something."

Van shook his head. "Linc is on his way to Missoula. He has a 5 a.m. flight back to New York."

"Oh," she mumbled. "He, uh, didn't stay long."

Van shrugged. "Gotta get back to business." He glanced in the back seat of her car and cleared his throat. "Can I help you take your groceries in?"

"Sure." She nodded. She pulled open the door and let Van take the bags out while she unlocked the door. He followed her inside, Soldier at his heels, and set the bags on the kitchen counter. He nodded at her and turned to leave.

"Would you like to stay for dinner?" she blurted.

"I wouldn't want to impose."

"No imposition. I promise. I'd love some company. It's no fun celebrating by yourself."

"Celebrating?" Van inquired, his head tipped to the side, one eyebrow raised. "What are you celebrating?"

"I got a job today." She grinned, bouncing on her toes. "The administrative assistant to Lakeside University's president."

"That's outstanding! Congratulations!" A smile lit up Van's face, and Serena couldn't help but think how gorgeous he looked.

"So, will you stay? I have chicken, vegetables, and a salad, plus two bottles of wine. I have more than enough to share."

"I'll stay." Van nodded. "Let me run Soldier home—"

"No." She interrupted. "He can stay. He'll behave himself, right?" She shot a playful, stern look in Soldier's direction. He barked in response, which made her laugh.

"He better." Van chuckled. "At least let me help."

Serena smiled. "You can clean and chop the vegetables while I change. The cutting board is in the cupboard, and the knives are in the top drawer." She left Van to work and went to change her clothes.

She slipped on a pair of jeans, a long-sleeved t-shirt, and a pair of fuzzy socks, then she pulled her hair into a low ponytail. By the time she got back to the kitchen, the salad was made, the vegetables cut, sprinkled with olive oil, and in the oven. Van had also poured two glasses of wine, set them on the table, and was poking around her fireplace.

"This is a mess," he stated. "I'll call Clint—ask him to come by and clean it. Don't use it until he does; it's a fire hazard."

"Okay." She nodded. "Thanks. I probably would have tried to start a fire and burned the place down." She handed him a glass and sat on the edge of the couch. She took a sip of the crisp white wine and sighed.

"Tell me about your new job," Van urged, sitting on the opposite end of the couch.

Serena launched into a brief explanation of her new position, which somehow turned into a discussion about how nervous she'd been and how badly she needed the job. Van listened intently, his gray eyes locked on hers. When she stopped talking, he was nodding.

"It's hard to start over." For the first time since they'd sat down, he didn't look at her, his gaze drifting to the large picture window facing the lake. "You think you can't do it, and every day you struggle to get through the day without losing it. It seems like it goes on forever until one day you wake up, and it's a little easier to make it through, and the next day is easier, and the next even easier. Of course, then you feel guilty because it's getting easier, which makes you wonder if you're forgetting what was once important in your life." He rubbed his hand over his left arm, and Serena could have sworn there were tears in his eyes.

"Van–" she began.

"Nothing's harder than starting over when you don't want to, though. When your entire world turns upside down and everything changes and you *have* to change, even when it kills you inside. Starting over after losing the person you loved more than anything in the world is the worst."

The timer on the stove went off, and Van shot to his feet, swiping at his eyes as he brushed past her to take the vegetables from the oven. She followed him into the kitchen, and together they dished up the food and refilled their wine glasses. They sat at the breakfast bar, the silence between them thick and uncomfortable. Serena shifted in her seat and stabbed her fork into her vegetables. She glanced at Van, who looked as uncomfortable as she felt. She took another sip of wine and decided to hell with it.

"Van? Can I ask what happened to your wife?" she asked. She knew he probably wouldn't want to answer, but she had to try.

Van laid his fork beside his plate and wiped his mouth with his napkin. He wouldn't meet her eyes. "I don't like to talk about what happened."

"I'm sorry. I understand if it's too difficult to talk about. Forget I asked."

Serena endured a few more minutes of uncomfortable quiet, nothing to fill the emptiness but the scrape of silverware across the plates and Soldier's snorts and yips as he dreamed. Just when she thought she couldn't endure another minute of the suffocating silence, Van cleared his throat.

"My wife was Adelaide Brooks."

"The actress?" Serena asked. "I love her movies. She was wonderful."

Van nodded. "She was amazing. Even though most of her work was in California or Canada, we lived in New York because it was home for both of us. She'd gotten popular enough I thought she should have security; she hated the idea. I won. Lincoln assigned one of our best men to head up the detail. Jasper traveled with her when I couldn't, kept an eye on her when I wasn't able to. I trusted him with her life." He picked up his wine and downed what was left in the glass, then he grabbed the bottle and filled the glass to the brim. "Six months after we assigned him to Adelaide, she went to Lincoln and begged him to take Jasper off her detail. After a lot of coaxing, she admitted he'd hit on her, rather aggressively. She didn't want to tell me. She told Linc she was afraid I would do something stupid."

"Did you?"

Van shook his head. "No. I did fire him. He was furious, claimed he and Adelaide were in love and she was lying to save my feelings. I didn't believe him; Adelaide would never do that to me. We'd been in love since high school; we were inseparable. I took over her security detail. For months we dealt with Jasper stalking Adelaide: phone calls, emails, showing up at movie premieres, on the set of a television show she was shooting, even at our apartment in New York. The only peace we got was a two-week vacation here. Once we were back home, it started all over. We got a restraining order. I took the security detail down to a bare minimum to keep her whereabouts a secret; I did everything to keep her safe. He terrified her. Absolutely terrified her."

"What happened?"

"Adelaide had gotten a part in a Broadway show, so we were in New York. She convinced me to take her to her favorite coffee shop, said she was tired of being cooped up at home, hiding from the world. I agreed. She was a bright light, so full of life and energy—the opposite of me. I couldn't resist giving her what she wanted." Van rubbed a hand over his face and exhaled. Tears glistened on his cheeks. "Sorry. I... I haven't talked about this in a long time."

Serena rested her hand on his arm and smiled gently. "It's okay. Take your time."

Van cleared his throat and took another drink of wine. "I got hung up outside talking to some street vendor, let her out of my sight for a minute. It was too long. I heard her scream... and... and..." He brushed at the tears streaming down his face, his voice dropping to a low whisper. "By the time I got to her, Jasper had covered her in gasoline and was standing beside her. He lit a match and dropped it, engulfing them both in flames. I threw myself at Adelaide, tried to grab her but... it... it was useless."

Van shoved up the sleeve of his shirt on his left arm, revealing the intricate tattoo she'd glimpsed several times. Loops and swirls covered his arms from the wrist to the elbow. Beautiful artwork hid the deep scars burned into his skin. Serena ran a finger over the markings, a tear sliding down her own cheek.

"I'm so sorry." The pain he must have suffered; she couldn't fathom what he'd gone through.

Van tried to smile, but it came across as a painful grimace. "After her funeral, I moved here. I can't go home."

"This is your home now," Serena said. "I'm sure Adelaide would be happy to know you've made a home here. You said she loved it."

"She did."

"Well, she'd want you to be happy."

Van chuckled. "That's what Lincoln always says."

"He's a smart man." Serena laughed. She squeezed his arm and decided it was time to change the subject. "Hey, how about we have some dessert and some more wine?"

"I think I'll take a raincheck," Van replied, pushing himself to his feet. "I should get home." He snapped his fingers to get Soldier's attention. "Soldier, *komen*." The dog jumped to his feet and went to his master's side. "Thanks for dinner."

Serena could only watch, speechless, as he left, closing the door quietly behind himself.

Chapter Six

Van

Van took Soldier for his morning walk before the sun was up, then he holed up in the house for the rest of the day, hiding from Serena. He told himself it was for the best; he wasn't the kind of person a woman like Serena needed in her life. She didn't need a trainwreck like him invading her space. As much as he was drawn to her, he knew staying away would be better for her.

The knock on the door came when he was heating a can of soup for dinner. He contemplated not answering it, but the knock came again, louder and more insistent. He turned off the stove and went to the door, Soldier at his feet.

"I know you're in there, Van," Serena yelled. "You might as well open the door."

Soldier barked, earning himself a dirty look from his owner. Van pushed a hand through his hair, gathered it at the back of his neck, and wrapped the rubber band from his wrist around it. Then he yanked the door open.

"Hey," he said. "What's up?"

"I know you're avoiding me," Serena said. "I think I even understand why."

"Serena—"

"Let me finish," she snapped. "I understand better than you can imagine. But right now, I think we could both use a friend. I like you; you're a good guy. And I think you like me—at least I hope you do. I guess all I'm asking is if we can be friends. Trust me, Van. That's all I want. A friend."

Van held the door open and gestured for her to come in. She snatched a paper bag off the ground by her feet and stepped inside.

"Chicken sandwiches," she explained. "And cake, since you bailed on me last night."

"Did you bring the wine?"

"I did. So I can stay?"

"I'm making soup. It'll go great with the sandwiches. You pour the wine, and we'll sit by the fire. It's warmer over there."

"Sounds great." She smiled.

———

Three weeks after Serena started her new job, she showed up at Van's door and asked him to take her to dinner.

"I need a night out," she explained. "My job is going great, I like the people I work with, and I think it's about time I get to know the town. People keep asking me if I've been to this place or that place, and I have to say no. And it's been forever since I've gone out and had fun. It's Friday, and I don't work tomorrow. I thought I'd let you take me to dinner."

"You'll *let* me take you to dinner? I don't get a choice?"

Serena's jaw moved and her eyes narrowed. A grin spread across her face when she realized Van was teasing her. "Come on, Van. Take me to dinner. It'll be fun. Please?"

Van shook his head and laughed. "Okay, but there's only one place I'll go."

"I'm at your mercy." She shrugged. "Give me an hour?"

"See you then," Van replied.

He hadn't realized he needed another friend until Serena came along. She was exactly what he needed, especially with Lincoln on the other side of the country. She demanded nothing from him, nothing more than his friendship, and it thrilled him.

They'd fallen into an easy, predictable pattern; dinner once or twice a week—sometimes at his place, sometimes at hers—walks with Soldier and breakfast on Saturday or Sunday morning.

Even though they were becoming friends—good friends—Serena held back a part of herself. She didn't talk much about her life before Montana. He didn't know what she'd done, where she'd lived, or even if she'd been involved with someone. No matter how much he pushed, or questioned, or hinted she could confide in him, she wouldn't budge. She was tight-lipped about her life before Lakeside.

He longed to get her to talk to him, like he'd done with her. Telling Serena about Adelaide—something he'd only spoken to Lincoln about—seemed to break down some emotional barrier that had been holding him back. For the first time in three years, he felt alive. He looked forward to getting up in the morning, and he looked forward to seeing Serena, spending time with her, talking to her. He hadn't felt like this in years, not since Adelaide.

Serena was back in one hour. His heart stopped when he opened the door and saw her. She wore a pair of black jeans, a cream sweater, and a red scarf. She had on a pair of high-heeled black boots, bringing her almost eye-level with him. Her long, caramel-colored hair was down, loose curls framing her face. She was gorgeous.

"You're staring," she murmured, blushing.

He chuckled. "Sorry. You clean up nice."

"As do you," Serena observed, eyeing him up and down.

He'd changed into clean jeans, a lightweight gray sweater, and a black leather jacket. He didn't dress up much; this was as close as he got. It pleased him to know Serena approved.

She looped her arm through his. "You driving?"

"Yes, ma'am." He pulled the door closed, then he led her to his truck parked at the back of the condo. He opened the door for her, took her elbow, and helped her inside.

"Where are we going?" she asked.

Van started the truck, backed out of the driveway, and waited for the security gate to open. "My favorite place to eat in this town is the Time Out Bar and Grill. It's close to the college on the water. It has a fabulous view. I think you'll like it."

"Sounds great." She stared out the window for a few minutes. "I can't tell you how much I appreciate this, Van. How much I appreciate you. Things haven't been normal for me in a long time. I've had a few tough years. Extremely tough. Being around you, being your friend, it... it means the world to me. Thank you."

Out of the corner of his eye, Van saw Serena wiping her eyes with a tissue from her purse. He bit his tongue; it was obvious someone had hurt her. Someone Van now wanted to hurt. He didn't speak, but instead reached across the seat and took her hand, his fingers intertwined with hers.

They drove in silence to the restaurant, but it wasn't awkward or uncomfortable. It was two friends leaning on each other, taking strength from each other. Van suspected his feelings for Serena were becoming more than friendly, morphing into something more. While the thought terrified him, kept him awake at night, he was doing his best to accept it.

Fear kept him from embracing those feelings, fear of the unknown, fear the feelings weren't returned, and fear of being disloyal to Adelaide. His wife had been the first and only woman he had ever loved and feeling something akin to that with another woman felt like a betrayal.

The Time Out Bar and Grill was busy. The parking lot was crowded with cars, and raised voices and loud music spilled out the open door. Serena took Van's hand and leaned into him as they walked to the door. It felt right, her hand in his. He liked it.

It seemed as if everybody was on the dance floor or shoved up against the bar. They weaved through the crowd to the tables at the back of the bar. Serena had a death grip on his hand, squeezing it so tight it hurt. He found a table as far from the crowds as they could get, pulled out Serena's chair for her, and eased into the one beside her.

Her hands shook, and her eyes darted around as if she were looking for danger. She exhaled a shaky breath.

Van slid his chair close to hers and rested his arm on the back of it. "Serena? What is it?"

She shook her head, her lip caught between her teeth, her eyes wide and terrified. "I... I just... I'm sorry, Van. I don't know if I can do this. There are so many people."

He rested his hand in the middle of her back and rubbed gentle circles on it. "Look at me, Serena. I won't let anything happen to you. I promise. But you have to tell me what's wrong."

She turned to face him, fear written in every worry line on her face. "You'll think I'm being stupid," she whispered.

"I won't. Tell me what's wrong."

She dragged in a deep breath, then another before she spoke.

"His name is Trace."

———

Serena excused herself to splash some water on her face, glancing over her shoulder at least twice on her way to the restroom. While she was gone, their server, Trista, took their order, beers and burgers, promising to get it to them as quick as possible, despite the crowds. Van thanked her. Serena returned a minute later.

"Okay, I'm listening," he said as she eased into the seat.

"Are you sure you want to hear this?" She pushed a shaking hand through her dark curls.

"Yes, I'm sure. As long as you're willing to tell me."

"Trace is my boyfriend... *was* my boyfriend. We were together for a little over a year. I've been hiding from him for almost two. Or trying to hide from him."

The hairs on Van's arms stood up, and a thick knot settled in his gut. "Why are you hiding from him?"

Serena stared at him, tears glistening in her azure blue eyes. She shrugged. "He hit me, Van. A lot."

Van closed his eyes and gritted his teeth. "He hit you."

"I made him angry—"

"No," he interrupted. "Do not blame yourself for what that piece of shit did."

Serena nodded, the tears now sliding down her cheeks. "I'm sorry."

"Don't apologize. You get to feel whatever you want." He sighed. "So, you came to Montana to get away from this Trace guy. He doesn't know about the condo?"

She shook her head. "No. I never talked about it. My dad thought it would be a good place to get away. To start over. I... I hope he's right. But I still get scared, you know? I've spent two years looking over my shoulder wondering if he was there. I don't feel safe anywhere. Crowds... a lot of people... they scare me. I worry Trace is hiding in the crowd. Who am I kidding? Everything scares me. I desperately want it to be over, I want things to be normal, I want to *feel* normal, but I'm afraid I never will."

Van took her hand and held it between his. "You don't have to be afraid. I will keep you safe. I won't let anything happen to you." The words tasted bitter on his tongue; he'd said the same thing to Adelaide.

"Promise?" Serena whispered.

"I promise."

"All right. Here we go." Trista set their beers and food on the table in front of them, interrupting their discussion. "Can I get you anything else?"

"No, Tris, thank you."

"Who's your friend?" she asked.

Serena smiled at their waitress. "I'm Serena. I'm new here. Van tells me you guys have the best food in town."

"Nice to meet you, Serena. I'm Trista. You can call me Tris." She wiped her hands on her towel then shook Serena's. "The reason Evan thinks we have the best food in town is because we're the only restaurant he'll eat at. But the service is always friendly, and the beer is cold." She patted Van on the shoulder. "Let me know if you need anything else."

"Evan?" Serena said, turning to look at him after Trista left.

Van chuckled. "Full disclosure: my first name is Evan. My nickname is Van."

"I can't believe I've known you for a full month, and I'm just finding out your actual name is Evan. Wow. You think you know people." She shook her head and took a bite of her burger. "Mm, these burgers are good, though."

"You okay?" he asked.

Serena nodded and gave him a half-hearted smile. Van took a drink of his beer and watched her. She tried to act like she was okay, but he could see the fear in her eyes, hear the tremor in her voice when she spoke. His blood boiled; if he ever got his hands on this Trace guy, he would teach him what it felt like to get the shit kicked out of him. Men like Trace were cowards and didn't deserve to have *any* woman in their lives, let alone a woman as good as Serena.

"You're not eating," she mumbled around the food in her mouth. "Not hungry?"

"Yeah, sorry. Off in thought." He grabbed the ketchup and drowned his fries in it, then he dug into his burger.

He let it go, even though he was curious about Trace. He wanted Serena to have a good time tonight. It hadn't escaped his notice when she said it had been a long time since things had been normal for her, and not only did it make him angry, it made him determined to give her some sense of normalcy. Trace may have destroyed her, but Van would fix her. It started tonight: excellent food, good beer, and good music. Anything to put a smile on her face.

Starting tomorrow, he would find out everything he could about Trace. And he would make sure the man never hurt Serena again. He would protect her, no matter what.

Chapter Seven

Serena

Serena leaned against Van as he unlocked her door and helped her inside. He flipped the light on in the kitchen and led her to the living room.

Her head spun, and her cheeks felt hot. She'd had too much to drink, but she'd had *fun*. For the first time in years. The food had been fantastic, the music had been loud, and the drinks had flowed. She'd beaten Van at pool, though she suspected he had let her win. Not that it mattered—they were having a good time. Van even smiled a few times. When they played darts, she switched to margaritas, swearing it would improve her aim. All it did was make her giggle and hit the wall beside the dartboard instead of the actual board. She didn't care; she had a great time.

Once Van released her, she leaned over to take off her boots, but all the blood rushed to her head, and she fell forward. Luckily, she landed on the couch, a hiccuping giggle leaving her. She flopped over, yanked her sweater off, leaving her in a light t-shirt, then she stretched out on her back, and stared at the ceiling.

"I need help, Evan." She laughed, kicking her feet.

"I'm gonna kill Trista for telling you my real name," he grumbled. He perched beside her on the couch and pulled her legs into his lap.

It took some maneuvering, but he got her boots off. He got up and set them beside the door, then he grabbed a blanket from the basket at the end of the couch and threw it over her. He crouched beside her and brushed her hair away from her face.

"Get some sleep. When you wake up, drink some water, and take a couple pain pills. I think I saw a bottle of ibuprofen in the kitchen. Otherwise, you'll have one hell of a hangover."

Serena nodded, wincing when it made the room spin. Van patted her arm and stood to leave, but she caught his hand, stopping him.

"Van, wait," she murmured.

"Hm?" he grunted, dropping to his knees beside her.

"Thank you."

"You already said thank you, sweetheart." He laughed. "Several times."

Serena shook her head. "Not for tonight. For everything, listening to me, understanding what I'm going through, and for promising to protect me. It's the first time I've felt safe in over three years. I can't possibly repay you for that."

"You don't have to repay a thing." Van sighed. He brushed a finger down her cheek. "I have to keep you safe; you mean too much to me to let anything happen to you."

A gasp escaped her, the air pushed from her lungs as Van's eyes locked on hers. His fingers drifted down her cheek to slide around the back of her neck. Sandalwood and spice washed over her, making her stomach flutter with unexpected need. Serena surged up, her mouth on Van's, the kiss intense, lingering. Her toes curled, her fingers twisted in the lapels of his jacket, her tongue darting out to trace his lower lip.

He abruptly released her. "I have to go," he said.

"You could stay."

Van kissed the corner of her mouth and pushed himself to his feet. "God, Serena, you tempt the shit out of me. But it's been a crazy, emotional night for both of us, and we've both been drinking. I don't think either of us is thinking rationally right now. So, I'm gonna go home. I'll see you in the morning. I'll bring coffee and bagels." He kissed her forehead and then he was gone, the door slamming closed behind him.

———

Serena shoved the blankets off and swung her legs over the side of the bed. Her stomach rumbled, either from too much liquor or the need to eat. She ran her hands through her hair, pulling it off her neck into a ponytail. She stared out the window at the winter storm rolling across the lake. The clouds touched the water, the wind blew in tremendous gusts, and snow swirled through the air.

She pulled on a pair of jeans, a sweater, boots, and her heavy coat, then she slipped out the door, intent on walking to clear her head. She hadn't slept a wink, not after the kiss, not after Van's revelation.

He cared about her.

At least, she thought it was what he meant when he said she meant too much to him to let anything happen to her. As much as it scared her, she felt the same thing for him. So much had happened in both of their lives—so much pain, so much hurt. Her heart ached for him, for herself, for everything the two of them had gone through, for everything that had broken them. Two broken people drawn to each other. She didn't know if they could make it work. *Why can't things be simple?*

The wind stung her cheeks, sharp needles of cold stabbing into her cheeks. She wrapped her arms around herself, climbed the hill, turned left at the gate, and started down the road next to the golf course.

She walked until she stood on the playground at the park near the water, staring at the lake and the dock, reliving every minute of the previous night. For the first time since everything with Trace, she felt alive. Van brought something to life inside of her, something Trace destroyed while they'd been together. She wanted to grab onto it and never let it go. She wanted Van.

After he'd left last night, she'd chastised herself repeatedly, wondering if she'd pressed him too hard, pushed him too far. Except she knew if she could go back and do it again, she would still kiss Van. And she wouldn't let him leave.

The dock went a hundred feet out into the lake, a wooden bridge floating on the water, secured by a few thin ropes tied to cement poles anchored in the lake. On the windiest of days, the dock swayed side to side; walking on it felt like walking a tightrope suspended over the Grand Canyon. She remembered chasing her sister up and down the dock, laughing, making a game of not falling in the water.

The wind blew through the trees, and the waves crashed against the shore, making the dock rock and sway like a crazy carnival ride. She shivered, zipped her jacket up to her chin, and chided herself for not grabbing her hat and gloves on the way out the door. She hadn't been thinking when she'd left; she had to move, to burn off some of this energy keeping her awake. Ever since she was a kid, she would take a walk when she needed to clear her head, so that had been the first thing she'd thought to do when she woke up for the hundredth time.

Serena followed the path from the playground to the dock and without hesitating, she stepped onto it. Van's anguish over the loss of his wife played like an incessant drumbeat in the center of her chest, ripping her heart to shreds with every tear she remembered falling from his eyes. She wanted to comfort him, to take away the pain she knew he lived with every day, but fear held her back. She wasn't good enough for him; she was too broken.

The stinging bite of the wind against her face drew her from her thoughts. She was steps away from the end of the dock. A strong gust of wind pushed her forward, forcing her to her knees. She stared into the murky depths of the churning waters of Flathead Lake. She hadn't realized she'd walked all the way to the end of the dock. A spray of icy cold water hit her in the face, and another gust of wind made the dock rock dangerously beneath her. Her fingers dug into the wood and splinters embedded themselves in the tips of her fingers. She dragged in a shaky breath and squeezed her eyes closed.

"Serena! What the hell are you doing?"

Fright propelled her forward, the sharp voice startling her, fear gripping her heart and sending her over the edge of the dock and into the freezing water. Her heavy coat sucked up the water like a sponge, and she immediately sank. She flailed her arms—she'd never been much of a swimmer—and tried to scream, but she swallowed the icy water, instantly freezing her throat and making her sputter.

"Serena!"

She heard someone call her name as a wave washed over her, pulling her under. She kicked her feet and reached for the surface, but there was nothing to grab onto. Another wave hit, more water went down her throat, her gasps and cries drowned out by the crashing waves.

Serena struggled to keep her head above water, feet kicking, arms pumping, anything to stay afloat. When she came to the surface again, she glimpsed Van racing toward her, then Soldier launched himself into the water, landing beside her and sending more water over her head. Instinct had her reaching for him, her fingers twisting in his coat, and he was beside her, his breathing loud in her ear as he turned to swim toward the dock with her arms wrapped around his neck.

Van laid down on the dock, his arms outstretched. As soon as she was close enough, he snagged her coat and hauled her out of the water, dragging her onto the dock beside him. A second later, Soldier was there too, his cold nose nudging her cheek.

"Jesus, she's gonna freeze," Van said. "Come on, boy." He leaped to his feet and picked her up, holding her tight against his chest. He hurried through the grass to his truck parked haphazardly in the parking lot. He set her on the passenger seat, then he ran around the truck and ripped open the door. Soldier jumped in and Van followed, slamming the truck into gear, the tires kicking up dirt and gravel as he backed up and turned toward the road. Serena's teeth chattered and her entire body shook as waves of exhaustion rolled over her. The heat in Van's truck wasn't enough to combat the cold seeping into her bones and taking over her body. He parked in his driveway, ripped open the passenger door, and hauled her out, holding her tight against his body. She buried her face against his chest, grateful for his warmth.

Van sprinted up the stairs and inside, pausing long enough to let Soldier in and to kick the door closed behind him.

"What the hell were you thinking? Walking on the dock in this weather. Jesus, Serena, you're lucky I saw you walking down the road, or you'd be dead. You scared the shit out of me." He set her on the floor in front of the fire and kneeled beside her. "We have to get you warm, okay?"

Serena nodded, unable to speak, her throat raw and frozen, her jaw aching thanks to her chattering teeth.

"Yeah, well, you might not be so cool with it when I take off your clothes. I gotta get you out of your wet clothes. Are we still good?"

"D-do it, d-d-d-dammit," she stuttered.

Van stripped off her clothes—jacket, sweater, boots, and jeans—leaving her in her bra and panties. He grabbed a faded quilt from the back of the couch and wrapped it around her. He stood up long enough to take off his jacket and kick off his shoes, then he threw another log on the fire and sat down beside Serena, his arm around her.

She rested her head on his shoulder and looked up at him. "Th-th-thank you," she said. A chill raced through her, the shivering intensifying.

"Thank me when you warm up. You're still trembling, and your skin is ice cold." He glanced around the room and pushed himself to his feet with an angry huff. "I'll be right back."

He disappeared up the stairs. Serena could hear drawers opening and closing and Van muttering curses. Soldier crept closer to her until his head rested against her leg. He stared up at her with his big brown eyes and whined.

Serena rested her hand on Soldier's head. "G-good b-b-boy." If it weren't for him, she'd be dead. She squeezed her eyes closed. She couldn't think about that right now.

The stairs creaked as Van came back down. He dropped another blanket, a sweatshirt, and two huge towels on the floor beside her. He'd changed into a pair of gray sweats and a plain black t-shirt, wool socks on his feet. He sat down behind her, took hold of her hips and pulled her between his legs, her back against his chest. He picked up a towel and dried her hair as best he could, then he helped her put on a heavy University of Montana sweatshirt.

"Come here, boy," he ordered, snapping his fingers until Soldier wearily pushed himself to his feet and trudged closer to his master. Van used the second towel to dry off the dog, then he ordered him to lie down before he pulled another blanket over Serena's legs and wrapped his arms around her waist.

Serena dragged in a deep breath. It hurt. Soldier nudged her hand with his nose, so she adjusted the blanket to cover him.

Van chuckled. "I'm sure he appreciates that."

"He saved my life," she rasped. She tried to clear her throat, but it hurt too much. "He can have anything he wants."

"Yes, he can," Van agreed.

Serena turned on her side and laid her cheek on Van's chest. She closed her eyes and relaxed, safe in Van's arms. His grip on her never loosened; he kept her tucked tight against his chest, his hands splayed across her back.

Chapter Eight

Van

Van dragged in a deep breath and squeezed his eyes closed. He held Serena close, rubbing circles on her back, holding her tight. He refused to think about what had happened. He'd come too close to losing her.

"Van?" she murmured.

"You shouldn't talk. You need to rest."

She shook her head. "What did you mean?"

"What?"

"You said I scared you. Why?"

Van tucked her wet hair behind her ear and kissed her temple. "I thought I lost you. The thought of losing you when I just found you—it terrified me." He pressed another kiss to her temple, his lips lingering. "I promised to protect you no matter what and instead, I almost lost you because of a damn storm—"

"It was stupid to go out on the dock," Serena interrupted. "I wasn't thinking. I'm so sorry."

"All that matters is you're all right," Van insisted. He took hold of her chin and tipped her head back, forcing her to look at him. "Don't scare me again." He brushed a kiss across her lips.

Serena stared up at him, her cerulean blue eyes staring right into the depths of his soul. He swallowed back the fear struggling to take him over, to devour him.

"Van? What's wrong?"

He shook his head. There weren't enough words to tell her what she'd done to him in the short time they'd known each other.

"I-I don't know," he mumbled.

Serena sat up and turned to look at him. "Do you know why I was out there, walking in the storm?" She inched closer to him. "I was out there thinking about you. About you and me." She grabbed his hands, holding them tight between hers.

"You and me, huh?"

"I don't know what to do, Van. I like you. I enjoy spending time with you. Our friendship makes me happy, happier than I've been in a long time. But I'm scared, too. Scared to let myself feel anything for anybody. I've been hurt, shit, more than hurt, I've been destroyed, terrorized, ripped to shreds." Tears glistened in her eyes. "I think you could help put me back together again."

Van closed his eyes and exhaled. "God, Serena, it's like you can read my mind. I've been feeling things for you I haven't felt since my wife died."

"Why didn't you tell me?"

"God knows I wanted to. So many things held me back. Guilt. Fear. Doubt. I wasn't sure you wanted me. But after I kissed you and you asked me to stay—" He shook his head and laughed. "You don't know how hard it was to walk away last night."

Serena surged forward and flung her arms around his neck, her mouth on his, the kiss desperate and needy.

Van returned the kiss, his fingers digging into her hips as he dragged her into his lap. "I want to make you whole again," he growled. "Let me make you whole again, baby."

"Yes." She nodded. "Jesus, yes. Please."

He kissed her lips, her cheek, moving down her jaw and her neck to her shoulder, her skin still ice cold. He hooked a finger in the sweatshirt's collar, pulling it aside and sucking gently where her neck and shoulder met. Serena's eyes closed, her head fell back, and her body relaxed under his touch.

Van slid his hands up her bare thighs, under the edge of the sweatshirt, pushing it up and off. Serena shivered. He ran his hands up and down her arms as he continued kissing her.

"Are you still cold?" he asked.

"Yes." She sighed. "Sorry."

"Stop apologizing, sweetheart," Van scolded. "You fell in freezing cold water less than an hour ago. It's going to take some time to warm up."

Serena grabbed the front of his t-shirt and pulled him down on the floor on top of her. "You could warm me up." She tipped her chin and pursed her lips, nodding at him, an invitation.

Jesus, she was going to kill him. She laid beneath him, her damp hair fanned out around her, a smirk on her face, and complete trust in her eyes. Van kissed her, exploring her mouth with his tongue, his fingers skimming over her bare skin, memorizing her perfect body. Goosebumps rose on her skin everywhere he touched, everywhere he kissed, her body trembling under his hands.

Her fingers tangled in his hair, urging him back to her lips. She moaned into his mouth, the sound shooting straight to his cock. He let out an answering groan, his entire body on fire with need for this woman. His lips roamed over her body—her breasts, her stomach, her hips. He kissed a trail up her legs, stopping to knead, lick, and suck her inner thighs. Serena's hips thrust forward, chasing his mouth, but he wasn't ready yet; he wanted to take his time with her, savor her.

Van took her hands, holding them at her sides as he worked his way up her almost naked body—kissing her stomach, licking the soft mounds of her breasts, his tongue dancing over the lace covering her nipples. He nipped the sensitive skin of her neck before catching her lips in his, pushing his tongue into her mouth to kiss her again.

"Van," she gasped when he pulled away. She trembled, her fingers digging into his hips, her breath tearing in and out of her throat. Her eyes were dark with lust, her lips swollen from his kisses.

He couldn't get enough of her; it might never be enough. He reached behind her to unhook her bra, sliding it down her arms, his lips trailing after it. He tossed it aside and took her breast in his mouth, suckling it.

"God, you're so beautiful," Van growled. "I want you so bad, sweetheart."

Serena nodded and tugged his hair, pulling him to her mouth, kissing him. "Yes, Van," she moaned. "God, yes."

Van scrambled to his feet and yanked off his clothes, then he dropped to his knees and pulled Serena's lacy black panties down her legs, his lips once again on her stomach. He settled himself over her, his head between her legs. He had to taste her.

"Van, what are you doing?"

"I want you, sweetheart. I want to taste every inch of you."

Serena gasped and squeezed her eyes closed, her head shaking from side to side. "I-I don't know. I've never—"

Her mouth snapped shut with an audible click when Van flattened his tongue and slowly ran it along her silken folds. He groaned as her taste flooded his mouth. Something snapped inside of him, his control slipping. He dove in, burying his tongue and two fingers in her pussy, desperate for more, desperate to give her as much pleasure as he could. He lost himself in her, lost himself in the sounds she made, the gasps and moans, the way her body moved, her hips rising to meet his mouth, her hands clenched in the blankets beneath her. Her chest rose and fell, her breathing ragged until she screamed her pleasure as she came in his mouth and on his fingers.

Van held her, lapping at her soaking wet pussy, his finger brushing her swollen clit until she collapsed in a boneless, out of breath mess. He kissed her stomach, sloppy, wet kisses that made her giggle as he moved back up her body and buried his face against the side of her neck.

"Shit," he muttered. "I don't have any condoms."

"I'm on the pill," Serena replied. "I trust you."

"Are you sure?" he whispered, his lips brushing against her ear.

"I need you, Van. Make love to me. Please."

Van didn't hesitate. He pulled her legs around his waist and slid into her, almost coming from the feel of her warm heat surrounding him. He clenched his jaw, groaning as she writhed beneath him. His cock ached with the need to fuck her senseless. He closed his eyes, his hips flexing, moving carefully, afraid of hurting her, afraid he wouldn't be able to control himself.

Fingers tangled in his hair and soft lips moved over his neck. "Don't stop." Serena sighed. "I want this. I want *you*."

That was all he needed. His restraint, his self-control, vanished at those words. He slammed into her, burying himself deep, her hips rising to meet his. Tangled together, bodies moving, hips thrusting, lips crashing together, breath mingling, indistinct murmurs of praise and reassurance coming from them. She dragged her nails down his back, marking him as another orgasm consumed her, her body thrashing with pleasure. Her name rumbled from his chest as he came, her walls clenching around him, milking his cock dry.

They collapsed together in front of the fire, wrapped around each other, exchanging kisses. Van brushed her hair away from her face, reveling in her beauty. He couldn't stop kissing her; she was too good to be true. He was afraid to move, afraid this would end up being some beautiful dream he would wake up from and she would be gone.

"Is this real?" Serena whispered, echoing his thoughts.

"It is." Van chuckled. "Doesn't feel like it, though, does it?"

A tear slid down Serena's cheek. He brushed it away with his thumb. "What is it?"

She shrugged. "It's nothing. I'm...I'm happy, I guess. For the first time in forever, I'm not afraid."

Van kissed her, hugging her close. "As long as you're with me, you don't have to be afraid. I promised to protect you, and I meant it."

Serena nodded. She rested her hand on his cheek and smiled. "Thank you, Van. For everything." She snuggled close to him, her head resting on his chest.

Van covered Serena with the quilt, brushed the hair from her forehead, and grabbed his phone from the table. Soldier opened one eye, huffed, and rolled to his back, bumping into Serena. She didn't move.

He took his phone and went up the stairs, ducking into his bedroom and pushing the door closed behind himself. He hit the button to call Lincoln, put the phone to his ear, and waited.

"Loser!" Lincoln greeted him. "What's up?"

"Hey, asshole." Van chuckled. "I need a favor. I need you to investigate someone for me. I don't have much information though."

"Hold on." Van could hear shuffling and grunting, Lincoln muttered something, and someone responded. "Alright, go ahead."

"His name is Trace. I don't have a last name."

"How the hell am I supposed to find some guy without a last name?" Lincoln grumbled.

"He lived with Serena. Find him through her."

"What's going on? Who is this guy?"

"It's her ex and the reason she's in Montana. He was abusive. I think it goes deeper than that. I want to know how deep. So, find any guy named Trace connected to Serena Chasey. They lived in California when they started dating."

"Is that all you know?" Lincoln asked.

"It is. I know it's not a lot to go on, but I want as much info as you can get me. Especially a current location, any restraining orders, reciprocity with Montana, anything you can find out." Van scrubbed a hand over his face. Always start with information: the more you knew about the enemy, the better equipped you were to handle him when confronted.

"Is Serena okay? Are you?"

"We're both fine. I'll be even better once you get me what I need. I can't protect her if I don't know what I'm going up against."

"Should I be worried?" his best friend asked.

"Not yet. I'm trying to be cautious."

"Does this mean what I think it means?"

Van laughed. "It might. You know I don't kiss and tell."

Lincoln let out a loud whoop. "You told me everything I need to know. Thank God. I knew there was something about her I liked. She is a gift, dude, and you better treat her like one. I like her. A lot."

"Yeah, so do I. And for some crazy reason, she likes me. Get back to me as soon as you can. I gotta go." Van disconnected the call before Lincoln could ask him any more questions. He wanted to get back downstairs to Serena.

She was still under the covers, the top of her head visible, Soldier curled up beside her. Van stepped into the kitchen and started a pot of coffee, then he poured some food into Soldier's bowl. The dog's head popped up at the sound, and he slowly padded into the kitchen, stopping to stretch beside his master.

Van crouched beside him and smoothed his fur, checking him over for any injuries. He'd been so concerned with Serena he'd forgotten Soldier had dived into the ice-cold water, too. The dog seemed none the worse for wear.

"You're a good boy, buddy," Van praised. "Good job today."

Soldier licked Van's cheek and yipped quietly as if he agreed. Van scratched behind his ears one more time before rising to his feet and gesturing for Soldier to eat.

"Do I smell coffee?" Serena mumbled from the floor.

Van crossed the room in two long strides, dropping to the floor beside her and gathering her in his arms. He caught her lips in his and kissed her, her arms coming up around his neck as he crushed her to his chest.

"Hi," she murmured when he released her.

"Hi." He grinned. "You hungry?"

"Starving." She extricated herself from his grip and grabbed the sweatshirt from the floor, tugging it on.

Van helped her to her feet, the sweatshirt falling almost to her knees. He pulled her back into his arms and kissed her again.

"I could get used to this." Serena sighed.

"So could I," he agreed. "Come on. I've got some coffee cake in the fridge. Let's get some food in you."

Serena nodded, her hand in his as he led her to the kitchen. He could definitely get used to this.

Chapter Nine

Serena

Dating Van was easy, simple. Pure. He cared about her, that much she knew, but he didn't burden her with the knowledge. Trace had used his love for her—if you could call it love—like a weapon, wielding it like a sword, holding it over her like an executioner preparing to remove her head from her body.

Is it possible to fall in love with someone in less than week? Because she thought she might be falling in love with Van. She thought falling in love again would frighten her; fear kept her from ever going down that road again. For Serena, love was abuse, love was terrifying, love was pain.

Van was the opposite of all the bad she'd known. He demanded nothing of her and gave her everything in return. She was happier than she ever thought possible. She felt free, content, *alive.*

"Earth to Serena," Van whispered, squeezing the hand he held in his. "You okay over there, sweetheart?"

"Yeah, sorry." She laughed. "Lost in thought." She turned to face him, tucking her foot under her leg. "Did I tell you thank you for this? Going to this faculty thing with me, I mean."

Van kissed the back of her hand. "You can thank me later." He chuckled.

Serena laughed and nodded. God, he made her feel good. "Oh, I will, trust me."

The "faculty thing" was a faculty party at Charles Ross's house. Every year, Charlie had an enormous dinner party for everyone who worked at the university. He claimed it was the one time of year he could get all the staff together under one roof. Ross wouldn't take no for an answer: everybody came, no excuses. He promised Serena if she showed up for this one party, he wouldn't bother her again for another year.

When she'd told Van about it, he'd offered to go with her. She hadn't even had to ask. She'd thrown her arms around him and kissed him, which had led to a satisfying round of sex up against the wall in his living room. That had been his first thank you. The other would come later tonight after they got home.

Van followed Serena's directions, coming to a stop in front of a huge three-story house on the edge of the lake. He whistled as he put the truck in gear and peered through the windshield at the brightly lit home.

"This is impressive," he said.

"Wow," Serena breathed. "I'm under-dressed for a place like this."

"You look gorgeous," Van told her. He gave her hand a tug, urging her closer. She slid across the seat, into his arms. He kissed her, his hand sliding up her leg, under her skirt.

Serena slapped his hand and nipped at his lower lip. "Later," she laughed.

Van groaned, pushed open the truck door, and helped Serena out. He wrapped his arm around her waist and led her to the front door. He tugged at the collar of his shirt, grimacing. Serena pushed his hand away and straightened his collar.

"You look great."

"I hate dress shirts. And jackets," he grumbled. "You're lucky I like you."

"More than lucky." Serena smiled, pressing a kiss to the corner of his mouth. "Blessed."

The door opened and Charlie ushered them inside. Serena introduced him to Van, then they followed him through the foyer and down the hall to the back of the house. The living room opened to a patio and a vast yard sloping downhill and right up to the edge of the lake. Strings of lights hung from the trees, portable heaters sat every ten feet, and fall foliage decorated the twenty-five tables at the edge of the patio.

Charlie showed them where the bar was, then he excused himself to greet more guests. A substantial crowd had gathered; some of them Serena knew, most of them she didn't. Even though Lakeside College was considered a small university, it had a large staff.

Serena greeted those she knew as they moved through the crowd, her hand in Van's. She stopped to hug Marcia and ask how retired life was treating her, she nodded hello to the town sheriff, Donna Willis, whom she'd met on a couple of occasions, and she waved at Professor Campbell and his best friend, Jacob, a young professor who would start at the university second semester.

They stopped at the bar where Serena got a glass of wine and Van got a beer, then they found an empty table and took a seat. Van slung his arm over the back of her chair, his fingers brushing her shoulder. Something so simple shouldn't have made her heart pound and heat rise in her cheeks. Knowing Van did it out of genuine affection rather than possessiveness presented a scenario she wasn't accustomed to.

Serena leaned into him and kissed the corner of his mouth, a smile dancing across her lips.

"What was that for?"

"For being you." She shrugged. "And for being so great. You make it easy."

"What do I make easy?" His arm slid off the back of the chair and circled her waist, his breath blew warm against her ear.

She almost told him how he made it easy to love him, but she bit her tongue and held back. Not now. Not yet.

"Everything," she said instead. "You make everything easy."

———

Serena had a great time. She'd worried they wouldn't have fun, that Van wouldn't, but those fears were laid to rest early in the evening. Van was quick to make friends; she was a bit surprised, considering how grumpy he'd seemed when they first met, but he was jovial and easygoing. He chatted with her colleagues like they were old friends, accepted invites to go fishing or off-roading. He even agreed to look at Charlie's ailing boat.

Food, drink, and dancing consumed the evening. Van twirled her around the dance floor and hummed quietly in her ear, his arms tight around her, holding her close as they danced to her favorite songs. She pinched herself several times to make sure she wasn't dreaming.

They were one of the last to leave, the party winding down after midnight. They chatted with another couple in the driveway for a few minutes, entertaining the notion of a couple's night out before saying their goodbyes and climbing into the truck. Van turned on the heat and pulled her against his side as they drove home. Serena rested her head on his shoulder, her hand on his leg, her face aching from smiling all night.

Van parked in his driveway, helped her from the truck, and led her across the street. She handed him the key to the condo and let him unlock her door. He paused outside the door.

"Aren't you coming in?" she asked.

"Was waiting for you to ask, sweetheart." He smirked, stepping across the threshold and pushing the door closed behind him.

Serena tossed her jacket over the chair and kicked off her boots. She sank onto the couch with a sigh, rested her head against the back, and closed her eyes.

Van sat down beside her, put his finger under her chin, tilted her head back, and kissed her, his tongue dancing across her lips until she opened her mouth, a breathy moan escaping her.

"I've been wanting to kiss you all night."

"I can't believe you waited so long," Serena mumbled.

"It took a lot of restraint." He chuckled. "I like your work friends."

"They liked you. A lot." She sat up, took his face in her hands, and kissed him, nipping at his lower lip. "Let's go in the bedroom."

Van laughed, gathered her in his arms, and carried her down the hall to the bedroom. She'd left the light on the bedside table burning—she always left a light on—so Van carried her inside and sat on the edge of the bed with her still in his arms. He held Serena tight as he stretched out across the bed, her head on his arm, his hand on her waist, his fingers under the edge of her sweater, cold against her skin.

Serena tucked herself against Van's side, her arm around his waist. He tangled his fingers in her hair, cupped her head in his hand, tugging her even closer. He took her leg and pulled it up over his, his leg between hers, his thigh grazing her center, his chest pressed to hers, his hand on her hip holding her in place. His kisses were soft, gentle, almost timid.

"You know I'm not breakable, right?" She giggled.

Van laughed, a breathy laugh that caused heat to pool in the pit of her stomach. "Oh, I know. But I want to take my time, sweetheart. Take you apart piece by piece."

Serena squeezed her eyes closed and groaned. Van slipped his hand under her sweater, his calloused fingers scratching at her skin as he stroked her waist. This time the kiss was deep, needy, scorching. He cupped her breast, circling her nipple with his finger, bringing it to a hard peak.

She gasped and arched into his hand. Van was always gentle, treating her with reverence and care, making her feel so special and so wanted even a simple touch pushed her to the edge.

"Is this okay?" he whispered against her mouth, his breath mingling with hers, his finger repeatedly brushing over the hard pebble of her nipple.

"God, yes," Serena moaned.

He rolled her to her back, settling himself between her legs, his mouth and hands touching and caressing her all over. Van's hips rocked into hers, the hard line of his erection pressing into her aching core. Serena squirmed beneath him, desperate for more. She slipped her hand between them and rubbed him through the thick fabric of his jeans. He groaned into her mouth, his tongue vibrating against hers, sending tingles of pleasure shooting through her.

"Mm, Jesus, Serena," he murmured. He pulled her sweater off, his lips moving down her neck and across her chest. "I want to feel your skin against mine, beautiful."

He slipped off her bra, lifting her effortlessly to toss it aside before he mouthed her tight, hard nipple, his tongue dancing and flitting over her breasts. She held the back of his head as his hot, wet mouth closed over her breast, making her heady with desire.

Serena twisted her fingers in the back of his shirt and tugged, wanting the same thing he wanted, skin on skin.

Van sat up between her legs, pulled off his shirt and unbuttoned his jeans before returning to his position between her legs. His bare chest pressed against hers, his hips flexing into hers, the button from his jeans scratching her bare stomach. Serena ran her hands up and down his back and sides, examining every inch of his bare skin. She rained kisses across his chest, her tongue flicking out to lick at the hollow of his throat, kissing every freckle, mark, and mole gracing his neck and torso. Her fingers danced over his back, sliding into the belt loops on his jeans so she could pull him into her.

The sound of their desire fused into one sound—a gasp and a moan, the shuffling of clothes being removed, skin sliding against skin—whispers of things to come. Every touch filled with want and need, every kiss a promise, every sound a symphony of lust.

Serena's body screamed for attention, for Van. She took him in her hand, stroking him, her hand sliding along his shaft, her thumb drifting over the head of his cock.

Van moved to her side, his hand drifting up her thighs, pushing her legs open, his fingers slipping into her folds, caressing her, his lips at her throat, suckling. He slid one finger inside her, taking his time, exploring her carefully. He cupped her, his palm resting on her clit, massaging it with the heel of his hand, until she was bucking and writhing, begging him to let her come. He pressed his mouth to her ear, words of praise and encouragement filling Serena's head as she orgasmed under his expert touch, arching so far off the bed the only thing touching it were her feet and head, her hands clutching desperately at his arm.

Serena fell back to the bed, wrung out, her breath tearing in and out of her throat, her skin hot and flushed. Van's hand stayed between her legs, his lips sliding down her cheek to her mouth, sucking her tongue into his mouth, moaning deep in the back of his throat, his cock hard against her hip.

She pushed him to his back and took his head in her hands, deepening the kiss. Van held his cock in his hand as she lowered herself onto him, his hips tilting up as she rocked back and forth until he was fully seated.

"Fuck, Serena. I need you to move, sweetheart," Van groaned. His hands were tight on her hips, his calloused fingertips biting into her skin as he held her, tugging her forward, urging her to move.

She leaned over him, her hands on either side of his head, her knees digging into the bed beside his hips. She moved, pushing herself down onto him, then sliding up his cock, holding the tip inside of her.

"Oh shit, that's what I want," Van growled, his head thrown back, droplets of sweat beaded on his forehead. His hips snapped up to meet hers, his thrusts hard and deep, the two of them moving faster and faster, racing toward their inevitable finish. Van thrust up one last time, his entire body tense, his cock throbbing as he came.

His fingers caressed her clit and then she joined him, her entire body alight with pleasure as she came, head thrown back, eyes closed, Van's name a curse on her lips.

Van pulled her down onto his chest and brushed her hair away from her face before placing a gentle kiss to her forehead. He pulled the blankets over her, wrapped his arms around her and held her close, his chin resting on the top of her head, his breathing steady and even as he drifted off to sleep.

Chapter Ten

Van

*S*he kissed him on the corner, damn the paparazzi, before she laughed and skipped up the street, smiling back at him and waving over her shoulder. He couldn't help but smile, her enthusiasm contagious as always. He shouted after her to wait, but she ducked into the coffee shop, her laughter floating back to him, sweet and vibrant over the sound of the busy New York streets.

Van sighed. What was the point of a bodyguard if she wouldn't let him protect her?

The first scream he heard wasn't hers, but it had him shoving the street vendor who'd stopped him out of the way and darting through the crowd, knocking aside the shocked bystanders. He reached her just as Trace dropped the match, the gas igniting with a giant whoosh that knocked the air out of him and sent him stumbling backward. He threw himself at her, the fingers of his left hand twisting in her blouse, the flames dancing up his arm—

"Serena!" he screamed.

"Van." A hand settled on his arm, cooling the heat flickering below his elbow. "Van. Look at me." Dark blue eyes locked on his, her chest pressed against his, her weight comforting, familiar. She exhaled, her breath warm against his skin.

His gaze held hers, and his hands settled on her waist. He inhaled, her scent filling his head, clearing the phantom stench of burning flesh. He cupped the back of her head, caught her lips in his, and kissed her breathless.

"Hey, you okay?" she asked when he released her. "You scared me."

"Sorry." He sighed, tucking her hair behind her ear. "Bad dream."

— 59 —

"Do you want to talk about it?"

"Not really," he said. "I've never been much of one to talk about personal stuff. Except with my shrink and the last time I saw him was about six or seven months ago."

"You can talk to me, Van. I *want* you to talk to me. If this is going to work—"

"We need to talk," he finished. "I know." Van sat up, leaned against the headboard, and pulled Serena between his legs, her back against his chest. He took her hands, his fingers intertwined with hers, resting on her stomach. He kissed her neck.

"Can I tell you something? Something that might freak you out?"

"Go ahead," Serena said. She squeezed his hands a little too tight.

"After Adelaide died, I was destroyed. Devastated. I came to Montana to hide, to leave the world behind, hoping it would forget about me and leave me to die, alone and miserable. Linc wouldn't let that happen. He kept bugging me, coming out here, refusing to leave me alone. He wouldn't give up on me."

"Thank God for Lincoln," she commented.

Van chuckled. "Then he had the audacity to bring a beautiful, enticing, mysterious woman to dinner at my place. And I fell for her. And I keep falling for her more and more every day. I've fallen so hard it's kind of scary how strong my feelings have become in such a short time. Scary and crazy."

Serena shook her head, a shaky breath leaving her. "If you're crazy, so am I." She tipped her head back to look at him. "It is scary, isn't it? I want to let myself go, let myself fall in love with you, Van, but I'm scared." A tear trickled down her cheek. "The last time I loved someone, I got hurt."

Van cupped her cheek and brushed away the tear with his thumb. "I will never hurt you. I promise." His lips drifted over hers. "And I won't let anyone hurt you, either. I love you, sweetheart."

"I love you, too," she whispered.

Van pulled her into his lap, their lips smashing together, tongues tangling. They broke apart, gasping for air. Serena pushed the blankets off him, her lips back on his, her hands all over him, running down his back, over his stomach and between his legs, taking his cock in her hands, her thumb smearing the pre-cum across the tip and down the length, stroking him roughly. She grabbed his hand and pulled it between her legs.

"Touch me," she moaned. "I need you to touch me, Van."

He did as she asked, his fingers grazing the lips of her pussy, seeking and finding her clit, circling it, smirking when her hips jerked under his touch, and she groaned into his mouth. The sound made his dick rock hard, achingly hard.

His need for her was off the charts, insane, scary, *crazy*. This woman woke something deep within him that had been lying dormant since Adelaide's death. He wanted her, needed her, ached for her. He had to have her. All of her, forever.

Serena broke off the kiss and slid down his body, kissed her way until she was nestled between his legs, his cock in her hand, her lips brushing it, her breath blowing over him. Van groaned and his fingers twisted in her hair as she slid him into her mouth, taking him until his cock hit the back of her throat. It constricted around him, and he nearly lost it.

"Fuck, sweetheart," he gasped, his hips rising to push himself deeper into her mouth, her hands splayed over his thighs, squeezing and releasing, her head bobbing as she worked him over, sucking and licking. He was close, so fucking close. His breath tore out of his throat, and his heart pounded in his chest, his balls drawn up tight, his stomach jumping in anticipation.

She released him before he came, moving to straddle him again, lowering herself onto his cock, rocking forward, leaning over to catch his lips in hers, kissing him. Van planted his feet on the bed, his hands on her waist, holding her in place as he thrust deep inside her. She moaned, the sound unbelievably sexy, unbelievably perfect. He wanted to be the only one to pull those sounds from her, the only one to make her moan, to make her cry out his name. He wanted to be hers forever.

He pulled Serena down on his chest, rolled her to her back, his cock still inside of her, his hips flexing, her legs wrapped around his waist as he pounded into her. She clawed at his back, her voice rising in a crescendo of yeses as he pushed her closer and closer to orgasm until she called his name as she came, her perfect skin flushed, sweat on her brow, her body convulsing around him.

He let out a long, stuttering groan as her walls tightened around his cock and her nails dug into his shoulders, his own orgasm pushing every thought, every doubt out of his mind, the only thing was Serena, her body, her scent, her taste on his tongue, those glorious sounds echoing in his ears. He collapsed on top of her, his lips on hers, consumed with her. She was his everything.

He never thought he could love again, but Serena changed all that. Serena healed him.

———

Van tossed the file and photos on the table and pushed a hand through his hair. Lincoln had sent the file as soon as he could, everything he could find on Trace Alvers. Thirty, well-educated, came from a privileged background. Serena had a standing restraining order against him, issued in California, but one that would likely hold up in a Montana court if needed. He had three separate assault charges—two while in college, ex-girlfriends, and one pending in

Arizona—along with several DUIs. Lincoln got his juvenile records unsealed, and they discovered he'd put a girl in the hospital after she'd broken up with him. His parents had buried it, and Trace had gotten nothing more than community service.

The man had a history, one Van didn't like. It made him sick to his stomach to read about all the people—all the women—Trace had hurt. There was no telling what lengths he would go to in order to get Serena back.

His phone chirped, a text from his shrink, reminding him of his appointment on Wednesday, an appointment he no longer wanted to keep. The last thing he wanted to do was go out of town and leave Serena alone.

Van hadn't seen his therapist in six months, ever since he'd packed up his practice and moved to Missoula. Dr. Sadler had been calling and emailing for two solid months, reminding Van he needed to pay him a visit. He'd agreed to drive down and meet with him, if only to get Sadler off his back.

He regretted it now, especially after reading Trace's file. An uneasy feeling had settled over him the last few days; something wasn't right. He couldn't put his finger on it, but his hunches were rarely wrong. He was unsettled. If he'd paid attention to this same feeling before Adelaide's death, he wouldn't have lost her.

He tried to cancel a few days ago, but Sadler refused to hear of it.

"Get your ass down here, Van. We can talk about why you don't want to come when you're here."

Van reluctantly agreed and promised he'd see Sadler on Wednesday. He figured he'd drive to Missoula, visit Sadler, grab lunch, take care of some business needs for Lincoln, visit Soldier's vet, and head back home. Hopefully, he'd be gone no more than eight or nine hours.

At least Serena would be at work all day, safe at the university. It wouldn't stop him from worrying about her.

Van showed up at her door bright and early Wednesday morning, carrying two coffees in metal tumblers along with a box of donuts. Serena had playfully pouted when he'd told her about his brief trip, teasing that she couldn't last one day without him. He'd promised to bring her breakfast and kiss her goodbye before he left.

Hands full, he tapped on the door with his foot. When she didn't answer right away, he looked at Soldier.

"Soldier, *een rede houden.*"

Soldier barked twice and scratched at the door. After a few seconds, Serena yanked the door open, still in her pajamas, her hair in a ponytail on top of her head. She gestured for them to come in, a huge grin spreading across her face when Van put the tumbler of coffee in her hand.

"You are a life saver, babe," she sighed.

Soldier leaned against her legs and stared up at her. Van thought the dog might love her more than his owner. She rubbed his head, scratching behind his ears. Soldier's tongue lolled out the side of his mouth, and if he could have purred like a cat, Van was sure he would have.

"You should leave him here with me."

Van shook his head. "I'm sure he'd love to stay here, but I don't know how Charlie would feel about you taking a dog to work."

"Charlie wouldn't care." Serena shrugged. "Come on. Please?"

It wasn't a bad idea. Leaving Soldier with Serena for the day would certainly help with his anxiety. Soldier would protect her with his life.

"Okay." He narrowed his eyes. "Promise you'll take care of him?"

"Of course, I will." She grinned. "Soldier, *ga liggen.*" The dog padded to the corner where Serena had put a blanket for him and laid down.

"You're getting better at Dutch," Van said.

"Lots of practice." She stepped close to Van and looked up at him. "Are you sure you'll be back tonight? I heard there was a storm moving in. It might make driving back difficult."

He kissed the tip of her nose. "I'll be fine." He wrapped his arm around her and pulled her flush against him. "I'll come over when I get home."

"You better. I'll be waiting. Don't leave me hanging." She brushed her fingers through his hair and pulled him down to kiss her. "Promise me you'll be careful."

"I wish you could come with me."

"God, I'm tempted. But Charlie has a meeting with the board of regents on Friday, and we have a lot of work to do before then. I can't go."

Van rested his forehead against hers and closed his eyes. "I know." He sighed.

"What's wrong?" she asked.

"I don't know." He shrugged. "I have a bad feeling I can't shake. It's eating at me. Just...promise me you'll be careful, okay?"

Serena nodded. "I will. Besides, I have Soldier. He'll take care of me." She pushed up on her toes, her lips on his. "Do you think you'll be back in time for dinner?"

"I'll try."

Her blue eyes sparkled, and she smirked. "Try really hard. I can guarantee you'll love what's for dessert."

Van growled low in the back of his throat, crushed her to his chest, and rained kisses over her face and throat. "Fuck, sweetheart, I think I'll have to do more than try." His pulse raced and his head spun. This woman drove him crazy and he loved it.

Serena walked him, to his truck, kissed him goodbye, and made him promise to text her when he got to Missoula and again when he left. He rolled the window down and waved as he pulled away, watching her in the rearview mirror until she went inside.

Chapter Eleven

Serena

Serena took her time getting ready. Thanks to Van, she was up early, far earlier than normal. She didn't mind; she would have been upset with him if he hadn't stopped to tell her goodbye before he left.

She couldn't wipe the smile from her face. She was in love, and she wanted to shout it from the top of the Mission Mountains. Her life was on the right track after years of derailment. It was time to leave Trace in her past where he belonged and embrace her future with Van.

She showed up early for work, Soldier in tow, made coffee, and got the office ready for the day, singing under her breath as she worked.

Her good mood and cheesy, lovestruck grin did not go unnoticed. Charlie mentioned it when he came in, Professor Campbell mentioned it when he stopped by, even a couple of students teased her during lunch in the student union. She laughed and brushed them off, joking with them for a few minutes before she sat in the corner with her food and a book she'd grabbed from the library. Soldier laid on the floor at her feet, gazing up at her.

Halfway through her lunch, an uneasy feeling came over her. Serena couldn't put her finger on it, couldn't figure out what bothered her; she felt *wrong*. She laid her book on the table and looked around the room.

A couple sat a few tables away from her, completely engrossed with each other. On the other side of the room, a young man was studying at a table by the wall. There were several students in line for food and several professors. Nothing seemed out of the ordinary, but something was off. Serena tucked her book under her arm, ordered Soldier to follow her, and hurried from the student union. She couldn't shake the feeling someone was watching her. She picked up the pace until she and Soldier were sprinting across campus and into the office. At least Charlie wasn't there; she didn't have to explain her flushed cheeks and heavy breathing. It was ridiculous to even think someone might have been following her.

Serena dropped into her chair, her head in her hands. She was paranoid. Things were going well and that meant any minute, it could go bad. Over the last two years, any time her life seemed to get back on track—new job, new home, anything good—Trace had swooped in and yanked it out from under her. It made sense she worried it would happen again, especially since she'd found Van. The thought of having it torn away, having Van torn away, terrified her. It was her imagination and the fear she'd continually lived with for two years playing tricks with her head.

Her phone vibrated on the desk beside her, making her jump and squeal. Startled, Soldier growled quietly, his ears up. Serena snatched up her phone, frowning.

[Van: Hey, sweetheart. I might not make it back by dinner. Some stuff came up that put me behind. I'll text when I leave.]

She sighed and pushed a hand through her hair. His absence fueled her paranoia. She'd gotten too used to having Van around. She missed him, needed him.

"The woes of being in love," she muttered under her breath. She couldn't help but laugh at herself. Most days she felt like she was having an out of body experience; it didn't seem real, the way she felt about Van or the way her life had changed in a short time. Serena had come to Montana to start over, and it was exactly what she had done. She'd hit the reset button and got a second chance at love.

Being in love with Van was so different than what she'd had with Trace. Now that she knew what genuine love felt like, she wondered if she'd ever been in love with Trace or in love with the *idea* of being in love with Trace. He'd been her entire world because he'd forced her to make him her entire world.

Footsteps running down the hall outside the office drew her from her musings. Soldier jumped to his feet and faced the door, his hackles up, another low growl leaving him. Her back stiffened and a sense of dread washed over her. She stared at the door, expecting it to burst open and Trace to be standing on the other side.

After a few seconds, Soldier backed away from the door and came to sit beside Serena's chair. He put his paw on her leg and stared at her with his big brown eyes.

"Good boy, Soldier." She wrapped her arm around his neck and chastised herself; it was probably a student late for class. She had to shake this feeling of being watched before it drove her insane.

The door opened and Charlie marched in, barking orders as soon as he stepped into the room. She grabbed her notepad and started scribbling notes as she followed Charlie into his office, Soldier on her heels.

If Van were going to be later than expected, she might as well stay at work and get some stuff done. Fortunately, she had a lot to do. She still had the paper to type up and the power point presentation to put together before Friday. If she got it done now, she might not have to work late on Thursday.

———

It was after seven when Serena pulled through the security gate. Van's truck wasn't behind the condo or in his driveway, which meant he wasn't back from Missoula yet. He'd texted her over an hour ago and said he was on his way home, giving her enough time to leave work, run by the condo to drop off Soldier, go grab some groceries, and get back home. He promised to come over as soon as he got back, no matter how late it was. Thank God. She missed him.

She parked next to her condo, climbed out of the car, and got Soldier from Van's condo. Out of the corner of her eye she noticed the light in her kitchen shining through the glass in the door. She thought she'd turned it off when she left for work; then again, she could be mistaken. Her head had been in the clouds, her lips still burning from Van's goodbye kiss. It was possible she'd forgotten to turn it off.

"Soldier, *zitten*," she ordered while she dug through her purse for her keys.

She stuck her key in the door, but to her surprise, it wasn't locked. She'd been diligent about locking it ever since Van scolded her about it. Her head must have been so far in the clouds this morning she'd forgotten. She pushed it open and reached for the light.

A rough, calloused hand wrapped around her upper arm and yanked her backward, her purse and jacket falling to the floor. The door slammed closed, leaving the dog outside. He immediately started barking. A startled squeak escaped her before a huge, clammy hand covered her mouth. The odor of stale whiskey and a familiar, expensive cologne washed over her.

"Hey, darlin'," A deep voice growled in her ear. "I've been looking for you."

Her gorge rose and her entire body went cold, goosebumps breaking out all over her. Tears gathered at the corner of her eyes and fear constricted her heart like a vise.

Trace.

Panic set in; she struggled to get away, kicking her feet and flailing her arms. Her elbow connected with his sternum, and he released her with a loud grunt. She threw herself forward and fell to her knees, crawled across the floor, and pressed her back against the kitchen cabinet, eyes darting around, looking for a way to escape. Trace stalked across the room and crouched in front of her, his hand pressed to his chest, rubbing the spot she'd hit, his face unreadable. He reached for her, and she flinched, bracing herself for the blow she knew was coming.

But Trace didn't hit her. His touch was surprisingly gentle, his finger drifting down her cheekbone. "God, I missed you," he murmured. "You're looking good, babe."

"Wh-what are you doing here, Trace?" she stammered, recoiling from his touch. "How did you...how did you find me?"

"I told you. I've been looking for you. It wasn't easy either. If you hadn't gotten the job at the university, I never would have been able to track you down."

"What? How?"

"Social security numbers, baby." Trace chuckled. "I tracked you here using your social security number. I knew where you worked, but it took me about a week to figure out where you lived. Took even longer to get you alone." He leaned over her, his faces inches from hers. "I don't know who the hell that long-haired hippie you're fucking is, but it is over. You got your fun, but it's time you remembered who you belong to. You're coming home with me."

She wrenched away from him, scooting across the floor, trying to put some distance between her and Trace. He followed her, hovering over her, arms crossed, a scowl marring his features.

"No use running, baby. Get your ass off the floor and go pack. Don't make me tell you again."

Serena burst into tears, heaving sobs tearing through her body, doubling her over. She gnawed on her knuckle, trying to hold back the tears, but they wouldn't stop. It was like she was shedding her new life, her new love, shedding it as her tears hit the tile floor.

Trace leaned against the counter, watching her, disgust written all over his face. It wasn't until her sobs subsided that he spoke.

"Are you done?" he asked. "Fuck me. Get moving. We're leaving. I hate these damn small towns. I can feel the redneck creeping up on me as we speak."

"No." Serena grabbed the edge of the counter and pulled herself to her feet. There was no way in hell she was leaving with Trace. Not in a million years. She straightened her shoulders and stared up at him.

"I'm not going anywhere with you," she told him, praying her voice wouldn't betray her fear. "Get the hell out of my house."

The slap knocked her into the counter, her lower back connecting with the edge, sending a sharp pain up her spine. She gasped and gripped the handle of the stove so hard her knuckles turned white. Fresh tears spilled down her cheeks.

Trace sighed and shook his head. "I don't know who the fuck you think you're talking to, Serena, but you better get your goddamn head on straight." He stabbed a finger toward the door. "I am walking out the door in five minutes. You can go voluntarily, or I can carry you over my shoulder. Either way, I'm leaving, and you are, too."

"Trace, stop!" she cried, shaking her head. "You have to stop. I am not going anywhere with you. I don't love you. It's over, and it has been for a long time. Get out of my house. Now."

This time he backhanded her, her head whipping to the side, her lip splitting, the coppery taste of blood flooding her mouth. She stumbled, clinging to the counter, desperate to stay on her feet, desperate to show him he would not intimidate her. She could hear Soldier barking outside; she prayed someone would hear him and come check on her.

"You little bitch," he seethed. "Why do you make me do that? Why do you have to make me angry? If you would do as I told you, I wouldn't have to hit you." He advanced until he was toe to toe with her, towering over her, his fists clenched at his sides, his face bright red, the vein in the center of his forehead throbbing. "Go pack your shit. I am not telling you again."

Lights splashed across the window, drawing Trace's attention away from her. Serena darted to the side and around him, running for the door. She had the doorknob in her hand when Trace grabbed her hair and yanked her to the floor. She screamed, the sound echoing through the house.

Trace hauled her to her feet and pushed her toward the bedroom, muttering obscenities under his breath. She stumbled into the wall, freezing in place at the sound of a knock on the door.

"Serena! You okay, sweetheart?"

"Fuck," Trace mumbled under his breath. He scrubbed a hand over his shaved head, grabbed Serena by the back of the neck, took the paring knife from the dish rack, and led her to the door. He pressed his mouth against her ear, squeezing her neck until she groaned.

"Open it and get rid of him. Or I will." He wiggled the knife in front of her face. "Understood?"

Serena nodded, took a deep breath, and opened the door to talk to Van.

Chapter Twelve

Van

The drive back to Lakeside from Missoula was a bitch. The storm started as soon as he hit the road, a thick, driving snow blanketing the ground within minutes. His need to rush, to hurry home to Serena, quelled thanks to the weather.

His visit with Dr. Sadler had gone better than he expected. His progress thrilled the doctor, especially when he heard Van was seeing someone. He'd tried to contain his excitement but had failed. Miserably. They'd spent the hour talking about Serena and Van's feelings for her. When he left Sadler's office, he felt better than he had in months.

It was almost eight when he pulled through the gate. He swung wide to pull into the driveway but to his surprise, the truck lights illuminated Soldier standing in the road between his condo and Serena's. He slammed on the brakes, threw the truck in park, and shoved open the door.

Van heard the scream as soon as he opened the truck door. Soldier heard it too because he spun around and raced to Serena's door, barking and growling before turning to look at his owner and whining loudly. He snatched his gun from the center console, tucked it into his waistband, and jogged down the road, whistling for Soldier to heel.

Serena's car was parked in her driveway, and her kitchen light was on. He went to the side door and knocked, three sharp raps on the glass. He tried to see inside, but the blinds covering the window were closed.

"Serena! You okay, sweetheart?"

He seriously considered breaking down the door, but before he could, Serena flung it open. Her eyes were red, her hair mussed and out of place. It looked like she'd been crying. Something was wrong.

"Hey," she mumbled.

"Are you okay?" Van asked.

"Yeah, I'm fine." Serena's eyes darted to the left, so quick he almost missed it, then back to him.

He put his hand on the door and one foot over the threshold, but Serena didn't move. She clung to the doorknob with both hands, gripping it tight. Soldier let out a low growl, his hackles raised, his body pressed against Van's leg.

"I...I had a crappy day. Charlie was an asshole all day, his usual self. Can I get a raincheck on dinner?"

A chill raced down Van's spine. Charlie was never an asshole; Serena had told him more than once Charles Ross was the kindest, sweetest, best boss she had ever had. He took a step back and cleared his throat.

"Sure, sweetheart. Call me if you change your mind."

Serena nodded and slammed the door without another word. Van took another step back, closed his eyes, and counted to ten. Then he opened his eyes and raised his foot, connecting with the door right beneath the knob next to the jamb. The door flew open and hit the wall.

Serena stood in the center of the kitchen, a tall, burly bald man behind her. Van recognized him from the photos Lincoln had sent him. Trace. As soon as the door hit the wall, he wrapped an arm around Serena's neck and dragged her back against his body, a small paring knife pressed to the underside of her chin.

Van's heart pounded, hard enough to hurt. If he weren't careful, he would lose Serena, like he'd lost Adelaide. He couldn't let that happen.

"Let her go," Van growled.

"Fuck you," Trace shot back. "She's mine. You had your fun with her, but now it's over. Tuck your dick back in your pants and haul ass back across the street. She's coming home with me."

Soldier growled at Van's feet; his fur stood on end and he crouched, ready to spring. Van held out his hand, silently ordering him to stay.

"I'm not fucking around, Trace. Let her go, and I won't kill you."

Trace snarled, his lip curling in an ugly sneer. He twisted the knife in his hand, pushing the tip into Serena's chin, a bead of blood appearing and sliding down the blade. Serena winced, a strangled cry escaping her.

"Fuck. You," Trace repeated.

A wave of nausea washed over Van, and black spots darkened his vision. He clenched his fists, his blunt nails digging into the palms of his hands. His throat constricted, and he couldn't get enough air.

Not again. He would not lose the woman he loved to another asshole. Not this time.

"Soldier. *Aanval.*"

The dog launched himself across the room, sinking his teeth into Trace's calf, clamping down tight. Trace screamed and stumbled back, releasing Serena and falling on his ass, the knife bouncing off the tile floor. Serena shoved herself away from him and tried to crawl to Van.

Trace kicked at Soldier, his steel-toed boot connecting with the dog's side, his hand landing on Serena's leg, holding tight. Soldier yelped, released Trace for a brief second, but he immediately latched back on. Serena ripped her leg free of Trace's grip, scrambled to her feet, and lunged at Van. At least he *thought* she was lunging at him.

Serena snatched the knife off the floor, turned around, and stabbed Trace in the upper thigh. He screamed and grabbed his leg, blood flowing from the wound, over his hands, and all over the kitchen floor.

"Soldier, *ophouden!*" Van shouted.

Soldier released Trace, but he stayed where he was, teeth bared, growling at Trace. Serena threw herself at Van, her arms around his neck, her face buried against his shoulder. Van pulled his gun from the waistband of his jeans and pointed it at Trace. With the other hand, he took his phone from his pocket and pushed it into Serena's hands.

"Call 911, sweetheart. Tell Sheriff Willis to hurry. And tell her we need an ambulance."

———

Sheriff Donna Willis was swift and efficient. She took statements from Van and Serena while the paramedics worked on Trace. When they loaded him in the ambulance, she climbed in beside him, read him his rights, and handcuffed him to the gurney. Van wasn't sure how much of it Trace understood; they'd drugged him to help with his pain. If Van could have had his way, he would have left him to suffer.

"Ms. Chasey, how are you?" Sheriff Willis asked when she returned to the house.

"I'm fine," Serena replied. She sat in one of her dining room chairs, staring out the picture window, Soldier beside her, her fingers twisted in his fur. The dog refused to leave her side.

Sheriff Willis didn't look convinced. She crouched in front of Serena and put her hand on her knee. "I want you to go to the hospital."

"I said I was fine," Serena insisted.

"She'll go," Van interrupted. "I'll make sure of it."

Sheriff Willis smiled at him, but she didn't move. "Will you go?"

Serena nodded. A tear slid down her cheek and she absentmindedly wiped it away. She held her hand out to Van, who took it. She held it so tight her knuckles were white. "Thank you, Sheriff Willis. I really appreciate everything."

The sheriff rose to her feet and shook Van's hand. "I'll be in touch."

Serena waited until everyone had cleared out before she spoke. "Take me to your place? I can't be here." Her eyes darted to the blood on the floor then back to him. "Please?"

Van put his keys in her hand. "Take Soldier and go to my house. I'll pack you some stuff. You can stay as long as you want."

"I-I can't." Serena shook her head, her hair flying around her head. "I don't want to be by myself."

Van grabbed her shoulders and forced her to look at him. "You won't be alone. Soldier will take care of you. If anything happens, say his name and *aanval*. It means attack. Say it, sweetheart."

"*Aanval*," she whispered.

Soldier's ears twitched, but he didn't move until Serena rose to her feet, then he followed her, staying right by her side. She walked past Van in a daze, the tips of her fingers brushing Soldier's fur, the defeated sorrow on her face breaking Van's heart, then she disappeared out the door. He stood at the window watching her as she climbed the stairs and entered his condo. He saw the light come on and watched as she sat on the couch. Soldier jumped up and sat beside her.

He went to her room, grabbed a duffel bag from the closet, and threw some clothes in it. He stopped in the bathroom and threw her toiletries in as well. If he forgot anything, he would come over here and get it for her. Before he left, he called Clint, the maintenance guy.

"Mr. Brooks, how are you?" Clint said.

"I'm good, Clint. I have a favor to ask you." He explained what had happened and asked if Clint could get some cleaners in to clean the place up. Clint promised to get it taken care of right away.

Van slammed the door closed behind him and hurried across the street to his place. He put Serena's things upstairs, then he helped her into her coat, put Soldier's vest and leash on him, and loaded them into his truck.

The hospital was near the university; it took them less than fifteen minutes to get there. Sheriff Willis must have given them a heads up because they ushered

Serena right back, the nurse ordering Van and Soldier to stay put. He did as he was told, but he wasn't happy about it and neither was Soldier. The dog whined and stared at the door Serena had gone through until Van scolded him.

"Soldier, *ga liggen. Komen*!"

The dog dropped to the floor, chuffing loudly, his focus on the door. At least he stayed quiet.

An hour later, Serena came out the door, a bandage on her chin where Trace had cut her, a small white bag clutched in her hand. Van rose to his feet and she threw herself into his arms, her head resting on his chest.

"Take me home."

Epilogue

THREE WEEKS LATER

Serena threw another log on the fire and picked up the box of ornaments. She wanted to get the tree decorated before Van returned. He wouldn't tell her where he went or what he was doing; he'd kissed her goodbye, jumped in his truck, and left.

She'd taken advantage of the opportunity to pull the tree and decorations from the trunk of her car and drag them in the house. She rearranged the furniture and set up the five-foot tree in front of the window. It wasn't even Thanksgiving yet—not for another three days—but she wanted to surprise Van. When she'd mentioned putting up a tree earlier in the week, he'd sheepishly admitted he didn't have any decorations.

"Decorating for the holidays was Adelaide's thing." He shrugged. "After she died—"

Serena had silenced him with a kiss, her fingers in his hair, tugging him close. The pain they'd both suffered over the years was too much, unbearable and unfair. She was determined to move past it, to help Van move past it. While she knew she could never replace Adelaide, she could love him in her own way. She planned to do it until the day she died.

She put the last of the decorations on the tree and plugged it in. It was perfect; the reflection off the window was better than she'd expected. She couldn't wait for Van to see it.

"What do you think, Soldier?"

The dog didn't move; he was sacked out on the floor in front of the fire.

She laughed and glanced out the window at her condo across the street. She'd been back over there to grab some clothes and clean out the fridge before returning to Van's. Despite Clint cleaning the place up and replacing her door, she couldn't go back. She could smell the blood and hear Trace's voice in her head as soon as she stepped inside. She didn't feel safe there anymore.

Van hadn't protested, not even a little, when she moved herself into his place. It had been a simple transition; she fit into his life so easily it was like he'd been holding a place for her. Not that they'd made anything official. She just never went home.

Serena finished decorating the tree, then she put the boxes downstairs in the basement. She put a roast in the oven for dinner and poured herself a glass of wine. All she had left to do was hang up the stockings—one for Van, one for her, and one for Soldier. She placed the holders on the mantel and hung them up, stepping back to see how they looked.

Pleased with what she'd accomplished, she sat down, pulled a blanket over her lap, and picked up her book. She managed to read a couple of pages before she heard the garage open and Van pull the truck inside.

He came up the stairs, his cheeks ruddy from the cold, a backpack slung over his shoulder. He stopped on the last step, a ghost of a smile on his lips. Serena pushed the blanket off her lap and rose to her feet, twisting her hands together as she tried to gauge his reaction.

"You've been busy," he murmured.

"Do you like it? I wanted to surprise you."

Van nodded. "It's beautiful. You did an amazing job. Come here."

She hurried around the couch and into Van's open arms. He pressed a kiss to her forehead and hugged her close.

"I have a surprise for you, too." He released her, tossed his backpack on the table, and shucked off his jacket. "I had a meeting with Charlie."

Serena stiffened, her eyes narrowing. "Why?"

"You are looking at the new head of campus security. Well, technically, B & D Protection Services is contracting with the university to provide security. I'll be overseeing it." He grinned. "But only if it's okay with you. I swear to God I'm not doing this to keep an eye on you or anything. I don't want you to think that. Me and Charlie talked about it a few weeks ago, a couple days after his party. I told him I had to think about it, though I was fairly certain I was gonna take it. My only condition is you sign off on it."

"Hm, would we be working together?"

"Not really. Charlie is giving me free reign to run things as I see fit, so I might see you if I have to meet with him." Van's grin faded away as he cleared his throat and shifted from foot to foot. "I won't take it if you don't want me there, sweetheart."

She cut him off, her mouth on his, her tongue dancing over his lips. "Can I at least steal you away for lunch once in a while?" she teased.

Van relaxed, the tension draining out of him. "I'd be upset if you didn't." He wrapped an arm around her waist and pulled her flush against his body. "There is something else we need to talk about."

"Okay." Serena drew the word out, wondering what else Van was up to. "What is it?"

"Your living situation." When Serena tried to pull away, Van held her tight, refusing to let her go. "I like having you here, sweetheart. A lot. I think we should make it permanent. What do you think?"

Her answer was a kiss that left them both panting. When they broke apart, her entire body was burning with need for Van.

"I'm gonna take that as a yes," he chuckled.

"It's definitely a yes," Serena breathed.

Van rested his forehead against hers. "Welcome home."

The Professor

Dedication

This one is for my kids. Your support (sometimes reluctant, thanks to the subject matter of my books) means the world to me! Without you, I wouldn't have the guts to follow my dreams. I love you guys!

Chapter 1

Jacob

"Did you know your house is the only one on the street without Christmas lights?" Luke slammed the front door, brushed the snow from his hair, and set the six-pack of beer on the kitchen table.

Jacob rolled his eyes. "I moved in two weeks ago. I don't even *own* Christmas lights. Not to mention, Christmas is a month away. I've got time."

"Add lights to your list." Luke laughed, tipping his head at the fridge, where Jacob had a to-do list for his new home.

Jacob chuckled and shook his head. "Are you gonna help me paint the living room or not? I'd like to unpack some time before the new year."

Luke shucked off his jacket and rolled up his sleeves. He gave his best friend a wry smile before grabbing a beer and heading for the living room. Jacob followed him.

It had been less than two weeks since he'd moved into his new place, and Jacob was still living out of boxes. He wanted to get some remodeling done before the second semester of school started. He suspected he wouldn't have much time once he went to work.

"Have you talked to Charlie?" Luke asked. He was on the ladder, edging the wall with paint below the ceiling; Luke had a steadier hand than Jacob, so he'd willingly given up the job to his best friend.

"His assistant called me. Serena, right?"

Luke nodded. "Yeah. She's sweet and new to town. Moved here in the fall, I think. Her boyfriend is the head of campus security. Nice guy. Evan something. Him and his friend own some big security company back east. What did she say?"

"Everything's ready. They set my classes and delivered my stuff to my office last week. Everybody is so excited to have me at Lakeside. Blah, blah, blah."

Luke stepped off the ladder and poked him in the shoulder. "What's wrong?"

Jacob scrubbed a hand over his face, scratching at the growing facial hair. He hadn't decided if he was going to keep the beard or not. He kind of liked it, and knowing his dad would have approved made keeping it even more appealing. He sighed and dropped to the tarp-covered couch.

"I never wanted to come back to Lakeside," he said. "I thought when I left for college, I was leaving it behind forever. Coming back is like admitting defeat."

"Seriously?" Luke chuckled. "You're one of the foremost experts in your field. How many people from our high school got a doctorate before they were twenty-five? Not one of them is a certified genius. Where's your Mensa card by the way? If I were you, I would frame it on my goddamn office door right beside my doctorate. We should call you Dr. Moore instead of Professor Moore."

Jacob scoffed. "Dr. Moore sounds so pompous. I'll stick with Professor Moore."

"Coming home isn't a failure, Jake. Maybe it was time. You spent the last three years hiding in Rome—"

"I wasn't hiding. I was working."

Luke grinned. "You're full of shit. You were hiding from Maggie."

"And I'm not hiding now?" Jacob wondered. "Coming home isn't running away from Rome and Gianna?"

"Is it?" Luke asked gently. "Or did you finally realize this is where you belong? It sucks your dad's death brought you back, but you're here now. You should make the best of it. After everything with Maggie and then Gianna—"

He rolled his eyes. "Can we talk about something else? Please?"

"Sure." An evil grin spread across Luke's face. Jacob didn't like it at all. "Are you ready to date? It's been, what, two months since you got back? Now that you're home, maybe it's time to find a new woman."

"You make it sound as easy as buying a new pair of shoes." Jacob sighed.

Luke laughed. "I'm not saying it's easy. I know it's not. But you could at least try."

"I wouldn't even know where to start."

"You don't have to find someone to marry. Just someone to date and have fun with." He smirked. "You know, I bet Bonnie has a friend." Luke took a sip of his beer and stared at his friend.

"I don't want to be set up."

"Just hear me out. Go out for drinks with me, Bonnie, and one of her single friends. We can go to Time Out, have a drink, maybe play some pool. Just friends hanging out, nothing more. It'll do you good to get out of the house. You need to quit moping around."

"I enjoy moping," Jacob grumbled.

Luke rolled his eyes and threw a roll of painter's tape at him. Jacob burst out laughing.

"I'll tell you what: I'll think about it, okay?" Jacob said. "At least let me get through the first few weeks of the semester, and then we'll talk about it."

"I'm considering that a promise. And I'm holding you to it."

Jacob ignored the remark, picked up a can of paint, and held it out to his best friend. "Finish the wall so I can unpack before Christmas gets here."

———

The wind stung his cheeks and nose, making his face burn and his eyes water. Each breath hurt and made his lungs ache. He forgot how cold it got in Montana. Winters in Rome were mild, rainy, and it rarely snowed; winters in Montana were like a punch to the gut. He regretted venturing out of his office in search of coffee. But the student union was closed for winter break, and Jacob was forced to find a place off-campus. Wet, thick snow grew heavier as he walked across campus, chilling his bones in seconds.

Jacob yanked open the door of the first cafe he came across—a small coffee shop near the university. It had been a burger place the last time he'd been in town.

The place was deserted—all the tables empty. He took a second to stomp the snow from his boots and shoved his gloves in his coat pocket before he cleared his throat, hoping to get someone's attention.

A young woman emerged from the back wearing a black apron and a name tag he couldn't read. She was short—maybe 5'4" or 5'5", much shorter than his 6'2"—with long, blonde hair and big, warm, chocolate brown eyes. Voluptuous, curvaceous, *gorgeous*. She plastered a smile on her face as he turned toward her, one of those *I-work-in-customer-service-so-I-have-to-be-here-and-pretend-I-like-it* smiles. Her eyes widened when she saw him, and he heard her sharp intake of breath. Jacob chuckled under his breath.

"H-hi," she stammered. "C-can I help you?"

"Can I get a cup of coffee while I wait for the snow to stop?" he asked, pointing over his shoulder at the burgeoning blizzard.

She leaned to the side and peered out the window. "Wow, it's really coming down. Um, sure. Just coffee? How do you take it?"

"Black, no cream, one sugar."

She grabbed a cup, filled it to the brim, and dropped in a packet of sugar, snapping the lid on and wiping the sides before handing it to him. He held out the cash, but she waved it away.

"On the house." A genuine smile lit up her face.

His heart thudded at the sight, and his breath caught in his throat. He propped a hip against the counter and gave her his best smile.

"You always give free coffee to strangers?" Jacob asked.

"Only the attractive ones," she quipped, the smile now accompanied by a flirty wink.

He laughed and shook his head. He was aware of the effect he had on others—he taught many classes filled with young men and women who were not always subtle about their attraction to him. Over the years, he'd learned to ignore it. The stares, the giggling, the blatant innuendos, even the occasional inappropriate social media post—he'd dealt with all of them over the years. He'd learned to close himself off and only let a few people in, like Luke. Those walls had protected him from any more heartbreak. But something about this girl made him want to break down those walls with a goddamn sledgehammer.

He stared; he couldn't help it. She was stunning with her full pink lips, the blonde hair skimming her waist, full breasts, and an impressive body, obvious even under her oversized sweatshirt and dowdy black apron.

"I'm Jacob." He held out his hand. "And you are?"

Chapter 2

Avery

She stared up at the insanely gorgeous man exuding masculinity. He wasn't like any of the boys she knew. He was all man. He wore clean, pressed jeans and a wrinkle-free, red plaid button up under his soft, brown leather jacket. He had on work boots, unscuffed and clean. His light brown hair was short and neat, spiked in the front, and he had a well-kept beard, short and neat like he'd grown it during the last couple of weeks. A light dusting of freckles covered his cheeks below a set of gorgeous emerald green eyes and a mouth that could stop traffic. Full, pink, utterly kissable lips. Heart-stopping, distracting lips. Avery imagined those lips wrapped around her—

Too late, she realized she was staring and biting her lip, lost in the fantasy playing in her head—a fantasy involving her, him, and a private room with a big, soft bed. He said something that she missed, too busy daydreaming. A smirk tugged at the corner of his mouth.

"I-I'm sorry. What was that?"

"I said I'm Jacob. Then I asked your name." He dropped his hand and smiled again, crinkles forming at the corners of his sparkling, green eyes.

"Avery," she blurted. "My name is Avery." She looked away, heat blooming in her cheeks. *God, is there anything about this man that isn't sexy?* His voice was deep and rich, the sound shaking her to the core. She took a sip of the tea she'd stashed under the counter and tried to look anywhere but those damn green eyes. They drew her in and wouldn't let her go.

"Nice to meet you, Avery," Jacob said. He raised his coffee cup in a salute.

"Thanks for this. I'm gonna hang out over there until the snow stops." He made his way to a table facing the window and took a seat.

Avery took another swallow of tea and burned her tongue. *I'm an idiot. And out of touch. Guys used to beg to take me out and offered the world on a silver platter.*

She chastised herself as she cleaned up behind the counter, getting ready for the next shift to come in. Once she had everything the way Ruby liked it, she slipped onto the stool behind the counter and stared out the window. She wanted to gaze at the handsome stranger in the corner, but she thought it might be creepy. It didn't stop her earlier fantasy from playing out in her head, her imagination in overdrive, her internal temperature rising with every scenario.

"Excuse me?"

Jacob stood in front of her. Busted again. She exhaled and smiled.

"Yes, sir?"

"I was wondering if you'd like to go out some time. Maybe grab some coffee or something?"

Avery snorted and rolled her eyes. It wasn't until she shot a glance around the coffee shop that Jacob realized what he'd said. He let loose a full, booming laugh. Avery's skin tingled.

"Okay, so I bombed that." He chuckled. He shrugged a shoulder and gave her a sheepish grin. "Forget I said anything." He yanked his gloves from his coat pocket and turned to go.

"I'd love to go out with you," Avery said, stopping him in his tracks.

Jacob turned and gave her a brilliant smile. He crossed the room in two strides and scribbled his number on the back of one of the paper menus. "I'll leave it up to you. If you decide I wasn't a total idiot, call me. If you think I'm insane, and you never want to see me again, toss it in the trash when I leave."

She giggled and took the menu from him. "Seems like a reasonable request."

His eyes sparkled, and his smile lit up the room. "I'll talk to you soon." He walked backward until he got to the door then winked at her. "I hope."

———

Avery hung her apron in the back, said goodbye to Jules and Ruby, and left without mentioning Jacob to either of them. She kept that information to herself, eager to get home and relax. She'd worked a double shift at the coffee shop by herself. Her body weighed a thousand pounds, her feet ached, and her head pounded. She needed food and sleep, in that order.

Her boss, Ruby, owned two locations of The Percolator in Lakeside, and Avery had worked at both since moving to town five years ago. When she moved out of the dorms at the university and into her own apartment, she started working at the one near the university, putting in as many hours as possible. It was within walking distance of her apartment and school, so she kept her car maintenance bill low, a necessity since she wasn't sure her crappy sedan would last until she graduated.

It took her ten minutes to walk home—her fingers and toes frozen by the time she closed the apartment door behind her. She stripped off her work clothes, put on her warmest pajamas—pants, a sweatshirt, and fuzzy socks—before settling on the couch with a heavy quilt. Fortunately, Nat wasn't home; she'd gone to Great Falls with her boyfriend for the holidays and wouldn't be back until the second semester. Avery let her mind drift to Jacob and whether she should take him up on his offer.

She hadn't dated in a while, not since Brent. After high school, unsure what she wanted to do with her life, she'd taken a year off and spent most of her time drinking and partying. One night, she woke up in a strange apartment with no idea where she was or who she was with, and it scared the crap out of her. She vowed to get her life together. She'd left Missoula, moved north to Lakeside, and enrolled at the university.

The change of scenery did nothing to stem her bad habits; she continued partying, rarely attended class, and scraped by with her grades. Avery came to her senses when Ruby sat her down and gave her an earful about her atrocious behavior. She quit drinking, stopped partying, and curbed her bad dating habits. No more frat boys, no more men she needed to tame. No more sex for the sake of sex. The last date she had was the end of her junior year, a blind date with a friend of a friend, one of the sheriff's deputies. She went on four or five dates with Brent before they agreed to end it.

Jacob was a temptation she couldn't afford. She had five months until graduation. She had to keep it together and forget the man that had consumed her thoughts since he walked into the coffee shop. She couldn't figure him out.

Jacob didn't look like a college student—he was too sophisticated and put together. He wasn't a local or a professor at the college. After living in Lakeside for the last five years, she knew most of the townies and people who worked at Lakeside University.

Locals, college students, and university faculty filled the town. College students were easy to spot—young, frantic, and stressed—while the locals had a perpetual look of reluctant acceptance. She couldn't blame them; summer brought the tourists, and the rest of the year they dealt with the constant influx of young adults learning their place in the world. The residents of Lakeside were undeniably patient.

Jacob was definitely a mystery. She had yet to decide if she wanted to unravel him.

———

Avery parked in the lot behind the coffee shop, yanked open the back door, and hurried through the kitchen, waving at Jules and her friend Carson before she darted into the employee bathroom to check her hair and makeup. Satisfied with what she saw, Avery went to the front counter and made herself a large vanilla latte. She looked around for Jacob.

It had taken her less than thirty minutes to call him and agree to a date. Their first phone call lasted almost an hour, and over the past several days, they'd texted and talked several times. She'd been looking forward to their date all week.

She had one slight panicky moment on the drive over, wondering if she made a mistake by agreeing to a date with someone she barely knew. But ignoring the little naysayer in her head, she'd crossed her fingers and hoped for the best.

Jacob sat in the back, in front of the large windows overlooking the university, jotting notes in a leather-bound notebook propped in his lap. He wore jeans again and the same work boots, along with a plain white button-down and a black blazer. He gnawed on his lower lip, concentrating on his writing.

Avery poured him a cup of coffee—no cream, one sugar—and crossed the restaurant, clearing her throat as she approached the table.

"Hi," she mumbled. Her stomach churned, and her hands shook. Men never intimidated her, never scared her. She always held the upper hand with them, but being in Jacob's presence made her feel as if she were walking on uneven ground. She didn't like it.

"Hey." He smiled, rose to his feet, and pulled out a chair for her.

She set the steaming mug on the table, sat down, and folded her hands on the tabletop.

"Thanks," he said. "You didn't have to—"

Avery waved his protest away with one hand. "I know the owner."

Jacob's laugh sent a tingle of desire down her spine. Even his laugh was sexy. She dragged in a deep breath and smiled at him.

I have nothing to worry about! Things will be fine.

Chapter 3

Jacob

Jacob enjoyed spending time with Avery. She was funny, smart, and stunning. Their relationship was uncomplicated—two people having fun. They went bowling, played pool at Time Out, tried ice skating in the park, and even caught a movie at the small theater downtown. It was exactly what Jacob needed. He felt normal for the first time since he left Rome. The weeks before second semester flew by.

The Saturday before the semester started, he invited Avery over for dinner—pizza from Roselli's. It had been three weeks since their first date and things were going well.

Avery's small, yellow sedan was parked in front of his house when he rounded the corner. He'd hoped to get back before she arrived, but the pizza place was packed, the line going out the door. By the time he got back to his place, it was almost dark.

He would have been on time, but Charlie Ross, the university president, called to ask him a favor. One of the other professors in Jacob's department, Walter Hess, had a family emergency and had to go home to Iowa. Charlie didn't know how long he would be gone, but Hess would miss several weeks of the second semester. Charlie begged Jacob to take on one of his senior level classes. It was too late to cancel it.

Jacob agreed. He wasn't teaching a full load this semester, only three freshman classes, so taking on another class wasn't a big deal. Charlie had been extremely grateful.

"If you need anything, Jacob, let me know. I mean it: anything."

He hit the garage door opener and turned into the driveway. Avery climbed from her car and waited outside, watching as he stepped out of his car.

"You're late."

"Hello to you, too." He smirked. "I got a late start, and the pizza place was packed."

"Roselli's? Yeah, they're always busy, especially before school starts. All the college kids are back in town. I guess I should have warned you." She shifted the bag she carried to her other arm.

"What's in there?" Jacob asked, nodding at the bag.

"Wine. And salad."

"Well, quit lurking in the driveway and get in here." He yanked open the passenger side door and pulled out the pizzas.

Jacob led Avery into the house and kitchen, set the pizzas on the table, and tossed his backpack into the corner. He showed her where he kept the plates and glasses then went to clean up. By the time he returned to the kitchen, Avery had set the table and poured the wine.

Avery leaned against the counter, staring out the window into his backyard, her lower lip caught between her teeth. He stopped beside her, rested his hand on the center of her back, and pressed a kiss to her cheek. She smiled up at him.

"Hi," she breathed. She wrapped her fingers in the front of his sweater, pushed up on her toes, and kissed him, her lips lingering on his. Desire twisted in his gut.

"Hi." His arm snaked around her waist, holding her close. "You hungry?"

"Starving."

Jacob laughed. "Me, too." He kissed her again and reluctantly pulled away. "Your choices are supreme or ham with pineapple. And if you make fun of my love of fruit on pizza, we are going to have a problem."

Avery's grin lit up her face. "You just sealed the deal. Ham and pineapple is my favorite."

"I knew you were the perfect woman." He winked and pulled out the kitchen chair with a flourish. "Have a seat."

After dinner, they cleaned up the kitchen, then Avery insisted on a tour. Jacob put his arm around her waist and led her through the house, pointing out the areas he wanted to remodel.

She paused outside his office, her eyes on the wall behind his desk. She stepped out of the circle of his arms and walked inside, coming to a stop in front of his desk.

"Jacob, what do you do for a living?" she asked.

It was a question she'd never asked him. In fact, they never talked about his work—it never came up. It hadn't seemed important.

"I'm a professor at the university."

Avery's shoulders slumped, and she shook her head. She muttered something indiscernible under her breath and turned to him. "At Lakeside? You're a professor at Lakeside University?"

"Yes. Avery, what's wrong?"

"I'm a student at Lakeside, Jacob." She shifted back a step and crossed her arms over her chest.

Jacob's head spun. He dropped into his desk chair and put his head in his hands. "Well, shit."

"That's all you have to say?" Avery snapped. "Well, shit?"

"I...I don't know what to say." He sighed. "I didn't know you were a student."

Avery's eyes narrowed, and her lips pursed. "You could have asked. You never did."

Jacob slapped the desk and rose to his feet. "Jesus, Avery, give me a break." He rubbed the back of his neck. "You don't look or act like a student. You're a wo—" His mouth snapped shut, and he closed his eyes. "How old are you anyway?"

"I'm twenty-five," she replied. "And you're right: I don't look like a student. I'm a senior. I graduate in May. I started college late and took things slow." She ran a hand through her hair, holding it off her neck. "I'm sorry. I shouldn't have snapped at you."

"It's alright. I'm sorry, too." He stepped around his desk and caught her hand. "Are you okay?"

"No." She shrugged. "I like you, Jacob. A lot. These last few weeks, spending time with you, it's been great. I thought maybe we—you and me—maybe we could...I don't know, I guess I thought there was something there, something between us. Don't you feel it, too?"

"I did. I *do*." He rubbed a hand up and down her arm. "But if you're a student—"

Avery took a step back, distancing herself from him. "But if I'm a student...what?"

"Avery, I could...I could lose my job. Dating a student, it's...well, it's wrong."

She laughed—a bitter, disdainful thing that hurt his head. "So, that's it then? Three weeks of fun and it's over?"

Jacob didn't know what to say. Being with Avery made him happier than he'd been since he moved to Rome. But he couldn't give up his job and everything he'd worked for to pursue a student. He just couldn't.

He opened his mouth, closed it, and settled for shrugging his shoulders. He didn't know what to say. Avery squared her shoulders and spun on her heels. She disappeared out the office door. A few seconds later, his front door slammed.

Chapter 4

Avery

*Y*ou're so stupid, Avery. How did you think you could have a relationship with a guy like Jacob?

His silence screamed his answer and told her everything she needed to know. She was a student, and he was a professor—it couldn't happen. *They* couldn't happen. It was better to leave than endure another minute with a man she couldn't have.

She hadn't expected anything to come out of their relationship, but the hope had been there. She liked Jacob; they connected in a way she'd never experienced before. The last three weeks had been fun and, she'd hoped, the beginning of something great. When she walked into his office and saw the diplomas and the books written by Dr. Jacob Moore, her stomach dropped to her toes.

"Over before it started," she muttered under her breath, swiping unnecessary tears from her cheeks. She swung into her parking space and hurried inside her apartment.

Nat wouldn't be back until tomorrow, so Avery had the apartment to herself. She took advantage, throwing on her favorite ratty pajamas and pouring a large glass of wine. A cheesy movie on the television made her feel a little better. She rested her head on the back of the couch and stared at the ceiling.

How did I not know Jacob was a professor?

She replayed every conversation they'd had the last few weeks, desperate to find a clue he might have given her. Nothing came to mind.

Avery picked up her battered laptop from the table. Her fingers hovered over the keys, her heart and head arguing with each other. *Let it go. Move on. Forget he existed.* Instead, she typed his name in the search engine.

Professor Moore—Dr. Moore—was thirty years old; he'd gone to college when he was seventeen. By the time he was twenty-four, he had his doctorate. He was a certified genius, a card-carrying member of Mensa. He spent the last five years in Italy, teaching anthropology at Sapienza Universita di Roma. Avery discovered he was one of the most well-known figures in his field, a feat rarely accomplished by someone his age. There were rumors he'd been engaged while he lived in Italy, though she couldn't find any other information about it. He did a good job of keeping his private life offline. Two months ago, his father died. Now he was back in Lakeside, his hometown.

Avery had no idea he was from Lakeside. He seemed so sophisticated. Shit, he was more sophisticated than anyone she knew in Montana. She wondered if anyone had known Jacob when he lived here before. It couldn't hurt to ask around.

Around midnight, she closed her laptop. Her eyes burned, and her head pounded. After looking up everything she could about Jacob, she took a chance and pulled up the employee handbook for the university. She clung to the hope that since Jacob wasn't her teacher, they could still see each other. She searched for over an hour but found nothing.

Avery dumped the rest of her wine in the sink and went to bed, vowing to forget about the handsome professor and the fun they'd had. She fell asleep with his laughter ringing in her ears.

———

Her last class on Monday—the first day of her final semester of college—was on the other side of campus, the farthest building from student parking.

As she hurried across the grounds, the chill in the air seeped into her bones, and her thoughts turned again to Jacob. He'd been constantly on her mind. Since dating him was forbidden—or likely forbidden—he became even more appealing. For the last two nights, she tossed and turned, unable to get him out of her head. He was driving her crazy.

Jacob left her brain as she stepped through the classroom door. It was nearly full, only a few empty seats scattered around the room. She sighed and made her way down a middle aisle, slipping into a seat in the center of the room.

"BILINGUALISM IN SOCIAL CONTEXT" was written across the old-fashioned chalkboard. Avery didn't see the professor anywhere, not that she would recognize Professor Hess anyway. She'd never been in one of his classes before this year; Hess only taught upper classmen and graduate classes. According to rumor, his class would be the most difficult she was taking this semester.

The door at the top of the stairs slamming closed pulled her from her thoughts. She glanced at the clock above the chalkboard. Looked like Professor Hess was tardy to his own class.

"Sorry about that, guys," a deep, familiar voice called. "Sucks to be late when you're the teacher."

Avery sat bolt upright, realization slamming into her. She turned to see Jacob striding down the stairs, an army green backpack slung over his shoulder. He wore a dark blue peacoat over a hunter green button up, jeans cuffed over his work boots. He looked phenomenal. Jacob dropped his backpack to the floor, tossed his coat onto the chair, pushed up his sleeves, and propped a hip on the wooden desk. He smiled at the class assembled in front of him.

"As some of you may know, I am *not* Professor Hess." A collective laugh echoed around the room and Jacob smiled. He hopped off the desk, crossed to the chalkboard, and wrote "Professor Moore" beneath the course name. "I will be teaching Bilingualism in Social Context for the next few weeks while Professor Hess attends to some personal matters. Hopefully, you guys don't mind putting up with me."

Another laugh filled the room, this one heavy on female giggles. Avery rolled her eyes and slumped in her seat. Maybe Jacob wouldn't notice her.

Sheer force of will propelled Avery to pick up her pen and follow along while Jacob lectured, going over the syllabus. He paced around the front of the room like a caged tiger—animated, excited, and unbelievably sexy—his green eyes bright with excitement and his smile dazzling the entire room.

Avery watched him in awe, frustrated and astonished that the world put the one off-limits man in Lakeside in front of her again.

Chapter 5

Jacob

Jacob spent Sunday at the university unpacking, organizing his office, and trying to get Avery out of his head.

It was stupid of him to not ask Avery if she was a student. He should have known better, living in a town filled with college students. But he'd been intentionally ignorant because Avery captured his attention like no one else. Being with her was uncomplicated and fun. He missed that in his life and didn't want to think about anything else.

It wasn't until his stomach rumbled that he looked at the clock on the wall. He'd been at it all day; he needed food and something to drink.

There was a burrito and a cold beer in his fridge at home, not to mention a comfortable bed. Maybe a good night's sleep would help him forget about the petite blonde with the chocolate brown eyes consuming his every thought. He grabbed his jacket, gathered some books from the table, and turned to go.

Margaret "Maggie" Hudspeth leaned against the door jamb, hip jutted out, examining her long red nails. She was something else. Tall, brunette, with a set of tits that would turn a dead man's head and deep blue eyes one could drown in. It was easy to see why he'd fallen for her all those years ago.

"Jacob," she purred. "It's good to see you."

"Mags."

"Nobody has called me that since you moved." She pushed past him, walking into his office like she owned the place. She went straight to his beat up couch and sat down, her long legs crossed at the ankles, a tight smile on her face.

"How are you doing?" Maggie asked.

He shrugged. "I'm okay." He set the books and his jacket on the desk.

"I was sorry to hear about your dad."

"Thank you," Jacob said.

Maggie cleared her throat. "You've been in town for what? Two months? You couldn't call or email or something? I have to show up in your office uninvited to get you to talk to me."

"Do you even want to talk to me, Mags? After everything that happened?"

"I'm here, aren't I? Besides, it was a long time ago. Things are different now."

Jacob eased into the chair across from Maggie. "True. How are you?"

She raised a shoulder, her eyes fixed on something behind him. "Not bad."

When Maggie lied, she refused to look him in the eye. It was how he'd known they shouldn't get married; she said "I love you" but hadn't looked at him. Her eyes told him the truth.

"Hm." He clasped his hands between his legs and got to the point. "Why are you here, Mags?"

"Can't I come say hello to an old friend? My former fiancé?"

Maggie never did anything without a reason. Jacob leaned back and crossed his arms. "Spill it."

Maggie rolled her eyes. "I hate it when you do that." She cleared her throat. "I want to know why you've been avoiding me."

"I didn't think you'd want to talk to me, Maggie. You said some harsh things when we split up. I believe one of them was 'I hate you and I never want to see you again.' Or am I wrong?"

Maggie shook her head. "No, you're not wrong. I said that. But I would like to reiterate that it was a long time ago, and things have changed. I'm not the same person I was when we broke up. You're not the only person who got out of this godforsaken town."

"Oh?"

"After you left, I moved to Denver. I taught high school for two years and a couple of community college classes. Getting away gave me some perspective."

"But you came back, like I did. How come?" Jake questioned.

"Ross offered me a job. Called and asked me to teach Science," she explained. "So, here I am. Like I said, I'm not the same person I was after our breakup. I doubt you are either."

Jacob nodded. "I'm not the same person. But I still don't understand why you're here."

"I wanted to see you, talk to you, and tell you I forgive you."

Jacob shifted uneasily. He hadn't expected this, maybe anger or disinterest, but not forgiveness. He scrubbed a hand over his face.

Maggie smirked. "Surprised?"

"You don't hate me?"

"I did for a long time. Until I realized our break-up was a good thing. For both of us. We were too young to get married. Neither one of us knew what we wanted or where our lives were going. I have no regrets, and I don't hate you." Maggie leaned forward, her elbows on her jean-clad legs, her tits on full display. "Do you forgive me? I said a lot of hateful things to and about you. Things I regret now."

Jacob forced himself to focus on her face. "Like you said, it's all in the past."

"Can we start over?" Maggie murmured.

There it was. His ex-fiancée was never subtle. She wanted something. He cleared his throat.

"What do you mean 'start over,' Mags?"

She sighed. "We could get dinner some time. Catch up?"

How the hell was he supposed to respond? If he told her no, old hateful feelings might resurface. But he couldn't tell her yes; he suspected she wanted more, and he didn't. He wasn't sure he'd ever want anything with Maggie. Their time had come and gone.

"Maybe." Jacob shrugged, hoping his noncommittal answer would dissuade her from pursuing the issue. "Look, I need to get home, get some rest before tomorrow."

"Of course," Maggie said, her eyes narrow and lips pursed. "I'll go." She rose to her feet, reached into her jacket, and pulled out a card. She set it on the coffee table in front of him. "Call me when you want to grab dinner."

Jacob watched her sashay from the room, her hands in her pockets, shoulders back, tall and proud.

What do you really want, Mags?

———

By the time Jacob's last class of the day rolled around—the class he'd agreed to teach until Hess returned—he was exhausted. He hadn't slept well the night before—nerves kept him up, and he spent the evening talking himself out of calling Avery.

He had office hours before Hess's class, but since classes had just started, he was free to get coffee. He needed the caffeine. In the student union, he ran into Luke, who insisted on hearing all about his first day. Jacob lost track of time and sprinted across campus, not making it to class until four minutes after the hour.

"Sorry," he muttered as he jogged down the stairs. "Sucks to be late when you're the teacher." He dropped his backpack on the floor next to the desk, threw his coat on the chair, leaned against the desk, and smiled at the assembled students.

Jacob loved teaching more than anything. He got a thrill out of sharing knowledge with his students and loved seeing the light in their eyes. And the first day of a new class was his favorite. It always seemed to go by in a blur of faces, voices, and questions—some of it not sinking in until long after class ended. Even though it was his last class of the day, and a class he would only teach for a few weeks, he was on a roll, the words coming easily as he paced across the front of the classroom, gesturing like crazy.

Class was almost over before he noticed Avery in the center of the class, slumped in her seat. He had taken the class syllabus and ran up the stairs, dropping a stack at the head of each row. When he stopped in front of the class, his eyes locked on hers. His gut twisted.

How did I not notice her before?

Jacob cleared his throat and clapped his hands together. "Sorry again for being late. I won't make a habit of it if you don't. Read through the syllabus, email me, or stop by during office hours if you have questions. We'll jump right in next class and get started. I expect everyone to be prepared."

He kept an eye on Avery as the other students filed out of the room. Several of them stopped to ask him questions—no surprise on the first day. Avery took her time putting her things in her bag, watching him out of the corner of her eye. The door closed behind the last student. She meandered down the stairs and stopped a safe distance away from him.

"Hi," he said. His damn hands shook, and his heart pounded painfully.

"Hello," she replied. She pushed a hand through her blonde curls, shoving them from her face. "I can't believe you're teaching this class."

"It's temporary, Avery. Only until Hess gets back." He spun around, entered his office, shoved the chair away from the desk, and dropped into it.

Avery followed him—small, angry, and irritated. She slammed the door closed and paced in a circle in front of him, her hair whipping around her face every time she spun around. "I'd drop it if I didn't need it to graduate. How am I supposed to sit here every day with you teaching the class? It's not fair."

Jacob leaned forward, his elbows on his knees. "You're right. It isn't fair."

"I'm so glad you agree with me," she mumbled. She stopped in front of his desk, crossed her arms, and glared at him. "How can you sit there and do nothing?"

Jacob rubbed a hand over his nape. He straightened his shoulders and locked eyes with Avery. His head spun. "I don't know what you want me to do, Avery. I like you. A lot. There was something between us, something special."

— *Jacob* —

Avery's eyes dropped to the ground, and she sighed. "I thought so, too. I guess we'll never know, will we? I should go." She yanked her bag higher onto her shoulder, sighed, and pivoted to leave.

Jacob shot out of his chair and lunged across the room. He grabbed her elbow, but when he opened his mouth, what came out was not at all what he expected.

"I don't want you to go. I want this. I want us," he whispered into her ear. Clean strawberry and vanilla fragrance wafted from her skin, filling his head. He closed his eyes and forced himself to concentrate. "Don't go. Stay here and talk to me."

Avery turned her head, their breath mingling as the air between them thickened with desire.

He wanted this woman, wanted to touch her, to kiss her, to do so much more to her. It didn't matter that she was a student or that he'd only known her a few weeks, not when she was inches away from him. So close, so tempting.

Jacob ducked his head and caught her lips with his. He hadn't felt like this in years. It was insane, the burning need coursing through his veins and overriding all rational thought. His arms slid around her waist and pulled her tight against his body. Her arms came up around his neck, her bag falling to the floor. She moaned in his mouth, the sound a punch to his gut.

"Professor Moore?"

The voice drifting through the closed door startled them and forced them apart. Jacob groaned, disappointment flooding him as he let her go and took several steps back. He cleared his throat and waited a heartbeat, trying to catch his breath. Grumbling to himself, he adjusted his shirt to hide his arousal.

"Stay here," he whispered. He stalked across the room, yanked open the door, and pulled it closed behind him.

The university president stood in the middle of Jacob's classroom. His smile widened when Jacob stepped out of his office.

"Mr. Ross? How are you?"

"I'm doing well," Charlie replied. "I stopped by to see how your first day was."

Jacob smiled. "It was great."

"I'd love to hear about it. Why don't you come to my office, and we can chat?"

"Sounds great. Let me gather my stuff. I can be there in ten minutes."

"Fantastic. I'll see you then."

Jacob waited until Charlie left the room before he returned to his office. Avery sat on the couch, her bag on the floor between her feet. Her cheeks were a delicate pink, and her chest heaved with deep breaths.

"I have to go," he said. "Can I call you later?"

Avery nodded and rose to her feet, her bag clutched in her hands. She walked past him without a word.

Chapter 6

Avery

*A*very's mind reeled. She kissed her professor, and Charles Ross, the university president, almost saw. Despite the cold of the January afternoon, sweat dripped down her back. Avery slipped the ever-present ponytail holder from her wrist and pulled her long blonde hair into a messy bun. She kept her eyes down, praying she wouldn't run into anyone while her brain was spinning out of control. She sprinted across the parking lot and slid to a stop next to her car.

Fumbling with the door handle, her nail caught on it and broke. Tears filled her eyes, and she cursed under her breath. She opened the door, threw herself inside, and shoved the key in the ignition. The car sputtered to life.

Five minutes later, she parked on the street in front of her building and hurried inside. She sprinted up three flights to her apartment, burst through the door, and ran right into her roommate Natasha.

"Hey, whoa," Nat gasped, stumbling backward and catching herself on a kitchen chair. "You okay?"

"No," Avery snapped. "I mean, yes. I guess. Sorry." She pushed past her and into her bedroom, slamming the door behind her.

She slumped on the edge of the bed, her bag falling to the floor with a loud clunk, and dropped her head into her hands. Everything was happening so fast. She was going insane. There was something about Professor Moore that drew her in like a moth to a flame. Avery had never been with anyone who made her want to throw all the rules out the window. She wanted to see him again, kiss him again, touch him again.

At least she didn't have class with Jacob—*Professor Moore* she reminded herself—until Wednesday. Bilingualism in Social Context met four days a week: Monday, Wednesday, Thursday, and Friday for an hour and a half. It would give her time to figure out what she was going to do.

She pressed her fingers to her lips, her eyes slipping closed as she recalled the kiss they'd shared. It held such promise. She'd gotten her hopes up, forgetting for a moment Jacob was a professor and she was his student. Things couldn't go any further between them.

———

An hour later, she emerged from the bedroom, determined to take her mind off Professor Jacob Moore. Maybe hanging out with Nat would help.

"Hey, stranger," Nat giggled. She jumped off the couch and hugged Avery a little too tightly.

The tiny redhead was a ball of energy, exhausting Avery with her positive attitude. She loved her roommate and best friend despite her nosiness and unending stream of over-the-top vivacity.

"How are your classes?" Nat asked.

Avery grabbed a bottle of water from the fridge and dropped to the couch beside Nat. "They're okay. Too early to tell."

"Do you have the new professor? Professor Moore? God, everyone is talking about him."

"He's teaching Hess's class for a few weeks," Avery said. Unexpected jealousy twisted in her gut.

"Is he as gorgeous as everyone says?" Nat asked.

"He is insanely handsome. Like stop-dead-in-your-tracks-to-stare-at-him handsome."

"You're so lucky!" Nat squealed. "I'd give anything to sit in class and stare at him all day. I guess he moved here from Rome because he was heartbroken or something. Did you know he's from here? Rumor has it he used to date Professor Hudspeth in the Science department when they were in high school. It wouldn't surprise me if they started dating again. Like a rebound thing."

Nat talked so fast it hurt Avery's head. She hadn't heard the rumors about Jacob. Or she hadn't been listening. She'd been in her headspace all day, upset over the loss of her relationship with Jacob and worried about her classes. She should have been listening.

Nat prattled on, even after Avery's phone chimed with an incoming message. She snuck a peek at it.

[Jacob: Meet me for a drink?]

With a sigh she hoped her roommate didn't notice, she picked up her phone and flicked her finger across the screen, keeping it out of Nat's eyeline.

[Avery: Are you sure that's a good idea?]
[Jacob: I just want to talk. Please?]

Avery squeezed the phone so tightly she was surprised it didn't break. *God, I want to say yes, but one of us has to be smart and do the right thing.* The phone chimed again.

[Jacob: Avery? Please?]

She closed her eyes, dragged in a deep breath, then exhaled slowly. She stared at the wall above Nat's head but didn't see the pale-yellow wallpaper with faded pink flowers. She saw Jacob's face smiling at her.

[Avery: Okay. Where?]

———

Nat gave her the third degree about where she was going and who she was seeing, but Avery refused to answer, telling her roommate it was private. Fortunately, a phone call from Nat's boyfriend, Brick, interrupted the interrogation and allowed Avery to sneak away.

An hour after Jacob's text, she stood outside Brannigan's Pub in Kalispell, twenty minutes north of Lakeside. Jacob suggested it. It was unlikely students or staff from the university would be there, especially on a Monday night. Avery saw Jacob through the window, sitting at a table with a beer in front of him.

She contemplated turning around and going home, ending it before it began. Instead, she yanked off her hat, her blonde hair tumbling around her shoulders, and stepped inside.

"Avery!" Jacob called.

She eased into the seat across from him with an uneasy smile. "Hi, Jacob."

"Thank you for coming." He grinned. "Do you want something to drink?" He waved at the server.

"Can I get a sparkling wine?"

Jacob ordered her drink, sat back in his chair, and tapped his fingers on the table. Avery didn't know what to say or how to act. What was the proper etiquette for a pseudo-date with one's professor?

The server returned with her drink and a plate of the pub's infamous black and tan onion rings. She sipped her wine and shifted in her seat.

"This is weird, huh?" Jacob said, picking at the corner of his napkin.

"Yeah, a little." She sighed. "Or a lot." A nervous giggle escaped her.

He reached across the table and took her hand, intertwining his fingers with hers. "I don't want to lie to you, Avery. I'm attracted to you. I haven't felt like this since—" His mouth snapped shut, and he cleared his throat. "It's been a long time."

"I'm your student, Jacob." She pulled her hand from his.

Jacob sighed and folded his hands in front of him. "Only because I'm teaching Hess's class. If I weren't, you wouldn't be my student."

"Would it matter if I wasn't in your class? I'd still be a student, and you'd still be a professor at the school I attend. It has to be against the rules, right?"

Jacob nodded. "I'm kind of afraid to find out."

"What do you mean?"

"I don't want to know. I've avoided looking it up or asking Luke about it. I guess I don't want some stupid rule telling me I can't be with you. I *want* to be oblivious."

"I don't understand," Avery said.

"I'm not making any sense." He grabbed her hands again, his emerald green eyes locked on hers. His thumb rubbed circles on her knuckles. "Let me put this as plainly as possible: I want to be with you, Avery. I want to give this relationship a shot. Despite the rules, despite everything. We can make this work. It won't be easy, though. You're the one who needs to decide what you want. If you don't want a relationship with me, then I'll settle for being your teacher, and hopefully, your friend. Your choice."

Avery's heart skipped a beat. She wanted more too. She was out of her mind—certifiably insane—but she wanted it. Wanted him.

"I want it as much as you do."

A grin spread across Jacob's face. "Yeah?"

"Yes," Avery replied. She picked up an onion ring and shoved it in her mouth. "This is going to be difficult, isn't it?"

"Yes." Jacob leaned over the table. "And complicated. Are you okay with that?"

Avery's heart thumped out of control. Jacob ignited something in her. When she was with him, she felt alive, beautiful, and wanted. She wasn't ready or willing to walk away from that. She dragged in a deep breath before she spoke.

"It's going to be hard, and sometimes I won't like it. I doubt you will too. We'll have to figure it out as we go along. But I think we can make it work, even if we have to keep it a secret. Let's give it a chance."

Jacob's smile lit up his face. He had gorgeous crinkles at the corner of his eyes and the green sparkled like dewy grass hit by morning sunlight. "Come here," he said.

Avery moved to the other side of the table and slid into the seat beside him. Jacob slipped his arm around her waist and tugged her against his side. He kissed her, his lips soft and sweet.

She sighed and snuggled closer to her professor. All complications disappeared when she was in his arms. She didn't think about anything else, only Jacob.

Chapter 7

Jacob

"Spill it, dude," Luke demanded. "You've been in a good mood for the last few weeks, and I want to know what the hell is going on." He took a sip of his cold beer and stared at his best friend, a smile playing around his lips.

"I don't know what you're talking about," Jacob said.

There was no way he was going to let Luke in on his secret. Everything was too new; he and Avery were still in the discovery stage. It had only been a couple of weeks since they had agreed to give their relationship a shot—rules be damned—and he had no intention of ruining it by opening his big mouth. He fiddled with his beer bottle, picking at the label, and refused to meet Luke's eyes.

"You're a shitty liar," Luke muttered, shaking his head. "I haven't seen you in this good of a mood in a long time. Since before Rome. Not since you and Maggie got—" His mouth snapped shut. "Sorry," he mumbled.

"I can talk about it. It won't break me." Jacob laughed. "It's been five years."

"You haven't mentioned it since you moved back to the states. You never explained what happened. One day everything was fine, and the next, you were packing your stuff and moving to Italy."

Jacob downed his bottle of beer and signaled their server, Trista, for another one. She set it in front of him, smiled shyly at Luke, then scurried away.

"Somebody has a crush." He snorted, nodding in Trista's direction.

Luke pointed at the center of his chest. "Engaged, remember? And you're changing the subject."

"There wasn't anything to explain," he said. "It was over between me and Maggie. End of story."

"I repeat, you're a shitty liar." His friend smiled and bumped his shoulder into Jacob's. "Tell me what happened."

Jacob exhaled, his fingers tapping on the bar top. "We were engaged."

Luke sputtered, beer flying from his mouth in a cascade of amber droplets. "You were what?"

He couldn't help but laugh; he'd never heard Luke screech. Sobering, Jacob scrubbed a hand over his bearded face and sighed. "I asked Maggie to marry me, and she said yes. We were engaged for almost a year."

Luke let out a low whistle. "How the hell did you keep it a secret?"

"We agreed to keep it quiet. Her parents wouldn't approve, not while we were both in school. We figured when we graduated, we'd get married."

"Jesus, Jake, that's crazy. What happened?"

He took a drink and wiped his lips with the back of his hand. "We fought all the time. About everything. She wanted to stay in Lakeside, settle down in our hometown, and make a life for ourselves. It wasn't what I wanted. Then I got the job in Rome."

"And you left."

"I left. I broke off the engagement, packed my shit, and took the job in Italy. I didn't think I'd ever come back here or see Maggie again."

Luke shook his head and chuckled. "Holy shit. She's probably pissed at you."

Jacob rolled his eyes. "Gee, thanks, Luke, I never thought of that. I can always count on you to make me feel better."

"Sorry." Luke grinned. "Have you talked to Maggie?"

Jacob nodded. "Yes."

"Shit, how did it go?"

"Okay, I guess." Jacob shrugged. "She wants something. I just don't know what."

"Maybe she wants to get back together?" Luke suggested.

Jacob shook his head hard enough to hurt his neck. "Oh no, not going down that road again."

"Are you interested in dating at all?" Luke asked. "Or are you putting your love life on the shelf?"

"You don't give up, do you?" Jacob chuckled. He downed the rest of his beer, set the bottle on the bar, and rose to his feet. "Right now, the only thing I'm interested in is settling into my job and my new place. The rest will come later."

Luke narrowed his eyes and shook his head. "I'm convinced there is a woman. You're too damn happy. But I'll drop it for now. You'll tell me when you're ready."

Jacob shrugged and clapped Luke on the shoulder. "Not likely," he joked. He pulled his wallet free and dropped some cash to the table. "I gotta go."

"It's early," Luke protested.

"I've got things to do." Avery was due at his place in a couple of hours. He still had to pick up dinner and straighten up before she got there.

"Uh, huh." His best friend shook his head. "There's something you're not telling me. I'm your best friend, asshole. You can trust me. Tell me what the hell has you so happy."

Jacob laughed. "Life, Luke. Life is good right now."

———

Avery perched on the edge of her chair, wine glass in hand, her brown eyes dark with worry. She'd been unusually quiet all night.

"You okay?" Jacob asked.

"I'm tired, I guess."

He kneeled beside her, took her chin between his fingers, and forced her to look at him. "We're already lying to the outside world, Avery. Let's not lie to each other. Something is wrong. Tell me what it is."

"You mean, aside from the fact we *are* lying to everyone? Which is a fabulous way to start a relationship." She took a sip of her wine with a shaking hand.

Jacob rested his hand on her waist and squeezed. "Is that what it is? The lying and secrecy?"

"Yes." She finished the wine in her glass and reached for the bottle, glass clinking together as she poured. "I want this to work. There's something about you, Jacob, something I can't put into words. There's a connection between us—"

He nodded. It was an indescribable connection. It pleased him that she felt it as well.

"Nat asked me where I was going when I left the apartment, and I couldn't tell her. On the way here, all I could think about was how happy I am, yet I can't tell anyone." Avery pushed a hand through her hair. "The secret keeping, it's just, well, it's hard to deal with. I can't tell anyone about us even though I want to scream it from the top of the Psych building. It...well, it makes me feel like I'm not good enough."

Jacob rubbed circles on her back, a poor attempt to soothe her. Guilt weighed heavily on his heart. He was the reason they had to keep their relationship a secret. It wasn't fair. To either of them.

"I'm sorry." He sighed. "You are perfect. You deserve the world, sweetheart, not someone who keeps you a secret."

Avery gave him a grim smile. "I want this, Jake. I want you. God, I'm sorry.

I'm ruining our date with all my doom and gloom." She kissed him, her lips lingering on his. "Forgive me?"

"There's nothing to forgive." Their lips brushed as he spoke. "Let's eat."

After they finished dinner, they moved to the living room with the wine. Jacob put a movie on, but instead of watching it, they talked with the television playing quietly in the background. It was a good start to filling in the gaps left by the early whirlwind of their relationship.

It was almost midnight when Avery pushed herself to her feet with a sigh and grabbed her shoes.

"I should go," she said.

Jacob walked her to the door, wrapped her in his arms, and kissed her. She clung to his neck, her face upturned, body flush against his. He held her close, not wanting to let her go. With one last kiss, she left.

Not tired, he decided to clean the kitchen. He opened a beer and put the leftover food in the fridge, staring out the window into the backyard as he waited for the sink to fill with water. He was so caught up in the thoughts running through his head, it took him a minute to realize someone was tapping on the back door. He dried off his hands and tossed the towel on the table before he opened the door.

Avery stood there, shifting from foot to foot, her lower lip caught between her teeth.

"Avery? Is everything okay?"

She didn't say a word. She stepped inside, dropped her bag to the floor, slid her arms around his waist, and kissed him.

Chapter 8

Avery

"I don't want to leave," Avery whispered.

The air was thick and tense, electric heat thrumming between them. Avery dragged in a shaky breath but was cut off by Jacob's mouth crashing into hers, kissing her long and hard. She pushed up into the kiss, her breasts pressed to his chest. A low moan escaped her. It had been too long since anyone kissed her the way Jacob kissed did—tender and sweet, with an underlying current of desperation and need. Her body burned with desire.

Jacob's hands slid down her sides and over her ass. He lifted Avery and set her on the counter, stepped between her open legs, and pulled her forward. His hips nestled against hers, his arousal hard behind the thick denim of his jeans. Avery's head fell back as he kissed her jaw, her neck, her mouth. Every touch of his lips made her ache for more.

She moaned and wrapped her legs around Jacob's thighs, her hand tangling in his hair, holding him close as the kiss deepened. Avery fumbled with the button on his jeans impatiently and tugged them open.

Jacob stepped back, his full, pink lips kiss-swollen, the pupils of his green eyes blown wide with lust. His chest heaved and his full cock strained for release behind his partially undone pants. His hands clenched into fists at his side.

"Jesus Christ, Avery, let me catch my breath," he panted. "Are you sure about this?"

Avery's stomach dropped and bile rose in her throat. If he turned her away, she wouldn't be able to handle it. She'd sat in her car for five minutes debating with herself, weighing the pros and cons of having sex with her professor. Despite the multitude of reasons not to take that step, she circled back to her inexplicable and desperate need for the professor. Screw the problems that might arise; she wanted Professor Jacob Moore more than she'd ever wanted anyone, and she would risk it all for him.

"Yes," she replied. "Aren't you?"

Jacob pounced and pressed his mouth on hers. The all-consuming kiss was the only answer she needed.

"I guess that's a yes," she giggled when he released her.

"It's a hell yes," Jacob growled. His arm slid around her and he pushed back between her legs, holding her on the counter with his body. His breath was warm against her skin. "Do you know how much I want you?"

Avery opened her mouth to speak; nothing came out but a weak squeak. She swallowed and tried again.

"Show me."

He kissed her, taking her breath away and making her heart race. She clung to Jacob as if she were drowning and he was her life preserver. It left no doubt in her mind about how much he wanted her.

Jacob yanked her t-shirt off and dropped it to the floor, moaning low in the back of his throat as he wrapped his lips around her lace covered breast and sucked. He kneaded the other breast, his thumb circling the nipple, flicking the hardening nub.

Heat pooled deep in the pit of her stomach, and a fine sheen of sweat broke out over her body. She hooked her leg around his ass and pulled him closer, writhing against him, desperate for some friction.

Jacob's lips moved up her neck and across her jaw. He intertwined his fingers with hers as he nibbled on her earlobe and pulled her hand between their bodies. "I need you to touch me, baby," he said. "Please."

Avery slipped her hand under his boxers and down the length of his shaft. Her hand wrapped around his cock, and a shaky groan left him. His hips moved with her hand, his kisses increasing in intensity as she caressed him. Jacob's hands moved all over her body, tugging at her clothes until she sat on his kitchen counter in nothing but panties. He buried his face between her breasts, kissing, licking, and nipping at her skin as his hands slid up her thighs, moving closer to where she needed them.

He dragged his fingers up her leg, skimmed the edge of her panties, and slipped a finger beneath them to caress her damp folds. She moaned and squirmed as her head fell back. Her hips rose off the counter as two of Jacob's fingers eased into her, caressing her until she saw stars and gasped his name. He didn't stop and dragged her to the edge of the counter, two fingers deep, the palm of his hand pressed against her. His mouth swallowed her obscene groans as she came on his fingers, her slick running over his hand.

Jacob released her long enough to kick off his shoes and remove his clothes. Then he eased a condom down his length and was back on her in an instant, sliding her wet panties down and tossing them aside before he entered her. He peppered her neck and shoulders with kisses as he slowly pumped his hips, giving her time to adjust to his substantial size. The hands on her ass yanked her closer with every thrust, so tight and perfect she wasn't sure how long she could take it. It was almost too much—a pleasure so insanely wonderful it bordered on painful.

"Lean back," he ordered.

Avery did as she was told and leaned back on her hands, heat rising in her cheeks as Jacob stared at her, devouring her with his eyes as his hands ran over every inch and curve of her body. He praised her—sweet words that made her head spin and her heart pound.

Jacob's fingers dug into her ass as he slammed into her, his cock dragging against her sweet spot every time he pulled out and his taut abs brushing her clit with each thrust.

Avery was on the edge, so close it wouldn't take much to push her over. She locked eyes with Jacob and slid her hand down her stomach and between her legs. She circled her clit with two fingers while Jacob pounded into her, his eyes blown wide. His cock twitched and pulsed as she climaxed, her orgasm exploding through her.

Jacob groaned and thrust harder, burying himself inside her, his tight, hard thrusts prolonging her pleasure, dragging it out until she was dizzy with the sensations overwhelming her. He came with a quiet grunt against her lips.

He held her, his lips gently caressing her neck and shoulder. He slid her off the counter, set her on her feet, and disposed of the condom. Avery held onto the counter, her head still spinning from the incredible sex.

Jacob held his hand out to her, a smirk on his face. She took it and returned his smile.

"Come on, let's go to the bedroom."

"Bedroom?" she repeated.

"Well, yeah," he chuckled. "I'm not done with you yet." He wrapped his arm around her waist and tugged her tight against his side. "If that's okay with you?"

Avery giggled and pressed a lingering kiss to his lips.

"I'll take that as a yes," he echoed her words back at her and winked, then he led her up the stairs to his bedroom.

Chapter 9

Avery

The shower turned off as Avery slipped her shirt over her head. Jacob walked out of the bathroom a few minutes later with a towel around his waist, his hair still wet and dripping down his broad shoulders and his taut chest. It should be illegal for one man to be so attractive.

"Hey, are you leaving?" he asked. He kept one hand on the towel, holding it in place as he rifled through the top drawer of his dresser. Boxer briefs in hand, he slammed the drawer shut with his elbow.

"Yeah. I have class in a couple hours." She tied her shoes and stood up, her eyes darting around the room, trying to remember where she'd left her purse. Her brain wasn't firing on all cylinders; the only thing she'd been able to think about was Jacob and all the things she wanted him to do to her. "Have you seen my purse?"

"I think it's downstairs in the living room. Or maybe the office." He leaned in for a kiss. "Or the kitchen or the hallway—"

"Is this where my purse might be or a replay of all the places we had sex last night?" She giggled.

Jacob chuckled and shrugged, an adorable smile on his face. Avery returned the smile and kiss, resisting the urge to yank off the towel and push Jacob down on the bed. She needed to get back and shower before her first class. She forced herself to break off the kiss and stepped away, patting his cheek.

"Hurry and get dressed so you can tell me goodbye," she said as she walked out of Jacob's bedroom. Downstairs, she found her purse on the couch, put on her jacket, pulled an orange juice from the fridge, and leaned against the kitchen counter. In less than five minutes, Jacob stood in front of her. She stepped into the hug he offered and rested her head on his shoulder.

"Are you okay?" He pushed her hair off her neck and kissed her throat.

"No, not really." Avery sighed. "I hate this."

"I'm sorry," he whispered against her neck.

"I know," she mumbled.

Jacob was always sorry; it seemed to be the only thing he'd said over the last few weeks since the first time they had sex. He was sorry he couldn't take her on a real date, sorry she had to sneak in and out of his house through the back door, sorry he couldn't call her, sorry they couldn't walk into class together as a couple, sorry, sorry, sorry, sorry. She'd heard him apologize more in the last three weeks than she'd heard anyone apologize in her entire life.

"Most of the time, I'm okay with how things are," Avery said.

Jacob rested his chin on top of her head and hugged her close. "Most of the time?"

"Yes, most of the time. Do I wish we could have a normal relationship and not hide it from everyone? Of course, I do. But I know it's not possible right now. I can wait. At least I think I can. I'll take what we've got for now. But I get angry and frustrated with the university's archaic rules forcing us to hide our relationship sometimes. If Professor Hess were here, he would be my professor, not you, and all of this wouldn't matter. We would be freely together."

"I'll make it up to you, sweetheart. I swear. As soon as I can."

"I know you will." She pulled him into a deep kiss. "I have to go. I'll talk to you later." She stepped out of his embrace, snatched her purse off the counter, and slipped out the back door. She could feel Jacob's eyes on her as she hurried across the lawn and out the side gate.

She'd parked her car a couple of blocks over next to a little neighborhood playground. Caught up in her thoughts, she stepped off the curb blindly. A black motorcycle sped down the street in front of her, and a startled squeak left her as she stumbled back to avoid getting hit. Avery cursed under her breath and pulled her coat tight around herself, shivering in the chilly morning air. She rushed to get in the car, turned on the heat right away, and checked the clock. She had less than two hours before her first class.

"Shit, shit, shit," she grumbled, checking her mirror before pulling into traffic. She'd be lucky if she made it on time.

Avery wasn't on time, and it threw her entire day off. She had to take a cold shower because Nat used all the hot water. Then she forgot to grab her English literature paper off the printer and had to skip lunch to detour to the library to print another copy. By the time she slid into her seat in Professor Moore's class, ten minutes late, she was in a terrible mood—tired, hungry, irritable, and her head felt like it might explode. She wanted to go home and take a nap. Jacob's disapproving look certainly didn't make her feel any better.

Doing her best to ignore Professor Moore and not make eye contact, she pulled her laptop from her bag, powered it up, and copied the notes from the board while she listened to the lecture. The headache pounded in the center of her forehead, and it only got worse by the minute. It was impossible to concentrate.

Her phone lit up with an incoming message. She slid her finger across the screen to find a message from Carson, her friend and co-worker.

[Carson: Come out with us tonight. We miss you.]

Avery smiled. She hadn't gone out with her friends in weeks, not since she started seeing Jacob. She typed a reply.

[Avery: Who's us?]
[Carson: Me, Brick, Nat. We're going to Time Out to shoot pool and drink beer.]
[Avery: I'm not sure I should. I've had a bad day. I'm tired, hungry, and I'm getting a headache. I wouldn't be much fun.]
[Carson: I have the perfect remedy for that. Come hang out with your friends. It will be fun. We miss you.]

Carson was right. Maybe she needed a night out to do something normal. Jacob would understand.

[Avery: Okay. But you have to feed me before we drink, otherwise, I'll be a mess.]
[Carson: Deal! Meet us at Time Out at 7.]

Avery scrubbed a hand over her face and sighed. The secrets were starting to have a toll despite her best efforts. Hiding her relationship with Jacob was getting harder, especially as her feelings for the professor grew. And though she told Jacob she would take whatever she could get from him, she couldn't help but long for a normal relationship—one where they could go on a real date, one where she didn't have to sneak in and out of his house, one where they could walk around town as a couple.

"Ms. Collins, may I speak to you for a moment?" Jacob interrupted her musings, drawing her attention back to the front of the class.

She jumped; she hadn't realized class was over. Avery cleared her throat and rose to her feet. "Of course, Professor Moore."

She shoved her things in her bag and pushed past the other students leaving the room, making her way past them down the stairs. Another student stood in front of the professor with her arms crossed and a hip jutting out, smacking her gum.

Jacob leaned against his desk, arms crossed over his chest in mirror, nodding at the young lady standing in front of him. He glanced at Avery and held up one finger.

"Three days, Ms. Small," he stated. "You can miss three days a semester. I made that clear in the syllabus."

The young woman—Avery thought her name was Becky—huffed and rolled her eyes. "I hoped you would make an exception for me." She took a step closer to Jacob and smiled up at him. "Just this once?"

Professor Moore shook his head. "I don't make exceptions. You can audit the class for no credit, or you can drop it and take it next semester."

"Fine," Becky huffed. She spun on her heel, her elbow smacking Avery as she pushed past her and stomped up the stairs.

"Wow," Avery mouthed.

Jacob straightened, towering over her. "Hey, you okay?" he asked, keeping his voice low. The door closed behind Becky, and he stepped closer to Avery, ducked his head, and pressed a kiss to the corner of her mouth.

Tears pooled in the corner of her eyes. She swallowed past the lump rising in her throat. She shrugged. "I'm having a crappy day. Whatever could go wrong, did."

"Oh, babe, I'm sorry," Jacob whispered. "Is there anything I can do?"

She shook her head. "No. You know what? I'm gonna go out with my friends tonight. I need...I need to do something normal, you know? Not hide out at your house for the night."

A pained expression crossed Jacob's face, gone so quickly she wondered if she'd really seen it. He nodded and kissed the top of her head. "Of course." He pushed a hand through his hair and chuckled. "Funny you should bring that up. Luke's been harassing me to go out with him for a beer. It might do us both good to have a night out."

Avery nodded and pushed up on her toes to kiss him. "I'll call you later, okay?"

"Have fun!" he called as she sprinted up the stairs.

———

Avery slumped in the booth and sipped her margarita, watching Carson and Brick play darts. She couldn't get the image of Jacob and his pained expression and the feeling she had upset him out of her head. It shouldn't bother her, but it did. She took her phone from her pocket, hoping he texted. He hadn't, so she sent him one, attempting to smooth things over.

[Avery: Having fun, miss you tho!]

So what if it was a lie? Half of it anyway; she missed him, but she wasn't having fun. He didn't need to know that. She shoved her phone into her back pocket. Nat appeared at the table with more drinks, french fries, and nachos in her hand. She set everything down and dropped into the seat across from Avery, a perfectly shaped red eyebrow raised and her head tipped to one side.

"Are you okay?" Nat asked.

"People keep asking me that, and it's getting old," Avery grumbled, shoving a fry into her mouth. "I'm fine."

"Okay, sheesh, grumpy, sorry," Nat said, hands up and a smirk on her face. "What? Are you tired from the late night you had?"

"What?" Avery feigned innocence.

Her friend rolled her eyes. "Please. When are you gonna tell me who he is?"

"What do you mean?"

"I know you're seeing someone, Avery. You're spending a lot of nights away from home, you act all secretive, and you hide in your room to talk on the phone. Are you going to tell me who it is or not?"

She shrugged. "I'll tell you when I'm ready. And I'm not ready." Except she was. She desperately wanted to tell someone, wanted someone to know how happy she was, how good Jacob made her feel, and how she might be falling in love with Professor Moore.

"Oh my God, is that Professor Moore?"

Avery's head snapped up. It was as if thinking about him had somehow summoned him to the bar. "What? Where?" She turned around, looking in the direction Nat pointed.

"Over there, on the other side of the bar."

Jacob was standing on the other side of the room with a couple of other professors, Luke Campbell and Margaret Hudspeth from the Science department, along with a brunette she didn't recognize. Avery turned back around before he saw her, ducking behind the high-backed booth.

Jealousy twisted through the pit of her stomach, and she had to resist the urge to throw herself out of the booth, stalk across the room, and slap Professor Hudspeth across her pretty face. Instead, she grabbed her drink and downed it in a few swallows. She wiped a hand across her mouth, grimacing as her head spun from the onslaught of alcohol.

"Are you okay?" The surprise on Nat's face would have been funny if Avery wasn't so pissed.

"I'm gonna need more margaritas," she muttered.

Chapter 10

Jacob

Jacob stopped inside the door and looked around, trying to find Luke in the crowd of people. Friday night at Time Out was busier than he expected. College students filled the place, along with a few townspeople he recognized and staff from the university. This was the place to be on the weekend.

"Jake!"

Luke waved at him from the other side of the bar; luckily, he towered over everyone at 6'5" and was easy to spot in a crowd. Jacob weaved through the crowd, elbowing people out of the way until he reached his friend.

Luke clapped him on the back and shoved a beer into his hand. "Don't be mad," he muttered.

Jacob narrowed his eyes and glared at him. "Why would I be mad?"

Luke didn't have time to answer because Luke's fiancée, Bonnie, appeared at Luke's side. "Jacob! You made it!" She pressed a kiss to his cheek and squeezed his arm. "Look who I brought!"

Maggie stood behind Bonnie, smirking. "Hello, Jacob."

"Maggie. Long time no see." He brought his bottle of beer to his mouth and downed it.

Maggie snorted, pushed past him to lean over the bar, and ordered a drink. She turned around and rested her elbows on the bar behind her, eyes narrowed, bright red lips pursed in irritation. She surveyed the room.

"Why are we here again? This place is filled with students." She said "students" as if the word left an unpleasant taste in her mouth. "Why don't we go to Ronnie's?"

"It's closed." Bonnie shrugged. "It's only open from June through August. The only other bar in town is the Elks' Lodge."

Maggie rolled her eyes and shook her head. She turned back to the bar, picked up her drink, and slipped onto a barstool, her head propped on her hand. She patted the seat next to her.

"Come here, Jacob. Sit down and keep an old friend company."

He ignored her, propping himself at the end of the bar and watched the crowd. Luke and Bonnie excused themselves to grab a pool table, leaving him alone with Maggie.

Maggie slid onto the seat beside him. She put her hand on his arm and bumped her shoulder into his. "Can't we try to get along? For the sake of our friends?"

"I wasn't expecting you to be here. I'm not trying to be difficult. I swear. But I don't want you—or anyone else—to get the wrong idea."

Maggie blanched, irritation crossing her face, but she quickly recovered. She cleared her throat. "I don't think anyone will get the wrong idea. We're just friends, Jacob. Nothing more. We can spend an occasional evening together without people thinking we're in love."

"We have a history, Mags—"

"One that no one knows about except Luke. We're adults, and we should act like it."

Maybe Maggie was right. Their relationship was in the past. Way in the past. It was time for them to move on. If she could act like an adult, so could he. All he wanted was an evening out with his friends and a chance to take his mind off his growing problems with Avery and their relationship. If he let this shit with Maggie bother him, it would only compound those problems.

Luke waved at him from the pool tables. He nodded, grabbed his beer, and said to Maggie, "I think they got a pool table. Come on. Let's see if I can still kick your ass."

Maggie raised an eyebrow but smiled before she hopped off the barstool and followed him to the pool tables.

The evening turned out better than he expected. Once he got past the frustration of Maggie had intruding on the night, he enjoyed himself. He and Luke played game after game of pool, getting more competitive as the evening wore on. Jacob nursed his way through two beers, intent on keeping his head on straight. It didn't stop him from having fun.

He tried to ignore Maggie flirting with him. Not that it was easy when she laid it on so thick—touching his arm, laughing too long at his stupid jokes, leaning against the table beside him, her expensive floral scent thick in the air. Everything was fine until Bonnie decided they should play two-on-two, teaming him up with Maggie. The flirting only intensified.

"Come help me line this shot up, handsome," Maggie teased, pointing at the pool table. "If I miss it, we lose."

Jacob exhaled, but rather than start an argument, or worse, suffer the wrath of an irritated Maggie, he leaned over her, positioned her hands on the pool cue, and helped her line up the shot. The shot cued up, he backed away, grabbed his beer, and moved to the end of the table. Ignoring Mags and her flirting was tiresome; he was ready to call it a night. After this game, he was going home.

Luke went next, then it was Jacob's turn. He took a swig of his beer, grabbed his pool cue, and turned toward the table. A pair of familiar brown eyes locked with his.

Avery stood near the bar, her face almost green. Without thinking, he took a step toward her, but she shook her head and turned away. He watched her wobble across the room, obviously drunk.

Jacob tried to concentrate on the game of pool, but he kept finding himself looking for Avery in the crowd, worried about her. After a few minutes, he watched her head for the front door. He took his last shot, propped his pool cue against the wall, and set his beer bottle down.

"I'll be right back," he said, pulling his jacket on.

He made his way through the crowd, ignoring Maggie and Luke calling after him as he followed Avery out the door. Consequences be damned, there was no way he would let her go home alone, not when she looked too drunk to make any wise decisions.

I need to take care of Avery.

Chapter 11

Avery

Avery did her best to ignore Jacob on the other side of the room, laughing and having a good time. But as the night wore on, she constantly looked over her shoulder, watching him. Bitter envy roared through her veins whenever Professor Hudspeth touched Jacob; the sight made her stomach roll. Every time Hudspeth brushed up against her professor, Avery reached for her drink, hoping it would help ease the pain and obliterate the jealousy. When Jacob leaned over her to help Professor Hudspeth line up a shot, Avery shoved herself out of the booth, stumbling over Nat's feet as she excused herself and hurried through the crowd to the restroom.

She stepped into the first empty stall, slammed it shut, and threw the lock just before her gorge rose and everything she ingested came flying out. Muffled "ews" and the sound of shuffling feet filled the room, then silence. She prayed the bathroom had emptied so she could puke in private, something she hadn't done since her freshman year of college.

Avery braced a hand on the stall door and pushed herself to her feet, grimacing at the filthy bathroom floor she kneeled on. She made her way to the sink, stopping every few feet when a wave of dizziness washed over her. She rinsed out her mouth, splashed water on her face, then left the bathroom.

Halfway across the massive room, she stopped and leaned against the end of the bar, her head spinning and her stomach clenching uncomfortably. Jacob stood beside one of the pool tables, his beer held between two fingers, a smile teasing the corners of his mouth. When he turned to line up his shot, his eyes landed on Avery. He straightened, concern coloring his features. He took a step toward her, but she shook her head, turned, and pushed her way through the mass of people.

Avery eased into the booth beside Carson and forced a weak smile onto her face. It was time to go. So much for a night out with her friends. She snatched an unopened bottle of water from the middle of the table and took a sip. She patted Carson on the arm.

"Give me my purse, would you, Car? I'm gonna go."

Before he could give it to her, Nat grabbed it and dumped it out on the table. She dug Avery's keys out of the pile, took her car key off the ring, shoved everything back inside, and set it in front of her.

"You're not driving," Nat said. "You've had too much to drink."

"Fine, whatever," Avery grumbled. She slid out of the booth, her purse clutched in one hand and phone in the other. "I'll call an Uber or Lyft."

She threw herself out of the booth and stomped out of the bar, ignoring her friends shouting after her, desperate to get away from them, from Jacob, from everyone.

Outside, she passed the window and saw Jacob and Professor Hudspeth. The gorgeous professor had a hip propped against the table and her arms crossed over her substantial chest, her perfect, blood-red lips pursed in what could only be irritation. Avery leaned against the wall beside the window, intent on staying there no longer than a minute or two to catch her breath. When she tried to push away, a wave of dizziness hit her.

"Damn it." She fell back against the wall, her cell phone falling to the ground. "Shit." She closed her eyes and concentrated on not throwing up again.

"Here."

Jacob stood in front of her, her cell phone in his hand. She took it from him and shoved it in her back pocket.

"What are you doing out here?" she asked.

"Hello to you, too." He put his hand on her arm, stroking it. "You don't look so good, sweetheart."

"I don't feel so good," she muttered. "I've had too much to drink, and I was trying to get an Uber..."

The door opened behind Jacob, and Professor Hudspeth peered around the corner. "Hey, it's your turn."

"Hey, Maggie." Jacob shifted on his feet. "This is Avery. She's one of my students."

"Hello," Professor Hudspeth—Maggie—said, her eyes flicking Avery's way before turning back to Jacob. "Are you coming? It's your turn."

"I think I'm going to drive Avery home," he told her. "Could you tell Luke and Bonnie goodbye for me?"

Maggie stepped outside, a confused look on her face. "Um, are you sure, Jacob?"

He nodded and took hold of Avery's elbow. "It's fine. Trust me, Mags, okay?"

Maggie grimaced, her chin tipping in a brief nod. "I'll talk to you later." It sounded more like a demand than a promise.

Jacob grunted and steered Avery away from the bar toward his car. He opened the passenger door, helped her inside, then jogged around the front and climbed in.

Avery snorted. "Are you sure you don't want to stay here with Maggie? I can still get a ride."

"No, I don't want to stay here with Maggie. I've never seen you like this. What is wrong with you?"

"It's called jealousy, Professor Moore," she snapped. She pressed her fingers to the center of her forehead and rubbed. "It's what happens when you spend the evening watching some woman fawn all over your boyfriend. Wait, I'm sorry, I'm not supposed to call you that, am I? You're not my boyfriend. You're the professor I'm secretly screwing." She hated herself even as the words came out of her mouth.

Out of the corner of her eye, she saw Jacob's mouth open then snap shut. He gnawed at his lower lip, his brow furrowed. His knuckles were white on the steering wheel. He exhaled loudly.

"That's not fair, Avery."

She sighed. "Nothing about this is fair. Fair would have been meeting you after I graduated, or you not being a professor at the university I attend. Fair would have been anything other than this. Sometimes it's too much to deal with, and today was one of those days." She scrubbed a hand over her face and looked out the window. "Where are we going?"

"Your apartment."

"We're not going back to your place?" She assumed when he'd offered to take her home, he meant his home. She was wrong.

"No," Jacob said. "You need to sleep off the alcohol. I think it's best if you go home."

Tears pricked the corners of her eyes, and her heart stuttered in her chest. She leaned her head against the frosty glass and closed her eyes, the soothing jazz music on the radio lulling her into a state of semi-consciousness. It was quiet until Jacob stopped in front of her apartment building.

"Drink a bottle of water and take a couple of aspirin," he said and leaned over her to push open the passenger door, his scent making her head spin. He didn't make eye contact.

Avery dragged herself wordlessly from the car, the heavy door creaking as she closed it. Jacob pulled back onto the street without so much as a glance back.

Her heart hurt as she watched him drive away. She dug her house key out of her purse, swung around, and tried to unlock the door, her shaking hands making it damn near impossible. A loud noise echoed off the wall. She squeaked and spun around so quickly she lost her balance and stumbled back against the door. A black motorcycle flew by, heading in the same direction as Jacob.

"Jesus Christ," she mumbled. "Asshole."

Another tenant came out of the building and pushed past her, so she grabbed the edge of the door and slipped inside. She raced up the stairs, her stomach churning, and frantically unlocked the apartment door, praying she wouldn't puke in the hallway. She ran through the apartment and fell to her knees in front of the toilet right before she threw up.

Avery fell asleep—passed out—and woke up shortly after curled in the fetal position on the bathroom floor, a wadded towel under her head. Her body ached, and her head throbbed. Sitting up caused another wave of nausea to wash over her. She waited for it to pass before pushing to her feet, mumbling curses under her breath when the room spun.

Avery dug through the medicine cabinet over the sink, grabbed the bottle of pain meds, and made her way to the kitchen. She swallowed two of the tiny white pills with some water, grimacing as they slid down her raw throat. The nausea crept back as she shucked off her clothes, fading only once she dropped to the bed and pulled the pillow over her head. She prayed Nat would stay at Brick's so she could get some sleep. The last thing she needed was her nosy roommate interrupting her sleep to interrogate her. If the look on Nat's face when Avery left the bar was any indication, that was exactly what she planned to do.

Avery fell into a restless sleep plagued with dreams of chasing Professor Moore through a dark forest, repeatedly losing him to a giant, red dragon.

———

She woke with the taste of stale beer and regret on her tongue. The room spun, and her head pounded. She dragged in a deep breath and blew it out.

I am never drinking again.

Avery grabbed her phone from the end table where she dropped it and slid her finger across the screen. There were no messages from Jacob, though there were a couple from her friends—Nat telling her she stayed over at Brick's and Carson checking on her. Her finger hovered over Jacob's name in her contacts for a second. Instead of calling him, Avery crawled out of bed to the bathroom. Forty-five minutes later, she'd showered, brushed her teeth, and had some toast and coffee.

It wasn't until she dug through her purse to find her car key that she remembered her car was at the bar and Nat had her key. It took her twenty minutes to find the spare key in a box under her bed. Then Avery ordered an Uber.

Twenty minutes later, she stepped out of the rideshare vehicle in the Time Out parking lot beside her car. She thanked the driver—a sweet, older lady who chatted about her favorite TV shows during the drive—one last time before she pulled the key from her purse and watched the car drive away. She brushed the snow from the windshield. The weather had taken a turn overnight, a storm moving in from Canada leaving a thick layer of snow over everything and bringing a bitter, chilly wind. Her fingers were numb by the time she climbed inside; she'd left her gloves on the kitchen counter.

She sent up a silent prayer the car would start and turned the key. To her surprise, it did on the first try. Avery waited for it to warm up while her head and heart waged a fierce argument over what she should do. After a few minutes, she pushed a hand through her hair, gripped the steering wheel tight, and pulled out of the parking lot.

Avery knew where she had to go and what she had to do.

Chapter 12

Jacob

*H*e went straight home after dropping Avery at her apartment, replaying their conversation—and his actions—in his head as he drove. Once he was home, he didn't bother to turn on any lights; he went straight to his room, peeled off his clothes, and fell into bed. Jacob's limbs were heavy, his throat thick, and his eyes dry. He was asleep seconds after his head hit the pillow.

The incessant tapping woke him, along with the sun shining through his bedroom window and his neighbor's barking dog. He sat up and checked the clock. It was after ten. No wonder he was disoriented; he hadn't slept this late since college.

The tapping continued. He pushed himself out of bed, yanked on his jeans and a t-shirt, and followed the sound to his back door. He yanked it open and a sharp wind hit him smack in the face, taking his breath away. Or maybe it was the woman standing at his door.

"Avery?" he mumbled. "What are you doing here? I was going to call you when I woke up." He pushed a hand through his sleep-tousled hair.

Avery smiled and shrugged one shoulder. Wisps of her blonde hair escaped her emerald hat, and her curves disappeared underneath her large, puffy jacket. She gnawed on her lower lip for a second before responding.

"I-I wanted to apologize."

Jacob shook his head before she finished speaking, grabbed her hand, and yanked her inside. The door slammed closed behind her. "No. You have nothing to apologize for. I would have reacted the same way if I had to watch someone—ex or not—putting their hands all over you. I'm the one who should apologize. I'm sorry you had to see that."

Tears glistened in Avery's eyes as she nodded. She smiled, but it didn't reach her eyes.

Jacob took her chin and forced her to look at him. "Avery, baby, there's something I need you to understand. *You* are the only woman I want. I have no feelings for Maggie. None. She is my past. You are my present."

Avery threw her arms around Jacob's neck, her body flush against his, and pressed a trembling kiss to his lips.

Jacob's mouth slanted over hers, his thumbs caressing the soft skin of her cheeks. He released her to drag her deeper into the house, down the hall, and into the living room. She dropped her heavy coat and hat on the couch, gasping in surprise when Jacob pushed her against the wall, impatient to get his hands on her. He slid his hand beneath her heavy sweater and up her side to cup her breast as he pushed his knee between her legs. He twisted his fingers in her hair and tipped her head back, his lips roaming over her neck.

"Mm, Professor Moore," Avery moaned.

"Fuck, Avery," he snarled and ripped open the front of her jeans. His hand slipped into her underwear and caressed her until she ground against his exploring fingers. He eased his middle finger into her, his thumb circling her clit.

"Touch me, sweetheart."

Avery unbuttoned his jeans and took him in her hand, stroking him, drawing a thick moan from him. He shoved her jeans and underwear down her legs. She pulled away from him, kicked off her shoes and pants, then yanked the sweater over her head, tossing it on the floor.

He wanted her, needed her. He couldn't wait a second longer. Jacob pounced. He pushed his jeans down to free his throbbing length, groaning when the sensitive tip brushed her leg. Yanking a condom from his pocket, he slid it on then lifted Avery and held her against the wall as he lowered her onto his thick cock, moaning as he filled her. His hips flexed and pressed into her before pulling out almost all the way, only to thrust deep into her again, moving in a quick staccato.

Avery threw her head back, slamming it into the wall, and gasped Jacob's name as her nails dug into his shoulders. He nipped at her bottom lip then sucked her tongue into his mouth, a low growl rumbling through his chest.

She came with a keening cry, her walls clenching around him. He thrust into her several more times, clutching and clawing at each other as pleasure consumed them.

As the sensations faded, Jacob used his body to hold her against the wall, kissing her. They clung to each other, breathless. He pushed a hand through her messy, blonde hair, kissed the tip of her nose, and set her on her feet.

"Are we good?"

Avery nodded. "Yeah, we're good."

He helped Avery gather her clothes, then he buttoned his pants and grabbed a sweatshirt from the closet.

"I'm hungry. Are you?" he asked.

Avery's lips pursed and her nose wrinkled. "Oh god, no. The thought of food makes me want to puke."

Jacob laughed and shook his head. "I'm not surprised. You had a lot to drink last night. How about some coffee?"

"I could drink coffee." She followed him into the kitchen and eased into a kitchen chair. She folded her arms on the table, laid her head down, and didn't move until he set the cup in front of her.

"Thank you," she mumbled, lifting her head long enough to take a sip before dropping it back to the table.

"Can I talk to you about something?"

"Hm?" She didn't look up.

"Would you be interested in tutoring a group of my freshmen?" Jacob sat down beside her and pushed her hair away from her face.

Avery turned her head and looked up at him. "How many?"

"I think there are seven of them. It would be two hours, once a week, whatever you want. It pays twenty-five dollars an hour." He rubbed her back, observing her. "What do you think?"

She sat up, tucked her hair behind her ear, and cradled her coffee in both hands. "I could use the money. Why are you asking me? Pity or something?"

"No," Jacob chuckled. "You're one of my best students, sweetheart. I looked at your transcripts, and your grades are phenomenal—aside from freshman year. I think you'd make a great tutor. You don't have to decide right now. Just think about it and let me know."

"I don't need to think about it. I can do it." Avery propped her head on her hand. "So, you're spying on me? Checking my transcripts?"

Jacob narrowed his eyes. "I check all of my students' transcripts. I want to see where they stand academically. It helps me be a better teacher."

"Hm, and it helps you check up on the woman you're sleeping with, too, right?"

"Okay, maybe a little." Jacob laughed. "But I swear I look at everyone's grades. I'm not being weird or stalkerish, I swear."

Avery kissed the corner of his mouth and smiled. "Thank God. I don't think I could handle a stalker, not even you. Too freaky."

Chapter 13

Avery

Avery parked in the student lot, wrapped a scarf around her neck, put on her hat, shoved open the car door, and hurried across the lawn to the library. The study group she agreed to tutor met once a week for the rest of the semester. Once inside, she headed straight for the information desk.

It took a second to place the student librarian behind the counter—Becky Small, the irritated girl from Jacob's class the previous week who tried and failed to flirt with Professor Moore. As soon as she glanced up, the warm smile on her face turned to ice. When Avery inquired where the study groups were, Becky gave her a snotty, clipped answer, directing her to the third floor. Ignoring Becky's impudence, Avery raced up the stairs and down the hall, finding the group of freshmen in a small room tucked in the back corner of the third floor.

She slipped inside, her eyes on the floor, mumbling apologies for her lateness as she took the empty seat at the head of the table. She dropped her backpack to the floor and turned to the group. Her eyes landed on Professor Jacob Moore.

Avery swallowed back a startled squeak and cleared her throat. "Professor Moore, what a surprise."

"Ms. Collins, how kind of you to show up."

She narrowed her eyes and gave him a wry smile. "My apologies. It won't happen again." She took a deep breath and tipped her head to one side. "I'm sorry. I didn't realize you would be here."

"I thought I would come to the first study session. While I'm sure you are

— 131 —

more than capable, I wanted to make sure everyone was on the right track. Pretend I'm not here."

Avery nodded. "I'd appreciate any insight you might give us."

Two hours later, the group was getting restless and so was she. Pretending Jacob wasn't in the room proved difficult, especially with his eyes following her every move. She checked her watch. The library was about to close. She quickly wrapped things up, scheduled the next study session, and sent everyone on their way.

Once the room emptied of freshman, Avery stacked the books on the table and tossed the garbage in the trash receptacle, all while glancing at her professor out of the corner of her eye. She leaned against the table beside him when she finished.

"What are you doing here, Professor Moore?"

Jacob chuckled, a bemused expression on his face. He stood in front of her and placed his hands on the table around her, caging her in. "I wanted to see you."

She stared, drinking him in. He wore a pair of worn jeans and a greenish-blue shirt, the color intensifying the green of his eyes. He must not have known the effect he had on her—or anyone else—no idea how his smile lit up any room, or how he drew admiring stares everywhere he went, including his classroom. She still couldn't believe he was with her.

"You wanted to see me?"

He nodded. "Yeah." Then he kissed her—a sweet thing that demanded nothing but promised so much.

He pulled away and Avery whined, wanting more.

"You are a fantastic tutor," he said. "I think you deserve to be rewarded."

Jacob's hands slipped beneath her shirt and up her sides as his lips moved over her neck, kissing and nipping at her throat. His thumb brushed across her nipple over her lace bra. She arched her back, pushing her breasts into his hands. His lips closed on the spot where her neck met her shoulder, biting and sucking, marking her. He popped open the button on her jeans and eased his hand past the waistband, his fingers sliding teasingly through her damp folds.

"Jacob," she gasped. "Someone might see us."

He cut off her protests with a kiss before pushing her against the edge of the table and holding her in place as he pressed open-mouthed kisses on her bare skin. She tingled everywhere, heat flooding her.

Jacob dropped to his knees in front of her and placed his warm lips on her stomach. He pulled off her shoes, tossing them aside one at a time. He hooked his fingers in the belt loops on her jeans and eased them down, kissing her bare legs as he went.

He looked up at her with a smirk, his green eyes dark with lust as he pulled one of her legs over his shoulder and nuzzled his nose into the curls at the apex of her thighs, groaning deep in the back of his throat. His tongue flicked out to lick her, circling her clit until her thighs trembled uncontrollably. Jacob slid his hands up the back of Avery's thighs and cupped her ass, holding her tight as he slipped his tongue into her, rolling it over and through her slick pussy. His tongue fucked into her at a maddening pace, his beard burning her inner thighs.

She gasped when his middle finger slipped in alongside his tongue, twisting and pressing the tiny nub of nerves, sending shots of intense, mind-boggling electricity screaming through her body.

The tightly wound coil in the pit of her stomach contracted, and her back arched as her fingers twisted in Jacob's hair, holding him close. Her hips came off the table to meet his mouth, a filthy curse leaving her as the orgasm rushed through her, every nerve in her body on fire with intense pleasure.

Jacob worked Avery through the orgasm, holding her in place so she wouldn't collapse, only pushing himself to his feet when the trembling in her body subsided. He caught her lips in his, still wet with her slick.

Avery hurried to release him from the confines of his jeans, pushing them down enough to take him in her hand and stroke his length. He slid a condom on, then she lifted her hips and guided him to her entrance, moaning as he slid into her.

He nuzzled the side of her neck and groaned as her nails sank into his ass, yanking him closer, urging him to move. With a growl, he tangled his fingers in her hair, tipping her head back and kissing her neck. He thrust into her, hard and deep, hitting her sweet spot with every tilt of his hips. His body tensed, and his hand tightening in her hair as he came, gasping her name.

Jacob pushed her shirt up, dropped his head to take her breast in his mouth, and sucked her nipple through the lacy fabric of her bra. He slipped a hand between their bodies and massaged her clit until she came with a desperate groan.

Avery clung to Jacob for a few minutes to catch her breath, her head resting on his shoulder. He tucked her hair behind her ear and kissed her temple.

"We should go, huh?" he said.

"I think that's a good idea."

Jacob helped her to her feet and back into her clothes, stopping for a moment to glance at the door and the dark library beyond.

"What's wrong?"

"Nothing." He shook his head. "I thought I saw someone. Probably a shadow playing tricks with my imagination." He pulled her into a quick hug and kissed her again. "Come back to my place?"

She nodded. "I'll meet you there."

Jacob squeezed her hand before slipping out the door. She shoved her things into her bag, stopping to catch her breath before she opened the door, and made her way through the eerily dark library.

Outside, fresh snow fell from above, covering the cars in a soft, white blanket. She scanned the lot, but Jacob's car was nowhere to be seen. He must have parked in the faculty lot in the back. It would explain why she hadn't seen his car when she arrived. A loud clanging noise behind her made her jump. She whipped around but she saw nothing. A security guard appeared at the door, just as confused as she was. Avery waved at him and hurriedly climbed in her car, grateful it started on the first try. She put it in gear and pulled out of the lot, driving carefully through the falling snow to Jacob's house.

Chapter 14

Jacob

Jacob hovered in the state between awake and asleep where everything felt like a dream yet wasn't. He wasn't sure if his phone vibrated or if he imagined it. It stopped after a few seconds, allowing him to dive back into dreamland, but it wasn't quiet for long. The multitude of vibrations sent it across the bedside table. He grabbed it, intent on turning it off, but the first few words of the text caught his eye.

[Unknown: Stop seeing her or I...]

He eased Avery onto her back and tucked the covers around her before he slipped out of bed, yanked on a t-shirt and sweats, and headed downstairs. In his office with the door closed, he opened the text message with shaking hands.

[Unknown: Stop seeing her or I will send these to Charles Ross.]

These were blurry pictures of him and Avery in the library earlier, one of them with his head between her legs, her head thrown back in ecstasy and fingers tangled in his hair. Another showed him buried to the hilt inside of her, a look of pure pleasure on his face. There were seven pictures total.

White fiery anger rushed through him. His vision turned crimson, and his ears rang. He squeezed the phone until the glass screen cracked then chucked it across the room with a strangled growl, watching it hit the couch and bounce to the floor with an unsatisfying thud.

Jacob dropped into his office chair, his head in his hands. He had no idea who sent the photos; he didn't recognize the number. He considered waking Avery but decided against it. She might as well get a few minutes of peace before he dropped this bombshell on her.

———

Avery stood in the middle of his living room, twisting her hands and pacing. Jacob sat a few feet away, his head resting against the back of the couch, eyes closed. He had said little since he'd woken her to show her the photo; he let her rant and rave, watching her anger turn from fear to confusion and finally dejection.

"Come here." He held his hand out.

She crossed the room and let him pull her into his arms.

He pressed his lips to her temple. "Are you sure you don't recognize the number?" he asked.

"I'm sure. What do you think they want?"

"Whoever it is wants me to quit seeing you. Why else would they threaten to send the pictures to Charlie? Maybe it gives them some kind of sick thrill knowing they have a hold over us."

"This is so stupid," she grumbled. "Who the hell do they think they are?"

Her body tensed in his arms, and her hands clenched into tight fists on her lap. The anger had returned. She twisted out of his grip, shoved to her feet, and resumed her pacing, muttering under her breath.

Jacob rested his elbows on his knees. "I'm sorry about all of this, sweetheart."

She spun around, blonde hair tumbling over her face. "What are you sorry for?"

He scrubbed a hand over the back of his neck and sighed. "This is my fault. I never should have put you in this position. I lose my mind when I'm around you, and I can't think straight. I should have waited, walked away when I had the chance, left you alone—"

"Is that what you want? You don't want to see me anymore? Do you...do you regret us?"

Jacob shot to his feet and pulled Avery into his arms. "Hell, no." He cupped her chin in his hand. "Look at me, sweetheart. I do not, nor will I *ever*, regret us. I wish all of this were easy. I wish I could tell the world how I feel about you." He pushed her hair away from her face and kissed the corner of her mouth. "God, I'm an idiot. If I weren't so selfish, maybe this would never have happened."

Avery shook her head, clinging to him. "It doesn't matter now. None of it matters. All we have to worry about is what we do from here on." She exhaled shakily. "What *are* we going to do?"

Jacob released her, spun on his heel, and took over pacing the room. "Maybe we should lay low for a while. Keep everything strictly student and teacher until we figure out who is behind the pictures. We shouldn't be alone together or do anything that might look questionable."

Avery perched on the edge of the couch and nodded. The pain in her eyes screamed at him.

He knelt in front of her and rubbed her arms. "I hate it, too, sweetheart. But I don't think we have any choice. I could lose my job and my tenure, everything I've worked for since high school. The college could suspend you, maybe even stop you from getting your degree."

"You're right, of course." She sighed. Avery rose to her feet and eased past him to grab her coat from the back of the chair and picked up her backpack. She didn't look at Jacob as she dug her keys out of her bag.

Jacob grabbed her arm, stopping her before she could get out the door. He wasn't about to let her leave upset, wondering if she'd ever meant anything to him. He couldn't let that happen.

"Hey," he said. "This doesn't change how I feel about you."

"How do you feel about me, Professor Moore?"

He pressed a kiss to the center of her forehead, the tip of her nose, her cheek, then slid his lips down her jaw to her mouth. He rested his forehead against hers, his eyes closed. Jacob struggled with the words to make this right.

"Avery, I...I don't know what to say."

"Of course, you don't." She pulled free of his embrace and bolted through the house. The kitchen door slammed behind her.

Chapter 15

Avery

The next week dragged along, the dreary weather of early March matching Avery's depressed mood. The day after Jacob received the pictures, she called in sick, told Nat she had the flu, and holed up in her room. She skipped her classes to wallow in her misery and binge-watch *Friends*.

She exchanged a few texts with Jacob, but she kept those to a minimum as well. Every time she talked to him, her heart broke all over again. The constant worry tore her apart. She couldn't sleep or eat and didn't want to leave her room.

Despite her misery, by the time Friday came around, she had to leave the apartment. There was a test in Jacob's class. She'd dreaded it all week—being in the same room as Jacob, breathing the same air, so close yet forced to keep her distance. She considered skipping, but it was the mid-term, her last test before spring break started next week.

Avery trudged across the snow-laden campus, her feet as heavy as her heart. Inside, Jacob watched her as she eased down the aisle and slipped into a chair in the top row as far from him as possible. She itched to touch him, to kiss him, to throw herself into his arms, push him into his office, and make love to him on his stupid, ragged, plaid couch. Instead, she kept her head down and busied herself yanking things from her backpack.

Jacob turned his back on the class and wrote on the board. She stared at the back of his head and gnawed on her pen, her stomach twisting and churning. When he turned around and leaned against his desk, she noticed he looked exhausted—his eyes red-rimmed and his hair tousled as if he crawled out of bed after a restless night. But he was still gorgeous.

"Alright folks, I've got some good news and some bad news for you." A hint of a smile played across his lips. "The good news is Professor Hess will be back after spring break, so you won't have to look at my ugly mug anymore."

His self-deprecating comment earned him a few laughs. He cleared his throat and continued.

"Now for the bad news. You still have to take the test."

The class groaned in unison, this time making him laugh. He grabbed the papers from his desk and passed them around, looking at Avery several times as he made his way around the room.

Only a few other students were left when she finished her test. She walked to the front of the classroom, set it on Jacob's desk, and turned to leave.

"Excuse me, Ms. Collins?"

Avery stopped short. The sound of her name in his deep voice sent a tingle down her spine. An ache built low in her gut.

"Yes, Professor Moore?" She locked eyes with Jacob.

"Have you scheduled another study session with my freshman group?"

Avery nodded. "I'm meeting with them Monday night. The test is next Wednesday, right?"

"Yes," he replied, staring at the floor for a few seconds. When he looked up, he had a hopeful expression on his face. "I wanted to ask you something. I was... uh, wondering if you...do you have a minute?" He pushed himself to his feet and pointed at his office door.

Avery shook her head. "I'm sorry. I have to get home." She spun on her heel, sprinted up the stairs, grabbed her coat and backpack on the run, and burst out the door, ignoring Jacob shouting after her. She didn't stop until she was outside. Assaulted by the stinging cold, she tugged on her jacket before hurrying across the parking lot.

Then stopped dead in her tracks. Her car leaned oddly to one side as if it was off balance. A large screwdriver protruded from the front driver's side tire. The passenger's side tire was deflated, a slash gaping across the rubber. A folded piece of paper fluttered under the windshield wipers. She plucked it free and took a deep breath before opening it.

Stay away from Jacob. Or next time it will be more than your tires that I slash.

———

"Drink this." Jacob pushed a hot mug into her hands.

Avery took a sip, wincing as the alcohol in the cup burned her throat. She blew out a shaky breath and closed her eyes. As soon as she pulled the cryptic note off her car, she had sprinted back across campus, ignoring her burning lungs as fear clutched wildly at her heart and drove her forward.

She burst through Jacob's office door, tears streaming down her face, babbling incoherently, and waving the note in his face. It took him several minutes to calm her down and figure out what happened.

Avery took another drink of the burning whiskey. She coughed, set it on the table, and hugged herself. She couldn't stop shivering. Dragging in a deep breath, she took her phone from her bag.

"I think we should call the police," she said.

"The police?"

"I know someone we can call," Avery explained. "A friend in the sheriff's department."

"You think that's a good idea?"

Avery nodded. "I do. Why? You don't?"

"I didn't say that," he huffed. "I just... this is gonna—" His mouth snapped closed, and he swallowed, his throat clicking. He exhaled and scratched the back of his neck. "Make the call."

Jacob sat beside her as she called. He listened as she explained what happened. When she disconnected the call, he tipped his head to the side, one eyebrow raised.

"Well?"

"My friend, Brent, is a sheriff's deputy. He'll be here soon to take our statements."

Less than ten minutes later, Brent Taft, her ex-boyfriend—if you could call him that—stepped through the door, his hat pulled low over his eyes, and his hand resting on the butt of the gun at his hip.

"Professor Moore?"

Jacob nodded and stepped around the table, his hand extended. Brent glanced at it and turned away. The deputy looked at Avery curiously. "Hello, Avery."

"Hey, Brent."

She and Brent went out two or three times, but there was no chemistry. They'd parted ways amicably, though she sometimes suspected that Brent's feelings were much deeper than hers had been. On the few occasions they'd crossed paths, she caught him looking at her with a longing that made her uncomfortable.

"What can I do for you folks?" Brent asked.

After a slight hesitation, Jacob told the deputy about the photos sent via text and the threatening note left on Avery's car. They spent the better part of an hour talking. When he left, Brent had the photos from Jacob's phone and a list of people who might have taken them: one of Avery's former roommates, an old boyfriend, and some students Jacob knew had a mischievous side. It impressed her that Brent maintained a professional demeanor; he only gave her a disapproving look once or twice. He seemed to reserve his irritation for Jacob, his questions clipped and accusatory.

"Deputy Taft?" Avery interrupted Brent's third repeat of the same question. "I'd like to go home, if there isn't anything else you need?" She glared at the deputy, hoping he got the hint. Enough was enough.

"Yes, ma'am," Brent said. He picked up the note, folded it in half, then in half again. He slipped it in his pocket and turned to Avery.

"I promise I will figure out who did this to you, Avery. You don't deserve to be tormented. Okay?"

"O-okay," she stammered. She didn't care for the expression on his face—oddly hopeful. "Can I ask you a favor?"

"Of course. Whatever I can do."

"Can you please keep this confidential? I know it has to go in the police report—"

"I'll tell you what," the deputy interrupted. "I'll wait a few days to file the official report, see if I can get some leads before I bring Sheriff Willis into the loop. Okay?"

The tension left Avery's body. "That would be great. Thank you."

Jacob walked Taft to his office door, shook his hand, and closed the door behind him. He exhaled loudly, crossed the room, and sat beside Avery on the couch. Taking her hand, he held it loosely, his shoulder touching hers.

"You should come back to my place tonight," he insisted. "I don't want you to go home alone."

"I wouldn't be alone," she scoffed. "Nat's there. Besides, we're lying low, remember?" She heard the frustration in her voice and immediately regretted it.

Jacob slipped an arm around her waist, his nose brushing against her cheek, his lips a breath away from hers. "I can't do this anymore. I don't want this...this guillotine hanging over our heads. I'm going to the university president."

"Jacob, you don't—"

He cut her off, his mouth slanting over hers. The kiss made Avery ache with need, hope bursting in her chest.

"I'll explain everything—how we met, how you're only my student because of Hess's leave of absence, all of it."

"And then what?"

"I beg Charlie not to fire me. Pray he lets me keep my job and my reputation isn't destroyed." Jacob rubbed the back of his neck and stared at the floor.

"I don't want you to do that," she said. She pushed to her feet and stood in front of him. "Let's see if Brent can do anything. Maybe you won't have to go to Ross."

Jacob sighed and stood up from the couch. He pulled her close, his warmth seeping into her. He brushed a kiss across her lips and rested his forehead against hers.

"I miss you, sweetheart."

"I miss you, too. I hate this. But please, Jacob, don't do anything crazy. Not yet. Promise me you'll wait."

Jacob closed his eyes and nodded. "I promise."

Avery sighed. She wasn't sure she believed him. "We can wait a few days, right?"

"I think so." He gave her a wry smile and kissed her again. "Call me when you get home?"

She nodded, hugging him close a moment longer, inhaling his scent, before she grabbed her stuff and hurried from the room, wiping tears from her cheeks.

Chapter 16

Jacob

Jacob promised Avery he wouldn't go to Charlie until Deputy Taft investigated who was behind the pictures and the note. He didn't like it, but he'd promised. Problem was he wasn't sure how long he could keep that promise. He wanted this to end. He wanted Avery.

Exhausted, he went home early, ate some leftover Chinese food, and drank a couple of beers. He tried watching TV, but he couldn't find anything interesting. Too many things crowded his brain.

He fell asleep on the couch fully dressed, his jacket shoved under his head, and one of his mother's afghans thrown over his legs. His dreams were memories of the last couple of days interspersed with whatever television show played in the background.

He slept like shit and woke when the sunlight shone through the thin curtains of his living room. He threw the blanket off and sat up, digging his fingers into the tight knots in the back of his neck.

He grabbed his phone and scrolled through his notifications. There was a lengthy voicemail from Avery.

"You're probably asleep, but I can't keep this in. I have to tell you. I hate this, Jacob. I hate not being able to be with you. I've tried to convince myself that we're nothing more than two people having fun. I told myself this is nothing more than a clandestine affair with my teacher." She giggled, and her voice dropped to a whisper. "This is so much more than a crazy, meaningless affair. I...I love you, Jacob." Another giggle followed by a loud sigh. "I can't believe I told you I love you over voicemail. How ridiculous am I? Don't answer that. I've been drinking, as if you couldn't tell. Shit. You know what, call me tomorrow, okay?"

Jacob stared at the phone in his hand. Jesus Christ, she *loved* him. The question was, did he love her?

It took him about five seconds to decide; he loved her, had for a while now, but he was afraid to admit it to himself, let alone to her. He'd let his fear get in the way.

Jacob was in too deep to turn back.

He regretted nothing. He never would. The more he thought about it, the more he knew what he had to do. He swiped his finger across the screen of his phone, pulled up his contacts, and dialed.

———

"Jacob, hi." Serena smiled at him from her desk. "How are things going?"

"Eh, not bad," he replied, shrugging a shoulder. "It's good to see you, again. How's Van?"

Serena's smile widened, and she blushed. "He's good. Enjoying his new gig as the head of security."

Jacob laughed. "He's enjoying it?"

"He said he's having fun. And I swear these damn college kids love him." She scrunched her nose and shook her head. "Especially the girls."

"You have nothing to worry about." Jacob chuckled. "Van loves you. Spend half an hour talking to him, and you'll know."

Serena giggled and pushed away from her desk. "Let me ask Charlie if he's ready to see you."

"Hey, wait. What kind of mood is he in?"

She paused in front of Charlie's door and lowered her voice. "Um, he's kind of grumpy. He's not happy about coming in on Saturday. I hope whatever you need to talk to him about won't piss him off."

"It might," Jacob groaned.

"Great," she mumbled. She took a deep breath and gave Jacob a less-than-cheerful look. "Give me a minute." She disappeared through a heavy oak door into an inner office, her "hey, Charlie" drifting over her shoulder as it swung shut.

Jacob sank into a plush chair against the wall. Out of the corner of his eye, he glimpsed a photo on Serena's desk—a picture of her, Van, and their dog, Soldier. He was looking forward to their wedding this summer.

Thinking about weddings reminded him it had been a while since he talked to Luke. He made a mental note to call his best friend.

He clasped his hands between his legs, his knuckles aching and hands clammy. His stomach rolled. He wanted this to be over. Charlie was a good guy, a great boss, and a hard-ass about his university's reputation. Nobody got away with improprieties on his watch.

Jacob pushed a hand through his hair, his knee bouncing, his brain creating all sorts of weird scenarios about this meeting. Most involved him getting fired.

The door opened, and Serena stepped out. "He'll see you now."

Charlie sat behind his desk, a faint smile on his face. Once Jacob sat down and Serena closed the door, Charlie tossed his glasses on the desk, sat back in his chair, and crossed his arms.

"Serena said I might not like this."

"You won't," Jacob replied.

"Let's hear it," Charlie grumbled.

Jacob wasn't sure what to say. He took a deep breath and opened his mouth. "I'm in love with a student."

The words he hadn't even said to Avery yet jumped out of his mouth on their own, eager to expose themselves. His mouth snapped shut as soon as it was out, and he leaned forward, his elbows on his knees.

"Go on," Charlie said, surprisingly calm.

He stumbled over his own words, unable to explain himself. He struggled to relax, to take his time, otherwise he would screw this up. Jacob sat back in his chair and started from the beginning, the first time he met Avery. By the time he finished, it was as if someone had lifted a weight from his shoulders.

"She's in Hess's class?" Charlie asked, swiveling in his chair.

Jacob nodded. "Yes. Which means she's no longer my student."

"When did you start dating?"

"Over winter break." Short, honest answers, no extraneous information. Charlie wouldn't want to hear it.

Charlie scrubbed a hand over his face. "You didn't know she was a student when you asked her out?"

"No," Jacob mumbled. "We met at The Percolator; she works there. I didn't know she was a student. I never asked, either. Not very smart."

"Damn right it wasn't smart," Charlie snapped, pushing himself to his feet. "You live and work in a college town, Jacob. Most of the town's population either works at or goes to the university."

"Yes, sir."

"Maybe you didn't ask because you didn't want to know."

Jacob cringed. Charlie was right. He looked at his boss and shrugged.

Charlie stopped pacing behind his desk and leaned over it, his palms flat on the surface. "I need some time to think things over. This is a complicated situation, Jacob. Not just because you're a professor and she's a student. You're esteemed in your field. This could be an enormous scandal neither one of us needs. Thank you for coming to me before it blew up in our faces." He dropped back into his chair, put his glasses on, and grabbed his tablet. "I'll call you tomorrow or Monday at the latest. Until then, don't do anything stupid." He looked at Jacob over his glasses. "That will be all, Professor Moore."

"Yes, sir," Jacob muttered, launching from the chair and striding out the door. He shouted goodbye to Serena over his shoulder as he hurried from the office.

At the bottom of the stairs, three floors down, he leaned against the wall, hands on his knees, panting as he tried to catch his breath. He took his phone from his pocket and dialed from memory, a smile spreading across his face when she answered.

It was the definition of stupid, and it flew in the face of everything Charlie said. But he needed to tell her what he'd done. It would affect her life as much as his.

———

As soon as Jacob pulled to a stop in front of Avery's apartment building, the front door opened and Avery appeared, a smile pasted on her face. She yanked open the door, climbed inside, clasped her hands together, and cleared her throat.

"Hi," she said.

"Hi, sweetheart." He wrapped a hand around the back of her neck, pulled her close, and brushed his lip across hers.

"I thought we were lying low."

Jacob rested his forehead against hers. "I had to see you." He released her and put the car in gear. They drove to his place in comfortable silence, her hand in his.

Once they were at his house, the curtains drawn, a glass of wine in Avery's hand, and a beer in his, he was ready to talk. He wrapped his arm around her shoulders, hugging her close, and pressed his lips to her temple.

"I have to tell you something."

Her voice shook when she spoke. "What is it?"

"I met with Charlie today. Charles Ross."

"The university president?" she asked. "We agreed you'd wait."

Jacob rubbed his hand over the back of his neck and sat forward, his elbows on his knees, his beer held loosely in his hand. He stared across the room at the TV. "I decided not to wait."

She set her wine on the table and wrapped her arms around herself, her face ashen. Her lower lip trembled. "I don't understand."

"I had to do something. Whoever is threatening us has too much power over us. I had to take that away. So, I went to Charlie and told him everything."

Avery slipped off the couch and kneeled between his legs, her hands resting on his thighs. "What happened?" she asked.

Jacob shrugged. "It was anticlimactic. He said he needed time to think things over and he'd call me tomorrow or Monday. Until then, I'm not supposed to do anything stupid."

"Your idea of not doing anything stupid is to call me, pick me up at my place, and bring me back here?"

He set his beer on the table, cupped her face, and pressed a hard kiss to her lips. "I told you, I needed to see you."

"What is Ross going to do?"

"I don't know," he admitted.

"This is all my fault," she muttered. "If I hadn't fallen in love—"

"This is on both of us. You can't help who you're attracted to. You can't help who you fall in love with. If I had to do it again, I would still get your phone number, and I would still ask you out." He squeezed her hands. "I would still fall in love with you."

Avery drew in a sharp breath and tears filled her eyes. "You love me?"

"Yes, I love you. I'm sorry I didn't say it sooner. I'm an idiot. I'm not making decisions based on what other people want. I'd give up everything if it meant being with you." He pulled her into his arms, kissing her neck as he hugged her against his chest.

"Can I ask you something?"

"Anything," Jacob said and stroked her hair, twisting the blonde curls around his fingers.

"You didn't do this because you're colossally stupid, right? You did it because you love me and can't live without me?"

Even though there was a playful quality to her question, he could see the underlying fear and worry in her gorgeous brown eyes. He hugged her tight, his lips pressed to her ear.

"I love you, and I can't live without you, sweetheart," he whispered. "I promise we'll figure it out. We'll make this work, no matter what Charlie says."

Chapter 17

Jacob

Late Monday afternoon, Jacob's phone rang, the sound shrill and jarring in the quiet of his office. He dropped his pen and snatched the handset.

"Professor Moore," he answered.

"Jacob? It's Serena. Are you available to come by and see Charlie?"

His heart skipped a beat, and he couldn't quite catch his breath. He swallowed back the fear rising in his throat and mumbled, "Yes."

Serena told him to come by in an hour. He hung up the phone with shaking hands, sat down in his office chair, then sent a text to Avery to let her know he was meeting with Charlie. She responded with a heart emoji and a reminder to tell her everything as soon as he could.

There was a chill in the air despite spring being weeks away. Jacob shoved his hands in his pockets as he trudged through the light snow covering the ground.

He was almost at the administration offices when his cell phone vibrated. He waited until he was in the building before taking it out of his pocket.

[Avery: I haven't heard from Brent. Still trying to reach him. Will let you know when I do. Have you seen Ross yet?]

[Jacob: I'm about to go in. What are you doing?]

[Avery: I'm at the coffee shop. Ruby needs help. Jules is out sick.]

[Jacob: Call me when you're off. I'll let you know what Ross says. Wish me luck.]

Avery sent him heart emojis along with a devil, which made him laugh. He tucked his phone in his pocket, tapped on the office door, and stepped inside.

Serena rose to her feet, a smile on her face as she came out from behind her desk to shake Jacob's hand.

"He's waiting for you," she said, pointing at Charlie's office door.

"Has he said anything to you?" Jacob asked.

She shook her head. "He's playing this one close to the vest. Come on." Serena opened the door and ushered him inside, giving him one last smile before stepping back out.

Jacob took a seat, leaned forward, and rested his elbows on his knees. His foot tapped incessantly until Charlie shot a look in his direction.

"Thanks for coming by, Jacob. You know, this hasn't made my life easy. I spent the entire weekend worrying about this."

"And?" Jacob asked.

"I'm not firing you. But you are on probation until further notice. If you screw up again, I will fire you. Understood?"

Jacob breathed a little easier. "Yes, sir."

"As for your relationship with Ms. Collins, I will not forbid it. To my unending surprise, it is not against the rules. There is no specific rule against fraternization between professors and students; the handbook merely suggests it *could* be inappropriate. But you and Ms. Collins are close in age, and you are no longer her professor, so it skirts the inappropriate suggestion. I am going to ask you to do your best to keep the relationship low-key. Can you do that?"

Jacob nodded. "Yes, sir."

A faint smile danced across Charlie's face. "You're lucky I like you, Jacob. And I did owe you one for taking over Hess's class. I didn't expect anything like this, though. Do me a favor and don't run around campus making a spectacle of yourselves, okay?"

"We won't," Jacob replied. "I promise."

"I'm holding you to that. Thank you again for bringing this to me before things got out of control."

"You're welcome, Mr. Ross. I appreciate your understanding." Jacob rose to his feet, shook Charlie's hand, and scurried out of the office.

On the way back to his office, Jacob decided he would call Deputy Taft himself. If he wouldn't answer Avery, maybe he would answer Jacob's call. As soon as he shut the door behind himself, he looked up the sheriff's number and dialed.

"Sheriff's office, Sheriff Willis speaking."

"Donna? Donna Willis?"

"Um, yes, this is Donna Willis. With whom am I speaking?"

Jacob cleared his throat. Donna graduated high school a couple of years before him; she probably wouldn't even remember him. "Donna, this Jacob Moore. We went to high school together."

"Jacob! Hi! I heard you were back in town. What can I do for you?"

"Is Deputy Taft available? I'd like to speak to him."

There was an awkward silence before Donna spoke. "May I ask what this is regarding?"

"I wanted to ask him if he has made any headway on the case involving myself and Avery Collins?"

"What case?" Donna asked.

Jacob explained the tire slashing and the photographs. Taft must not have told Sheriff Willis yet; he had said he would wait a few days.

"Are you sure it was Taft? Absolutely sure?"

"Yes. Avery called him herself."

Sheriff Willis exhaled. "Jacob, Deputy Taft has been on administrative leave since Christmas. He shouldn't be investigating any cases. Did you call our office to report it?"

"I'm...I'm not sure. Avery called it in—"

There was silence on the other end of the line, silence Jacob didn't like.

"Donna?"

"I'll call you back, Jacob."

Before he could say anything, the line disconnected. He stared at the phone, dumbfounded, before hanging it up. A thick fog invaded his brain. He picked up his cell phone and called Avery. It went straight to voicemail, so he texted her.

[Jacob: Avery. Call me. Now.]

———

Jacob gunned the engine, speeding through the twenty-five mile per hour speed zone in the middle of town. His conversation with Sheriff Willis made him uneasy, and Avery not answering her phone had his head in all the wrong places. He needed to find her.

He stopped in front of the coffee shop, slammed the car into park, and sprinted to the front door, leaving the car running with the door open. He burst into the building, but the coffee shop was empty.

"Avery!" he shouted.

"Jacob! Back here!"

Jacob darted through the swinging door, following the sound of Avery's voice. He caught sight of Avery going out the back door. She glanced back over her shoulder, her overly bright eyes locking on his and her face ashen. He took a step forward, but she was suddenly gone as if she had never been there.

He followed her, stumbling over boxes stacked near the door and knocking them to the floor. He had to get to Avery. The fear in her eyes had chilled him to the bone.

Jacob burst through the door into a short alleyway. Thirty yards up the street, Avery was being dragged toward her car by a man he couldn't make out. The man shoved Avery into her car and climbed in behind her.

"Avery!"

Her brake lights flashed, and the car pulled away from the curb, fishtailing on the damp street.

Chapter 18

Avery

Avery shoved her phone into her purse and shut down the engine. She stared out the windshield. *I shouldn't have told Ruby I would work.* All she would do was worry about Jacob's meeting with Mr. Ross and watch the clock until she could call him. Ruby had a strict "no cell phone" rule when working, so she wouldn't be able to talk to Jacob until she was off.

With an irritated sigh, she pushed open the car door and hurried inside. She snatched her apron off the hook by the door, tucked her silenced phone in her back pocket, dropped her things in the office, and made her way out front.

"Avery, thank God." Ruby pushed a hand through her hair and gave her a weak smile. "You're a lifesaver. Thank you for coming in."

She patted Ruby's arm. "I'm happy to help. Now, don't you need to go? Something about a soccer game?"

"Yes. Carson should be here in less than an hour. Can you handle things until then?"

Avery looked around the empty coffee shop. "Uh, I think so." She laughed and pushed Ruby toward the swinging door leading to the back. "Go, take J.J. to his game."

Ruby yelled goodbye over her shoulder, and a few minutes later, Avery heard the back door slam closed.

"Can I talk to you, Avery?"

She gasped and spun around, one hand grasping the counter to keep from falling.

"Brent! You scared the crap out of me." She leaned against the counter. "I've been trying to call you."

"I know," Deputy Taft said. He glanced over his shoulder then stepped behind the counter. "I have to tell you something."

"Um, okay. Is it...is it about my tires? Or the pictures? Did you find out anything?"

"I don't think you should date Jacob anymore," Brent snarled.

"Wait? What?" Her chest tightened, and sweat dripped down her back.

"You need to stop seeing Jacob. If you don't, I'll have to tell the university."

Realization hit Avery like a hard slap. Brent took the pictures and slashed her tires. She jerked her arms down, gripped the counter behind her, and tried to not to scream.

"I think you should go," she gritted out through her teeth.

"Give me a minute," Brent snapped. "Hear me out."

Avery shook her head. "I don't think we have anything to talk about."

He was right in her face. Avery took a step back but was blocked by the counter. She cleared her throat and inched to the left, hoping she could get around Brent.

Brent's hand closed around her upper arm. "Five minutes, Avery. That's all I'm asking."

Avery shook her head again. "No. You need to go." She tried to pull away, but Brent's grip tightened painfully.

"Please?" Brent begged.

"Let me go." She tried to yank free, but he wouldn't let go.

Brent mumbled something unintelligible under his breath and looked around. After a second, in which she hoped he might give up and let her go, he pushed her through the swinging door and into the back of the shop, ignoring Avery's protests.

"What are you doing?" she cried, struggling against his grip.

"I want to talk to you. I need you to listen to me for five minutes. That's it." His lip curled, his handsome face turning demonic.

Avery's heart pounded, and her entire body shook. Brent dragged her toward the back door. She heard the bell over the front door ring, then Jacob called her name.

"Jacob! Back here!" she yelled.

"Shit." Brent yanked her out the door, but not before she saw Jacob, her eyes locking with his. She whimpered and tried again to yank free, but Brent wasn't letting go. He hustled her down the alley to her car, pushed her into the driver's seat, and climbed in beside her.

"This isn't funny, Brent," she snapped. "Let me out of the car."

Brent popped open the glove box and pulled out her extra set of keys. He dropped them in her lap, reached into his pocket, removed his service revolver, and pressed it against her side. "Start the car and drive, Avery. Now."

She did as she was told, her hands shaking as she put the car in gear and hit the gas, the ass end of the car fishtailing as she accelerated on the wet street.

———

Avery swiped at the tears sliding down her cheek and gnawed on her lower lip, the faint coppery taste of blood on her tongue. She didn't want Brent to hear her cry. He'd been babbling on since they left The Percolator, telling her why she had to break up with Jacob and give him another shot.

The depth of his obsession with her sank in as they drove. He knew everything: how she met Jacob, how many times they'd gone out over the winter break, even the first time they had sex. It was obvious he'd been watching her. Following her. Stalking her. Fear crawled over her, bringing goosebumps to the surface of her skin.

"Turn there." Brent pointed at a barely visible dirt road up ahead, a mere gap in the trees.

She turned and followed the seldom-used road, the car bouncing and dipping on the dirt tracks. It ended two hundred yards into the trees. She stopped the car, put it in park, and left the engine running.

Oppressive silence filled the car, thickening the air with tension. Avery cleared her throat and turned to Brent with a watery smile.

"What are we doing out here, Brent?" She tried to keep her tone pleasant and accommodating, scared she would anger the sheriff's deputy if she didn't stay calm.

"I told you—I wanted to talk to you." He pushed the gun hard into her stomach.

Her smile wavered, but she did her best to hold it in place. "What do you want to talk about?"

"You and Jacob. The two of you, you're not...you're not meant to be. But you and me, we are."

Avery shook her head before she could stop herself. The look Brent gave her made skin crawl. She swallowed back the biting remark on her lips.

Brent's eyes narrowed, but he continued. "I know it's hard to understand, but *our* lives are meant to intersect, *our* lives are meant to be joined. We will be together. I will do anything I have to to make that happen."

"Brent, we only went out a couple of times—"

"That doesn't matter!" He slammed his fist down on the dashboard, leaving a considerable dent.

Avery slapped her hand over her mouth and cowered against the door, her eyes on the gun.

"When I saw you in the library…when I saw what *he* was doing to you, my anger got the best of me. I was going to go to the university and tell them, even if it meant Jacob losing his job or you getting kicked out of school." Brent scrubbed a hand over his face. "But then I realized maybe I could make you break up, which would give me a chance to prove to you I am the person you belong with. If you would just try to understand, then I could breathe again. I could *live* again."

Anger flooded her. "So, this is what you do?" she yelled. "You kidnap me and drag me to the middle of nowhere? You think this is going to make me want to be with you?"

"Avery, just listen to me—"

"I listened to you, Brent. I listened to you tell me you've been following me, obsessing over me, and you tried to blackmail me into dating you. That's what I heard."

Brent sighed and shook his head. "You never gave me a chance. You broke up with me and forgot about me."

"That's not true."

"Stop. Don't patronize me." He moved the gun, pulling it away from her side to set it on the seat between his legs, his hand resting on his thigh, inches from the weapon. "If you'd just given me a chance, maybe things would be different."

Speechless, Avery shifted restlessly in her seat. The corner of her phone jabbed her in the ass. She'd forgotten it was in her pocket. She glanced at Brent out of the corner of her eye, but he was staring out the passenger window, muttering incoherently under his breath.

Without taking time to think, Avery shoved open her door and threw herself on the ground. She scrambled to her feet and took off at a dead run, not sure where she was going. All she knew was she needed to get away from Brent. She heard a pop and felt a sharp sting on her right arm then a warm gush, but she kept running. With another pop, she felt her hair move as a bullet sailed past her and hit the tree a foot to her left. She ducked, fell to her knees, and crawled into the brush. Low to the ground, she crawled on her hands and knees through the trees, rocks embedding into her hands and branches scraping her arms and face, until she couldn't hear Brent anymore. Only then did she stand up and start running again, her hand pressed to the bleeding wound on her arm. She checked to make sure her phone was still in her pocket and sent up a quick prayer that it would work this deep in the woods.

It has to work. It has to.

Chapter 19
Jacob

Jacob sat in the corner, a steaming cup of coffee in front of him. He watched Sheriff Willis on the other side of the room talking with Ruby. He glanced at his watch; it had been two hours since Avery disappeared with Deputy Taft. Sitting here doing nothing was killing him.

"Professor Moore?" Sheriff Willis slipped into the seat across from him.

He gave her a weary smile. "You can call me Jacob, Sheriff."

"Only if you call me Donna." She set her notebook on the table and cleared her throat. "Is it okay if I ask you a few questions?"

Jacob bit his tongue and nodded. Donna shouldn't be here asking questions; she should be looking for Avery. He rubbed the center of his forehead and forced himself to be patient.

"How long have you two been seeing each other?"

"Since winter break," he responded. "So, what's that? Three months."

Donna scribbled in her notebook, her eyebrows scrunched together. She did that in high school when concentrating.

"When did you receive the photos you told me about?"

"Um, I guess about two, two-and-a-half weeks ago."

"And when did Miss Collins call Deputy Taft?"

He was sure of this answer. "A week and two days ago after she found her tires slashed. She came back to my office and called him from there. We both assumed he filed the report and the incident was being investigated."

"I can't tell you how sorry I am." Donna sighed. "I suspended him in

— 156 —

December. I wrongly assumed he wouldn't do anything stupid, so I didn't take his badge or service revolver. Rookie mistake. But we are doing everything in our power to find her."

"Who is *we*, Sheriff?" Jacob snorted. "I've seen you and Taft. So that leaves you."

"I have two other deputies I've pulled in, along with the state police. I promise you we will find her. And we'll find Deputy Taft."

"Sheriff Willis?"

A young, female deputy stopped a foot away from the table, a hand on the butt of her gun, the other on her hip. She didn't look old enough to drink, let alone carry a weapon.

Donna excused herself, patting Jacob on the arm as she walked past him to join the deputy. They put their heads together and whispered, then hurried out the front door of the shop.

Jacob followed, yanking his jacket on as he pushed through the people crowding the small coffee shop. He stepped out the front door as the sheriff's car flew past, lights on and siren wailing.

Natasha appeared at his side, her face pale, dark circles under her eyes. Her boyfriend—Jacob thought his name was Brick—stood off to one side, arms crossed and glaring at everyone.

"Any word?" Natasha asked.

Jacob shook his head. "No. But Sheriff Willis took off like a bat out of hell. I don't know why."

Natasha wrapped her arms around herself. "You know, Avery didn't tell me she was seeing you. She usually tells me everything."

Jacob squeezed her shoulder. "We didn't tell anyone. I didn't even tell *my* best friend. It was...*is* complicated."

Natasha shrugged, obviously unconvinced, and wandered off. Jacob scrubbed a hand over the back of his neck and wondered for the millionth time if Avery was okay. This was all his fault. If he hadn't been so stupid...

"They found her." Luke came out of the coffee shop and stopped in front of Jacob. He'd come down as soon as Jacob called him, no questions asked. Luke was incredibly supportive despite his obvious curiosity. It was a temporary reprieve; the third degree would start as soon as Avery was safe.

"What? Where?" Jacob asked.

"An old logging road north of town. She's been wandering the woods for hours, no cell service, alone, hurt, and near hypothermia."

"Hurt?" Jacob snapped. "What do you mean, hurt?"

"I overheard someone say it was a bullet wound. They're taking her to the hospital."

"Shit." Jacob turned and sprinted to his car, gesturing for Luke to follow. He pulled away from the curb before Luke even shut his door.

———

"When can I see her?" Jacob demanded.

The nurse behind the counter rolled his eyes again. "Mr. Moore, you're going to have to be patient. You aren't family or listed as an emergency contact, so I cannot let you back to see her. Not unless she agrees to see you."

Jacob leaned over the counter. "Then go ask her," he snarled.

"She's with the sheriff. Talk to her when she comes out." The nurse spun on his heel and disappeared through a door behind the counter.

Luke grabbed Jacob's arm and dragged him back to the waiting area. "Stop bugging the staff." He pushed Jacob into a chair and sat beside him. "They have enough to worry about without you harassing them."

Jacob slumped in his seat, head in his hands. "You know, you don't have to babysit me."

Luke chuckled. "Apparently, I do. Otherwise, you'll keep bugging that poor nurse."

"I'm serious. Go home to Bonnie. I'm sure she's wondering where you are."

"I doubt it," his friend muttered. "We...well, the wedding is off."

Jacob sat up straight in his seat. "What? You're kidding, right?"

"Nope. We broke up two weeks ago."

Jacob scrubbed a hand over his face. He was a shitty friend. He'd been so wrapped up in his own world and problems that he hadn't realized his friend's life had gone to hell.

"Christ, Luke, I'm so sorry."

Luke shrugged. "I'm okay. I think it's for the best. We weren't good together."

"Why didn't you tell me?" Jacob asked.

"You seemed distracted, worried about something and dealing with your own problems. I didn't want to burden you with mine." Luke smiled. "I guess it was because of Avery, huh?"

"Yeah. I love her. But she's a student. Made it—"

"—complicated," Luke finished. "I think it's time we got a beer and talked. We have a lot to discuss."

"Jacob?" Sheriff Willis—Donna—came out of the emergency room door. "Ms. Collins is asking for you."

He glanced at Luke, who nodded his approval. He jumped to his feet and followed Donna back down the hall.

"How is she?" he asked.

"She got lucky. We found her before the onset of hypothermia. It was close. She has a bullet wound on her arm and scrapes and bruises from running through the woods. She's understandably freaked out from being kidnapped."

"Did you find Taft?"

Donna nodded. "Yes. Lost in the woods, looking for Avery. He's at the station. The state police are processing him, and then they'll take him to Missoula." She stopped in front of a closed curtain and pulled it back.

Avery was on a bed piled high with blankets, her eyes closed, purple circles under her lashes. She stirred and turned, her warm brown eyes locking with Jacob's.

"Hi." Tears welled in her eyes. She held out her hands to him.

Jacob strode past Donna to sit on the side of the bed. He took Avery's face in his hands, tilting it back to examine the scratches and bruises, his thumb brushing over her lips. He closed his eyes and kissed her forehead. She sagged against the pillows, the tears sliding down her face.

"I'm so sorry, baby," he said, holding her close and stroking her hair.

He held her until she stopped trembling and her tears dried up, then he tucked the blanket around her and rose to his feet. "I should let you get some rest." He swept her hair behind her ear and kissed her.

Avery grabbed his hand, squeezing it so tight her knuckles turned white. "Don't leave." Panic laced her words. "Please, Jacob. Stay with me."

She didn't have to ask twice. Jacob wasn't sure he'd ever be able to leave her again. He stretched out on the bed and wrapped his arms around her, careful not to jostle the IV in her arm. She rested her head on his chest and closed her eyes. Within minutes, she was asleep in his arms.

Chapter 20

Avery

"How'd it go yesterday?" Nat dropped her backpack in the booth and slid in. "It sucked," Avery replied. "Thank God Jacob was with me. I was a wreck. Testifying in front of a grand jury is nerve-wracking. But I don't have to see Brent again until the trial. Unless the asshole pleads guilty."

"Do you think he'll do that?"

Avery shook her head. "No. Jacob thinks it will go to trial. I just want it to be over. I want them to find Brent guilty and put him in jail. I only wish it could be for the rest of his life."

Nat took Avery's hand and clasped it between hers. "Me too, kiddo. Me too. That jerk deserves it after what he did to you."

"Let's change the subject, okay?"

Nat laughed and dropped her hands. "Sure. How goes the job hunt?"

Avery crossed her eyes and stuck out her tongue. "That sucks, too. I think I might have found something with the high school up in Kalispell. I'm waiting to hear from the principal. What about you?"

"Say hello to the newest member, co-director, stage manager, and head of marketing for the Lakeside Thespians Dinner Theatre." Nat jumped to her feet and curtsied with a grand sweep of her arms.

"Aw, Nat, that's awesome! I'm so jealous."

"Don't be." Nat giggled, returning to her seat. "It's not as grand as it sounds. But the theatre is under new management, and they hope to make a name for themselves. They have big plans for the summer and the influx of tourists. I'm part of those plans. I don't think it hurts that Daddy threw a bunch of money at them, and my brother, Nate, offered to let us use Time Out for some big fund-raising get-togethers. Thank god he owns the place. But it's a job. I'm just glad I don't have to go back to Great Falls and live with my parents."

"Brick wouldn't have liked that," Avery added.

"Yeah, well after you moved out, I wasn't sure I'd have much choice."

Avery had moved out of the apartment she shared with Nat after graduation. She would have left sooner, but she wanted to wait until she graduated. Jacob asked her to move in with him the day they let her out of the hospital. It had taken her days to convince him it was a bad idea while she was still in school. Fortunately, she had Luke backing her up, as well as Charles Ross's directive to keep things low-key. Jacob had reluctantly agreed.

Avery narrowed her eyes and gave her friend a playful glare. "I doubt that. Brick was pretty much moved in by the time I left. I had to step over his beer bottles to get out the door."

Nat rolled her eyes. "Not all of us live with the perfect man."

Avery didn't like the tone of Nat's voice. It wasn't jealousy; it was something else. "Natasha, what's wrong?"

Nat glanced around the coffee shop then pointed at the door. "Speak of the devil. Perfect man headed this way." She snatched up her backpack and rose to her feet. "I'll see you later." She gave Avery a hug and mumbled "hello" to Jacob as she headed out the door.

Jacob slipped into the booth beside Avery and slid his arm around her waist. "Hey, sweetheart. How you holding up?"

"Okay." She rested her head on his shoulder. "I'm glad it's over. Or mostly over, I guess."

He kissed the top of her head and hugged her close. "I feel like I can't apologize enough."

"Yeah, well, you need to knock it off," Avery quipped. "You need to stop blaming yourself for what Brent did. He's off his rocker, living in his own reality that doesn't include the truth in any way, shape, or form. I thought he was my friend, and he was trying to help us. You didn't know he was obsessive and crazy any more than I did."

"If we hadn't been dating—"

"He would have still done it," she interrupted. "It wouldn't have mattered if I was dating you or not. It would have happened either way. And if it wasn't for you, no one would have known Brent took me, and who knows what would have happened. I owe you my life."

Jacob rested his forehead on hers. "I love you, Ms. Collins."

Avery wrapped a hand around the back of his neck and brushed a kiss across his lips.

"I love you too, Professor Moore."

The End

Our Two-Week, One-Night Stand

Dedication

This one is for DeDe. Thank you for being the best mother-in-law in the world. I miss you every day.

Chapter 1

Cecily

*C*ecily stared out the window. She hated New York, hated it. She didn't understand why her father insisted she accompany him on his annual trip to the Big Apple. They spent no time together outside of the office, and they didn't talk when they were together anyway. Since her breakup with Lawrence, her father barely spoke to her. His disappointment was palpable and hurtful. She couldn't even bring Sebastian to keep her company. But worse than any of that, her father wouldn't allow her to join him at the board meetings, insisting she wait in his office. Her position in the company—director of company events—didn't require a seat at his board meetings.

Honestly, she was nothing more than a glorified party planner for the company, so coming to New York was a waste of time for Cecily. Behind her, Claude Devereaux, her father, dropped his pen and shoved himself away from his desk. "Have the proposal for the acquisition party on my desk by the time I come back. I want to look it over." His indignant tone mixed with the thickness of his French accent signaled his irritation with her.

Cecily put a smile on her face and turned away from the window. "Of course, Daddy." She took a step toward the door her father was walking toward. "I would love to go with you to the board meeting."

"You're not ready for that kind of responsibility yet, princess," Claude Devereaux said.

"I'm thirty years old, Daddy, with an MBA in business from Stanford. When exactly am I going to be ready?"

— 169 —

"I'm not having this discussion again, Cecily." He straightened his jacket and tie.

"At least let me go to the board meeting with you. You never know, I might have some ideas worth talking about."

"There's no need to attend today's meeting. We're discussing cybersecurity and meeting with the firm that helped us set up the firewalls and safeguards. Nothing to worry yourself about."

"Daddy, if you would give me a chance—"

Claude forcefully interrupted Cecily. "Enough, Cecily. My business is very important to me. I won't entrust it to just anyone."

"But I'm your daughter. No one knows the company or the business like I do. I'm the perfect person to trust. When are you going to realize that?"

Her father rolled his eyes and left without answering her. Cecily paced the room like a caged animal, back and forth in front of the floor-to-ceiling windows, looking out over the skyline she hated.

Six years of college and an MBA, all for nothing because her father would never allow her to run his company. She wasn't the son he'd always wanted so he'd pinned his hopes on a son-in-law, but Cecily crushed those dreams when she dumped Lawrence. Claude pinned all his hopes on Lawrence, the first boyfriend Cecily ever had that her father liked. This was another point of contention between them. No matter how hard she worked or how much she begged, Devereaux Industries was forever out of her reach.

Cecily snatched her purse off the chair and headed for the elevators. She wanted a drink some place where her father wasn't. Outside, she hailed a taxi and asked the driver to take her to the closest bar, where she'd drown her sorrows in vodka martinis.

——

The bar was a little more than half full when Cecily walked in. She pushed through the crowd, nodding and smiling, as she made her way to a seat at the bar and ordered a drink. She smiled gratefully at the bartender when he set her vodka martini in front of her. A sigh of relief escaped her when the cool liquor slid down her throat.

Cecily watched the five o'clock, after work crowd fill the dance floor, as her foot tapped with the thumping beat of the music. When a cute guy asked her to dance, she readily agreed. It had been too long since she'd had any fun. If Cecily had to be in this godforsaken city, she could at least enjoy herself.

Hours passed; the sun set, and the dark bar grew darker. She lost track of how many songs she danced to and how many drinks she had. Free of her father's disapproving glares and archaic ideas—if only for a little while—Cecily let herself go.

Suddenly, a man drew her eye as soon as he walked through the door. He was tall, maybe 6'3", blond, muscular, mid-thirties, and drop-dead gorgeous in a Captain America-kind of way. Tight jeans clung to his thick thighs and a black leather jacket covered his bulging arms and broad shoulders. Both the men and the women stared at him, stopping in their tracks with their mouths hanging open to stare at the blond god making his way across the room. The crowd split to let him pass, and he walked right through them like he owned the place. He yanked his jacket off and sat at the corner of the bar.

Cecily kept an eye on him as she danced until the crowd grew and merged in front of her, obscuring her view. She danced for a few more minutes before making her way to the edge of the dance floor. He stared at her, and heat flooded her cheeks. Eyes downcast, she eased into her seat on the opposite side of the bar. When Cecily looked up, she looked right into a pair of gorgeous dark blue eyes. Nerves overtook her, and she looked away. She caught the bartender's attention and ordered another drink.

"Put her drink on my tab." His voice was deep, one of those voices you never tired of hearing. He stood beside her chair, close enough that she could smell the spicy scent of his aftershave and see the rippling muscles under his shirt. Cecily couldn't stop staring at him.

He was the most gorgeous man she had ever seen. Even though he stood well over six feet, he moved with cat-like grace and ease. He had broad shoulders that tapered down to a tiny, tight waist, where she could see his well-toned abs through his too-small shirt. He pushed a hand through his short blond hair as his cobalt blue eyes danced over her.

"Mind if I sit down?" he asked, gesturing to the empty seat beside her. One side of his mouth pulled up in a sexy, little smirk and in that moment, Cecily knew exactly how her evening would end.

She hadn't expected to meet someone, not in New York, but she wouldn't look a gift horse in the mouth. It would only be for one night, like the other men she'd slept with during the last few months. She would talk to this guy and have some fun, maybe a lot of fun if the evening went as she hoped.

"Not at all." She held out her hand. "My name is Cecily."

"Nice to meet you, Cecily." The smirk grew into a grin. "I'm Lincoln." His large hand encompassed hers. He held it longer than necessary, squeezing it before releasing it.

Lincoln sat on the stool beside her, and they chatted for a few minutes about nothing important while they sipped their drinks: the weather, the crowd in the bar, and the score of the Mets game playing on the bar TV.

The music swelled, and an upbeat song she loved pumped through the speakers in the corner. Cecily swayed side to side, her foot tapping. "What do you say we dance?"

Lincoln laughed and shook his head. "I don't know; I'm not much of a dancer."

Cecily stood up and grabbed his hand. "You've never danced with me. It'll be fun, I promise."

He shrugged, set his beer on the bar, and let her lead him by the hand to the dance floor. She took his hands, placed them on her hips, and eased closer to him. She took a deep breath and shimmied to the music, sidling closer to Lincoln and letting the music control her movements.

Lincoln stood in front of her, stiff and unmoving. He squeezed her hips so hard, it hurt.

"Relax, Lincoln."

"I'm not so good at this," he muttered. "Are you sure about this? Maybe we should go back and sit down."

Cecily laughed, pushed up on her toes, and pressed her lips to Lincoln's ear. "Shut up and dance with me."

Lincoln gulped and pulled her tight against his body, his focus on her and her alone. He squeezed her hips again as she wiggled against him. He bit his lip, and a faint blush colored his cheeks.

Despite his reluctance, Cecily kept Lincoln on the dance floor for several songs, the two of them moving fluidly with the music. Lincoln was a fabulous dancer. Even though he hadn't wanted to dance with her, he appeared to be enjoying himself.

Emboldened by the way Lincoln looked at her, and how the heat of his stare caused a tingling ache between her legs, she put her hands on his cheeks and kissed him. It was gentle at first, her way of testing the waters and gauging his interest. The kiss only lasted a few seconds before it exploded, and they began exploring each other with reckless abandon.

It was as if they were alone in the crowded room: hands all over each other, her tongue in his mouth, the taste of beer and mint gum filling her mouth. Unable to stay quiet, Cecily moaned quietly.

Lincoln pushed away from her, glanced around, and then he pulled her down a dimly lit, secluded hallway leading to the bathrooms. No one was coming or going, so they were alone.

With one more glance over his shoulder, he pushed her against the wall between the bathroom door, grabbed the bottom of her skirt, and hiked it up. He put his hand on her ass and squeezed, groaning when he grazed her bare skin. His mouth covered hers with a kiss like nothing she'd ever experienced. He kneaded her breast through the silky fabric of her blouse, drawing a groan from her as her nipples hardened. She squirmed against him and her back arched as she pushed herself against Lincoln's warm body.

"Let's get out of here," he whispered in her ear. He kissed her neck, his lips sliding down to her collarbone where he nibbled at the space where her neck and shoulder met.

Her brain—along with her mouth—shut down as Lincoln's lips moved over her skin. She threw her head back so he could have better access to her neck. The stubble on his cheeks and chin rubbed deliciously against her, burning in the best way possible and obliterating all coherent thought. There was only Lincoln.

Cecily felt the hard line of his erection as Lincoln pressed his hips into hers. He tangled his fingers in her hair and nipped at her bottom lip.

"Cecily. Look at me."

She looked at him with hooded eyes, her heart pounding, and the whoosh of blood rushing in her ears.

Lincoln licked his lips. "If we don't get out of here soon, I'm gonna take you right here against this wall, and I won't give a shit who sees it."

That was what she'd been hoping to hear. She smiled, slid her hand between their bodies, and rested it on Lincoln's hard shaft trapped between them. Raising up slightly on her toes, she wrapped her hand around the back of his neck, pulled him down, and kissed him.

"Do you think you're man enough to handle me? I might be more of a woman than you're used to." She squeezed him gently, his cock twitching behind the zipper of his jeans.

Lincoln growled low in the back of his throat and moved in to kiss her, but at the last second, she turned her head with a teasing smile on her lips. He moaned, grabbed her wrists, and held them over her head, his grip like an iron vise. He pushed his hips into hers, grinding against her and drawing a moan from Cecily, as unexpected heat shot through to her core and settled in the pit of her stomach. She ached with need.

"I don't think it'll be a problem, sweetheart. I will leave you spent and more satisfied than you can even imagine. You'll scream my name when you cum." His hips moved in a slow circle, his enormous cock straining to be released. "The question is, do you want me to do that right here, against this wall, or do you want me to take you back to your place so I can give you the ride of your life?"

"My hotel is around the corner," she whispered breathlessly.

Lincoln kissed her throat, right beneath her jaw. "Good choice." He took a step back, straightened her blouse and skirt, then he took her hand and strolled back to the bar.

"Before we go, I have to tell you something," Cecily said.

"Okay."

"This is a one-time thing. Just tonight. I'm not interested in anything more or anything permanent. I'm just looking for some fun."

"Perfect, because that is all I'm looking for, sweetheart. I'm not interested in any kind of relationship, either. One night only." Lincoln said. "And trust me, I promise it will be fun."

Cecily downed her drink and picked up her purse. "I'm down the street at the Conrad."

He pressed a kiss to her cheek. "Let's go."

Chapter 2

Cecily

ecily didn't remember the walk back to the hotel. All she could think about was her hand in Lincoln's, the way her lips still burned from his kisses, and how her body was on fire everywhere he had touched. He kept his distance as they walked through the lobby and took the elevator upstairs, only holding her hand. After they got off at her floor, he put his hand on her waist and waited patiently behind her as she unlocked the hotel room door. Once they were inside, Lincoln held her hand while he slipped the "Do Not Disturb" sign over the handle and pushed the door closed. He spun around and pounced on her, a gleam in his eye.

"Bedroom?"

Cecily pointed over her shoulder. Lincoln took her hand and led her through the hotel suite to the adjoining bedroom. She stopped at the end of the bed while Lincoln walked to the other side of the room, turned on the bedside table lamp, and turned back to her.

He removed his shirt, tossing it on the floor as he toed off his shoes, unbuckled his belt, and unzipped his jeans. Cecily caught a brief glimpse of dark blond hair dropping into the top of the v behind the zipper. Her heart skipped a beat when she realized he wasn't wearing any underwear. He kept his eyes on her as she crossed the room to stand in front of him.

"Why are you still dressed?" he asked gruffly.

She shrugged her shoulders and shook her head. Her stomach flipped, and her hands shook, something she didn't expect. One-night stands didn't make her nervous; they never had. But Lincoln was different. She did not know why, but he was.

"Cecily?"

"Sorry," she mumbled. She reached for the lamp Lincoln had turned on, but he caught her hand and stopped her.

"What are you doing?" he demanded.

"I'm turning off the light."

Even though Cecily had grown to love and accept herself the way she was, she didn't have sex with the lights on. That confidence and acceptance slipped when she was in the bedroom. Years of teasing and self-doubt were hard to shake, especially with feeling sexy. Her last boyfriend, Lawrence, hadn't helped; he never made her feel sexy. They never made love with the lights on because he said he didn't need to see her when they had sex.

"I love you *despite* your flaws," Lawrence would tell her. Those flaws Lawrence referred to were nothing more than her curvy, larger-than-average body.

The damage Lawrence did was the reason she hadn't dated anyone seriously since their breakup six months earlier. She didn't trust anyone. Most men only cared about sex, something that could be done with the lights off and forgotten about the next day. She was forgettable, so it was easier to sleep with them and walk away; that way, she stayed whole.

"Leave it on," Lincoln said. "I want to see you."

Cecily opened her mouth to argue, but he cut her off with a kiss, his hands sliding over her body. He cupped her ass and dragged her close, emphasizing his desire for her by rubbing his body against hers.

"Now take off your clothes."

The tone of his voice left no room for argument. She hurried to remove her skirt and blouse, dropping them on the floor beside his. She resisted the urge to cover herself with her hands. Before she took off anything else, his mouth was on hers, his tongue buried in her mouth. Lincoln sat on the edge of the bed in front of her, removed her bra and tossed it aside. He thumbed her nipple as he kneaded her breast, then his tongue darted out and caressed the erect nipple. Lincoln hooked his finger in her lacy, black underwear and pushed them down her legs as he kissed his way down her body.

Cecily jumped and tried to push him away when his tongue flicked against her warm center at the apex of her thighs. Lincoln wrapped his arm around her thighs, holding her in place. He looked up at her, confused.

"What's wrong?" he asked. His voice was deeper, gruffer, sexier.

"I ... I ... just let me turn off the light," she answered. Cecily reached for it again, but in one swift move, Lincoln tossed her onto the bed and trapped her beneath him.

"I said I want to see you," he reiterated, his blue eyes boring into hers.

"But why?"

"You're gorgeous, Cecily," he whispered. His breath was hot against her ear, bringing goosebumps to the surface of her skin. Lincoln slipped his hand between her legs and caressed her as he talked, making it difficult to concentrate on his words. "I want to watch you come undone, watch your beautiful face as you cum, and watch this gorgeous body move as I ... do ... this."

His long middle finger slid slowly inside her, the palm of his hand pressed against her, as he moved in tight, small circles.

She moaned while her hips grinded against his hand, her eyes rolling back in her head as he massaged her. Lincoln smiled, his dark blue eyes sparkling as he watched her.

His mouth closed over her breast and his tongue swirled around the nipple, sucking it greedily. Cecily clutched the blankets in her hands as the tension built, and wound her body tighter and tighter, bringing her closer to the edge with every movement. Lincoln moved down her body, kissing her everywhere, as his finger continued to pump, sending tingles storming through her entire body. No one had ever done this to her; no one had ever brought her to the peak of climax so easily. He hovered over her wet core, his warm breath blowing over her. He glanced up at her, with that damn, sexy smirk on his face.

"Hold on to something, sweetheart," he said. His tongue flicked out, dancing over her sensitive nub and driving her wild with need. He thrust another finger into her, and her hips leaped off the bed. He pushed her back down, positioned his head between her legs, and worked her open with his mouth.

Cecily held the back of his head, grinding against his face. Her startled gasps interspersed with cries of his name, filling the room as she hurtled toward her climax. When he put his palm flat on her stomach and moved forward, pushing his tongue deeper into her, she lost it. Something between a scream and a squeal burst out of her, as an orgasm to beat all orgasms blew through her.

When Lincoln pulled away, Cecily trembled, her heart pounding out of control and she couldn't catch her breath. He licked his lips as he crawled back up the bed and laid beside her. Cecily took a few moments to catch her breath and collect herself before she rolled to her side, eased her hand past the waistband of Lincoln's jeans, and took hold of him. She stroked his cock, silently marveling at his size as his hips moved, thrusting into her hand.

"Mm, that's it, gorgeous. That's perfect." He rested his forehead against hers and squeezed his eyes closed, with his mouth open and lips glistening.

She loved the sound of his voice, deep and sexy, praising her as she touched him. She pushed his pants down over his hips, giggling as he impatiently kicked them off. He took a condom from his pocket, sat up, and moved to the top of the bed, his back against the headboard.

"Come here," he said, as he slid the condom down his length.

Cecily shook her head. "No. It's okay, really—"

Lincoln grabbed her arm, pulled her close, and cut her off with another kiss. "I want this, Cecily. I want you like this, right now. So, stop talking and get over here. I want to hold on to that pretty ass while you ride me."

Cecily crawled into his lap and straddled him, moaning as she slid down his hard cock. He filled her completely. She slid forward and moved carefully, not sure how much Lincoln could take.

He moaned, one hand gripping her ass so hard she was sure it would leave marks. His fingers tangled in her hair, tugging her head back to stare into her eyes. He yanked her forward, thrusting into her, hard.

"No need to be gentle. I can take whatever you want to give me," he said.

Cecily nodded, pressed her knees into the bed on either side of his hips, and ground down onto him. His hips jerked, pumping into her. She planted her hands on his shoulders, dug her nails into his shoulders, and rode him hard. She didn't let up, her breasts bouncing up and down as they brushed against his naked chest. As her clit pressed against his pelvic bone, the sensation pushed her toward another orgasm. Lincoln pulled her hips down and thrust so deep into her, she thought she might pass out.

Lincoln groaned. "Fuck yeah, that's it. Just like that. That's what I want." He panted and sweat ran down his neck and chest, the muscles in his thighs hard and tight as his cock slid in and out of her. "Come on, let me feel you cum all over me." He slipped a hand between their bodies, pushed his back against the headboard, and braced himself with his feet while he pounded into her. His cock brushed her sweet spot while he thumbed her clit until she let go with an obscene moan, coming harder than she ever had before. Her nails dug into his shoulders as she held on, wave after wave of unbelievable pleasure washing over her.

Lincoln grunted and thrusted up into her one more time, groaning as his own orgasm swept over him. His head fell to Cecily's shoulder, and his entire body shuddered as he came.

"Wow," she mumbled once she could breathe again. She kissed his neck several times before she sat up. She tried to move off him and cover herself, but

Lincoln held her against him as he rolled to his side. He kissed her, his hands running over her curves while his eyes followed his hands.

"I'm not done with you," he whispered.

"Oh, yeah?"

Lincoln smirked. "Yeah. I hope you didn't have any plans tonight."

"Nothing I can't cancel."

"Great, let's spend the rest of the night right here."

"That sounds amazing," she whispered as she laid her head on his shoulder.

———

The incessant buzzing of her cellphone dragged her from sleep. She opened one eye, but it wasn't on the bedside table where she usually kept it. Maybe it was in her purse. Not that she had any intention of getting out of bed and answering it. Thankfully, after a few seconds, it stopped.

Cecily rolled onto her back and stretched. Her muscles ached, but in the best way possible. She looked to her right but saw she was alone in the bed.

"Lincoln?" She sat up, the covers pooling in her lap. "Lincoln, are you here?"

No answer. He was gone.

She wasn't surprised. Cecily made it quite clear this was a one-night situation and nothing more, and he'd agreed. She didn't mind; she was flying back to Montana today, so New York could kiss her ass.

A loud pounding on the door startled her and dragged her from the bed. It had to be her father, come to collect her for her flight back to Montana. She was halfway across the room when she heard her Claude. "Cecily Camille Devereaux! Open this door right now, young lady."

She rolled her eyes. It was going to be a long ride to the airport.

Chapter 3
Cecily

Three Months Later

"Cecily!" Nate shouted. "Where's Sebastian?"

She slipped onto the barstool and gave Nate, the bar's owner and bartender, a smile. "He's home," she answered. "He was being an asshole. I wasn't in the mood to deal with him, so I told him to stay home and think about his attitude."

Nate laughed and set a vodka martini in front of her. "Think it'll work?"

"Probably not. He's stubborn as hell. He doesn't enjoy staying home, though, so he might behave for a few days. I'll see what kind of mood he's in when I get back."

"Are you hungry?" Nate asked. "I could make you something to eat."

"I'm fine. Thanks."

Nate narrowed his eyes. "When's the last time you ate?"

Cecily rolled her eyes. "I don't know. Two, maybe three hours ago. What difference does it make?"

"I'm just looking out for you, that's all." Nate wiped down the bar in front of her, even though it wasn't dirty. He kept his bar spotless.

"I'm a big girl. I can take care of myself." She grabbed her drink and took a swallow, doing anything to not look Nate in the eyes.

Her friend frowned. "How long have we been friends?"

"Too long?"

"I'm serious, Cecily."

She smiled at Nate. "Since your dad bought the bar and you moved to town. So, a little over two years? Why?"

"I know you, and you don't look fine," Nate said. "You look tired."

"I'm fine," she repeated. "I promise." She knew Nate didn't believe her, but she didn't have the energy to argue.

Nate didn't need to know the stress was killing her. For the last three months, Lawrence had called her nonstop, all day every day, begging for another chance. Her father threatened to cut her off if she didn't patch things up with Lawrence and get a proper job—which, to him, meant taking back her old job as Devereaux Industries' glorified party planner. Living alone in the mansion on the lake was depressing and, more than anything else, it reminded her that her mother had passed away. She missed her mom.

A loud cheer erupted from the corner, making Cecily jump and her drink slosh over the side of her glass. "Damn it."

Nate laughed. "Are they too loud for you, princess?"

Cecily snorted and threw a straw at Nate. He knew she hated that—her father sometimes called her princess, and it drove her crazy. Nate liked to tease.

"What's going on over there?"

"Van's bachelor party."

"Van's bachelor party? I should have known. I just came from Serena's bridal shower; it was tamer than those guys watching the Mariners and Yankees, though. I can't believe the wedding is Monday."

"Seems like yesterday that Serena started working at Lakeside College, doesn't it?" Nate said. "I can't believe she's lived here for almost a year."

"Has it been a year already?" Cecily asked. "I met her and Van six months ago when I moved back to town and interviewed for a teaching position at the college. We hit it off, immediately. She's so sweet and perfect for Van. I can't wait for the wedding."

"It came up fast, didn't it? Are you going?"

"Yeah, you?"

Nate nodded. "I agreed to tend bar for Van, my wedding gift to the couple. And my roommate, Mason is taking the wedding photos. Hey, how's the job hunt going? Any luck?"

Cecily took another drink. "No. My father is to blame for that. I think he's sabotaging my efforts to find work with another company. I've done a few things for Lakeside College, but with it being summer, the university president, Charlie, doesn't have much for me to do."

"So, your father is keeping you from getting a job with another company, and he won't let you work for his?" Nate shook his head. "I'll never understand Claude Devereaux."

She sighed. "It's a power trip thing. He wants me under his thumb, but he doesn't want to give me anything meaningful to do. Making me a party planner is supposed to appease me, but he hates the fact that I want more. In his eyes, I *am* working for him, but it's not anything important."

"I'm sorry." Nate patted her arm.

Cecily shrugged, uncomfortable with someone feeling sorry for her. She cleared her throat and pointed to the bottles of alcohol behind Nate.

"Can you get me another drink? Actually, on second thought, how about some fries?"

"You got it." Nate poured her another drink before heading toward the kitchen, stopping every few feet to check in with the other customers in the restaurant.

She picked up her drink and took another sip. Exhausted, she closed her eyes and took a deep breath. The last time she'd had a good night's sleep was in New York. Thinking about New York inevitably led to thinking about Lincoln, and that was never good.

Lincoln was always on her mind since their time together, and it scared her. Never once had a one-night stand gotten under her skin like this one had. She couldn't stop thinking about him and the things they'd done. She wished it could happen again. Spending the night in bed with Lincoln had been amazing. If only she'd gotten his last name, his number, something. She longed to hear his deep, sexy voice whispering in her ear.

Someone backed into her and jostled her elbow, knocking her out of her seat and spilling her drink onto the bar and into her lap. Cecily stumbled to her feet, praying she wouldn't land on her ass. She cursed under her breath and grabbed a stack of napkins.

"Oh, my God. I'm so sorry."

Cecily froze, choking on the words she'd been about to say. It wasn't possible, not when he was over two-thousand miles away on the other side of the country. It couldn't be him, unless thinking about him had magically summoned him. If that was the case, he would have shown up three months ago. She turned as everything was moving in slow motion.

Standing in front of her was the tall, blond, muscular, drop-dead gorgeous in a Captain America-kind of way man she had first seen three months ago.

"Lincoln?"

"Holy shit! Cecily?"

"What are you—?"

"How the hell—?"

Lincoln seemed just as surprised to see her as she was to see him. One hand brushed against her arm as he moved closer to her, a smile spreading across his chiseled face.

Cecily stepped into his personal space and kissed his cheek, anxious to get close to him. It wasn't easy to keep her hands to herself. She wanted to touch him, caress him, and remind herself why this man was constantly on her mind. Lincoln gestured for her to speak.

"What are you doing here?" she asked.

"My best friend is getting married in two days." He took her hand and rubbed his thumb across her knuckles. The simple gesture sent a tingle of desire down her spine and reminded her of their time together.

"Van?"

The surprised look on Lincoln's face made her giggle. "I'm not a mind reader or something," she said. "I know Serena, and the bar owner, Nate, is a friend of mine. He told me about the bachelor party."

"Of course," Lincoln said. He guided her to her seat and sat down beside her. "I can't believe you're in a tiny town in Montana. I never expected to run into you here, or anywhere. What a small world."

"I could say the same thing about you. Lakeside, Montana, is pretty far from New York City."

Lincoln chuckled. "Van loves this place; it's his home, and I would not miss my best friend's wedding because it's in the middle of nowhere."

Cecily laughed. "It is off the beaten path. I'm glad we ran into each other, though."

"Okay, so you know why I'm here," Lincoln said. "What are you doing in Montana?"

"I live here," she explained. "My family owns a home nearby."

"I never would have guessed. You don't seem like a Montana kind of girl."

"I'm not really a Montana girl; it's more like an adopted home. We have a vacation home on the lake. I sort of borrowed it six months ago and haven't left. My family is from France. My father moved to the United States before I was born. We've lived all over the world."

"Military?"

Cecily shrugged. "Something like that."

She wouldn't answer that question. She didn't tell people—especially men she slept with—who her father was. It complicated things when they found out she was the heir to a billion-dollar empire. The way things had gotten complicated with Lawrence and the reason he wouldn't leave her alone.

Lincoln didn't press the issue but leaned on the bar and propped his head up on his hand. "It's good to see you, Cecily. Fantastic."

Cecily brushed a hand through Lincoln's messy hair and stroked his face. "I'm glad to see you too. More than you know."

"I've been thinking about you a lot since that night in New York," he said.

"Really?" she asked.

"Really." Lincoln ran his hand up her leg. "You're pretty unforgettable, sweetheart," he whispered.

Heat rushed through her from head to toe. Lincoln's presence was a dream come true, the man she'd thought about nonstop for the last three months sitting right in front of her. "I could say the same about you," Cecily replied coyly.

Lincoln cleared his throat and his cheeks flushed pink. "I am sorry about your drink. Let me buy you another one. Vodka martini, right?"

He remembered what she drank. *God, could he be any more perfect?* She swallowed and nodded.

"Yep. Vodka martini."

Chapter 4

Lincoln

*H*is trip from New York was a nightmare. The connecting flight to Chicago landed late, causing him to miss his flight into Kalispell, Montana. He spent an uncomfortable night in the airport, waiting to catch a standby flight into Missoula, Montana. It wasn't his first choice and it was a longer drive, but there was nothing else he could do. It was eight hours before a seat on another flight was available. Once Lincoln landed in Missoula, the rental company didn't have an SUV available so he settled for a compact car that was far too small for his 6'3" frame. By the time he pulled into Van's driveway at nine the next morning, his legs, shoulders, and back ached so much. He wanted sleep, a shower, and a beer, not necessarily in that order.

When he approached the door, Lincoln knocked once, even though he was sure no one was home. He and Van had talked several times during his layover in Chicago, so his friend knew he would be late. Van told Lincoln to make himself at home while he and Serena were at work. Fortunately, Lincoln had his own key to Van's place, so he let himself into the small condo.

It was quiet: no Serena and no Van. Soldier, Van's Belgian Malinois, wasn't there either; no doubt he was at Van's side. Lincoln breathed a sigh of relief and trudged upstairs, dumping his things in the spare bedroom and ducking into the bathroom. If he wanted to enjoy himself at Van's bachelor party tonight, he needed to sleep.

Lincoln still had a hard time believing Van was getting married. After Van's first wife, Adelaide was murdered, Lincoln wondered if Van would ever leave his house again, let alone meet someone, fall in love, and get married. Then Serena came into his life and changed everything for the better. He couldn't have been happier for his best friend.

He showered and shaved, downed a bottle of water from the fridge, and fell into bed. After closing his eyes, he passed out in a deep sleep.

———

A wet, sloppy tongue sliding up his cheek drew Lincoln from sleep. He groaned and opened one eye. Soldier stood over him, his tongue hanging out of his mouth.

"Hey, boy," Lincoln mumbled. "Where's your owner?"

Soldier bounded out the door, stood in the hall, and barked once. Lincoln dragged himself out of bed and followed the dog downstairs.

"He lives!" Serena jumped off the couch and hugged him tight. "It's so good to see you."

"What time is it?" he asked.

"Almost four," Van answered. He grabbed Lincoln's hand, shook it, and pulled him into a hug. "It's good to see you, brother."

"You too."

It wasn't just good to see Van; it was great. They'd been friends since childhood, grew up together, joined the army together, and started a security consulting business when they returned to New York. Lincoln tried to keep their friendship together when Van moved to Montana after Adelaide's death, but it was a struggle. Van pushed everyone away, except his dog, after his wife's death. Thank God Serena came along and pulled Van out of his self-imposed imprisonment.

"You ready for tonight?" Lincoln asked.

Van rolled his eyes. "I guess. You know how I love to be the center of attention."

"It's a bunch of guys getting together for drinks at the bar," Serena interjected. "It's not like Nate is having a parade down Main Street for you."

Lincoln laughed, as he loved how Serena called Van on his shit. He clapped his friend on the back. "It'll be fun. A bunch of guys shooting the shit. No pressure, no demanding women around—."

Serena punched Lincoln playfully on the arm. "Watch it, mister." She wrapped her arms around Van's waist and kissed him on the cheek. "It's only for a couple of hours. You don't want to be here with a bunch of giggling women oohing and ahhing over lingerie, do you?"

"I do," Lincoln cheerfully interjected.

"We need to find you a girlfriend," Van muttered.

Lincoln shook his head. "Nope; that is not happening. I am not interested in a relationship. Too complicated."

Serena opened her mouth—probably to ask why—but Lincoln turned and sprinted up the stairs. He wasn't interested in opening those old wounds. "I'll go change so we can go," he called over his shoulder.

———

According to Van, Time Out was the most popular bar and grill in Lakeside. He didn't bother to mention it was the only bar and grill in Lakeside, but no sense in bringing up the obvious.

Time Out was owned by Nathan "Nate" Owens, a twenty-three-year-old entrepreneur from Great Falls, Montana. His father helped him buy the bar when he was twenty-one and he'd turned it into a thriving business in less than two years. Van said he was a "nice kid," and he wasn't wrong.

Nate sectioned off the back corner of the bar and laid out quite the spread—stuff like burgers, nachos, fries, and chicken wings. If it was bad for you, it was there. The drinks flowed nonstop: beer, wine, water, soda, you name it, it was available. Nate assured them if they needed anything, he would get it.

Lincoln was thrilled Van agreed to have a bachelor party. Van had always kept to himself, especially after the death of his first wife. He'd been a hermit when he met Serena, and obviously things had changed since he took the security job at Lakeside College. While it wasn't an enormous party, there were still nine people in attendance, including Nate. It eased Lincoln's mind that Van had friends he could turn to other than him, even if they were people from work.

"Are you having fun?" Van asked after two hours of pool, baseball, food, and drink.

"Yes, of course." Lincoln slapped Van on the shoulder. "What about you?"

"Don't tell Serena, but yes, I am."

Lincoln chuckled. "I'm totally telling Serena you said that. No secrets between married couples."

"Speaking of no secrets, my lovely fiancée wants to know why you don't have a girlfriend."

Lincoln rolled his eyes. "Did you tell her I don't *want* a girlfriend?"

"Yes, but Serena is ... persistent."

"She's not going to set me up, is she?"

Van shrugged. "I can't make any promises."

Lincoln chugged his beer. "I need another drink." He needed something stronger than a beer, so he spun around and headed for the bar.

"Bring me a scotch and soda!" Van called after him.

Lincoln turned around and waved at Van. A second later, not realizing how close he was to the bar, he bumped into someone behind him. A startled squeak erupted in his ear, followed by a lot of cursing. A young woman stood beside him, her back turned, as she muttered curses under her breath and wiped her clothes with a stack of napkins.

"Oh, my God. I'm so sorry," Lincoln apologized.

The woman swung around, a startled look on her face and her gorgeous mouth hanging open.

"Lincoln?"

"Holy shit! Cecily?" He couldn't believe his last New York one-night stand was in a little town in Montana and that he had run into her.

"What are you—?"

"How the hell—?"

Montana was the last place in the world he expected to run into this woman, as he thought he'd never see her again. But Cecily had lingered in his mind since they'd met. It was the first time he regretted not getting a woman's number so he could call her again.

Now she stood in front of him, her long black hair plaited in a braid down her back, her gray eyes sparkling, and her mouth open in surprise. He wanted to kiss her. Hell, he wanted to do more than that.

Cecily stepped close—so close the sweet smell of her pomegranate and vanilla perfume enveloped him—and kissed his cheek. God, she was too close. He clenched his hands and reminded himself they were in a public place.

"What are you doing here?" she asked.

Lincoln grabbed her hand, desperate to touch her, and rubbed his thumb over her knuckles. He forced himself to concentrate and answer her question. "My best friend is getting married in two days."

The dimple in her cheek became more prominent when she smiled. "Van?"

Is she a mind reader?

He must have looked surprised because Cecily giggled. "I'm not a mind reader or something. I know Serena, and the bar owner, Nate, is a friend of mine. He told me about the bachelor party."

"Of course." *How was it she could echo his thoughts?* He kept hold of her hand and guided her back to the bar. He sat on the stool beside her. "I can't believe you're in a tiny town in Montana. I certainly never expected to run into you here, or anywhere. What a small world."

Nice going, Linc. Remind her a few more times that she was just a one-night stand.

Her cheeks turned a faint shade of pink. "I could say the same thing about you. Lakeside, Montana is pretty far from New York City."

He laughed. "Van loves this place; it's his home, and I would not miss my best friend's wedding because it's in the middle of nowhere. I thought it would be a good time for a vacation, too."

She couldn't argue with him. "It is off the beaten path. I'm glad we ran into each other, though."

"Okay, so you know why I'm here," Lincoln said. "What are you doing in Montana?"

"I live here. My family owns a home nearby."

Lincoln shook his head. "I never would have guessed. You don't seem like a Montana kind of girl."

Cecily volunteered some more information, though she dodged his more probing questions about her family and her childhood. He decided not to push the issue. Let her have her secrets; she must have a reason.

Lincoln leaned on the bar, thinking, *Maybe this trip to Lakeside wouldn't be a complete bust.* "It's good to see you, Cecily. Fantastic."

Cecily pushed a hand through his hair and stroked a finger down his face. "I'm glad to see you too. More than you know."

"I've been thinking about you a lot since that night in New York."

"Really?" The smile on her face made his heart leap.

Lincoln nodded. "Really." He stroked her leg, leaned close, and dropped his voice to a whisper. "You're pretty unforgettable, sweetheart."

A flirty smile danced across her lips. "I could say the same about you."

He cleared his throat. "I am sorry about your drink. Let me buy you another one. Vodka martini, right?"

Chapter 5

Lincoln

"I'm going to the ladies' room," Cecily said, after he ordered her drink. She kissed Lincoln's cheek, grabbed her purse, and disappeared down the hall.

Warmth spread through his chest, and his heart pounded. No woman had ever done that to him. Since his ex-wife Cat broke his heart, ten years ago he'd become the perpetual bachelor, destined to be alone forever. He was okay with that; serious relationships weren't his cup of tea, not anymore. However, these feelings for Cecily were different and unexpected. *Cecily* was different and unexpected.

What the hell is this?

Van eased into the seat Cecily just vacated across from Lincoln, and Soldier laid down next to his feet. He smiled at his best friend. "You disappeared," he said. "I thought you left."

"Shit. Sorry, I was talking to—."

"I saw her." Van cleared his throat and shifted nervously. "Pretty girl."

"Yes, she is."

"Do me a favor and don't sleep with her, and then blow her off right away, okay? She's going to the wedding."

"Wait, you know her?" Lincoln said in shock.

"She's a friend of Serena's. I think she works at Lakeside College. So, yes, I know her."

"Holy shit." Lincoln scrubbed a hand over his face and shook his head.

Van's eyes narrowed. "What did you do?"

— 190 —

Lincoln glanced around before he leaned forward and dropped his voice to a whisper. "I already slept with her."

Van pinched the bridge of his nose. "You slept with her? How the hell did you manage that? You've been in town less than twenty-four hours."

"I didn't sleep with her *here*. I slept with her in New York. Three months ago. I met her in a bar, and we went back to her hotel."

"You slept with her three months ago? And now you run into her in a bar in Lakeside, Montana? Jesus, talk about a small world."

Lincoln shook his head. "It was the day of my last meeting with Devereaux. The bar was close to his New York office. The meeting stressed me out, so I went there to unwind—."

"Met Cecily and slept with her. How do you do it, Lincoln? Only you could find the one woman in New York City who lives in Montana." Van snapped his fingers. "You didn't think you'd see her again, did you?"

"Would you stop doing that?" Lincoln sharply replied. It drove him nuts that Van always knew what he was thinking, sometimes before he knew it.

Van chuckled. "Sorry. But I know you better than you know yourself."

"Which pisses me off. You're right. I didn't think I'd see her again, okay? I'm glad I did, though. We had a great time. A really great time. I wouldn't mind spending time with her while I'm in Lakeside."

Van raised an eyebrow, then changed the subject. "I came over here to tell you I'm gonna head home. I've had enough of being the center of attention for one night." He put a set of keys on the bar in front of Lincoln. "These are the extra keys to Serena's condo, since she kicked us out of my place until after the wedding."

He slipped the keys into his pocket. "Thanks."

"Just do me a favor, okay?" Van said.

"Okay. What?"

"Don't do anything stupid." He whistled, and Soldier moved to his side. The dog pushed his head against Van's hand. "I might have to spend time this woman after you go home."

Lincoln chuckled. "I won't, I promise."

———

This qualifies as stupid.

Lincoln had Cecily pushed up against her car in the bar's parking lot, one hand on her ass and the other under the edge of her sweater, gripping her waist. She groaned into his mouth as he kissed her. He broke off the kiss, but he didn't release her.

"I should go," he whispered.

"I don't want you to go," Cecily said. "Stay here." She wrapped her arms around his waist. "Better yet, come back to my place."

That would definitely be stupid.

"I can't," he said. "I should go."

She pouted, her bottom lip pushing out looking plump and pink. "Am I going to see you again?"

He took her chin in his hand and kissed her. "Hell, yes."

Stupid.

Lincoln pulled his phone out of his pocket. "What's your number?"

Cecily rattled it off. She checked his screen to make sure he had it correct. "You'll call me, won't you?"

"Definitely. And if you don't hear from me, you call me." He typed his name in a message and sent it to Cecily's number, then he kissed her one last time, opened her car door, and helped her inside. He didn't climb into his rental car until she rounded the corner and was out of sight.

Lincoln wasn't tired when he returned to the condo. Soldier met him at the door, his hackles raised and growling until he realized it was Lincoln. The dog huffed, turned around, and headed down the hall. Lincoln followed Soldier down the hall to the master bedroom where Van was sound asleep. Soldier dropped to the floor beside the bed and closed his eyes.

Serena relegated the two of them to her old condo across the street from Van's until after the wedding. Lincoln wasn't familiar with her place, so he took a few minutes to look around until he found his stuff in the room across from Van's. He wasn't tired after sleeping all day, so he grabbed a beer from the kitchen and went out onto the patio. The view was almost as good as Van's, so he took a seat and stared at the water of Flathead Lake lapping against the shore.

Lincoln checked his watch. It was after eleven on a Friday night and he was exhausted. He was in Lakeside for two weeks, his first real vacation in years. Coincidentally, that was how long it usually took him to decide he didn't want to date one of the multitude of women he'd slept with over the years. Cecily would be no different: they could hang out, have fun, and, of course, have sex. When it was over, he could go back to New York and back to living his life without Cecily taking up any more space in his head. It would be a good way to cleanse his system of her.

He leaned his head back on the chair and stared at the stars. They always seemed so much brighter in Montana, especially without the skyscrapers, smog, and bright lights of New York dimming their intensity.

Maybe I should move up here.

It wasn't the first time he'd thought about giving up the insanity of the Big Apple for small-town life in Montana. Now that they'd taken care of the business by selling it to the security company in Hollywood, he could seriously consider getting out of New York. Of course, that was before he knew Cecily was here. If he moved to Montana, she might get the idea he was interested in some kind of relationship.

Would that be such a bad thing? Maybe it's time to —

He cut off the voice in his head by downing the rest of his beer. He scrubbed a hand over his face and rose to his feet.

Two weeks; that's it. Just two weeks. Like a two-week one-night stand.

He dropped the empty bottle in the recycle can and headed for bed, falling asleep before his head hit the pillow.

Chapter 6

Cecily

C ecily heard Sebastian before she saw him. He didn't like to be left home alone and was making sure she knew it.

"Alright, alright, shut up already," she muttered. She pushed the heavy oak door closed and threw her purse on the foyer table.

Sebastian sat on the stairs, looking at her. He wasn't happy.

"What?"

He bounded across the floor, stopped in front of her, and stared up at her. After a few seconds, he wagged his tail.

"I guess I'm forgiven." Cecily scooped him up and hugged him. He turned his face to look up at her, and she kissed him. He rested his head on her shoulder and sighed.

"You're spoiled rotten."

Sebastian grunted in response, so Cecily put him on the floor and headed for the kitchen, with the dog right on her heels. Once the spoiled Shih Tzu had a treat and she had a glass of water, she pulled her phone from her pocket. It had been on silent all night, and the reasons why stared her in the face.

First up, one missed call and a voicemail from her father. It was probably another phone call meant to chastise her for her choices in life—like breaking up with Lawrence or quitting her meaningless job with his company to pursue other interests. She wasn't in the mood to listen to it.

As usual, there were five missed calls from Lawrence, several text messages, and a voicemail. Just like every other day, but at least he was predictable. Six months after their breakup and he couldn't let go or wouldn't let go. Not that he was desperate to hold on to her out of love or even lust. His was an even more basic need.

Money.

Once upon a time, she thought Lawrence loved her. They met three months after she went to work for Devereaux Industries. Lawrence worked in accounting, while she worked as the company's overpaid party planner. She kept her familial relationships to herself to fit in with her co-workers and spent a lot of time hanging out with them—club-hopping, parties, late-night dinners. Lawrence was always there. He pursued her, intent on dating her. She found him to be quirky, attractive, and fun to be around, so they hit it off. Six months after they met, they were officially a couple.

Lawrence didn't know she was Claude Devereaux's daughter and the heir to the Devereaux's billion-dollar empire. At least Cecily thought he didn't know. When she told him, nine months after they started dating, he was unfazed and claimed he didn't care she was worth billions of dollars. He shrugged it off and told her money wasn't important to him.

Lawrence proposed on their one-year anniversary and of course, she accepted. Three months later things changed between them. His interest in her father's business intensified, and he sought out Claude to talk business regularly, both at work and when he was supposed to be spending time with her outside of work. Before she knew what happened, Lawrence was in line for a big promotion with Devereaux Industries, and her father couldn't stop singing her fiancé's praises. Lawrence pulled away from her, spending less time with her and more time with her father. He claimed he was "learning the ropes" of the business, but Cecily felt betrayed. He knew how contentious her relationship with Claude was, yet he didn't seem to care or want to help it.

His attitude toward her changed too. When they first started dating, he'd been doting and sweet, fawning over her. As his interest in Devereaux Industries increased, his attitude toward Cecily changed to where he ignored her phone calls and texts, made excuses to get out of lunch and dinner dates, and frequently commented unkindly on her looks and weight. It was so much like her father's attitude toward her that she began to wonder if Claude had somehow turned Lawrence against her.

The phone in her hand vibrated, yanking her out of her memories. Lawrence again. She hesitated for a minute before she hit the button and answered.

"I told you to stop calling me," she said instead of offering a greeting.

"CeCe! Thank God."

Cecily cringed, and her stomach rolled. "Don't call me that."

Lawrence sighed, and his voice took on that condescending tone she hated so much. "Cecily. I'm sorry. I'm just glad you answered. Can we talk?"

She perched on the edge of a kitchen chair, put her phone on speaker, and her head in her hands. "We are talking, Lawrence. What do you want?"

"Don't be like that."

"Like what? Irritated? Frustrated? Angry? Hurt? I don't think we have anything to talk about. You cheated; you lied; you're a shitty human being. See, nothing to talk about."

"We have a lot to talk about, honey—," Lawrence started to say before Cecily interrupted.

"I'm not your honey, Lawrence. I'm not anything to you, except maybe your ex-fiancée or, if that's too fancy for you, your ex-girlfriend. But I am not now, nor will I ever again be your honey." Cecily took a drink of her water. "Are we done?"

"I'm coming to Lakeside to see you," he explained.

"That's not a good idea—."

"We need to talk. Clear the air and set things right."

"We have nothing to talk about, Lawrence. I said everything I want to say to you six months ago. Stay in New York; I don't want you here." She ended the call and tossed her phone on the table.

It started ringing again. Cecily ignored it, shoved her chair away from the table, and got up. When was Lawrence going to get it through his thick head that she would not marry him? She contemplated calling him back and chewing him out, making it clear once and for all she wouldn't marry him. But it wasn't worth the headache.

Cecily whistled and patted her leg, getting her dog's attention. "Come on, Seb. Let's go to bed."

———

She woke up thinking about Lincoln. Knowing he was so close had her tingling all over, and she wondered if he'd call today.

Once the coffee was brewing, and Sebastian had taken several laps around the backyard, Cecily sat at the table with her phone in front of her. It rang, startling her. She checked the number on the screen before she reluctantly snatched it off the table. Might as well get it over with.

"Hello?" she answered.

"Cecily?"

"Hello, Daddy." She sat up, her shoulders back, and straightened the placemat under her coffee. "How are you?"

"I'm well." Her father cleared his throat. "You didn't return my call yesterday."

"I got in late last night and didn't want to wake you."

"Were you at that bar?" Her father's disdain was obvious even through the phone.

Cecily sighed. "Yes, I was at the Time Out bar. I like to hang out there. My friends are there."

"Perhaps you need better friends," her father suggested.

"I'm not having this argument with you again, Daddy." It was her turn to clear her throat. "I'm sure you called for a reason."

"You talked to Lawrence yesterday?" he asked.

He knows I did.

"I assume you talked to him too?"

"I did. You should sit down and discuss your issues with him. Give the boy a chance."

Her blood boiled. "I don't want to give him a chance, Daddy. I don't know why I need to keep saying this, but my relationship with Lawrence is between me and him. You have nothing to do with it. It's none of your business."

"I beg to differ. You are my daughter; therefore, it is my business. I like Lawrence—."

"Daddy."

"On second thought, maybe the three of us should talk. Sit down and talk it out."

"I don't want to—."

"You're acting like a petulant child, Cecily, and it's growing tiresome. You know what? I'm coming to Lakeside. We'll discuss the situation when I get to town. I'll let you know when I will be there. Don't even consider going anywhere; I expect you to be in Lakeside when I get there." The line disconnected.

"Nice talking to you too," she muttered to herself.

Dealing with her father was a nightmare, as his idea of a discussion was to guilt her to do what he wanted. Unfortunately, her father was on Lawrence's side and would do anything to get her to do what he wanted.

Claude Devereaux claimed to Cecily he was doing what was best for Devereaux Industries. He decided Lawrence was good for business, therefore Cecily marrying Lawrence was good for business. He considered it a business arrangement because love didn't matter, and what Cecily wanted didn't matter.

If only her mother were alive. Claude was much easier to handle when Deirdre Devereaux was alive because she kept him in check. Since her sudden death from a heart attack, Claude was impossible.

Cecily picked up her phone and squeezed it, as if she could somehow make it ring. She wanted Lincoln to call her, for he was a calm in the storm. Being with him and taking him to bed would help her forget her problems. She was determined to make it happen before her father and Lawrence arrived, a bit of fun before a lot of misery.

She pulled up a number from her contact list and hit the button. It only rang twice before the woman answered it.

"Cecily! Long time, no talk."

"Hey, Tia, I need a favor."

"Anything for you, you know that. Tell me what you need, and I'll make it happen."

Cecily grinned. "Let's start with one of your cabins."

Chapter 7

Cecily

y five o'clock on Saturday, just one day after seeing Lincoln, her plan was in place. Thank God she wasn't above taking matters into her own hands. Tia, owner of Stoner Creek Cabins, reserved the Stillwater cabin for the night for Cecily and promised to have it unlocked and ready as soon as she got Cecily's call. All she had to do was get Lincoln there.

After she fed Sebastian, she leaned against the kitchen counter and texted Lincoln.

[Cecily: Hey, heartbreaker. Are you free?]

It took less than thirty seconds to get an answer back.

[Lincoln: Yes, I am. Just finished helping Serena and Van at the Ross's place.]
[Cecily: I want to see you. I know a place we can meet. I'll send you the address and directions.] You game?
[Lincoln: Absolutely.]
[Cecily: I'll meet you there in an hour.]

Cecily sent Lincoln the address, directions, and the cabin number. She got Sebastian settled in his room under the stairs, grabbed the bag she'd already packed, and left a note for her housekeeper and the island caretaker, Mr. and Mrs. Tuttle, to let them know she was out for the night.

She had hoped to get to the cabin first, but when she rounded the corner, she saw a truck parked next to the cabin and Lincoln leaning against it.

As she got out of the car, she grinned at him. "Hey."

"Hey, yourself," he replied. "Get your ass over here."

Cecily reached into the car, grabbed her bag, and followed Lincoln up a short set of stairs to the porch. Lincoln took her hand, intertwined his fingers with hers, and kissed her. Her heart skipped in her chest at the touch of his fingers against hers and the warmth of his lips on her skin. She tugged him toward the double doors leading inside. A shaky breath escaped her, as she sent up a silent prayer for strength. She was going to need it.

Cecily led Lincoln inside. The door swung shut behind them, and Lincoln was on her in an instant, his arms around her and his lips on hers, shoving his urgent and impatient tongue into her mouth.

She giggled but the sound was swallowed by Lincoln's mouth on hers. "Impatient much?" she mumbled.

"I can't resist you, sweetheart," Lincoln grumbled. "I need you." He yanked at the button on her jeans.

"Let's take a shower," she said. She took his hand and led him through the cabin to the bathroom down the hall.

Lincoln's lips never left her skin, even as she turned on the shower and stripped off her clothes. Once she was out of her clothes, she held Lincoln's head in her hands, kissing him as he yanked off his jeans and shirt.

Free of their clothes, Lincoln pushed her into the shower and shoved her against the tile wall. His body was flush against hers as steam billowed around them, the water falling over his broad shoulders and covering them.

Cecily ran her hands over his back and stomach, loving the feel of him. Last time they were together, it had been insane. The night went by so fast, she didn't have time to explore Lincoln's muscular body. Now she had the opportunity to memorize every inch of him—every scar, every mark—and she planned to take full advantage.

Lincoln moaned, the sound vibrating through his chest. Cecily continued her exploration, running her fingers over the taut muscles in his stomach and caressing his inner thighs. When she took his cock in her hand and stroked him, Lincoln's eyes rolled back in his head and a satisfied grunt escaped him. Cecily took her time brushing her thumb over the tip of his shaft with each upward swipe, drawing out his pleasure and savoring every one of Lincoln's gasping breaths as she ran her hand up and down his length.

After a few minutes, Lincoln grabbed her hands and held them over her head with one of his. He licked the water droplets from her neck and breasts, nipped at the sensitive skin beneath her ear, and rubbed his body against hers. Lincoln's hand drifted over her breasts, down her stomach, and between her legs. A smirk danced across his full, pink lips as his fingers teased at her entrance. He ducked his head and caught her lips in a kiss, a deep, soul-scorching kiss, distracting her as his fingers slipped inside her.

He released her, allowing her to take hold of him again. They moved in sync, moaning, gyrating, and grinding against each other. Lincoln's hips flexed as he thrust into Cecily's fist, while she pushed herself down on his long, thick fingers, trembling with every brush against her sweet spot.

"I want you to cum for me," Lincoln growled in her ear.

His words pushed her over the edge. Cecily gasped his name as she came, her walls clenching around his fingers. Her head fell back against the tile, and she squeezed her eyes closed as the sensations overtook her.

"I want you inside me, Lincoln," she whispered. "I *need* you inside me."

"Shit. We can't. Not now. I didn't bring a condom in here."

"It's okay. I'm on birth control. And I trust you." She squeezed his dick, twisting her hand at the last second, drawing a groan from him.

Lincoln's eyes closed, and he dragged in a shaky breath. "Fuck. Okay. I trust you too."

He slipped his arms around her, lifted her, and lowered her onto his throbbing shaft, filling her completely. He held her against the wall, legs spread, with one hand braced above her head and one arm still around her waist.

Cecily dragged her nails down his shoulders, leaving deep, red marks on his skin. He attacked her neck, biting and sucking, as he fucked her, his hips thrusting at a near maddening pace. She slid her hand down her stomach and between her legs, teasing herself as Lincoln's cock slipped in and out of her.

Lincoln growled, his voice wrecked with lust. "Jesus, sweetheart, that's fucking hot."

He slammed into her, his forehead pressed to hers and his cock buried deep inside her, pulsing as he came. Cecily dropped her head to his shoulder and gasped as her own climax rushed through her, sending her reeling with the onslaught of pleasure.

Lincoln set her on her feet, but he kept her in his arms, kissing her. They finished cleaning up and stepped out of the shower. He wrapped Cecily in a giant, fluffy towel, stopping every few seconds to kiss her cheek or shoulder.

Cecily dried her hair while Lincoln made drinks and checked out the cabin. When she was done, she found him in the bedroom, staring out the window at the lake through the trees, both drinks in his hands. She plucked her drink from his hand and sat cross-legged on the bed.

"Thanks for meeting me," she said. "I wasn't sure you would come, what with the wedding in a couple of days. You weren't busy?"

"I was, but I snuck away when I got a break."

"Won't Van be mad?" she asked.

Lincoln shrugged. "Maybe." He set his drink on the bedside table and crawled onto the bed. "But you're worth it." He tugged at her towel and pushed her down on the bed. He kissed her breasts and moved down her stomach until he hovered over her warm core.

Cecily giggled. "What are you doing? I thought we could have dessert. Tia put something in the fridge."

"You're my dessert." He pushed open her thighs and settled himself between her legs.

The first touch of his tongue caused a delicious tightening of the muscles in her stomach and a satisfied sigh to slip past her lips. When his mouth closed over her, she couldn't hold back a scream of pleasure, nor could she stop the obscene noises she made as he repeatedly brought her to orgasm. By the time he pulled away, she was shaking and breathless.

Lincoln rolled her to her stomach and entered her from behind, thrusting hard and deep. Cecily pushed back against him and took every inch of his substantial length, the pillow under her head swallowing her screams.

They collapsed to the bed, limbs tangled together, face to face. Lincoln tucked her hair behind her ear and pressed a kiss to her forehead. She fell asleep beside him soon after, his hand on her waist and hers on his chest.

Cecily woke three hours later, the blankets on the bed covering her nakedness. Lincoln laid on his stomach, his arms wrapped around the pillow under his head, as light snores came from him. After checking the clock on the bedside table, she grabbed her bag from the floor and quickly dressed; it was much later than she thought. She jotted a note on the pad by the phone and dropped it on the pillow by Lincoln's head.

Cecily paused at the door and looked back over her shoulder at him. She knew she would see him in a couple of days at Van and Serena's wedding, but she liked this look on him, satisfied and sleepy. Maybe they could get another round or two in before he went back to New York; that should be enough to get him out of her system.

She sighed. If only her life wasn't so complicated, things could be different between them. But Devereaux Industries would always and forever stand between her and love. She would always wonder if any man who professed to love her actually loved her or was more interested in her for her connection to one of the most powerful companies in the world. It was the reason she hadn't told Lincoln who her father was.

The news would taint what they had, and what they had was damn near perfect. Walking away while things were good would be the wise thing to do, and her heart would stay intact.

"See you later, handsome," she murmured. She pulled the door closed and left.

Chapter 8

Lincoln

The ceremony was over, Mason, the wedding photographer, had taken the wedding photos, and the DJ had introduced the newlyweds as husband and wife to the waiting crowd. It was time to mingle while they waited for dinner to be served. Lincoln found Van's mom and sister and spent a few minutes talking with them before excusing himself to search for the open bar. He needed a minute, a stiff drink and to catch his breath; it had been a long day.

Lincoln had been up before the sun, joining Van in a run along the lake. They used to run through Central Park before going to work, but it had been a long time ago. It was a relief to see Van working out and taking care of himself, better than the days after Adelaide's death when he drank himself to oblivion and barely slept. Though Lincoln grumbled when Van dragged him out of bed, he had to admit the run and the fresh Montana air rejuvenated him.

Good thing too, because it had been nonstop madness for the last twelve hours. But the wedding was over, and the party had started, so Lincoln wanted to kick back and have some fun, which would start with a stiff drink.

While he waited for the bartender, he pulled his phone from his pocket to see if Cecily texted him back. He didn't know whether they invited her to the wedding or not. He tried to look for her during the ceremony, but the sun shone in his eyes standing at the altar and he could not see past the first row of seats.

Lincoln couldn't get Cecily off his mind. The last two nights, he fell asleep with the image of her in his head. It annoyed him when he woke up at the cabin and she was gone, but part of him understood; staying overnight was a step toward commitment and feelings. He got the impression Cecily was about as uninterested in a relationship as he was, though spending more time with her appealed to him. He was sure it would get her out of his system before he left.

Lincoln put his phone in his pocket. He'd spend a few minutes looking for her, but if he couldn't find her, he'd get drunk and have fun at his best friend's wedding.

Charlie Ross, Serena's boss and the owner of the home they currently partied in, clapped him on the back and leaned against the bar beside him.

"Van tells me you need a job."

Lincoln burst out laughing. "I hate to be the one to break it to you, Mr. Ross, but I don't need a job. Van is looking for a way to get me to move out here."

Ross chuckled. "Please, call me Charlie. I'll tell you what, if you ever need a job, I'd love to bring you on at the university. Van tells me you have an extensive background in security consulting. We could use someone like you at the university."

"You have Van," Lincoln said. "He's the one who's good with all that stuff."

"According to him, you're better. I would love to have both of you working for me."

"A crack team of two?"

"Yep." Charlie laughed. "Think about it. If you guys ran Lakeside College's security, I wouldn't have anything to worry about. Nothing."

Lincoln smiled. "I'll keep it on the back burner. Now, if you'll excuse me, I'm trying to find a friend." He picked up his drink, thanked the bartender, and wandered back through the house.

He was almost back outside when he spotted a voluptuous, gorgeous body wrapped in an emerald-green dress twenty feet in front of him. A black braid hung down her bare back, swinging between her shoulder blades. He recognized the swing of those hips.

"Cecily!"

She froze, turned around slowly with her hands on her hips, and gave him a sexy smile. "Lincoln. I've been looking for you."

He reached out and caressed her arm. She stepped closer to him and kissed his cheek, lingering with her hand pressed to his chest. The smell of orange blossoms filled his head.

"You smell delicious," he whispered. His lips brushed the shell of her ear, and she shivered.

Cecily laughed. "You are insatiable, aren't you?"

"Only when I'm with you, sweetheart." He took her hand. "I wasn't sure if you were here or not."

"Serena and I are friends. I work part-time at the college for her boss, Charlie. We've gotten to know each other working together the last six months. She's sweet; Van's a lucky man."

"Yes, he is." He leaned over her. "What are you doing later? Van and Serena are staying in Charlie's guest house tonight, and I have the condo to myself. You should come over. I believe I owe you dessert."

Cecily sighed. "God, I wish I could." Her face pinched like she was sucking on a lemon.

"What's wrong?"

Cecily glanced around at the people hanging around the bar before she spoke. "Nothing. I'm fine."

Her pinched face and furrowed brow told Lincoln she was lying. Something or someone had upset her. He sighed, took her arm, and steered her through the house, looking for an empty room. He spotted an open door, pulled Cecily inside what looked to be an office, and pushed the door closed.

"Okay, we're alone." Lincoln crossed his arms over his chest and stared her down. "Tell me what's wrong."

Cecily snorted and shook her head. "I told you, it's nothing." She spun on her heel, stalked across the room, and stopped a few feet from the window. She wrapped her arms around herself and shivered.

Lincoln followed her, stopping a foot behind her. "You're a lousy liar, Cecily. It's obvious that something is wrong. What is it?"

Cecily laughed ruefully and shook her head. "I am a lousy liar." She smoothed the front of her dress. "I'm expecting company later this week, my father and, I assume, my ex-fiancé. I am not looking forward to it. It's bugging me enough that it shows on my face; I'm not good at hiding my emotions. Right now, I am in a bad place and doubt I'd be much fun."

"Do you want to talk about it?"

Cecily huffed. "No, not really."

Lincoln moved closer and rested his hand on the small of her back. "Okay, we won't talk about it. How about you forget about whoever is coming to visit? I know that's a lot to ask, but I'm asking, anyway. Let's go have a good time celebrating my best friend and his wife. We'll drink, party, and forget about everyone else."

Cecily turned around and grinned at him. "How do you see this evening ending? Both of us drunk and passed out somewhere?"

"God, I hope not." He took her arm and spun her in a circle, twirling her around until he ensconced her in his arms. He pushed her against the window, took her chin in his hand, and kissed her. When they broke apart, they were both panting. "I'd like the evening to stretch into morning. In fact, I'll be in Lakeside for the next two weeks on vacation" Lincoln slid his hand down her back and cupped her ass. "We can spend the next two weeks drowning in each other, and when it's over, we can part as friends, lovers, or we can forget the other person exists. But let's make the next two weeks worthwhile." His lips drifted down the side of her neck as he lightly kissed her.

Cecily moaned, and her head fell slightly against the window. She gripped Lincoln's shoulders tight. "Two weeks?" she asked. "Then we walk away, no hard feelings if one of us doesn't want more?"

"Two weeks, Cecily. What do you say?"

Cecily nodded, wrapped her hand around the back of his neck, and pulled him in for a kiss.

"I think it sounds like a fabulous fucking idea."

———

Lincoln dropped his fork on the table and picked up his drink. He signaled one of the wait staff to bring him another one, then he leaned back in his chair and smiled at Cecily.

"So, how long have you lived in Lakeside?" Lincoln asked.

Cecily tapped her chin. "Off and on for years. At first, it was just summers. When I was in junior high—I guess I must have been about thirteen or fourteen—my mom tired of moving all the time because of my father's business. She decided that the two of us would come live here so I could go to school. Mom wanted me in public school, making friends and living a normal teenage life. Daddy suggested boarding school, but Mom was adamant we come here. She didn't want to be away from me. We stayed until I graduated from high school and left for college. After I left, she moved to New York with my father. They kept the house, and I spent most of my summers in Lakeside. Six months ago, I moved here for good."

"So, you graduated from high school here?"

"Lakeside Unified, grades seven through twelve. I can tell you, being the new kid in a school where the other students have known each other since kindergarten isn't easy. Being the rich kid compounds those problems."

Lincoln raised an eyebrow. "The rich kid?" Maybe it was the alcohol or maybe she was finally comfortable with him, but it pleased him that she was sharing with him.

Cecily signed and nodded. "I guess I didn't mention that my father is worth a lot—it's more like a substantial amount—of money. It made things difficult growing up." She didn't elaborate, and he didn't press. She would tell him when she was ready. "I was also a bookworm and painfully shy. I was fat, at least according to the girls in school."

Lincoln pursed his lips. "Kids are jerks."

Cecily laughed. "You're not wrong. They are jerks, especially when you don't fit the mold. I wasn't athletic, I didn't ride horses, or hang out with everybody at the lake. I was used to being alone or being the only kid around a bunch of adults. At a young age, I learned to entertain myself. I was happy to stay home and read my books. I liked to study, and yes, I was overweight. Not fat, per se, but I was heavier than most girls my age. Kids don't know how to handle people who aren't like them. They don't understand, and they don't want to take the time to understand. It's not until they're older that they learn to be tolerant of people who aren't like them." She made a face like she'd sucked on a lemon or a sour grape. "Or at least you hope they do."

Lincoln caressed her arm. "I'm sorry. People are assholes."

"It was a long time ago," Cecily said. "I'm over it."

Lincoln narrowed his eyes. "It doesn't seem like it. You're not still bothered by a bunch of teenage jerks, are you?"

Cecily laughed. "No. Now I'm bothered by the adult jerks in my life: Lawrence Bronson and Claude Devereaux."

"Claude Devereaux? You know Claude Devereaux of Devereaux Industries?"

Cecily snorted. "I'd say so. He is my father."

"Wait a minute." Lincoln's heart thumped in his chest, and he had to swallow back a groan of frustration. "You're Claude Devereaux's daughter?"

Shit.

Cecily cleared her throat. "I am. I take it you've heard of my father?"

"Who hasn't? He's one of the richest men in the world, in the news and tabloids all the time. I can't believe—." His mouth snapped shut.

"You can't believe what?"

"I just ... I can't believe you're his daughter. I've never seen *you* in the news or the tabloids."

"My parents were extremely careful about keeping me out of the spotlight. And I don't make a habit of telling people I'm his daughter. Too many complications."

"I can imagine," Lincoln mumbled.

After the way he'd ended his business arrangement with Devereaux, Cecily Devereaux was the last person on earth he should be involved with. He opened his mouth to tell her as much and tell her he knew her father—had in fact worked for him—but the music cut out and the DJ called for the crowd's attention. Lincoln scrubbed a hand over the back of his neck; it was time for his speech.

He downed his drink and dropped his glass to the table. He'd tell Cecily later when he wasn't making speeches and a bunch of people able to eavesdrop on their conversation surrounded them. Instead, he leaned over her, wrapped a hand around the back of her neck, and tugged her close. He pressed his lips to her ear. "When this night is over, you're coming back to my place, and I'm going to make you forget all about your troubles. Sound good?"

Cecily sighed. "That sounds amazing."

Lincoln kissed the shell of her ear and got to his feet. Cecily smiled up at him, so he couldn't resist bending over and kissing her again. She giggled and pushed him away, mouthing "go" at him. Reluctantly, he turned back to the stage. He could listen to her laugh all day and all night. At least she was smiling.

I'll do anything to keep that smile on her face. Anything.

Chapter 9

Cecily

"Come home with me."

When Lincoln purred those words in her ear just after midnight, she melted. *How could she resist?* That deep, sexy, blow-her-clothes-off-with-one-word voice was why she was in his bed, snuggled under his arm and half asleep. Before they dozed off, he made her promise she wouldn't sneak off, as he wanted to wake up next to her.

They had the condo to themselves. Van and Serena were on their way to Glacier for the next week with their dog in tow. Lincoln told her he planned to stay in Montana not only to babysit Van and Serena's two condos, but because he needed a vacation, and Lakeside was the perfect place to escape the madness of New York City.

The next morning, Cecily didn't wake up with Lincoln; to her surprise, she woke up alone, buried under a pile of blankets. She sat up, stretched, and checked the clock. It was early, not even eight. Noises came from the kitchen, noises that sounded a lot like someone cooking. Cecily crawled out of bed, pulled the down comforter around herself, and followed the sounds.

"Hey, gorgeous," Lincoln said. "How did you sleep?"

"Um, I actually slept well," she replied. "What are you doing?"

"Making you breakfast. There's a T-shirt and a pair of my sweats in the bathroom. They might be a little big, but you're welcome to them. I thought that might be more comfortable than your party dress."

"Toothbrush?"

"Extra one in the bathroom next to the clothes. Hurry, though. The food will be ready in a few minutes."

Cecily made her way down the hall to the bathroom and closed herself inside. She dropped the comforter to the floor and grabbed Lincoln's shirt and sweats. They were more than a little big; they were huge, but not uncomfortable. She brushed her teeth and smoothed her hair, then she returned to the kitchen and sat at the table.

Lincoln kissed the top of her head and set a plate in front of her of eggs, bacon, and toast.

Jesus, he cooks too? Damn it, why is he so perfect?

"Do you want coffee, tea, milk, or orange juice? I've got all of them."

"How about a glass of orange juice?"

Lincoln poured her a glass, then he sat next to her with his own plate of food. He was a hearty eater, devouring several eggs, bacon, and two pieces of toast in short order. He belched quietly and grinned at her.

Cecily laughed. "Were you hungry?"

"Good sex makes me hungry." He winked at her.

"You're incorrigible," she mumbled.

"I know." He cleared the plates off the table and dumped them in the sink. "What are your plans for the day?"

She sighed. "I need to go home, let my dog out, and get ready for my company." She rolled her eyes. "Getting my head in the right place takes time."

Lincoln leaned against the counter and crossed his arms. "Tell me about your company."

"Trust me, you don't want to know." She sipped her juice.

"Sure, I do. Tell me."

Cecily snorted. "Okay, but it's a mess. Remember, you asked." She took a deep breath and exhaled before she spoke. "My father is coming to town. And I have a sneaking suspicion my ex-fiancé Lawrence will be with him."

Lincoln narrowed his eyes. "Why?"

Cecily shrugged. "A hunch. My father might be a savvy businessman, but with me, he's predictable to a fault. He'll bring Lawrence with him."

"Why would he do that to you?"

"Because Daddy thinks I should have married Lawrence. He desperately wanted me to marry him. Daddy *likes* Lawrence—scratch that—Daddy loves Lawrence. My father has plans for him, and I ruined those plans by breaking off the engagement. He is extremely upset with me for ending the relationship."

"You obviously had a reason for doing it."

She nodded. "I did." She narrowed her eyes. "Are you sure you want to hear this?"

"I wouldn't have asked if I didn't."

Cecily sighed. Recounting her past with Lawrence made her queasy. "Lawrence is a jerk. When we first started dating, he seemed sweet and attentive. Looking back, I realize I ignored a lot of stupid stuff he did and said. I think at the time my feelings blinded me."

Lincoln nodded. "I get it. Love is blind. We don't see what people are really like until it's too late."

Cecily tipped her head and narrowed her eyes. This was the first time Lincoln had hinted at any previous relationship. *What does he mean when he says he gets it?*

Lincoln didn't offer any additional information, so Cecily continued. "I hid who I was for a long time and when I finally told him I was Claude Devereaux's daughter, it didn't go as I expected."

"Were there complications with Lawrence?"

Cecily shook her head. "No. It was weird. He didn't seem surprised, and he claimed he didn't care who my father was or that I was the heir to a billion-dollar empire. It sealed the deal; I agreed to marry him. But once we got engaged, he changed. Suddenly, everything in Lawrence's life was about my father and Devereaux Industries. It didn't take long to realize he didn't love me; he loved my father's money and the idea of being in control of that money."

Lincoln raised an eyebrow. "Oh?"

"I guess Daddy promised him a big promotion or something after we were married. I was nothing more than a means to an end, but I'm better than that. I'm not someone's meal ticket. I broke off the engagement and moved out here. My father has been on my case ever since."

"Jesus, Cecily. He sounds like a real ass."

"Lawrence or my father?"

Lincoln grunted. "Both."

"You're not wrong." Cecily pinched the bridge of her nose. "You know what? I don't want to talk about it anymore. This whole thing is a colossal pain in my neck."

Lincoln shrugged. "Okay." He grinned at her. "Let's talk about something else. Can you stay for a while?"

She laughed. "I think I can stay a little longer." Her voice dropped to a conspiratorial whisper. "But only if I can get you to take me back to bed."

"Sounds like a plan to me," Lincoln said. He grabbed her, pulled her out of the chair, and kissed her all the way to the bedroom.

Sebastian was all over her when she arrived home. She felt bad leaving him home all night for the second time that week, but it wasn't like he had been alone. Mr. and Mrs. Tuttle were more than happy to take care of him. Not that Sebastian was happy about it. The second Cecily came through the door, he was under her feet and following her everywhere, even into the bathroom. He brought her toy after toy, barking at her until she tossed them across the room. It took almost an hour to wear him out.

She was on her way to take a shower when her phone rang; it was her father. She sat down at the top of the stairs and answered her phone. Sensing her tension, Sebastian curled up in her lap.

"Hi, Daddy."

"I'll be there on Thursday," her father said.

"Hello to you too," she mumbled.

"Cecily, I don't have time for your nonsense. We'll be in Kalispell in the morning and at the house two hours later. Have Mrs. Tuttle get my room ready. I will see you on Thursday." The phone disconnected.

Cecily pushed herself to her feet, tucked Sebastian under one arm, and went to find Mrs. Tuttle. She informed the housekeeper that her father would arrive on Thursday, to which Mrs. Tuttle promised to have his room ready. Confident Lawrence would be with her father, she suggested Mrs. Tuttle get one of the guest rooms made up as well. Cecily encouraged her to prepare one on the opposite side of the house from her room. The further away from her, the better.

Cecily took a quick shower, grabbed a book from her room, a pitcher of Mrs. Tuttle's fresh lemonade, and went out onto the patio. After her romp with Lincoln, she was tired. Within a half hour, she was asleep on the lounge chair, with Sebastian next to her.

If her cellphone had stayed quiet, she would have slept for hours. Instead, it rang incessantly, pulling her from a pleasant dream about Lincoln. She snatched the phone off the table where she'd left it and answered it without looking at the number.

"Hello?"

"Let's go out to dinner Thursday night," Lawrence said. "I'm sure there's someplace decent in Kalispell."

Christ. Seriously?

She scrubbed a hand over her face. She wasn't awake enough for this conversation. "I don't want to go to dinner with you, Lawrence. Besides, how do you know I don't have plans?"

"Plans? With whom? Those friends of yours at the bar? I'm sure you can cancel any plans you have with them."

Cecily squeezed her cellphone so tight, she heard the case squeak. "It's not with my friends from the bar," she blurted. "I have a date. For your information, I've been seeing someone."

She didn't know why she said it or why it came out of her mouth so easily; it was a lie.

Not really. I have been seeing someone. I see him every time we have sex.

Lawrence seethed; she could hear it through the phone, the sharp, repeated intakes of breath and the smacking of his lips. She'd grown accustomed to those sounds when they'd dated. After thirty seconds of silence, he cleared his throat. "You're seeing someone."

It wasn't a question; it was her chance to back out of it, to correct herself; it was her chance to tell him she wasn't really seeing someone, and they were only friends. Instead, she said, "Yes, that's what I said. His name is Lincoln, and we've been seeing each other for about three months."

And just like that, it was out there, and she couldn't take it back. Cecily rubbed the center of her forehead.

What did I just do?

Lawrence huffed. "Well, I can't wait to meet him. I'm sure your father would like to meet him as well. I'll tell him you have a new boyfriend when we fly in. See you Thursday, CeCe."

The line disconnected.

"Shit!"

Sebastian grunted, opened one eye, and stared at her, annoyed she woke him up. He jumped off the chaise lounge, made his way across the yard to plop down beneath one of the lilac bushes, and promptly went back to sleep.

"Yeah, buddy, join the club. I'm annoyed with me too."

Cecily put her head in her hands and rubbed her temples with her thumbs. *Holy hell. What am I going to do?*

Chapter 10

Lincoln

ecily's panicked phone call forced him off the couch, away from the ball-game, and into action. When he'd last seen her Tuesday morning, she was fine. She was wary of her father's visit but wasn't the desperate woman who called him now. A lot changed in twenty-four hours, and she begged him to meet her at the Time Out Bar and Grill because she needed to talk to him right away. He promised to be there in ten minutes.

Lincoln parked in the lot's corner and jumped from the truck. He strode quickly through the parking lot and, once inside, his eyes darted around, taking in everything. Cecily was at the bar, a little white dog with brown spots curled up by her feet and a drink in her hand. She looked as if she'd lost her best friend. He pushed through the crowd and stopped beside her, his hand on her back.

"Are you okay?" he asked.

Cecily finished her drink, dropped the glass to the bar, and shook her head. "No."

Lincoln eased into the seat beside her. The dog looked up at him and yipped before putting his head on his paws and staring up at Lincoln, like he was assessing his character.

"Who's your little friend?"

"That's Sebastian. He's all bark and no bite, trust me. He's just making sure you know he's here."

Lincoln held out his hand so the dog could smell it. Sebastian rose to his feet and sniffed Lincoln's fingers. Apparently satisfied with what he smelled, he huffed and laid down. Lincoln turned his attention back to Cecily.

"Okay, what's wrong? You've got me worried."

"I screwed up, Lincoln. Big time."

He gestured to the bartender, pointed at Cecily's empty glass, and held up two fingers. Drinks ordered, he turned back to Cecily.

"What did you do?"

She grabbed his hand and squeezed it. "I need to ask you a huge favor, Lincoln. And when I say huge, I mean huge. I'm begging you to say yes."

He narrowed his eyes and sat up straight, his shoulders back. He cleared his throat and rubbed the center of his forehead. Huge favors never ended well for him.

"Tell me what you need, and then I'll decide whether I'll say yes." The bartender, his name tag said Andy, set their drinks down, took one look at Cecily's face, and scurried away.

Cecily gave him a weak smile. "I guess I shouldn't assume you'll do it just because we're having sex, should I?"

Lincoln chuckled and shrugged. "Never assume, but I didn't say I wouldn't help. Tell me what you need, Cecily." He took a sip of his drink.

"I want you to be my boyfriend."

Lincoln sputtered and choked on his drink. He wiped his mouth with the back of his hand and stared at Cecily.

"I'm ... I'm sorry, what?"

Cecily laughed, a hollow, twittering gasp that sounded like a choking bird. "I know how it sounds. I do, and I swear I'm not suddenly in dire need of a relationship. Jesus, that's the last thing I need." She exhaled. "Okay, let me try to explain." She twisted a napkin around her fingers and stared at it instead of looking at him. "Lawrence *is* coming with my father."

"Okay." Lincoln drew the word out. "What does that have to do with me?"

"I might have told him you're my boyfriend." She put her face in her hands and burst out laughing. "Oh my God, I'm so sorry." She scrubbed her face, straightened her shoulders, and turned to face him. A tear slid down her cheek, and she absentmindedly wiped it away.

Lincoln took her hand and intertwined his fingers with hers. "Don't apologize." This wasn't the woman he knew. Normally, she exuded a confidence he admired. She always knew what she wanted and how she would get it. However, this wasn't the Cecily who swept *him* off his feet and took him into her bed.

She gave him a weak smile. "I feel like an idiot. I shouldn't have said anything to Lawrence, but he sets me on edge. It just came out, you know. He wanted to go to dinner and talk about us. I got sick of being bombarded with his stupid requests to talk about *us,* so I blurted out that I had a boyfriend." She shrugged. "Now I need one."

"Cecily—."

"You know what? Forget I said anything. I'll figure something out."

What is wrong with me? She's asking for help.

"I'll do it," Lincoln said.

"Seriously?"

"Yes, seriously."

Cecily threw her arms around his neck. "You're the best, Lincoln. I mean it, the best. I owe you."

Lincoln hugged her close and pressed his mouth to her ear. "Trust me, sweetheart. I plan on collecting that debt."

———

They moved to a booth in the back corner of the bar, ordered food, and a pitcher of beer. Now would be the perfect time to confess to Cecily that not only did he know her father, but he'd worked for him as well. Just because they were going to lie to other people about the reality of their so-called relationship didn't mean they should lie to each other.

He was about to tell her but then their server, Trista, appeared with their order. She also brought Sebastian a cut-up hamburger, a dish of water, and a small squeaky toy. Sebastian jumped around the booth and onto the floor, desperate to get his paws on the toy. Cecily took the toy and spent a few minutes tossing it around for Sebastian before she returned to the table. Sebastian jumped onto the seat and set to work devouring his hamburger.

Cecily poured their beers, picked up an onion ring, and nibbled on it. "You're really okay with this?" she asked.

Lincoln took a healthy swallow of his beer, leaned back in the booth, and smiled at Cecily. "Alright, let's talk details."

"Details?"

"It would help if we got our stories straight. How we met, where, when we met, how long we've been dating, that kind of thing."

Cecily pushed a hand through her hair and shifted in her seat. "Maybe this was a bad idea; it's too complicated. I'm not a talented liar."

"It doesn't have to be complicated, and you won't have to tell too many lies." Lincoln tapped his fingers on the tabletop. "We shadow the lies in the truth."

"What do you mean?"

"We tell the truth, or at least most of the truth, about how we met. In New

York, three months ago, at a bar. We hit it off and dated." Lincoln shrugged. "The lie mixed with the truth."

Cecily munched on an onion ring. "You make it sound so easy." She narrowed her eyes and looked him up and down. "Why are you so agreeable about this whole thing? You didn't have to say yes. You could have told me to shove it."

"Where's the fun in that, babe?"

Cecily giggled and shook her head. "You're incorrigible."

Lincoln winked. "I know."

———

He threw himself on the bed, his arm over his eyes.

What the hell am I doing?

Agreeing to pretend to be Cecily's boyfriend was a bad idea. It meant spending a lot of time together while her father was here. He still hadn't told her he had worked for her father, a secret he would not keep much longer. Once Claude Devereaux saw him, the cat would be out of the bag. He and Claude had parted ways less than amicably; in fact, it had been damn near an all-out war once Lincoln confronted Devereaux about his nefarious business dealings.

At first, Claude shrugged it off, claiming it was no big deal and he could walk away any time he chose. Lincoln knew that wasn't the case, especially given the people he'd gotten himself tangled up with. He tried to explain that to Claude, but the stubborn businessman thought he knew best and refused to listen. When Lincoln explained he would no longer be working for Devereaux Industries because of his business associates, Devereaux had exploded, vowing to destroy Lincoln's business and reputation if he quit.

It had taken all his self-control not to let loose on Devereaux. He explained that Brooks and Dunn Security would no longer work for Claude's company. Then he walked out of the building and straight to the bar, where he met Cecily.

But there was more to it than the massive lie of omission hanging over his head. He felt an overwhelming attachment to Cecily that he did not want to feel. Acting like her fake boyfriend would make it a lot harder to walk away from her. He contemplated picking up the phone, calling her, and telling her he changed his mind. Except he couldn't stop thinking about the look on her face, the pain and even fear.

Lincoln sat up and scrubbed a hand over his face. This was stupid. He didn't get attached; he didn't get involved. After Cat, he put all that behind him.

Catherine Crowley was Lincoln's high school sweetheart and ex-wife. They'd married right out of high school, six weeks before he and Van left for boot camp. They were deeply in love, or so he thought.

After boot camp, the army whisked him away for additional training and then sent him to Afghanistan. He didn't get to see Cat before he left, something he always regretted. They kept in touch via snail mail, email, and infrequent phone calls. As time went on, Cat pulled away. The letters stopped, and the emails dwindled to once every week or two until they eventually stopped altogether. Lincoln brushed it off as a wife's fear and difficulty of being married to a military man.

When he could finally go home between his first and second tour, it seemed like a good idea to surprise the wife he hadn't seen in nine months. He'd gone straight to their small apartment from the airport, unlocked his front door, and walked into his home that was filled with another man's belongings. He was the surprised one. His entire world, his entire belief system, and his faith in love conquering all disintegrated on the spot. Cat served him with divorce papers two days later. She married Todd, her boss and new boyfriend, two months after the divorce was final.

Lincoln vowed to never fall in love again. The heartbreak Van suffered after his wife's death only solidified his decision. Love was messy, complicated, and not worth the heartache. Avoiding any kind of long-term relationship was easy; any time a girl got too close or too clingy, he walked away. Most of the time, he didn't stick around long enough to get to the clingy stage. Van teased him about being a one-and-done-kind of guy, which was a reputation Lincoln welcomed.

"Nine days until I'm gone. I'll put Cecily Devereaux behind me and get on with my life," he said out loud. Hearing the words made it seem more definitive. He would help her out of this jam, then go back to New York and back to his life of no emotional commitments and no heartache.

"Easy peasy," he mumbled.

Chapter 11

Cecily

*C*ecily paced the back patio with Sebastian at her feet. She checked her watch every few minutes, eager to get past the mundane and tedious greetings accompanying a visit with her father. They were embarrassingly awkward with each other, almost like they weren't related.

It was worse after her mother passed away. Once she was gone, Cecily and her father had nothing in common and nothing to talk about. Her father's focus shifted to getting her married off to an appropriate suitor, wanting to pawn her and the problems she caused him off on someone else.

Every few seconds, she glanced across the lake, but she didn't see the boat crossing the water. She grabbed a glass of lemonade off the patio table and chugged half of it, then wiped the back of her hand across her mouth.

I will not survive this.

Since the phone call with Lawrence and her meeting with Lincoln, she'd teetered on the edge of a nervous breakdown. Fear twisted her stomach into knots: fear of getting caught in a lie, of disappointing her father, of screwing up and giving into her father's demands. It had always been difficult to stand up to him, more difficult than she would admit out loud. If he pressured her to reconcile with Lawrence, she feared she might give in to his demands.

The roar of a speedboat's engine caught her attention. Cecily pushed a hand through her hair and squared her shoulders.

Here we go.

Her father was at the helm, their caretaker in the passenger seat, and Lawrence was in the middle of the boat, ensconced in a large life jacket with a death grip on the edge of his seat. Her ex-fiancé hated large bodies of water—the ocean, lakes, even large rivers. He had never visited the home on the lake, especially after he discovered it was on an island three miles offshore. Cecily tried many times to get him to visit her home in Montana, but he always refused.

If he will come all the way out here, he must be desperate to look good for my father.

Cecily raised her hand and waved. Claude Devereaux returned the wave, but Lawrence maintained his hold on the boat. She picked up Sebastian, pressed a kiss to the top of his head as she attached his leash to his harness, and wrapped it around her wrist. She then stepped through the recently installed gate, put in to keep Sebastian from running off. He liked to take off into the woods surrounding the house, so she never let him outside the gate without his leash, even if she carried him.

As she made her way down the path to the dock, she watched Claude pull the boat alongside the floating wood, jump out, and secure the line to the moor. Lawrence didn't move until her father completed his tasks.

"Cecily." Her father kissed her cheek and gave Sebastian a cursory pat on his head. The dog allowed it, even though Cecily knew he didn't like her father.

Lawrence climbed off the boat and stumbled over a raised board on the dock, the too-large life jacket hitting him in the chin. He pushed his glasses up his nose and plastered one of his fake smiles on his face.

"CeCe, love! It's so good to see you." He descended on her, his hands outstretched as he leaned in to kiss her.

Sebastian snarled and nipped at Lawrence, catching the corner of the life jacket between his teeth. He tugged on it and growled.

"Sebastian, no," Cecily said half-heartedly.

The dog looked up at her, but he released Lawrence with one of his irritated huffs. Cecily took a step back, avoiding Lawrence's damp lips, and smiled at him.

"Lawrence," she said. She turned to her father. "How was the flight, Daddy?"

"Bumpy," he grumbled. "Let's get up to the house. I could use a drink."

Cecily nodded and followed her father up the dock. Lawrence paused long enough to remove the life jacket and toss it in the boat before joining them. Mr. Tuttle followed them, two suitcases in his hands.

Once they reached the lawn, Cecily set Sebastian on the ground, removed his leash, and pulled the gate closed behind her father and Lawrence.

"The fencing looks good, Cecily," her father commented. "Did Will do it?"

"Yes, sir. All I ask is that you remember to keep the gate closed; otherwise,

Sebastian gets out and heads straight for the water or into the woods. I don't want him to get hurt, so please keep it shut."

Lawrence snorted. "You put a fence around the back patio to keep your dog in? Isn't that a little excessive? Why not keep him inside?"

"He likes to play outside," Cecily said.

"We will keep the gate closed," Claude interjected. "I know how much you like that little dog. Now, let's get that drink before we go to dinner. My secretary made us reservations at The Montana Club."

Cecily headed for her father's office, with Sebastian at her feet, while Claude and Lawrence settled themselves up in their rooms. Lawrence came down first and walked right up to Cecily. Sebastian growled at him as Lawrence passed the dog. Her ex took her arm, dragged her close, and pressed a damp kiss to her cheek.

"I missed you," he whispered.

She yanked her arm free and stepped back until there were several feet between them. "No, you missed my father's money and the prospect of a promotion in the company."

"Don't be like that," Lawrence muttered. "I *missed* you. We should sit down and talk, see if we can work something out."

"I don't want to work anything out, Lawrence, because I don't want to get back together. Marrying you is no longer in my best interests. When we broke up, I thought I made that clear. And every time we talked every day for the last six months."

Lawrence sucked on his bottom lip. "Do you think you can do better than me? Look at you, CeCe. You haven't changed. You're still overweight—."

"I'm fine the way I am," she snapped.

"You've put on a lot of weight."

Cecily pinched the bridge of her nose. "I'm not having this discussion with you, not again. This is one reason we aren't together anymore. You made it perfectly clear how you felt about my weight gain. Obviously, you haven't moved past it."

Claude entered the study. "Moved past what?" he asked.

"Nothing, Daddy. It's not important." Cecily moved to the other side of the room and sat on the recliner. Sebastian followed her and sat beside her, with his head resting on her calf.

Claude raised an eyebrow, but he chose not to comment. He made himself a drink, then he sat behind his enormous mahogany desk. He leaned back in his chair and crossed his arms.

Cecily mirrored her father, crossing her arms as she leaned back. Two could play his game.

"Lawrence tells me you've been dating someone," Claude stated. "Invite him to dinner tonight. I'd like to meet him."

She opened her mouth and closed it again; there was no sense in arguing with her father. Besides, she and Lincoln planned for this. Putting off the meeting wouldn't do any good; it would get Lawrence out of her hair too.

"I'll call him and have him meet us there." She shoved herself to her feet. "I'm going to get ready. Come on, Sebby, let's go."

The Shih Tzu got up and followed her, giving both her father and Lawrence a wide berth. Cecily pulled her phone from her pocket and dialed Lincoln's number. He picked up on the first ring.

"Showtime," she whispered.

———

Cecily watched the restaurant door, half-listening to her father and Lawrence talk. Lincoln was late.

"I'll make the arrangements." Claude cleared his throat. "Cecily? You are available, aren't you?"

Cecily dragged her gaze away from the door and turned her attention to her father. "I'm sorry, available for what?"

"To come back to New York with us. You have had enough fun in Lakeside; it's time to come back to New York and resume your job with Devereaux Industries." Her father jutted a finger in Lawrence's direction. "Also, we need to discuss your ridiculous decision to break off your engagement to Lawrence."

Cecily shook her head about her father and his impossible demands. She exhaled and started with the job. "You mean my meaningless job as the company party-planner? That job?"

"It's not meaningless—."

"My master's degree is in business, Daddy, and you used me to plan company get-togethers. I am worth more. I can *do* more." She glanced at Lawrence smirking on the other side of the table. "As for my so-called ridiculous decision to break off the engagement, I believe that is none of your business."

"You are my daughter, Cecily Camille, so it is my business."

"No, it's not. It's my life and my decision. I am doing what is best for me—."

"Maybe it's time to realize you need to do what's best for the Devereaux family name and my company."

Cecily closed her eyes and rubbed her forehead. A headache throbbed in the center of her head.

"Cecily? Are you okay?"

Lincoln stood behind her father, frowning. She hadn't noticed him come in.

"Lincoln! Thank God!" she blurted. She jumped to her feet and threw herself at him. She kissed his cheek.

He squeezed her waist. "Sorry I'm late."

"My hero," she whispered in his ear. "I'm so glad you're here."

Her father swung around, snorted loudly, and rose to his feet. "Dunn? What the hell are you doing here? Cecily, is this a joke?"

"Wh-what?"

"You didn't tell me your friend was Lincoln Dunn."

"You know Lincoln?" Cecily asked.

"Of course I do," her father said. "He works for Devereaux Industries."

Lincoln shook his head and grimaced. "Not anymore, Claude." He extended his hand, and Claude gripped it. "It's good to see you again, sir."

Cecily couldn't move. She stood frozen in place, staring at Claude and Lincoln. *He works for Devereaux Industries.*

Lincoln nudged her, took her arm, and guided Cecily back into the booth. He reached for her hand, but she tucked the hand closest to him under her leg and picked up her drink with the other. Her head spun, and her appetite was gone. She downed her drink in two swallows and signaled their server for another. *Lincoln works for Devereaux Industries.*

Her father narrowed his eyes and pursed his lips when their server set the second drink in front of her. She stared at him as she picked it up and took a sip.

Lawrence cleared his throat; Cecily had forgotten he was there. Her ex put his shoulders back and his chin jutted out, as he reached across the table to shake Lincoln's hand.

"I'm Lawrence, Cecily's fiancé." he said.

Cecily groaned and shook her head. "Ex-fiancé, Lawrence. You're my *ex-fiancé.*"

Lawrence shrugged. "My apologies. There seems to be some confusion regarding our relationship status."

"No confusion," Cecily muttered. "We aren't engaged anymore. End of discussion."

Lawrence huffed. "Problem, CeCe?"

"Don't call me that," she snapped.

"Cecily, don't be rude," her father interjected. "It's unnecessary."

She pushed a hand through her hair and sighed. Lincoln slipped his arm around her shoulder and pressed a kiss to her temple.

"I don't think she was rude," he said. "She doesn't like being called CeCe. My guess is she was only reminding Lawrence not to call her by an unwanted nickname." Lincoln stared at Lawrence.

Her ex squirmed in his seat and scrubbed a hand over his face. He looked like he'd eaten a lemon as he mumbled, "Sorry."

Lincoln intimidated Lawrence, and Cecily loved it. Discovering her father's working relationship with Lincoln irritated her, but she pushed it aside. She focused on making her fake relationship with Lincoln seem real. Right now, she needed to convince her father and Lawrence that she was head over heels for Lincoln Dunn.

Cecily leaned into him, pressing herself tight against his side. She put her hand on his leg and squeezed, grinning at Lawrence and her father.

"What do you say we order dinner?" Cecily said.

Chapter 12

Lincoln

Lincoln glanced over at Cecily. She plastered herself against the passenger door, leaving two feet of distance between them and stared out the window, refusing to look at him. Cecily could have caught a ride with her father and Lawrence, but she went with Lincoln. It was obvious she didn't want to be in a car with her father or ex-fiancé, but Lincoln wasn't sure she wanted to be in the car with him either.

He couldn't blame her for wanting to avoid Claude and Lawrence; her father was overbearing, and Lawrence was an ass. Lawrence was also the fakest person Lincoln ever met, and he'd worked with politicians, musicians, and actors. The fake, deep voice he'd used most of the night—unless he forgot—made Lincoln repeatedly chuckle. The man had babbled incessantly about every topic under the sun, not allowing anyone else to speak. Lincoln could have dealt with those minor annoyances, but Lawrence's obvious disdain for Cecily was enough to make Lincoln want to take the guy out. And he wanted to make it hurt.

While dinner had been awkward and downright annoying, the car ride home felt like being suffocated with a wet blanket.

Lincoln cleared his throat. "Cecily?"

She refused to look at him; instead, she continued staring out the window with her chin propped on her hand.

"Will you talk to me, please?"

Cecily turned to look at him, and her voice broke when she spoke. "Why didn't you tell me you work for my father?"

He held the steering wheel with one hand and with the other hand, he rubbed the back of his neck. There it was; he'd waited all night for her to say something. He exhaled.

All right. Here we go. Honesty is the best policy.

"First, it's *worked*, not work. I am not currently employed by Devereaux Industries."

"Thanks for clarifying." Cecily's voice dripped with sarcasm.

Lincoln sighed and continued. "When we met, I didn't know you were Claude Devereaux's daughter."

"You didn't know? You worked for my father, and you didn't know I was his daughter? That seems unlikely."

"No, I swear." He chuckled nervously. "You told me your father kept you out of the spotlight. I gather he kept you out of his business dealings as well, or I would have seen you in a board meeting or something." He gripped the steering wheel so hard, his knuckles ached. "When I met you in New York, you were a gorgeous woman I wanted to spend the night with. And when I saw you at Time Out, you were the same gorgeous woman I still wanted to spend the night with. That's who you are to me, Cecily, a beautiful woman I am insanely attracted to. I didn't even know your last name. Believe me, I didn't know Claude Devereaux was your father until you mentioned it the other day. And I don't care who your father is."

Cecily snorted. "I've heard that before, Lincoln. You aren't the first man to feign a lack of knowledge about my father and my inheritance. I don't have the patience to deal with that again."

"What do you mean, again?"

Cecily pinched the bridge of her nose and stared at the lights flashing by the car window. "Every man I have ever dated is only interested in one thing—my father's money. It's difficult being the daughter of a billionaire. The last straw was Lawrence. I thought he loved me, but he was another guy using me to get to my father. Breaking off the engagement and moving to Montana hasn't staunched the love between my father and my ex-fiancé. It's a never-ending battle to prove to my father that Lawrence isn't who Daddy thinks he is; it's a battle I'm tired of fighting. I'm sick of it."

"I imagine you are. It can't be easy."

"No, Lincoln. It sucks. And now, apparently, I need to do it again."

"What?"

Cecily snorted. "You worked for my father. You're a successful businessman too. My father loves that, because it means a big, strong, smarter-than-her man could take care of his little girl. This whole fake relationship thing was a bad idea. I never would have asked you if I knew you worked for my father."

Lincoln grimaced. "I can assure you your father does *not* like me."

"He doesn't?"

"No, he doesn't. Trust me." He wasn't about to go into detail; Cecily had more than enough issues with her father. He didn't need to tell her the real reason he no longer worked for Claude Devereaux.

Cecily rolled her eyes, but a hint of a smile teased the corners of her mouth. "Okay, this is going to sound awful, but my father not liking you is good for our fake relationship. It takes the focus off Lawrence and me."

"And puts it on me."

She inched closer to Lincoln. "What? Do you think you can't handle it?"

Lincoln chuckled. "Oh, I can handle it. Your father doesn't scare me."

"Thank God, because sometimes he scares me." Cecily took Lincoln's hand and traced her fingers over his knuckles. "Did you really not know I was Claude Devereaux's daughter when we met?"

"I didn't, I swear. When we met, I didn't know who your father was. I like you for *you*, Cecily, not because you have money. I don't need *or* want your money."

Cecily laughed. "I've heard that before too."

"I'm sure you have. But this time it's true."

"What did you do for my father, anyway?"

He could tell her that much. "Cybersecurity consultants. After Van's wife died and he moved to Lakeside, we stepped away from personal security and started working in cybersecurity. There was a need, and we took advantage of it. It was easier with Van here and me in New York. Devereaux Industries hired us to clean up their computer systems and increase their online security."

"How long did you work for him?" Cecily asked.

"Six months. Once we had the system up to par, we handed it off to his tech services and in-house security. We were back-up only, you know, in case of emergencies; that was three months ago."

Cecily took her hand out of his. "Wait a minute, we met three months ago."

Lincoln nodded. "Yes, we did. We met an hour after I left the board meeting." An hour after, he gave her father the finger and quit. He glanced at her out of the corner of his eye. The defeated look on her face broke his heart. Before he could react, she pointed out the window.

"Turn right at the stop sign."

Lincoln followed her directions, coming to a stop in a parking lot next to a long dock with several boats moored next to it. He put the truck in park, reached across the seat, and took Cecily's hand.

"I'm sorry someone with an ulterior motive has hurt you. But that's not me. This isn't some grand scheme to fool you out of your fortune or get in good with your father. Trust me, that is the *last* thing I want to do. When I say I don't want or need your money, I'm not lying. I do not need your money. Van and I recently sold our business for an enormous sum of money, enough that neither of us will ever have to work again."

Cecily tilted her head to one side and raised her eyebrows. "Really?" she whispered.

"Yes," he replied. "We sold the business two weeks after I met you. We were negotiating the sale while we still worked for your father."

"Okay, so you're not after my father's money. How come you didn't say something once you knew who I was?"

Lincoln shrugged. "I'm a chickenshit?" At least that earned him a genuine laugh. "Honestly? Every time I tried to tell you, something would happen—like best man speeches and servers playing with your dog. After two or three times of not saying anything, I figured it was too late. I was afraid you would hate me for not telling you, and you wouldn't want to spend time with me anymore. For that, I apologize; it was stupid and selfish."

Cecily squeezed his hand. "You are telling me the truth, right, Lincoln? I need to know because I can't handle any more deception, from anybody. I've been used too many times."

"I'm telling you the truth, I swear." He kissed the back of her hand and said, "I do not want or need your money. Now, are we okay?"

She sighed. "I guess so. But I need you to promise you won't withhold the truth from me again. Okay?"

"Yes, ma'am." He looped his pinky with hers. "Pinky swear." His gut clenched at the white lie slipping past his lips. Cecily didn't need to know her father was an ass and not quite legitimate with some of his business dealings. He would keep that from her, for the time being.

Cecily giggled, pulling his attention back to her. "You're a charmer, Lincoln Dunn. A real charmer."

"That's what I've been told." He wrapped his hand around the back of her neck, dragged her close, and kissed her. When he released her, he rested his forehead against hers and breathed her in, the intoxicating scent of orange blossoms filling his head. After a few seconds, he lifted his head and looked around.

"Where are we?" he asked.

Cecily smirked. "Um, the boat dock."

Lincoln rolled his eyes. "Obviously. I thought I was taking you home?"

She shook her head. "The boat is taking me home." She pointed at a sleek black-and-gold speedboat. "I live on the lake."

"Like, literally on the lake?"

Cecily laughed and waved her hand at the lake. "I live on an island, Devereaux Island. It's about three miles offshore."

He chuckled. "You never cease to amaze me."

Cecily kissed Lincoln's cheek, grabbed his hand, and clasped it between hers. "Thank you for the ride, and the explanation. I feel a lot better. Will you come to the house for brunch tomorrow? Please?"

Lincoln took her chin between two fingers, tipped her head back, and gave her a soft, lingering kiss. "Yes. What time?"

"I'll meet you here at ten." She pressed another kiss to his lips before she shoved open the truck door and jumped out. She jogged up the dock and climbed aboard the boat.

He sat and watched her get the boat ready until her father and Lawrence pulled into the parking lot and parked beside him. He tapped the horn twice, waved at Cecily, and left.

———

"How's the vacation?" Van asked. "Are you lying low?"

"Kind of," Lincoln replied. He propped the phone between his ear and shoulder while he drove. He didn't want to get lost in Lakeside trying to find his way back to the condo from the dock where he'd dropped off Cecily. The town looked a lot different in the dark.

"What do you mean by kind of?"

"I've been spending time with Cecily."

"Oh?"

"You don't have to sound so happy about it."

Van laughed. "You hear one syllable, and you think I sound happy."

"Yeah. You do, maybe even gloating a little."

"So, does this mean your total ban on relationships and love is over?"

Lincoln chuckled. "Hell, no. Cecily likes relationships about as much as I do; it's a mutual attraction. She's sexy and amazing in bed."

"TMI, brother."

"Sorry," Lincoln said. But he wasn't, not really. He'd been wanting to brag about Cecily for days, not just her prowess in the sack, but her personality, her determination, everything. He liked a strong woman, and Cecily fit the bill. "She's great, Van. Really great."

"Hmm," Van hummed.

"I know you want to say something. Spit it out."

"I think you're falling for this woman, Linc. This isn't like you. Spending time with women is not something you do. Ever since Cat screwed you over, you're a love 'em-and-leave 'em kind of guy."

"Nothing has changed," Lincoln snapped. He turned into the parking spot next to the condo and shifted the phone to his other ear as he parked the truck. "I'm on vacation, and I'm spending time with an attractive woman. The sex is great, and the company is great. In two weeks, I'm going back to New York: no attachment, no relationship. End of story." He slammed the truck door, unlocked the side door of the condo, and went inside.

"Are you trying to convince me or yourself?"

"I don't need to convince anyone of anything. I'm not getting attached. Cat taught me a lesson I will never forget. Look, I gotta go. I'll talk to you later." He disconnected the call and tossed his phone on the kitchen counter. It drove him crazy that Van knew him so well, the perils of being best friends for twenty-five years.

I am not falling for Cecily. Not at all.

Chapter 13

Cecily

awrence squeezed her shoulder before he sat on the chaise lounge beside her the next day. He glanced at the cup of coffee in her hand and smiled.

"There's coffee?" he asked.

Cecily looked at him over the top of her sunglasses. "In the kitchen, in the coffeepot. Mugs are in the cupboard to the left of the sink."

He snorted, rose to his feet, and stomped across the yard back to the house. Cecily giggled under her breath. She checked her watch; thirty minutes until she could take the boat to get Lincoln. He made an excellent buffer. Plus, she was pretty sure Lawrence was afraid of him.

Sebastian growled, signaling Lawrence's return.

"What is that dog's problem?" Lawrence muttered.

"He hates you," Cecily said.

"Wow, okay. Blunt much?" He sat back down and cleared his throat. "How did you sleep?"

"Fine."

"I saw Mrs. Tuttle making brunch."

"Yes."

"Is every conversation we have going to be like pulling teeth?"

Cecily shook her head. "Probably."

"Jesus, Cecily, enough already. You're pissed at me, I get it. I screwed up. I'm sorry. You've made your point."

"What do you mean, 'I made my point'?"

"I get it. I acted like an ass. It won't happen again. Can we move on?"

Cecily pulled her sunglasses off and stared at Lawrence. "I have moved on."

Lawrence took her hand. "I meant move on together. We can put the past behind us where it belongs and plan our future together."

"We don't have a future together, Lawrence. How many times do I have to tell you that?"

"Your father thinks we have a future."

"I don't care what my father thinks. He isn't in charge of my love life. I choose who I want to be with, not Claude Devereaux." She put her sunglasses back on and stared at the lake. "And I have Lincoln, now. I don't need or want you."

Lawrence waved his hand like he was shooing away a fly. "Both your father and I think Lincoln is a passing fancy. He'll move on soon enough, and you'll be alone again."

"Do you hear yourself when you talk, Lawrence? The things you say to me—."

"I'm trying to be honest," her ex snapped. "One of us should be." He looked pointedly at her.

Cecily shoved herself to her feet, snatched her sweater off the back of her seat, and picked up Sebastian. "I'm taking the boat to shore; Lincoln's coming for brunch. I'll be back in less than an hour."

The slam of the gate behind her left a satisfying ring in her ears. She unmoored the boat, put Sebastian in his life jacket, and secured him with his leash to the seat beside her. Within minutes, the speedboat skipped across the water, the wind blowing her long, black hair away from her face.

Cecily loved the water, and she loved the lake. Several times a week, she would take the boat out on the water and forget about her problems for a while. The ice-cold sprays of water hitting her skin revitalized and energized her, while the wind ruffling her hair and clothes reminded her of the power of nature. Flathead Lake was beautiful, a beauty difficult to explain to anyone who hadn't experienced it in person. She would never understand how her father could resist the charms of the lake. She wanted to stay here forever.

It took less than fifteen minutes to reach the dock. Lincoln lounged against one of the roof supports: sunglasses on, arms crossed, and muscles bulging.

How can this man look so incredibly delicious without even trying?

She waved at him as she pulled the boat alongside the dock. Lincoln waved back and jogged down the length of the dock to meet her.

"Are you ready?" she asked.

He grinned. "As I'll ever be." He jumped off the dock onto the bow, wrapped a hand around the back of her neck, and dragged her close. He leaned over her, his lips brushing hers as he spoke. "You look utterly delectable." He caught her lips in his and kissed her breathless before moving down her neck and sucking at her pulse point.

Cecily's head fell back, and a shiver raced through her at the feel of Lincoln's lips on her skin. For a moment, she considered skipping brunch and going back to Lincoln's place. Sex with Lincoln would be more fun than brunch with her father and Lawrence.

She wrapped her arms around his neck and hooked a leg around the back of his thigh. "God, you're sexy," she whispered. "I could do you right here."

"Tempting offer, babe, but don't we have someplace to be?"

Cecily grimaced. "Yes. Unfortunately." She released Lincoln and returned to her seat at the helm. She looked over her shoulder at him. "You can sit back there. Seb rides shotgun. Do you want a life jacket?"

Lincoln chuckled and shook his head. He sprawled across the bench seat in the center of the boat, his long legs stretched out in front of him and his arms thrown over the back of the seat. "I'm good."

Cecily eased away from the dock. Once she cleared the dock and moved past the boats cruising the shoreline, she let loose, pushing the speedboat to the max. They sped across the water, bouncing across the waves, as sprays of water soaked into their clothes. She glanced at Lincoln several times; he had his head thrown back, and a huge smile on his face.

Why does he have to be so perfect?

When the house came into view, her stomach twisted uncomfortably. Brunch with Claude Devereaux and Lawrence was not as appealing as spending the day on the lake with Lincoln. She would have loved to show him the small cove with its gorgeous stretch of beach hidden on the other side of the island. It was easy to picture the two of them swimming in the clear blue water and making love on the sandy beach. Anything was better than what was to come.

Once she safely moored the boat, she tucked Sebastian under her arm and gestured for Lincoln to follow her up the dock. He took her hand, intertwining his fingers with hers. It felt right, natural. She swallowed past the lump rising in her throat.

What the hell is he doing to me?

Lawrence greeted them at the gate, a mimosa in his hand. He was unsteady on his feet as he reached for Lincoln's hand, wincing when Lincoln squeezed too hard.

"Are you drunk?" Cecily asked. "How is that possible? I was gone less than an hour." She put Sebastian on the ground and latched the gate.

Lawrence's eyes widened, and he snorted. He gave her a disgusted look before he turned to Lincoln. "How wonderful you could join us, Lincoln. We didn't get much of a chance to talk last night."

"Nobody had much chance to talk, Larry," Lincoln responded. "You talked enough for all of us."

Lawrence's eyes narrowed, and he waved the hand holding the mimosa in a circle. "I was only making conversation. Anyway, I have so many questions about how you and Cecily met." He gave her another pointed look before he gestured to a table by the pool laden with food. "I hope you're hungry; Mrs. Tuttle made enough food to feed an army."

Lincoln grinned. "I'm starving. A vigorous ride always makes me hungry." He winked at Lawrence, threw his arm over Cecily's shoulder, and headed for the table next to the pool.

Cecily slapped her hand over her mouth to muffle the laughter attempting to escape. She grabbed Lincoln's hand and squeezed it as a silent thank-you.

When Claude saw them coming up the walkway, he rose to his feet and extended his hand. He greeted Lincoln with a tight smile and gestured for him to sit. Cecily gave her father an odd look, but she bit her tongue.

"Good to see you, Dunn," Claude said.

Lawrence snorted, dropped into the chair beside Claude, and finished his drink. He grabbed the pitcher on the table and poured himself another one.

Claude eyed Lawrence up and down, then he tapped him on the shoulder and ordered him to move, so Lincoln could take his seat. His tone left no room for argument, so Cecily's ex got up and stomped to the end of the table. He sat down, grabbed a plate, and piled it high with food, glaring at Cecily, Claude, and Lincoln as he shoveled food into his mouth.

"What brings you to Montana, Lincoln?" Claude asked.

"Cecily."

"My daughter?"

Lincoln took a seat at the table next to Claude, reached for the plate of fruit and cheese, and popped a grape into his mouth. "Yes, sir."

"May I ask how you two met?"

"We met in New York—."

"I met him at a bar down the street from the hotel," Cecily interjected. "We got to talking and hit it off."

Claude crossed his arms over his chest. "When was this?"

Cecily sighed. "Daddy."

Lincoln smiled at her and squeezed her hand. "It's okay; it was three months ago, sir. Right after your last board meeting, I believe."

"No shit? Is that true?" Lawrence asked. "That's crazy."

"Why yes, Larry, it *is* crazy," Lincoln said. "Crazy that I saw a gorgeous woman drinking alone at a bar and wanted to get to know her better. One thing led to another, and here I am."

"Do you often fly across the country to visit women you've only known for three months?" Claude asked.

Lincoln chuckled. "Well, no sir. Turns out, it's a small world. As luck would have it, my best friend lives here in Lakeside. It was easy to plan a trip when I knew I could see both Cecily and Van."

"So, you're not here just for Cecily," Lawrence said. "Your friend is here too."

Lincoln took Cecily's hand and kissed the back of it. "Oh, trust me, I'm here for Cecily."

Cecily grinned at Lawrence and settled back in her seat. She poured herself a drink, as she listened to her father and Lincoln talk. The topics ranged from business to soccer, her father's favorite sport. Lawrence interjected occasionally, but mostly they excluded him from the conversation.

Once the food was gone and the pitcher of mimosas empty, Cecily excused herself and headed for the kitchen. She needed a break from her father giving Lincoln the third degree and Lawrence pouting. It was a testosterone-fueled nightmare on the patio, and Cecily had had enough.

"Cecily, are you hiding?"

Cecily popped up from behind the open refrigerator door, seeing her father standing in the doorway. She grabbed a bottle of water, pushed the door closed with her hip, and sat on the stool at the large island.

"I'm not hiding; I needed a break."

"A break from what?" Claude sat on a stool opposite her.

"Everything." She cleared her throat. "So, do you like Lincoln?"

Claude shrugged. "Are you asking for my approval?"

She made a face. "No."

"I didn't think so." He cleared his throat. "He's suitable husband material."

Cecily rolled her eyes. "That's not what I asked."

"He will make someone a good husband someday."

"Someone?"

Claude nodded. "Yes, someone. It will not be you, though."

She took a sip of water and forced it past the lump rising in her throat. "Why is that?"

"I've heard rumors he's a bit of a ladies' man. My guess is that you are nothing more than a brief fling. Once he is done with you, he will move on."

Cecily recoiled, as if he had slapped her. "Daddy..."

"I know it hurts to hear that, princess. But it's true. You're better off with someone reliable, like Lawrence."

"Are you *ever* going to let that go? I don't love Lawrence."

"Be reasonable, Cecily; it's not always about love. You're thirty years old. It's time for you to quit messing around, hanging out on this stupid island in the middle of nowhere doing nothing with your life. Maybe if I cut off your trust fund—."

"You know what? Cut me off." She got to her feet. "I do not care." She emphasized each word with a tap of her index finger to the countertop.

Claude scowled. "I'm serious."

"So am I."

She wanted to say more, wanted to tell her father exactly what she thought of him, but before she could, she heard Lincoln outside.

"Sebastian, come back here!"

Cecily spun on her heel, sprinted through the house, and out the patio door. The back gate was open; Lawrence was on the dock; Lincoln was halfway across the lawn; and for the love of God, Sebastian was down by the water and headed for the woods.

"Sebastian!" she screamed.

Her dog froze and turned to look at her. He dropped his head and trotted back up the hill, his tail between his legs. She forced herself to stroll down the hill, so as not to spook the Shih Tzu and send him running away. When she reached him, she scooped him up and squeezed him hard enough to make him yelp in protest.

"Bad dog," she mumbled, as she plastered him with kisses. "Bad, bad dog."

Lincoln appeared at her side and slipped his arm around her waist. "I'm sorry. I tried to catch him. He wouldn't come to me; I don't think he trusts me yet."

"How did he get out?"

Lincoln looked at Lawrence. "Larry left the gate open."

Cecily shook her head. "Why am I not surprised?"

Lawrence met them at the gate. "Whoops. Thought I closed that gate." He winked at Cecily and took a swallow from the glass in his hand.

Out of the corner of her eye, Cecily saw Lincoln shake his head. She glared at Lawrence. "When are you going home?" she asked.

"We're leaving Tuesday morning," her father interjected from the patio. "I have a meeting in San Francisco in the afternoon."

Cecily gave both Lawrence and her father dirty looks. "It's not soon enough."

Chapter 14

Lincoln

After he returned from Cecily's, Lincoln took Van's boat out on the lake. He went to the spot Van considered the best fishing spot on the lake and spent three hours fishing. By the time he got back to shore, the sun was going down. A breeze kicked up, bringing a slight chill to the air. Every time he visited Montana, he forgot how cold it could get, even in the middle of the summer.

Back at the condo, he cooked a frozen dinner in the microwave and threw on a sweatshirt. Lincoln grabbed a six-pack of beer, the barely edible food, and went out on the patio. It might be cold, but the phenomenal view of the lake was worth sitting outside in the chilly breeze.

He wasn't sure what or how it happened. Cecily wormed her way into his brain and took up permanent residence. When he wasn't with her, he wanted to be. He thought about her all the time. He woke up with her on his mind, fell asleep thinking about her, and dreamed about her during the night. Cecily Devereaux consumed his every thought.

It scared the hell out of him.

Lincoln couldn't deny that they were good together. She made him laugh, made him feel like a kid, and she was by far the most gorgeous woman he had ever been around. When he acted like an ass, she called him on it. Cecily understood him on an emotional level he'd never experienced with anyone, other than Van. The physical side of their relationship was indescribable. Everything he had ever wanted in a woman was embodied in Cecily.

Dammit.

He had to tell her. After his marriage to Cat went south, he went to a therapist. During that time, he promised he would always be honest with himself and with the people in his life. Hiding his feelings from Cecily would not do either of them any good. If he was falling for her—and he was—then he owed it to himself, and her, to be honest about it. He had to tell her.

Lincoln pushed himself to his feet, grumbling under his breath about women worming their way into his head.

And my heart.

He threw his half-eaten microwave dinner in the trash and poured himself a glass of bourbon. He downed it and poured another glass. Back outside, he made himself comfortable with the bourbon and his remaining beer while he watched the sun drop below the horizon.

———

The fog of an alcohol-induced sleep weighed down Lincoln's body, and his head pounded like a mallet hitting a gong. He scrubbed a hand over his face and struggled to sit up. The bottle of bourbon had been a mistake.

With a loud grunt, he shoved himself upright. He groaned and clutched his head. It was too early, or he was too hungover. Probably the latter. He pinched the bridge of his nose, then he rubbed the sleep from his eyes.

Lincoln snatched his phone off the bedside table and checked it, seeing it was almost one in the afternoon. He'd slept half the day away. He dropped the phone back on the bed and made his way to the bathroom.

After his third glass of bourbon, the night became a blur. He wasn't even sure how he got to bed.

Lincoln stripped off his clothes and turned on the shower. He stepped over the edge of the tub and yelped as the frigid Montana water hit his skin, jolting him into full consciousness. He grabbed the soap and scrubbed himself clean. A shiver raced through him, as he stepped from the shower and wrapped a towel around himself.

The cold water woke him up, but it didn't stop his head from pounding. He needed a cup of strong black coffee. He threw on a pair of sweats and a T-shirt, grabbed his cellphone, and made his way to the kitchen. Once he had the coffee brewing, he opened the sliding glass door and stepped outside.

Lincoln took a deep breath and raised his face to the sun. Getting drunk last night hadn't helped him figure out how to handle the situation with Cecily; all it had done was give him a massive hangover.

In eight days, he was supposed to fly back to New York. He had eight days to figure out what he was going to do about this woman who had unexpectedly taken over his life.

As if on cue, his cellphone rang. He yanked it out of his pocket.

Speak of the devil, and she appears.

"Hey, gorgeous, how's it going?"

Cecily's garbled words were barely coherent. All he got out of her was it had something to do with Lawrence, and she was terrified.

"Whoa, whoa, slow down. What happened?"

Cecily choked back a sob. "I-I need your help. Can you come to the house? Please? I can send Mr. Tuttle to meet you at the dock."

"I'll meet him there."

"Thank you, Lincoln. Thank you so much."

"Anything for you, baby." The words were out of his mouth before he could stop them. He took a deep breath and chose his next words carefully before he blurted out something just as telling and stupid.

"Stay calm, and I'll see you in a while."

Shit. Damn woman, getting under his skin.

He shoved his phone in his pocket and headed for the bedroom to change. Lincoln to the rescue.

"So much for my coffee," he muttered.

———

Mr. Tuttle was in the boat, waiting for him when he got to the dock. Lincoln moved to the seat beside the caretaker and leaned close to be heard over the roar of the engine and the boat hitting the waves.

"What happened?" he asked.

"Sebastian appears to have gotten out last night," Mr. Tuttle explained. "Miss Cecily didn't realize he was gone until this morning. Mr. Lawrence left the gate open while he was in the garden, and Sebastian darted out. Mr. Lawrence claims he didn't notice the little dog leave the safety of the backyard, but he is not in the house or anywhere within the gates we've installed. We've looked all over, but the missus and I can only do so much. Miss Cecily is in a panic."

Lincoln shook his head. "I can imagine."

"She's been looking for him all morning. Alone. Neither her father nor Lawrence have bothered to help her. Mrs. Tuttle and I have tried, but neither of us can go too deep into the woods." Mr. Tuttle glanced at Lincoln out of the corner of his eye. "She didn't want to bother you, but she felt she had no other choice. She's worried you'll be angry with her or, worse, think she's being ridiculous."

Lincoln sat up straight as the boat approached Devereaux Island. "She loves that little guy. I get it. Dogs have the power to heal a person."

Cecily stood at the end of the dock, shifting from foot to foot, gripping her left hand with her right, and rubbing her palm with her thumb. She offered him a pained smile as he stepped off the boat.

"Thank you for coming, Lincoln."

He grabbed her elbow and pulled her into a hug. She buried her face against his chest, and, within seconds, gasping sobs escaped her. He held her close, rested his chin on top of her head, and rubbed her back.

"Hey, it's okay. We'll find him."

Cecily shook her head. "He's been gone so long. I'm not sure we'll find him. I mean, what if he went into the water or got hurt in the woods? What if a wild animal got him? He must be hungry and thirsty."

Lincoln had nothing to say. Cecily could be right, but he would do everything he could to find the little dog before he gave up hope.

"Where do you want to start?"

Cecily shook her head. "I don't know. I looked everywhere, but it was sporadic. I was all over the place."

Lincoln released her. "Let's get started."

Taking charge was in his nature, so he divided the area around the house into quadrants and handed out assignments. Mr. and Mrs. Tuttle oversaw the area around the mansion and inside the fence in case Sebastian came back. He and Cecily would search outside the fenced area, along the water and into the woods. He brought everyone together and gave them their instructions, then they set to work.

Two hours later, no Sebastian. They had walked along the edge of the lake, searched all the way around the huge Devereaux mansion, and gone a hundred yards into the woods, but he was nowhere to be found.

It didn't go unnoticed that Lawrence and Claude Devereaux were nowhere to be seen while everyone else searched. Cecily said her father was "busy working," and Lawrence was nose deep in his laptop. According to Cecily, neither of them had time to help her look for Sebastian. She shrugged it off, but Lincoln knew it bothered her. Now and then, he noticed Lawrence watching from the window. He never saw Claude.

Lincoln stood at the end of the path leading into the woods, waiting for Cecily. She had gone inside to get them something cold to drink. The temperature had jumped, especially after the chill in the air last night had worn off. It was close to ninety degrees.

He took several steps into the woods, off the path, into the trees. He hoped to hear a branch break, or maybe a bark or a whine, something, anything, that would lead him to Sebastian. Unfortunately, there wasn't anything.

"This is useless," he mumbled. He turned to head back to the house, but a faint yip stopped him in his tracks. He froze and strained to hear. Maybe it had been his imagination.

Then he heard it again, the distinctive whine of a dog. He took off in the direction he heard it coming from, pushing through the trees and bushes, calling Sebastian's name.

"Seb? Sebastian?"

A louder bark came from deeper in the woods. Lincoln followed the sound. Another fifty yards, and he saw a flash of white. He pushed through the brambles, bushes, and tall grass until he got to the dog.

Sebastian laid on the ground next to a tree, hidden under a large bush. His tail thumped weakly against the ground when he saw Lincoln, and he whined faintly.

"Hey, buddy," Lincoln whispered. "Are you okay?" He brushed a hand over the dog's back, wincing when Sebastian yelped. His left leg was oddly bent and covered in burrs, with long strands of grass wrapped around it.

"Alright, let's get you out of here." He gently brushed leaves and dirt off the dog, then he worked to untangle him. Sebastian watched him with his big brown eyes, whimpering quietly.

Lincoln scooped up the dog and hurried back through the woods. Cecily saw him coming up the path as she came out the back door, and when she saw her dog, she dropped the tray she carried on the table and ran down the path to meet them.

"Oh, my God, is he okay?" She reached for him but pulled her hands back at the last second when she saw his leg.

"I don't know. His left leg looks funny. I'm sure he's dehydrated too. Do you have a vet in Lakeside?" Lincoln asked.

"Dr. Schaffer. I'll call her." She pulled her phone from her back pocket. "Let's get him in the boat. You hold him, and I'll drive. The vet's office is on the water. She has a dock where we can put the boat."

Lincoln followed Cecily to the dock. As he settled himself and Sebastian on the boat, he glanced back at the house. Lawrence stood at the window, watching them with his arms crossed and a smirk on his face. If he'd been closer, Lincoln would have punched the smarmy look off his face.

Later.

Chapter 15

Cecily

"Thanks, Freddie. I'll pick him up Tuesday morning." Cecily ended the phone call and set her phone on the table. She stared out the sliding glass door at the moon shining on the lake.

Sebastian had been at the vet for hours. Dr. Winifred "Freddie" Schaffer had shooed her out of the office an hour after Cecily brought him in, promising to call as soon as she assessed his injuries and started treatment.

Cecily and Lincoln went to Lincoln's condo to wait; she wanted to be close in case Freddie wanted her to return to the office. Cecily paced and stared out the window while Lincoln watched a baseball game on the TV.

"How's Sebastian?" Lincoln asked from the couch.

Cecily smiled at him. "Sebastian's doing okay. He's sleeping, ate something, drank some water, and the vet tech gave him some pain meds. Freddie thinks the leg is broken. She's waiting for the swelling to go down to take the X-rays. If it is broken, he'll be in a cast for about six weeks. I can pick him up on Monday." Cecily swallowed past the lump rising in her throat. "I can't thank you enough for helping me find him. Nobody understands what Seb means to me—."

"I do," Lincoln interrupted. He rose to his feet and took two steps closer. "I know how a dog, or any pet, makes a difference in a person's life. Van's dog, Soldier, saved my best friend's life, more than once. Until Serena came along, Soldier was Van's only reason for living."

"Serena said Soldier saved *her* life."

— 243 —

Lincoln nodded. "He did. That dog, he's a hero, in more ways than one. So, I get it. Seb is important to you, so it was important that I help you find him."

Cecily crossed the room and threw herself into Lincoln's arms. She needed to feel his body against hers, fill her head with his scent, and have his powerful arms wrapped around her. She wanted him.

He hugged her close. "Hey, are you okay?"

"Yes. Thanks to you." She buried her face against his chest and inhaled. She took a second to center herself before she looked up at him. "Can I stay here tonight? I don't want to go back to the island. I am in no mood to deal with my father or Lawrence. Not tonight."

"Yeah, of course you can." He kissed her forehead.

Lincoln took her hand and led her to the couch. He sat down and pulled Cecily down with him, setting her between his legs. She toed off her shoes, rested her head on his chest, and closed her eyes. Lincoln put his hands on her shoulders, his thumbs digging into the knots at the base of her neck.

Cecily sighed and let her head drop, her chin resting on her chest. "That feels amazing," she whispered.

Lincoln worked his fingers into the stiff muscles in her shoulders and neck. It hurt, but it felt amazing. Her body went limp, relaxing under Lincoln's adept touch.

"How is it you make everything better?" she whispered.

Lincoln chuckled. "Do I? I thought I was just being a good friend."

Cecily tipped her head back and looked into Lincoln's gorgeous blue eyes. "You *are* a good friend. A fantastic friend."

Lincoln's lips brushed against the back of her neck. "Get some rest, sweetheart."

Cecily closed her eyes and exhaled. She rested her hands on Lincoln's thick thighs and let her head fall back against his chest again. She concentrated on Lincoln's hands on her neck and shoulders, the feel of his chest rising and falling under her head, and his manly scent washing over her. Within minutes, she was asleep.

———

"I appreciate you coming back to the island with me," Cecily said. "You didn't have to."

Lincoln squeezed her knee. "After you told me about your discussion with your father last night, I wasn't about to let you come back alone. I can only imagine what he and Lawrence have been plotting. You need a buffer."

The conversation Lincoln referred to had been more of a lecture on her father's part. It miffed him that she wasn't returning to the island after what he called her "adventure with that damn dog." He spent a half an hour going on and on about her responsibilities, his irritation with her, and her lack of respect for him, his money, and her place in his world. It took all her self-control not to hang up on him.

Lincoln helped Cecily dock the boat, then he took her hand as they walked to the house. She was grateful for the gesture, especially when she saw her father and Lawrence seated on the patio. Claude's crossed arms and scowl frightened her. Lawrence looked gleeful. She sighed and squeezed Lincoln's hand.

"Here we go," she muttered.

"Cecily," her father said, as they stepped through the gate.

She forced a smile onto her face. "Hello, Daddy."

Claude Devereaux rose to his feet. "Thank you for seeing Cecily home, Lincoln. Mr. Tuttle will take you back to town. Cecily, Lawrence, and I have things to discuss."

"What exactly do we have to discuss?" Cecily asked.

"Cecily's future," Lawrence said. "Something that is not any of your business, Mr. Dunn."

Lincoln took a step toward her ex-fiancé, but Cecily put her hand on his arm, stopping him. "My future is not anyone's business but mine," she said. "Therefore, there is nothing for us to discuss. Lincoln and I are going to the other side of the island. I am going to show him the cove, and we're going to have a picnic lunch."

Claude shook his head. "I don't think that's a good idea. There are things we need to talk about. Today."

This time it was Lincoln who shook his head. "I think Cecily has made it clear how she feels about staying here to discuss her future with two people who don't care what she wants. Come on, Cecily." He led her past them into the house and slammed the door.

"Are you tired of hearing me say thank you yet?" she asked.

Lincoln pulled her into his arms. "You can show me how thankful you are when we get to that cove you mentioned." He kissed her hard on the mouth and released her. "How fast can we get out of here?"

Turns out, they could get back on the boat in under an hour. Cecily avoided her father and Lawrence as she got everything together for a picnic and swimming, sticking to her bedroom, the linen closet, and the kitchen. She breathed a sigh of relief once they were back on the water and heading toward the opposite side of Devereaux Island.

She'd been wanting to take Lincoln to the secluded cove for days; it was the most beautiful spot on the entire island. Twenty-foot-high cliffs surrounded the crystal blue cove and trees dotted the small beach.

They dropped anchor twenty yards offshore. Cecily shucked off her cover-up, spread a towel on the bow of the boat, and stretched out. Lincoln pulled two bottles of beer from the cooler, sat down beside her, and handed her one.

She drank half of it, burped loudly, and wiped her mouth with the back of her hand.

Lincoln chuckled. "Have I told you how great you are?"

She turned to look at him, leaning on her elbow. "No, but I'm willing to listen to you expound on my greatness."

Lincoln cupped her face and brushed his thumb over her cheek. "You are great. Absolutely amazing."

"Lincoln," she whispered.

He put his thumb on her lips, silencing her. "Let me get this out before I chicken out." He leaned over her, his nose brushing hers. Her breath caught in her throat, and heat raced through her veins.

"I'm falling for you, Cecily. I know that's not what we agreed to or what you want to hear, but it's happening." He dragged in a deep breath. "You've consumed my soul, sweetheart, and I will not fight it. You can have me, all of me. I'm yours if you want me." He lightly kissed her, his lips just brushing hers, but it might have been the best kiss she'd ever had.

Cecily closed her eyes and focused on breathing. *Lincoln was falling for her. When did that happen? And how come the thought of her and Lincoln together, maybe forever, didn't send her running into the lake?*

"Lincoln, I—."

He cut her off, his mouth on hers, kissing her breathless. His hand was on her hip, squeezing and releasing repeatedly. Despite the sun beating down on them, goosebumps broke out across the surface of her skin.

Lincoln broke off the kiss and rested his forehead against hers. "How secluded is this place, sweetheart?" he whispered.

Cecily shrugged. "Nobody comes here; the island is private. We've worked hard to keep it that way."

Lincoln pushed her to her back, his hand between her legs, caressing her through her swimsuit. He was impatient, his lips on the inside of her thighs and the scruff of his unshaven chin scratching at her sensitive skin, sending exciting tingles through every nerve ending. He twisted his fingers in her plain black swimsuit bottoms and pulled them down her legs. A lusty moan escaped her when his lips touched her pussy.

His breath was hot as he lapped at her aching sex, while his fingers teased at her entrance. Cecily squirmed, desperate for more contact, desperate to get closer to him.

Lincoln planted one knee beside her leg and held tight to her hips, his fingers digging in and holding her brutally tight. He pushed himself forward as he tasted her, his tongue sliding deep into her. He pulled her close, his head moving from side to side, as the scruff on his face burned and his nose hit her clit.

Jesus Christ.

Lincoln moaned, hums of satisfaction coming from him that vibrated through her core. He slipped two fingers in beside his tongue and caressed her inner walls as his fingers moved in a come-hither motion.

"Oh, fuck, Linc, right there." Cecily gasped as he hit *that* spot, the perfect spot. She wrapped her hands around his head, her nails scraped his scalp, and her thighs closed around him, holding him in place.

Lincoln growled low in the back of his throat and his head came up, his eyes locking on hers. "Yeah, baby, that's what I want to hear." He dove back in, devouring her like she was everything he wanted and everything he needed. Muffled moans of sheer arousal came from him, adding to the vibrations rocketing through her.

Her hands flailed and reached for something, anything, to hold on to as unbelievable sensations rolled through her. She ended up grabbing the towel beneath her and holding it in a death grip as Lincoln fucked her senseless with his sinful mouth, her body completely at his mercy.

Wave after wave of pleasure assaulted her as Lincoln pushed her to impossible heights, and the orgasm exploded through her, so intense and so strong that for a brief second, she blacked out.

Cecily came to her senses a few seconds later to find Lincoln hovering over her, his hips nestled between her legs, his hands in her hair, and his lips on her neck.

"Holy shit," she whispered. "That was incredible."

Lincoln laughed. "It was fucking hot. And thank you for inflating my already substantial ego." He pressed a kiss to the underside of her jaw and rocked his hips into hers, his arousal rubbing against her sensitive center.

"Lincoln, about what you said."

"Not now, sweetheart. Later. I said my piece, and we're done." He kissed her again and intertwined his fingers with hers. "Let's just enjoy the rest of the day with no pressure."

Cecily nodded, but she had no intention of letting it go. They would talk about it before he flew off into the sun and headed east.

Chapter 16

Lincoln

Lincoln stood on the dock, locked in an embrace with Cecily, while Claude Devereaux stared down at them from a top-floor window of the mansion and the late afternoon sun shown down on them. His skin crawled like a thousand bugs had landed on him. He knew from experience that Claude was not a man to be reckoned with; not that he gave two shits about Claude Devereaux or his feelings about Lincoln's relationship with Cecily. It was obvious Claude didn't have Cecily's best interests in mind, or he wouldn't push her to marry a man she didn't love.

He was reluctant to leave Cecily, but she insisted she would be fine; she planned to go straight to her room and sleep through to the next day. It sounded like a great idea, one he intended to replicant once he was back at the condo. Not that it would be easy to fall asleep, as professing his feelings for Cecily had done a number on his head. He had a lot to process.

Cecily broke off the kiss and took a step back. "I'll call you tomorrow after I pick up Sebastian. I think we need to talk."

Lincoln sighed and nodded. He kissed Cecily one last time and turned to the boat where Mr. Tuttle waited to return him to the mainland. He waved at Cecily as the boat pulled away from the dock.

"Miss Devereaux seems quite fond of you, Mr. Dunn," Tuttle said.

Lincoln grinned. "You think so?"

"Oh, yes. Seeing her with you differs a great deal from seeing her with Mr. Bronson."

"I'm quite fond of her too," Lincoln said.

Mr. Tuttle smiled. "That's good to hear. It's been a long time since Cecily had someone on her side. After her mother died, her father changed. And Cecily was alone. Even after Lawrence came into her life, she was alone. It's good to see her smiling again."

Mr. Tuttle said nothing else as he pulled the boat up to the dock and Lincoln stepped off. He gave the caretaker a wave and headed for his truck.

Lincoln checked his watch as he parked in front of Serena's condo. After everything that had happened the last forty-eight hours, he'd forgotten what day it was. Van and Serena would be back Tuesday, which was tomorrow, and he was supposed to be back in New York on Friday.

He needed to talk to Cecily. He needed to know how she felt or if she was even interested in anything more than a sexual relationship.

Tomorrow. We'll talk tomorrow and figure everything out.

———

The knock on the door came far earlier than he expected, just after eight. He hadn't even poured himself a cup of coffee. Lincoln yanked the door open, expecting to see Cecily with Sebastian in tow, but he came face to face with Claude Devereaux.

Startled, Lincoln stepped back. "Mr. Devereaux. What are you doing here?" *And how did you find me?*

"I need to talk to you, Dunn. About Cecily."

Lincoln's guard went up. He drew in a deep breath and exhaled. "What about Cecily?"

Claude pushed past Lincoln into the kitchen. "I want you to break up with my daughter. This nonsense has gone on long enough. Let her down easy and walk away. Lose her phone number and forget she exists."

Lincoln closed the door and turned to look at Claude. He kept his fists clenched at his sides. "I'm sorry. Nonsense? What nonsense?"

"You and Cecily. She has messed around for far too long. It's time for her to get back to work and settle down. No more games, no more dating random men to piss me off."

"Is that why you think she's dating me?" Lincoln interjected. "To piss you off?"

Claude gave him a terse nod. "Why else would she choose to date an ex-military man with a floundering security business?"

Lincoln snorted. *If only he knew.*

"Despite what you might think, Mr. Devereaux, your daughter is *not* dating me to piss you off. In fact, she didn't know that I knew you until a couple of days ago. Our relationship has nothing to do with you, nothing at all."

Claude glared at Lincoln and shook his head. "How much do you want?"

"What?"

Claude sighed and pinched the bridge of his nose. "I'm talking about money, Dunn. How much will it take to get you to walk away from my daughter?"

Lincoln's blood boiled. "There isn't enough money in the world, Mr. Devereaux." He pulled open the door and gestured to Claude's car in the driveway. "I think it's time for you to go."

Claude didn't move. He crossed his arms over his chest and waged a silent battle of wills with Lincoln, brown eyes locked with blue. Neither of them broke contact for almost a full minute.

Claude was the first to look away. He cleared his throat before speaking. "I don't think you understand. Cecily will marry Lawrence; it is non-negotiable."

"This conversation is over, Mr. Devereaux. Thank you for stopping by."

Claude stalked past him, not looking back until he was standing beside the car. He rested his hands on the roof of the car, hit the top of it with a fist, and turned back to Lincoln.

"End it, Dunn. Today. Or else." He didn't expound on what the "or else" might be. Instead, he climbed into the car and drove away.

———

Lincoln paced the back deck, his cup of cold coffee gripped tight in his hand. Cecily had texted him an hour ago to let him know she would be there soon.

He didn't know what to do. He wanted to tell her what happened with her father, but he feared it would upset her and push her to cut herself off from her father, the only family she had left. Lincoln didn't want to break up a family.

Out of the corner of his eye, he saw Cecily coming up the patio steps with Sebastian in her arms. The little dog looked half asleep and quite grumpy. Lincoln dropped his coffee cup to the table and held out his arms.

"How is he doing?" he asked.

Cecily handed Sebastian to Lincoln. "Good. The cast will be on for six weeks, then it will be more X-rays and possibly surgery to strengthen the leg. Freddie is worried he'll re-break it. She said if she puts a metal plate over the break, it should keep it from breaking a second time."

Sebastian stared up at Lincoln with his big brown eyes. He huffed and rested his head on Lincoln's shoulder. Lincoln rubbed a hand down his back several times before putting him on one of the padded patio benches. With his broken leg jutting out awkwardly from his body, Sebastian laid down and closed his eyes.

Cecily wrapped her arms around Lincoln's waist, pushed up on her toes, and pressed a kiss to his cheek.

"Hi," she whispered.

Lincoln smiled down at her. "Hi, gorgeous. How was your night?"

She shrugged. "I hid in my room, like I said I would. Mrs. Tuttle even brought my dinner upstairs so I didn't have to endure another meal with my father and Lawrence. She told them I was sick. They left early this morning without even saying goodbye."

Lincoln rolled his eyes. "Your father left without saying goodbye??"

"Yes. Lawrence didn't come and bug me, and when I came downstairs this morning, they were gone. I had to wait for Mr. Tuttle to come back with the boat before I could get Seb."

He tightened his hold on Cecily, pulled her tight against his body, and kissed her, hard.

"What was that for?"

"I just wanted to kiss you." He cleared his throat. "I need to tell you something."

Cecily took a step back and pinched the bridge of her nose. "Is it going to be something I'm going to lose sleep over? Because the last thing you told me kept me awake all night."

"I'm sorry about that—."

Cecily waved her head, dismissing his apology. "Don't apologize. I'm grateful you were honest with me. I prefer that to hiding your true feelings from me. It just gave me a lot to process and think about." She sat on the patio bench beside Sebastian, rested her hand on his flank, and scratched him. "What did you need to tell me?"

"Your father stopped by on his way out of town."

Cecily's eyes widened, and her shoulders stiffened. "I'm sorry, what? My father stopped here? Why would he do that?"

Lincoln sighed. "He asked me to break up with you. He insisted your marriage to Lawrence was inevitable."

The look on her face broke his heart. She sighed and stared out over the lake as she spoke. "I do *not* understand him. He refuses to let go of this thing with Lawrence. He sabotages all my efforts to get a job, and he won't be happy until I'm back in New York, working for his stupid, precious company."

Lincoln sat down beside her and slipped his arm around her waist. He pressed a kiss to her temple. "Maybe it's because he worries about you? Maybe he thinks if you're in New York, he can monitor you and keep you safe."

Cecily snorted. "My father isn't that noble, Lincoln. It's a control thing for him. Plain and simple. If I'm in New York, he can keep me under his thumb and force me to do what he wants." She rested her head on Lincoln's shoulder. "He refuses to let me live my life. You know, he's threatened several times to cut me off if I won't abide by his rules. Maybe it's time I let him. I don't want his stupid money, anyway. It causes me nothing but grief."

"Is that what you want?" Lincoln asked.

She shrugged. "Maybe. I don't know. I'm not sure what I want. Speaking of which, let's talk about what you want."

"What?"

"I know you're trying to avoid talking to me—."

Lincoln shook his head. "No, I'm not, I swear."

Cecily smiled. "Okay, whatever you say. But we need to talk. You sprung some serious stuff on me yesterday."

Lincoln tried to interrupt her again, but Cecily put her finger on his mouth and shushed him.

"I'm not done." She took a deep breath. "I like you, Lincoln. A lot. Far more than I should like you. Whatever this is between us wasn't supposed to be anything more than a minor fling, a blip on my radar. You were supposed to be out of my life in two weeks. We were going to walk away, remember? Maybe as friends, maybe not. Instead, you swoop in and tell me you have feelings for me. You tell me I've consumed your soul. How the hell am I supposed to respond to something like that?"

"Tell me how you feel," Lincoln whispered.

Cecily shook her head. "That's just it. I don't *know* how I feel. I haven't allowed myself to think about it." She pulled herself out of his arms, rose to her feet, and stared at the lake. "I'm scared to think about."

He had to ask the obvious question. "Do you want a relationship?"

Cecily shrugged. "If you asked me that question two weeks ago, before you got here, the answer would have been an adamant no. But now, I don't know."

Lincoln jumped to his feet and crossed the patio in two long strides. "Take everything else out of the equation: the money, your father, Lawrence. If none of that was clogging up your brain, what would your answer be?"

Her shoulders slumped, and she shook her head. "I can't process this without that stuff. It's impossible." She scooped up Sebastian and turned back to Lincoln. "I should go. The last twenty-four hours left me feeling ... discombobulated. I need to think. I'll call you later."

"Cecily."

She froze at the top of the patio steps, but she didn't turn around. "Give me a little time, Lincoln. Let me figure out what I want."

Instead of following her around the side of the house or trying to convince her to stay, he let her go. She took her little dog and left.

You can't force someone to love you.

If anybody knew that, it was Lincoln Dunn.

Chapter 17

Lincoln

"Lincoln!"

He swung around just in time to catch the enormous ball of fur flying at him, stumbling back several steps when the Belgian Malinois's full seventy pounds hit him. Lincoln hefted him into his arms and endured thirty seconds of having his face licked before he set Soldier on the ground.

"What are you feeding him? He weighs a ton."

Van laughed and reached out to hug his best friend. "Serena sneaks him table scraps when I'm not looking. She thinks I don't know, but I do."

"When did you get back?" Lincoln asked. "I didn't see you coming from your condo."

Van clapped him on the back. "An hour ago. I was on my way over when I saw you headed for your car. Where are you going?"

"I thought I'd go to Time Out for a burger and some beers. You should come with me."

"I'm here to ask you to come over and have pizza with us. Serena ordered one from Roselli's. And we've got beer."

"I don't want to intrude."

"You're not. I'd like to spend some time with my best friend before you head back to New York. You're leaving Friday, right? Besides, we are insanely curious to hear about you and Cecily."

"We? So, you told Serena?"

"Yeah, of course. No secrets between married couples, right?"

Lincoln raised an eyebrow and snorted.

Van grinned and shrugged. "Cat doesn't count; she never loved you like you deserved."

Lincoln flinched. "Thanks for the reminder."

"Come on. Quit being an ass and come have dinner with us. Right, Soldier?"

Soldier barked and wagged his tail.

"Fine. I'll come have dinner with you." Lincoln rolled his eyes. "Promise me no third degree, though, okay? I know you're curious about Cecily and me, but it's still new. Different. I'm not even sure where it's going or if it's even going anywhere."

"Take my dog for a walk and meet me back at my place." Van tossed Soldier's leash to Lincoln. "I'm going to go pick up the pizza."

———

"Start talking."

"Serena." Van made a slicing motion across his neck and tapped her leg with his foot.

"No, don't 'Serena' me. We've waited long enough. Lincoln got to hear all about our honeymoon. We ate pizza, and we drank beer. Now, he talks."

Lincoln laughed. "What exactly am I talking about?"

Serena gave him a dirty look, but a smile teased the corners of her mouth. "Cecily. I want to know everything."

"Everything?"

Serena giggled. "Maybe not everything. You can leave out anything about sex." She made a face.

Lincoln jumped to his feet. "Great. I'll see you two later."

"Sit down!" Van ordered. Soldier barked his agreement.

"I'm going to need another beer for this." He stepped into the small kitchen and pulled one out of the fridge. "Anyone else?"

Van raised his hand, but Serena declined. She sat back in her chair, crossed her arms over her chest, and waited.

Lincoln made them wait, staring out the window, stopping to pet Soldier, and drinking his beer. It wasn't until Serena cleared her throat that he talked.

"I like Cecily. A lot."

A grin spread across Serena's face. "You do?"

Lincoln nodded. "Yes, Serena, I do."

"I'm going to be a buzzkill and ask the obvious question," Van interjected. "I know your history, bro. All of it. So, I have to ask. Are you serious about this woman? Or are you going to go home to New York on Friday and forget she exists?

Lincoln scrubbed a hand over his face. "Always asking the hard questions. I like her, Van. I will not forget she exists."

"Do you think she might be *the one*?"

He shrugged. "I don't know. Do I want her to be the one? Yes, I do. Does she want to be the one? I don't know."

Serena's mouth fell open. "You don't know?"

Lincoln laughed. "No, Serena, I don't. Cecily wasn't—or isn't—any more interested in a relationship than I am. I really took her by surprise when I told her I have feelings for her. I think I scared her." He sat on the couch next to Van. "Then there's her father."

"Claude?" Van asked.

"Yep."

Van sat forward, his elbows on his knees and a scowl on his face. "What did Devereaux do?"

"He offered to pay me off if I broke up with his daughter."

Van shook his head. "Why am I not surprised?"

"What kind of person does that?" Serena said.

"Claude Devereaux," Lincoln replied. "He is *exactly* that kind of person. Manipulative and controlling. He will do anything to keep Cecily under his thumb, which includes making her marry Lawrence."

"Who's Lawrence?" Van asked.

"Her ex-fiancé," Serena explained. "They broke up six months ago and from what she's told me, her father won't let it go."

Lincoln nodded. "It's true. I cannot understand why. I had the pleasure of meeting Lawrence, and honestly, he's a jerk. He treats Cecily with aloof disdain, scoffs at her every word while also begging her to take him back. And her father sees how he treats her, witnesses it firsthand, but he wants them to get married. Devereaux doesn't give a shit what Cecily wants. It's crazy."

Serena let out a low whistle and shook her head. "I knew Cecily had issues with her father, but I did not know it was that bad."

"I'm assuming you told him to piss off," Van said.

Lincoln chuckled. "In not so many words. He wasn't impressed. But guess what? I don't give a shit."

Van laughed. "I figured as much." He leaned forward and put his elbows on his knees. "So, what are you going to do about Cecily?"

"I'm going to let her decide what she wants. I don't think she needs another man in her life telling her what to do." Lincoln checked his watch and pushed himself to his feet. "Look, it's after ten, and I have imposed on you long enough."

"You're not imposing." Serena said.

Lincoln squeezed Serena's shoulder and smiled down at her. "Yes, I am. You don't need me hanging around. You're still on your honeymoon."

Eyes downcast and a blush coloring her cheeks, Serena patted his hand and giggled. She jumped to her feet, grabbed her beer, and said, "Come on, Soldier. Let's get your leash and go for a walk."

Van caught her around the waist, pulled her close, and kissed her softly on the cheek. "I'll catch up with you."

Serena brushed a kiss across Van's lips, then she snapped her fingers, drawing Soldier to her side. She headed for the door, grabbed Soldier's leash off the table, and waved goodbye to Lincoln. Van watched Serena from the patio overlooking the lake until she disappeared into the shadows.

Lincoln envied him. Van's love for Serena and her love for him was the purest, sweetest, greatest love he'd ever seen. He didn't think he wanted love; shit, he didn't think he deserved love, but it snuck up on him and punched him in the gut. And damn it, he wanted it, and he wanted it with Cecily.

Van stepped back inside and returned to his seat. He leaned forward, his elbows on his knees. "It seems odd that her father is pushing for the marriage, despite Cecily's reservations."

"You mean despite her outright refusal? You're right. It is odd."

"Have you investigated Lawrence? Done a deep dive into his history?"

Lincoln shook his head. "It seemed invasive."

"Would you object to me running his name through the system?" Van asked.

"You think you might find something?"

Van shrugged. "Maybe, maybe not. But it can't hurt to look. Maybe he's got money issues, or he's power-hungry. Maybe he has some shit on Claude. Who knows? Let me check him out."

It took him two seconds to decide. "Do it."

Lincoln said his goodbyes and crossed the street to Serena's old condo. His eyes were heavy, and his head felt like he stuffed it with cotton. Sleep beckoned him. Hopefully, it didn't elude him.

Once he stripped off his clothes, he fell onto the bed and within seconds, he was asleep and dreaming of Cecily.

Chapter 18

Cecily

Cecily delivered Sebastian to the island, leaving him with Mrs. Tuttle to fuss over his injuries. She returned to the boat and headed for open water, pushing the throttle open until the boat flew across the crystal blue lake. The wind tied her long black hair in knots, and water drenched her clothing. She didn't stop until there was no land or other boats to be seen.

It was a gorgeous day, one of those rare Montana days where the temperature hovered around ninety degrees and there wasn't a cloud in the sky. Cecily cut the engine, dropped the anchor, pushed her hair out of her face, and climbed onto the bow of the boat. She stretched out and stared at the endless blue above her.

This was her safe space; it had been for years. She came out here when the thoughts in her head became too much to sort out. It had been a crazy ten days. Everything jumbled together, making it hard to focus on one thing: Lawrence; Lincoln; her father; the never-ending arguments about her canceled engagement; sex with Lincoln and unwanted feelings developing. Even Sebastian fought for space in her head.

Cecily sat up, raised her head to the sky, and screamed as loud as she could. She didn't stop until her throat was raw and the sound faded to almost nothing. She flopped back on the bow, spreadeagle. Her heart pounded, and her breath tore in and out of her throat.

Lincoln wasn't supposed to fall in love with her. This was supposed to be a fling; two weeks, in and out, and then they moved on. Instead, Lincoln threw a monkey wrench in the system and announced he had feelings for her.

— 258 —

Feeling's mutual, buddy.

There it was, the thing she avoided facing for the last eighteen hours.

I'm in love with Lincoln Dunn.

Cecily closed her eyes and turned her face toward the sun. "I'm in love with Lincoln Dunn," she said out loud. She wanted to hear the words, feel them wash over her as she admitted to herself that she was indeed head over heels for Lincoln.

"Dammit," she muttered. "How did that happen?"

There was no question how it happened. Lincoln was sweet, protective, handsome, and an unbelievable lover. He saved her dog, and he helped her out when he didn't have to. The real question was why had it taken her so long to realize she loved him?

The next question was, now what? Should she run to Lincoln like a woman in some cheesy movie, jump into his arms, and the two of them could live happily ever after? Was it even possible?

This was unfamiliar territory for her. Lawrence had pursued her, not giving up until she agreed to go out with him. Her love for Lawrence grew while they dated, but it never became a deep, gnawing need in the pit of her stomach. Not like Lincoln. He owned her mind, her body, and her soul. Lincoln possessed her.

She sighed, and her worries seemed to float away like a child's balloon stolen by the wind. A calmness settled over her, and her worries disappeared. Figuring out what she wanted was half the battle. She wanted Lincoln Dunn; the rest would work itself out.

The gentle rocking of the boat and the warm sun lulled her to sleep.

———

Cecily woke when cold water droplets hit her bare skin. She shot up, worried the boat broke anchor, and had drifted close to shore, but it was a late afternoon rain sprinkling the watercraft. Typical Montana weather; gorgeous in the morning, rain in the evening. She scrambled off the bow and into the driver's seat.

It took thirty minutes to get back to Devereaux Island. Fortunately, the rain wasn't heavy, and it was still light out, though the chill in the air made her shiver. Her stomach growled, and her throat was dry. After lying in the sun for hours, she probably had a sunburn too.

Cecily docked the boat and checked her phone as she made her way to the house. There were no calls, no texts, and no voicemails. It was unfathomable to her that neither her father nor Lawrence had contacted her since they left. But rather than relief, a sense of foreboding had settled over her. She didn't trust her father or Lawrence, and her fight with them was far from over.

It's just the beginning.

"Mrs. Tuttle?" she called, as she pushed open the enormous oak door and stepped into the foyer. She threw her bag on the table by the door. "Mrs. Tuttle?"

The only answer was a faint bark. Cecily followed the sound until she found Sebastian contained in the small room under the stairs she had converted into the dog's bedroom. She equipped it with a large, soft bed, food, and water dishes, and a basket full of toys. Taped to the bottom of the Dutch door was a note.

Ms. Devereaux-

Mr. Tuttle and I have gone to town for dinner.
Sebastian will need to be fed. He was very mopey this afternoon
and wouldn't eat.
Also, your father left a note for you on his desk. You should read it.

Have a wonderful evening!

Mrs. Tuttle

Sebastian hobbled to the door and stared up at her. She opened the Dutch door, scooped him up, and planted a kiss on the top of his head. In the kitchen, she prepared his food while he watched her. Once he had his food, she went down the hall to her father's office, pushed open the door, and stepped inside.

Propped in the center of her father's desk was a letter, her name written across the front in his neat, almost-perfect handwriting. She sat in the enormous leather chair behind the mahogany desk and stared at the letter for a full minute before she picked it up, holding it between two fingers as if it might bite her.

Cecily took a deep breath, opened the envelope, removed the letter, and unfolded it.

Cecily-

I know you are angry and frustrated. I understand your independent streak, perhaps better than you. But I've indulged the fun and games long enough. It's time to give up the childish wares and take on your adult responsibilities. Lawrence is suitable marriage material, far better than Lincoln Dunn, a going-nowhere former military man with a reputation as a ladies' man. An alliance with Lawrence will be an asset to you and, ultimately, to Devereaux

Industries. I expect you to return to New York by the end of the month or forfeit your trust fund. No further discussion is necessary.

Sincerely,

Claude

She wanted to scream. *An alliance with Lawrence? What did that mean?* Her father worded it like she was some damsel being sold to a suitor to benefit her father's kingdom.

Cecily sat up straight, the letter falling from her fingers and fluttering to the ground.

"Son of a bitch!"

———

Four hours and a pounding headache later, Cecily sat at the dining room table, leafing through page after page of internal Devereaux Industries communications, as well as her father's private notes. Her father's use of the word "alliance" had seemed odd, odd enough that it prompted her to suspect something nefarious might be happening at the company.

It took her an hour to get into the private accounts and notes on the Devereaux servers. Thankfully, her father was a creature of habit and had never changed his password from "deirdreandclaude"; it had been the same thing for years. She memorized it in grade school to access the home internet. It hadn't taken much detective work to find her father's private files. From there, she searched her name, and then Lawrence's name, and discovered a wealth of information.

Lawrence Bronson was the son of Gerald Orville Fortuna. The Fortuna crime family was well known up and down the East Coast. They had ties to drugs, prostitution, and illegal gambling. Her father had done business with them for years, using Devereaux Industries' various companies to launder their illegal money. Gerald Fortuna paid her father insane amounts of untraceable cash in return.

According to the emails Cecily uncovered, Claude had second thoughts about his business dealings with Fortuna. He wanted to break free, but Fortuna refused to let him out of the business. The tone of the emails changed from mildly worrisome to downright threatening. Claude backed down and apologized for suggesting they part ways.

Unconvinced, Gerald Fortuna threatened to ruin Claude's business and his reputation. He demanded a promise from Claude, a deal to keep their business dealings intact in perpetuity. Gerald's suggestion—a marriage between their children.

Cecily dropped the papers to the table and pushed herself away from the table. She stumbled into the kitchen, leaned over the sink, and vomited. She rinsed out the sink, sank to the floor, and put her head on her knees.

Her father traded her to keep his business and reputation from falling to ruin. She was nothing more to her father than an object meant to be used as he saw fit. Her marriage to Lawrence was an alliance between a prominent crime family and a powerful entrepreneur. Love had nothing to do with it.

Bile rose in her throat again, but she forced it back down. She'd had enough information for one night, so she dragged herself to her feet and pulled open the cabinet next to the sink. She grabbed four ibuprofen and a sleeping pill, filled a cup with water, and swallowed them. Sebastian was asleep under the table, so she picked him up and carried him to her room.

It wasn't until she was in bed, buried under the blankets, that her mind turned to Lincoln. The recent revelations about her life had her second-guessing everything. *Did she really love Lincoln?* After what she'd just discovered, she wasn't sure she knew what love was. They had fooled her once. She wouldn't be fooled again. Maybe loving someone or even someone loving her wasn't meant to be. For all she knew, it was all another lie.

Chapter 19

Cecily

The phone rang six times before Cecily gave up.

His phone must be on silent.

It was early, just after seven, and she had only been awake for about five minutes. She hadn't been able to wait another minute to talk to Lincoln.

Not only did she need to talk to him about their relationship and where it was going, but she needed his advice. He knew her father, he'd worked for her father, and he'd implied that he didn't care for her father's business practices. She convinced herself talking to Lincoln would make her feel better. Maybe he could ease her mind and tell her she was wrong, that her engagement to Lawrence wasn't a penance her father had to pay to crime boss Gerald Fortuna. Better yet, maybe he had proof she imagined the whole thing.

Just the thought of being used as a pawn in a business deal drove the nausea from the previous night back to the surface. She scrambled out of bed and rushed to the bathroom, her head hanging over the toilet for several minutes, though her empty stomach kept her from vomiting.

She scooped up Sebastian and headed for the kitchen, where she grabbed a bottle of ginger ale. Her stomach settled after a few sips. She distracted herself by getting Sebastian's food ready for the morning and making a pot of coffee.

Maybe I should call my father.

Even contemplating talking to her father made her nauseous all over again. *What was she supposed to say? "Hey Dad, I found out you were trying to use me as a bargaining chip in your dealings with a known mobster."* Cringeworthy.

A faint bark drew her attention to the back door. Sebastian stared at her, then he scratched at the door, a forlorn look on his cute, little face. He wanted out, and she was ignoring him. Cecily opened the door and followed him out. He limped across the yard, the leg in the bulky blue cast stuck oddly out behind him. He spent a few minutes sniffing around the patio table, did his business under the bush, and laid down under one of the chaise lounges.

Cecily checked the gate to make sure she latched it before she went inside for coffee. She took a mug out of the cupboard and some cream from the fridge.

"Good morning, Ms. Devereaux."

Cecily jumped and swung around, a high-pitched squeak leaving her.

"Mrs. Tuttle! You scared me to death!"

Mrs. Tuttle laughed. "My apologies. How was your day yesterday?"

Cecily grimaced. "It kind of sucked."

Mrs. Tuttle made an odd face. "I'm sorry to hear that. Anything I can do?"

"I don't think so," she replied. "By the way, thank you for watching Sebastian."

"It was my pleasure. You know I love that little dog almost as much as I love you."

Cecily set her mug on the counter, bounded across the room, and pulled Mrs. Tuttle into a tight hug. Mrs. Tuttle gasped.

"I love you too," Cecily mumbled. She kissed the woman's cheek, then released her.

Mrs. Tuttle patted her hair, as if her tightly woven braid would dare release a stray hair. She cleared her throat. "I think I heard your cellphone ringing. Did you leave it upstairs?"

Cecily rolled her eyes. "Yes, I did. Thanks. I'll go grab it."

Her phone was on the bathroom counter. She checked her missed calls. The only one she had was from Lincoln. She hit the button to call him back.

"Hey, sweetheart," he answered.

"Thank God, Lincoln. I need to talk to you."

"I gathered as much since you called me at seven in the morning. Are you okay?"

"Yes." She dragged in a deep breath. "No, that's not true. I'm not okay. In fact, I am so not okay I want to scream. I need to talk to you, and I don't want to discuss it on the phone. Can you meet me? Please?"

Lincoln warily agreed. She couldn't blame him; he'd bent over backwards for her during the last week, helping her with her father and ex-fiancé, her dog, and now she needed him again. He probably thought they were going to talk about his feelings for her and if she reciprocated them. Instead, she needed yet another favor from him. Maybe she should clarify what she needed from him.

"Cecily?"

She snapped back to reality. "Sorry. My mind drifted. Meet me at The Farmhouse on Stoner Loop. Do you need directions?"

"I'll find it. What time?"

"In an hour?" she asked.

"See you then." Lincoln disconnected the call.

Cecily sighed as she shoved her phone back in her pocket. She didn't like Lincoln's short, clipped sentences and irritated tone.

I might have pushed my only ally too far.

If he walked away from her at the end of his two-week vacation and never talked to her again, she wouldn't blame him one bit.

———

Lincoln pushed open the door, looked around the small restaurant, and headed for the table Cecily grabbed at the back of the restaurant. He slid into the booth across from her and folded his hands in front of himself, squeezing them so tight she heard his knuckles crack.

"Hi."

After tipping his chin in her direction, he signaled their server and ordered a coffee. He picked up the tiny cup and downed the black coffee in three swallows. He winced and set the cup back down.

"Sorry. I didn't sleep well. I need a heavy dose of caffeine." He gestured to their server and pointed at his coffee cup.

"I understand; I didn't sleep well, either."

Their server took their breakfast order and refilled their coffee. Lincoln waited until the young man walked away before he spoke. "All right, I'm here and slightly caffeinated. What's up?"

Cecily cleared her throat. "I have a question for you." She shifted in her seat, sitting up as straight as possible, her back resting against the cold vinyl of the booth and her toes just brushing the floor. "How much do you know about my father's business?"

Lincoln sighed. "Quite a bit. Why?"

He was being intentionally evasive. "I want you to tell me why you quit. Tell me why you dislike my father so much. Most people love him, think he's charming and wonderful. Not you."

His eyes narrowed and his shoulders stiffened. "Cecily, I can't discuss my business dealings with your father. Devereaux Industries required an NDA when Van and I went to work for them. I will say that my ideas about proper business practices did not mesh well with your father's. Aside from that, I cannot share anything with anyone, including you."

Cecily huffed and crossed her arms. "This is my father's company. I have a right to know what he is doing."

"Then ask your father. I can't tell you."

"Lincoln, come on."

He scrubbed a hand over his face. "I'm serious, sweetheart. I can't tell you anything, not unless I want to cost Van and myself a crap ton of money."

"My father is in deep with Gerald Fortuna. You know who that is, right?"

It was Lincoln's turn to clear his throat. "Yes, I do. I can tell you that Fortuna is not a man to be trifled with. If your father pissed him off..."

"Lawrence is Fortuna's son."

Lincoln jerked in his seat, his knee hit the table, and his coffee sloshed over the side of the cup, staining his napkin. "How did you find out?"

"Wait? You knew?"

"I know *now*," Lincoln said. "I didn't know before this morning." He cleared his throat. "Van offered to investigate Lawrence. I told him to do it. I called him on my way over here, and he filled me in. Lawrence used his mother's maiden name to avoid complications with the law."

Cecily sighed. "I didn't know he was Fortuna's son. I had no idea. Fortuna and my father were behind the engagement, a deal to guarantee their business arrangement lasted forever. I found paperwork, emails, a bunch of stuff that made it clear my father used me to keep Fortuna happy. But since I broke it off, I messed everything up. No wonder my father is desperate for us to get back together."

"You think your father arranged your marriage to Lawrence? As what, a payment to Gerald Fortuna?"

"Yes. Sick, huh?"

Lincoln pushed himself out of the booth and slid in next to her. He put his arm around her and squeezed. "Jesus, Cecily, I don't know what to say. 'I'm sorry' doesn't seem like enough."

She rested her head on his shoulder and closed her eyes. "I don't want it to be true. What kind of person uses his child as leverage in a sick business deal?"

Lincoln grunted. "What are you going to do?"

"I don't know. The thought of talking to my father terrifies me."

"I could talk to him. I'm going back to New York tomorrow—."

Cecily cut him off. "Thank you, but this is something I need to take care of myself. If I don't stand up to Claude, I'll always be afraid of him. My father treats me like I'm a helpless, clueless female. I need to prove to him I'm not. I'm going to stand up for myself. He will be told who is in charge of my life." She squeezed his arm. "So, you're leaving tomorrow?"

"I couldn't get a flight out of Kalispell, so I'm going to Missoula tonight. My flight leaves early tomorrow morning." He propped his arm on the back of the booth and turned to face her. "I guess that means our two-week one-night stand is over."

Cecily twittered nervously. "Cute."

"Cute? Okay, if you say so." He chuckled. "So, tell me, did you think about us?"

"I did." She picked at the napkin on the table, shredding it to pieces. Her stomach rolled and her head spun. This wouldn't go well.

He twisted a strand of her hair around his fingers. "I wonder, what conclusions did you reach?"

"My life is upside down, Lincoln. I don't know whether I'm coming or going. I don't even know if I can trust you."

Lincoln closed his eyes and snorted. "You *know* you can trust me."

She sat up straight and stared into those damn deep blue eyes of his, refusing to let herself fall under their spell. "That's just it, Lincoln. I don't know if I can trust anyone. I thought Lawrence loved me, but it was bullshit. My father cares about himself more than my interests. I'm sick of people taking advantage of me."

Lincoln dropped her strand of hair, and a scowl marred his gorgeous face. "Is that what you think? That I've been taking advantage of you?"

Cecily grabbed his hand out of fear he would bolt. "Wait. That's *not* what I think at all." She held tight to his hand. "Last night, I was all set to come in here and tell you I was falling in love with you. I was going to tell you we could give the relationship thing a shot."

"What changed?"

"I'm scared, okay? Everything I believed to be true isn't. I feel like I can't trust anybody right now, not even you. I just need some time—."

Lincoln ripped his hand from hers and stood up. "Time? I think we're out of time, sweetheart. Sorry." He spun on his heel, pushed past the server carrying their food, and walked out of the restaurant.

Chapter 20

Lincoln

*H*is hands shook as he drove. After all this time, after everything he'd done, Cecily still didn't trust him. What more could he do to prove his love to her? *Why did I think this time would be different?*

A horn blared behind him, drawing his attention back to the road. He swerved over the double yellow line, one tire in the other lane, before he twisted the wheel and skidded to a stop on the shoulder. He put the truck in park and scrubbed a hand over his face.

This is bullshit.

There was a reason he didn't get involved with a woman for longer than one night. Relationships were nothing more than a punch to the gut. The pain and the heartache were too much. He should have learned his lesson after Cat. Love worked its way into your heart and then blew it to pieces.

"I never should have told her how I felt," he muttered to himself. "So much for honesty."

He ignored the voice in his head telling him to calm down and not jump to conclusions. That voice hadn't helped when he divulged his feelings for Cecily; it wouldn't help him now. He had to face the truth. If Cecily believed he was like Claude and Lawrence, there was nothing else he could do.

Lincoln checked his watch. If he hurried, he could get to the condo, pack, and be on the road within the hour. He wanted Lakeside in his rearview mirror as soon as possible. The sooner he got out of town, the sooner he could get Cecily Devereaux out of his system.

Back on the road, he concentrated on driving through the small town. He hadn't thought it possible, but he was going to miss this place. Small-town life suited him, more than he'd ever imagined. The leisurely pace with which people lived their lives appealed to him. Deep down, he'd thought he could make a life in Lakeside, and part of him hoped that life would include Cecily.

If only...

He stopped himself from going down that rabbit hole. "If only" would tear him apart. No sense dwelling on what could have been; he needed to look forward.

Lincoln eased into the parking spot beside the condo. If he hurried, he could be out of Lakeside before dark and on the road to Missoula. He'd stay in a hotel on Reserve Street and board his plane bright and early tomorrow morning. Before too long, Cecily would be a distant memory.

Inside the condo, he went straight to the bedroom and shoved his clothes in his duffel bag. A quick stop in the bathroom for his toothpaste and deodorant, then he was back to the bedroom for one last look around.

Two sharp raps on the door drew him from the bedroom. He zipped his duffel bag shut, hefted it over his shoulder, and pulled open the door.

"Hi," Serena said. "You got a minute?"

"Sure," Lincoln nodded. "Come on in."

Serena shook her head and pointed over her shoulder. "Can we talk out here?"

He stepped outside and pulled the door closed behind him. He forgot Serena hadn't stepped foot in her condo since her abusive ex-boyfriend had attacked her inside and tried to kidnap her. Asshole move on his part.

"Sorry."

She smiled at him. "It's okay." Serena cleared her throat. "Van and I are heading out on the boat. We thought you might want to come with us."

Lincoln shook his head. "I don't think so. I'm leaving." He dug the condo keys out of his pocket and handed them to her.

Serena scowled as she stared at the keys in her hand. "I thought you were staying for a couple more days."

"I'm catching a flight out of Missoula early tomorrow morning. I'm leaving Lakeside tonight to stay in Missoula." He shrugged. "It's the easiest thing to do."

"I don't understand," she said. "What about Cecily?"

"Cecily has a lot going on right now. She found out some stuff about her father and his involvement in her engagement."

"Hey!" Van jogged across the street, Soldier on his heels. "What's going on?" He glanced at the duffel bag in Lincoln's hand. "Are you leaving?"

"Yeah."

"Did you talk to Cecily? Tell her what we discovered about Lawrence?"

Lincoln nodded. "She already knew, though."

"She did?" Van said. "How? I had to dig deep to find out he was Fortuna's son."

Lincoln explained his conversation with Cecily and what she had discovered. Once he was done, he said, "So, as you can see, it's probably best for both of us if I give her some space and time to figure out what she wants."

Van crossed his arms over his chest and shook his head. "Whenever you say you want to give a woman time to figure out what she wants, that's Lincoln speak for 'I'm done with this before it gets serious.'"

"Van—."

His friend held up his hand. "You know how I always bitch about it bugging me that you know me so well? Well, guess what? *I* know *you*, Linc, and you're bailing. When it gets hard, you bolt."

Lincoln shot Van a dirty look, tossed his bag in the truck, and slammed the door. "Cecily made it clear she isn't interested in a relationship."

Serena stomped her foot and glared at him. "She said she needed time; that's not the same as not being interested in a relationship. Give her a chance."

Lincoln glanced at Van, but his friend stared past him at the lake, his hand resting on Soldier's head.

"You're right, Serena. But I don't think she wants a relationship, especially after everything she just discovered. Besides, it's been two weeks. I think that's enough time. If she doesn't know what she wants by now, she never will."

"That's not fair," Serena snapped. "She just got devastating news. You can't ask her to make a life-altering decision right now."

"Can you help me here?" Lincoln pleaded with his best friend.

Van shook his head. "Nope. She's got a point. Cecily's father is an ass, her ex-fiancé is an ass, and she literally just discovered they were co-conspirators to control her life. She deserves some time to figure out what she wants."

So much for friendship. Lincoln looked at his watch and yanked open the truck door. "I gotta go. I want to get to Missoula before dark."

"Why don't you stay two or three more days, maybe talk to Cecily again?" Van suggested. "We don't mind. You can stay in Serena's condo for as long as you want."

"I need to get home," Lincoln muttered.

Serena gave him a dirty look, spun on her heel, and stomped across the street. He didn't enjoy making her angry—it wasn't his intention—but he needed to get out of Montana and get his head on straight. He turned to Van.

"Your wife is mad at me."

"She'll be fine. I'll talk to her."

"Will you explain to her—?"

"I'll try. I can't promise she won't still be mad at you, though. Go home to New York and figure out what *you* want. I know that's what you want and need to do." Van held out his hand.

Lincoln grabbed it and pulled him into a hug. "Thank you." He took a deep breath. "I'll be back, I swear."

"I know."

Lincoln crouched down, took Soldier's head in his hands, and scratched the dog behind his ears. He gave him one last pat, stood up, and climbed into the truck. As he turned the corner, he looked in the rearview mirror and saw Van raise his hand in a half-hearted wave.

Chapter 21

Cecily

Cecily stared at the picture of her father and mother on their wedding day. It was one of the few times she'd seen her father with a sincere smile on his face. *What happened to him?*

Her mother wouldn't know the man her father had become. A tear slid down her cheek, and she brushed it away. She missed her mother every day, but lately it had been an indescribable ache. Her father never understood her, but her mother always had her back. When Claude Devereaux was being his worst and making Cecily's life impossible, Deirdre Devereaux made things better.

"Cecily."

Her father stood in the doorway with Lawrence right behind him, peering over his shoulder with a salacious, triumphant smirk on his face.

She pushed herself to her feet and stepped around the desk. "Daddy. I see you brought Lawrence along."

Her father strode into the room, his head held high, his shoulders back, and a fierce scowl on his face. "Don't start, young lady."

Cecily sighed. "I came back to New York to discuss the letter you left me."

"I assume that means you've come to your senses. Your old position is still available with the company. I secured a temporary lease on an apartment overlooking Central Park for you, and I arranged a tour of the Four Seasons next week as a potential wedding venue."

She crossed her arms and dug her nails into her biceps, a reminder not to let her father intimidate her. It irked her that he assumed she was prepared to do as he said. She glanced at Lawrence, now smirking in the corner, and cleared her throat.

"I'm here to discuss Gerald Fortuna."

Lawrence coughed and, for a brief second, her father's tightly controlled façade slipped. Claude clenched his fists, and his shoulders sagged the tiniest bit. He pulled himself together before he spoke.

"I do not know what you are talking about."

Cecily opened her briefcase, pulled out the folder of information she carried all the way from Lakeside, and dropped it in the center of Claude's desk. Her heart pounded, and her palms were sweating.

Her father didn't move. He stared at the folder on the desk, his lower lip caught between his teeth. When he looked up, it wasn't Cecily he looked at but Lawrence.

"Lawrence, please excuse us?"

"I—."

"Now, Lawrence."

He huffed, but he did as Claude asked. He paused at the door, glanced back at Cecily with a pinched look on his face, then he opened the door, stepped out, and slammed it.

She turned around to find her father sitting at his desk with the folder open, flipping through the papers. She eased into the chair across from him and waited.

It took Claude almost ten minutes to go through the folder. When he was done, he closed it and sat back in his chair.

"Where did you find this?"

Cecily shrugged. "I looked for it, Daddy. After reading your letter, including the line about an 'alliance' with Lawrence, it occurred to me why you pushed this engagement so hard. I'm not as stupid as you think."

"Obviously." He shifted in his seat. Cecily had never seen her father so uncomfortable. "I wish I could say this isn't what it looks like, but clearly it's not worth denying."

"You're right. There is no need to deny it."

Claude folded his hands on top of the desk and squeezed his eyes closed. "What do you want?"

"I want to be left alone. I don't want you interfering in my life anymore."

Her father opened his eyes. "That's it?"

Cecily nodded. "What else could I possibly want from you?"

Claude sighed. "A job? Money? That stupid island in the middle of nowhere? You don't want anything?"

"I don't want to be beholden to you for anything," she snapped. "It would be more stuff for you to hold over my head and another way to make me miserable."

"How did we get to this point?" he whispered. "You're my little girl. I love you."

Tears pricked the corner of her eyes. "You haven't said that in a long time."

Claude sighed, and his shoulders slumped. He leaned back in his chair. "After your mother died, I wasn't sure I could love anymore. She was my entire world. My everything." Claude scrubbed a hand over his face. "The biggest mistake I ever made was shutting you out. My focus was on the business. I lost touch with you and thought supporting the engagement to Lawrence would bring us closer. It didn't matter how or why the engagement happened, only that it did. I thought you were happy. Or maybe I so desperately wanted you to be happy that I was blind to the fact that you weren't."

"Even though I told you time and time again I wasn't happy with Lawrence, you wouldn't let it go. You kept pushing me to stay with him and to marry him. Keeping your business solvent was more important than my happiness."

Claude shook his head. "It wasn't, I swear."

Cecily sighed. "You know what's funny about all of this? If you had come to me and told me what was going on, I might have been able to help you. We could have figured something out." She waved her finger in a circle. "We could have saved all of this, saved Devereaux Industries. Together." She rose to her feet, walked around the desk, and kissed her father on the cheek. "I'm going back to my life in Montana."

She turned to leave, but her father grabbed her hand and stopped her. "Wait."

"There's nothing else to say."

"Maybe there is. Maybe there is still a way to save my company. *Our* company." He hit the intercom button on the phone. "Becca, could you get a lawyer from the legal department in here, please? As quick as possible."

"What are you doing?" Cecily asked.

"Righting my wrongs," Claude replied.

———

Cecily's face hurt from smiling. She had expected to walk into Devereaux Industries, tell her father off, and walk out destitute and homeless. Instead, she carried paperwork in her briefcase that gave her a controlling interest in her father's company. Now it was her company.

To say it shocked her would be an understatement. Not only had Claude signed over his interest in the company to her, but he also agreed to step down for the good of the company. Her head spun with all the things she needed to do. She would have to stay in New York for at least a month to get everything squared away.

"Cecily!"

Lawrence slid to a stop in front of her. She had hoped to make it out of the building without running into him, but luck was not on her side.

"What did you do?"

She feigned ignorance. "I'm sorry? I'm not sure what you're talking about."

"Your father told me to clean out my desk and be out of the building by the end of the day. What the hell is going on? Two hours ago, he told me you and I were getting married, and he would put me on the board. Now I'm fired?"

"To be fair, it wasn't my father who fired you; it was me. He delivered the message, but I made the final decision."

Lawrence took a step back. "You can't do that."

Cecily's smile widened. "Oh, but I can. I now hold the controlling interest in Devereaux Industries." She wiggled her briefcase. "The lawyer is filing the paperwork as we speak. First on my agenda is removing any trace of you and your mob boss father from my company."

Lawrence grunted and took a step toward her. "Do it, and you'll regret it. Trust me."

Cecily didn't back down; instead, she stepped closer until she was mere inches from Lawrence's face. "I'm not afraid of your father, Lawrence. Not even a little. His hold over Devereaux Industries is finished."

Lawrence blinked and backed up. He spun on his heel and walked away without a word. Cecily watched him until he got on the elevator, then she crossed the lobby to the security desk and got the attention of the young lady sitting at the monitors.

"Yes, Ms. Devereaux?"

"Can you make sure Lawrence Bronson is out of the building by five p.m., please?"

The woman nodded. "Of course, Ms. Devereaux."

"Please, call me Cecily." She pulled off her visitor's badge, set it on the counter, and walked out the door.

———

For the third night in a row, she walked to the bar down the street from her hotel. She sat in the same spot, ordered the same drink, and kept her eyes on the door. She deflected the attention of other patrons, politely declining offers to buy her a drink or take her on the dance floor. After two hours, she dropped some money on the bar and left.

Call him.

The little voice in her head wouldn't shut up, no matter how often she told it to be quiet. The problem was the voice was right. She should call him. Hoping to run into Lincoln at the bar where they met was a lesson in futility. If she just picked up the phone and told him she was in town and wanted to see him, he would come.

Maybe.

"Shut up," she muttered under her breath.

It had been six weeks since she'd seen Lincoln or spoken to him. Cecily *wanted* to call him. She wanted to talk to him, kiss him, make love to him, *be* with him. But the thought scared her. Hell, it terrified her.

What was she supposed to say? "I'm sorry" wasn't enough, and "I'm ready now" seemed lame. She'd asked for time, and he'd given it to her. Eight weeks. There had been no communication—no texts, emails, or phone calls. Not that she hadn't picked her phone up dozens of times, intent on calling him or at least texting him, but one day bled into another and another until her one-month stay in New York had turned into two.

She stepped into the elevator, hit the number five on the panel, and stabbed repeatedly at the button to close the door until it eased shut. She pulled her phone out of her purse and checked for messages: five from her administrative assistant, one from her father, and another from her lawyer, but nothing from Lincoln. Cecily unlocked her room, tossed the phone on the bed, and grabbed her suitcase from the closet. Her plane left at eight tomorrow morning, so she wanted to get packed tonight.

Tomorrow she would be home, back in Montana. There was still a lot of work to do, but she'd put a great New York team in place, and she knew she could do the same in Lakeside. She couldn't wait to get home. She missed her dog, the Tuttles, and the island.

Cecily sat on the bed with her phone in her hand and stared at the screen. It was now or never. She hit the button, put the phone to her ear, and waited.

"You've reached Lincoln Dunn. Please leave a message, and I'll get back to you as soon as possible."

She cleared her throat. "Um, hi, Lincoln. It's me. Cecily. I, uh, wanted to say hi." She closed her eyes and took a deep breath. "I miss you. I'd love it if you called me back."

Cecily ended the call, packed her bags, and showered, then she crawled into bed and pulled the blankets up to her chin. Lincoln was front and center in her mind as she drifted off to sleep.

Chapter 22

Lincoln

Lincoln stopped dead in his tracks, unable to look away from the beauty in front of him. He crouched down and held out his hand. The tiny ball of fur stretched out its neck and sniffed his fingers.

"She's cute, isn't she?" the young lady sitting on the park bench said.

Lincoln smiled. "She's adorable. Is she a Shih Tzu?"

The girl nodded. "Her name is Sadie." She licked her lips. "I don't suppose you're interested in a dog, are you? I'm trying to find her a home."

"You're getting rid of her?"

"She's the last of the litter. Unbelievably sweet, even-tempered, and house-broken. Obviously, she likes you."

Lincoln laughed. "You're a great salesperson."

The girl shrugged. "I don't have to be when she's so cute." She narrowed her eyes. "Are you interested?"

An hour later, he walked out of the PetSmart on Broadway with three bags of dog necessities—a bed, toys, food, harness, leash, dog bath products, a crate, and training treats. He juggled them and his new dog as he hailed a cab. He kept Sadie tucked under his arm while she surveyed the world around her. Now and then, she would lick his arm, either to remind him she was there or to make sure he was real; he wasn't sure which.

The doorman at his building—Arnold—raised a wary eyebrow when he climbed from the cab, but he hurried over to help him pull everything out of the cab.

"Mr. Dunn, what did you do?"

"I bought myself a dog." Lincoln held her up, as if Arnold hadn't already noticed her. "She's cute, huh? Her name is Sadie."

Arnold shook his head. "I hope you know what you're in for. Puppies are like newborn babies. I don't think you'll be getting much sleep."

Lincoln didn't have the heart to tell him he hadn't been sleeping much anyway, not since leaving Lakeside. Maybe Sadie would bring him some peace. He kissed the top of her head.

"She'll be a good girl, won't you, Miss Sadie?"

"You're smitten," Arnold laughed. "It's nice to see you smile, sir."

"Thanks, Arnold. It's, uh, nice to smile again." He cleared his throat. "Can you get all this stuff upstairs for me? I'm going to take her for a walk."

He took the harness and leash out of the bag and put them on Sadie. He set her on the ground and burst out laughing when she twisted herself up in the leash and flopped down on the ground.

"Don't worry, baby girl; we'll work on it."

Lincoln coaxed her down the street. It took Sadie a few minutes, but she got the hang of it about five blocks from his apartment. They were a hundred yards from the bar where he met Cecily—a place he'd avoided for two months—when he noticed a curvy, raven-haired woman come out the door.

Holy shit. Cecily.

Before he could even think about yelling Cecily's name, Sadie turned around and darted between his legs, tangling her leash around his ankles. Lincoln grunted and slid to a stop, one hand on the wall beside to keep himself from falling to the ground. He swore under his breath, snatched up the puppy, and untangled himself. When he looked up, the woman was nowhere to be seen.

"Probably just my imagination," he muttered.

Lincoln tucked Sadie under his arm and headed back to his apartment. Arnold had taken everything upstairs and left it on his kitchen table. Beside it was the day's paper, folded neatly in half. He put Sadie on the floor so she could explore, grabbed a beer from the fridge, and set to work putting away her things.

He couldn't stop thinking about Cecily. While he didn't think the black-haired woman that he saw leaving the bar was her, it had certainly dredged up memories. Not a day went by that he didn't think about Cecily. As much as he hated to admit it, he missed her. Coming home to New York was supposed to get her out of his system and he was supposed to move on, but he found himself stuck, unable to do anything other than regret the choices he made.

Maybe I should call her.

Lincoln chastised himself for even considering it. Cecily hadn't contacted him, which solidified his belief that she was not interested in a relationship with him. Calling her would only end in heartache. He was sure of it.

He grabbed the paper and moved to the couch. A few seconds after he sat down, the tiny Shih Tzu wandered over, curled up on his feet, and fell asleep. He chuckled and scratched the top of her head. Van would lose his mind when he found out Lincoln had bought a dog. He couldn't wait to tell him.

He searched for his phone so he could call his best friend, but the headline under the fold of the newspaper caught his eye.

Devereaux Industries Taken Over by Billionaire Entrepreneur's Daughter.

He snatched up the paper and skimmed the article. According to the story, Claude Devereaux had signed over control of his company to Cecily two months earlier. She swooped in and made broad changes across the company, which included ending a long-term financial arrangement with Fortuna Financial, a company owned by the known mobster, Gerald Fortuna.

> *"I'm bringing integrity back to Devereaux Industries," they quoted Cecily. "This will be a company people will be proud to work for, one that will make money, and one that will lead the business world into the future. I can't wait to get started."*

They filled the article with glowing comments about Cecily and her plans for the company, which included moving the CEO offices out of cold, impersonal New York and to her adopted hometown in Montana. She was confident it would go well because she had put a crack team in place to keep the New York office running. Technology would allow her to be part of the business from the other side of the country.

"Wow, nice work, sweetheart," he whispered. "I knew you could stand up to your father."

The puppy's head popped up, and she stared at Lincoln with her big brown eyes. He picked her up and set her in his lap. She curled up and went back to sleep.

Lincoln rubbed his hand down her back, ruffling her soft fur. "You know what, Sadie? I have a friend named Sebastian who I think you would like."

His cellphone beeped from the kitchen table, but Sadie looked so comfortable, he opted not to get up. He would check it later.

———

"Are you ready for this?" Van asked.

Lincoln laughed. "Is anybody ever ready for something like this?"

Van laughed along with him. "True. You got everything you need?"

Lincoln patted the bag sitting on the floor by his feet. "I think so."

"Call me if you need me to bail you out."

"Of jail?"

Van snorted. "Well, if things don't go as planned, you might *need* bail money."

"Ha-ha." Lincoln opened the truck door and climbed out. He grabbed the bag from the floor, double-checked to make sure he had everything he needed, and headed inside.

He'd put a lot of thought into how the next few minutes of his life would play out. The decision hadn't been an easy one, but it was the right one. He just wished it hadn't taken him three months to figure out what he needed to do.

It took a minute for his eyes to adjust after he stepped inside. He only took a few steps inside the Time Out Bar and Grill before he sat at a table by the door. He hefted his bag onto the table with a grunt and unzipped it.

Sadie popped her head out. She'd grown a lot in the last month, putting on three pounds since he'd brought her home. She licked his face and gave him her adorable grin.

"Hey, Sadie Sue. You're a good girl, aren't you?" He straightened the bow on her collar, attached her leash to her harness, and took her out of her carrier. He took the folded papers out of the side of the bag, tucked them into his back pocket, checked his front pocket one more time, and then set Sadie on the floor.

"Come on, girl."

Sebastian noticed him first. He bounded to his feet, rushed across the bar, jumped up, and put his paws on Lincoln's leg. He barked once.

"Hey, buddy! It's good to see you." He reached down and petted the little white dog. "No more cast, huh?"

"He got it off last month," Cecily said.

Her voice was music to his ears. He closed his eyes for a second before he opened them and smiled at her.

"Hey, Lincoln."

"Hey, gorgeous. How's it going?"

Cecily grinned. "Good. Great." She hopped off her barstool, kneeled, and held out her hand. "Who is this little one?"

"That is Sadie. I thought her and Sebastian could be friends."

Sebastian ducked under Cecily's hand and sniffed Sadie's ear. He stretched, rested his head on his paws, and barked. Cecily patted his flank, whispered "be nice," and stood up.

"Oh, yeah?" She tipped her head to one side. "Are you planning on hanging around long enough for them to become friends?"

Lincoln pointed at the barstools. "Can we talk for a minute?"

Cecily nodded and eased onto the stool she'd just vacated. Lincoln sat beside her and cleared his throat.

"Congratulations on acquiring your father's company," he said.

"Thanks." Her smile widened. "I thought it was time for me to stand up to my father and let him know who was in charge of my life."

Lincoln laughed. "Just like you said you would. Is everything going well?"

"It's getting there. We have a lot of work to get done, a lot of changes to make, but it's coming together. I'm excited about the future."

"You should be."

"Thank you." She took a sip of her drink. "Now, what did you want to discuss?"

He pulled the papers from his back pocket, unfolded them, and slid them across the bar to Cecily.

"What is this?"

"Read it."

She picked up the papers, her eyes widening as she read them. When she was done, she swallowed, gripped the papers tightly in both hands, and turned to look at him.

"Lincoln?"

He put his hand over hers. "It's a prenuptial agreement."

"I know what it is. What I want to know is why? What are you ... what are you doing?"

"I want you to trust me. This was the only way I know how to prove to you I *can* be trusted." He tapped the paper in her hand. "I'm not interested in your money or your company. My only interest is you."

Cecily bit her lower lip. "This might be the most romantic thing anybody's ever done for me." She turned her hand over and took hold of his.

"One more thing." With his free hand, Lincoln reached into his front pocket and pulled out the velvet box. He opened it and set it in front of Cecily. "It's not an engagement, not yet anyway, but it is a promise." He leaned close, his lips brushing her the shell of her ear. "I love you, Cecily Devereaux. And I promise to love you for as long as you want me. Forever, if that's what you want."

"Forever sounds good," Cecily whispered. "In fact, it sounds a lot better than a two-week one-night stand."

Lincoln laughed, took hold of her chin, and pulled her close. His mouth closed over hers, and it was the best kiss they ever shared; it was the kiss that sealed the promise.

THE END

About the Author

Mimi Francis is a sassy and confident romance writer known for her steamy tales of passion that leave readers breathless. Her creative writing style is filled with vivid imagery and bold characters that make her stories come alive. Born and raised in Montana, Mimi has always had a passion for writing and storytelling.

Mimi's love for writing began when she was a teenager and she honed her craft by penning countless short stories and journaling. As an adult, she turned to fan fiction as an outlet for her need to write. But it wasn't until she started writing romance novels that she truly found her niche. Her books are filled with sizzling chemistry, well-developed characters, and laugh-out-loud humor.

When she's not busy crafting her latest heartstopping romance, Mimi can be found sipping margaritas and indulging in her favorite Marvel movies. She's a self-proclaimed fangirl who can't get enough of superheroes and epic battles. But her true obsession lies with the TV show Supernatural, which she has watched from beginning to end more times than she cares to admit.

Mimi is also a wife, mother, and grandmother as well as a loving dog mom to four adorable Shih Tzus named Sebastian, Sadie, Sasha, and Sophie. Her furry companions keep her company while she writes and provide endless entertainment with their playful antics.

Mimi's writing career started with her first novel, "Private Lives," the first book in her Second Chances in Hollywood series. Since then, she has published eight more books, including the Loves of Lakeside series, set in her home state of Montana. Mimi enjoys writing strong female leads and steamy romance scenes that leave readers wanting more.

Connect with Mimi on Instagram, Threads, and Facebook at @author.mimi. francis, on TikTok at @authormimifrancis, or on her website mimifrancis.com.

Book Club Questions

RUN AWAY HOME

1. Do you think Serena's decision to move to Lakeside to get away from her ex is a good decision?

2. Van has built walls around himself due to the grief of losing his wife. What does Serena's arrival do to those barriers he has put up?

3. How does Soldier help bring Serena and Van together? Do you think their "meet cute" was realistic?

4. Both Van and Serena are dealing with significant past traumas. How do they help each other heal?

5. Do Van and Serena find it difficult to open up to each other, considering their experience with trauma?

6. Flathead Lake and the town of Lakeside are places of refuge for Serena. Why does she feel safe there?

7. How do Serena and Van's past experiences shape their decisions and the actions they take? Is this especially noticeable in their interactions with each other?

THE PROFESSOR

1. What do you think initially drew Jacob to Avery, despite his intention to start fresh in Lakeside?

2. Avery was determined to stay focused during her final year of college. Does her relationship with Jacob change her goals?

3. The story involves a power dynamic between a professor and a student. How did you feel about their relationship, and how does the author handle this dynamic?

4. How did you feel when Jacob's relationship with Avery was revealed in the story, and what impact did it have on both characters?

5. How does the theme of secrecy affect both Jacob and Avery throughout the book?

6. In what ways do Jacob and Avery each grow or change by the end of the story?

OUR TWO-WEEK, ONE-NIGHT STAND

1. If you had to trade places with one character in this book, who would it be? Why?

2. How did the setting impact the story? Would you want to read more books set in Lakeside, Montana? Would you want to visit Lakeside based on this book?

3. If you were making a movie of this book, who would you cast as Lincoln? How about as Cecily?

4. If you had to pick another character to be the protagonist, who would it be? Why?

5. To which character did you most relate or empathize?

6. Did Lawrence make a good "villain"?

7. Which dog was your favorite? Soldier, Sebastian, or Sadie? Which one would you want as a pet?

8. If you were Cecily, what would you do when you found out what her father did?

9. Were you rooting for Lincoln and Cecily to get together? Why or why not?

10. What songs did you think of while reading this book? (For extra fun: make a playlist!)

Discover more at
4HorsemenPublications.com

10% off using HORSEMEN10

9 798823 206778